# A VILLAGE VACANCY

Julie Houston

An Aria Book

First published in the United Kingdom in 2020 by Head of Zeus Ltd
This paperback edition first published in 2021 by Head of Zeus Ltd
An Aria book

9 7 5 3 1 2 4 6 8

A CIP catalogue record for this book is available from the
British Library.

ISBN (PB) 9781800246478
ISBN (E) 9781789546651

Cover design: Cherie Chapman

Typeset by Siliconchips Services Ltd UK

Head of Zeus
First Floor East
5–8 Hardwick Street
London EC1R 4RG

www.headofzeus.com

For all my lovely women friends
(You know who you are!)

# Prologue

Westenbury village, Yorkshire

The evenings were so much darker now the season was turning and summer moving forwards on its inevitable cyclical journey into autumn once more. One minute it was cricket, the intoxicating smells of BBQ smoke drifting over from next door and seemingly endless days when he didn't even have to think about school, never mind be at the beck and call of those in charge. And then, almost without warning, they were halfway through September and several weeks into the new term with the heady smell of brand-new files and folders, as well as the uncertainty of new friendships, different teachers and kids who didn't like him and didn't understand why he sometimes behaved like he did.

But there was always football. Autumn was football and he *loved* football.

He jumped up from the cold stone wall in the shadows of Westenbury Church on which he'd been sitting for seemingly hours but was, in reality, no more than fifteen minutes, as the other two approached. The taller of the pair glanced behind him and, without speaking or any other indication of recognition, slipped the large brown package into his hands before he and his companion walked off in the direction of Midhope, the train station and the trans-Pennine route back to Manchester.

He stuffed the bulky envelope down the back of his jeans, pulled the T-shirt and oversized cagoule down over the bump and jumped on his bike.

He was glad the autumn evenings were so much darker now.

# Once upon a time in Westenbury village there was:

GRACE STEVENS, 43 – teacher, separated from husband Dan and mother to Jonty and Pietronella.

HARRIET WESTMORELAND, 43 – Grace's best friend since the age of 11, wife of Nick, mother to Libby, Kit, India and five-year-old twins Fin and Thea.

JONTY HENDERSON, 5 – Grace's son from a brief relationship with Seb Henderson.

PIETRONELLA STEVENS, 4 – Grace and Dan's adopted daughter. Has Down's Syndrome.

DAVID HENDERSON, 47 – Local wealthy businessman and chair of governors at Little Acorns school. Married to Mandy and father of Seb.

SEB HENDERSON, 27 – Son of David and Mandy. Father to Grace's son, Jonty but now partner to Libby Westmorland and father of two-year-old Lysander.

MANDY HENDERSON, 47 – David's wife and Seb's mum. Was head girl when at school with Grace and Harriet.

CAROLINE HENDERSON, 67 – David's mother. Lives in London.

LIBBY WESTMORELAND, 22 – Harriet's daughter, Seb's partner and mum to Lysander. At Leeds university studying medicine.

KIT WESTMORELAND, 20 – Harriet's son. Lovable rogue, working for his father and David Henderson's textile company.

DR JUNO ARMSTRONG, 37 – GP at Westenbury surgery. Recently divorced. Mother to Gabriel, 13 and Tilda, 11. In love with, and partner of, Dr Scott Butler.

ARIADNE, PANDORA and LEXIA – Juno Armstrong's sisters, all living in Westenbury village.

SCOTT BUTLER, 44 – GP from New Zealand at Westenbury surgery and Juno's lover.

DR IZZY STANFORD, 44 – Senior partner with husband, Declan at Westenbury surgery.

CLEMENTINE AHERN, 35 – owner, together with David Henderson, of Clementine's restaurant in Westenbury village.

CASSIE BERESFORD, 42 – headteacher at Little Acorns, Westenbury's village school.

DEIMANTE MINIAUSKIENE, 28 – teaching assistant at Little Acorns.

PROFESSOR PATRICK SUTHERLAND, father to Juno and her sisters as well as to their half-brother, Arius, 17. Renting a cottage down at Holly Close Farm.

Esme Burkinshaw, 62 – Mother to Maya, 22 and recently moved into the area and renting the cottage next to Patrick Sutherland.

# I

## September

The sublimely pretty village church in Westenbury, itself a cut-jewel nestled invitingly in a sheltered valley among the heather-covered moorland of West Yorkshire, was looking particularly welcoming this warm morning towards the end of September. Guests, as well as those not officially invited but who had felt unable to stay away, made their way up through the immaculately kept churchyard in which the heady scent of late-summer roses, Salvia, Phlox and in particular the Buddleias whose purple flowers were alive with the soporific thrum of bees, tempted and teased noses as effectively as any exclusive French perfumes.

Those able to find a seat to rest high heels, recovered from the backs of wardrobes after a summer of comfortable sandals, sat gratefully, turning to nod briefly at acquaintances and neighbours before reaching for the order of service printed on expensive embossed cream card and meticulously laid out on the ancient oak pews in front of them. For those knowing her only by sight or repute, but nevertheless compelled to show their presence in the church, (she was, after all, one of them) the transept at the back of the mediaeval building was thought a fitting gathering place and the crowd of well-wishers stationed there grew as the church clock tower began laboriously to toll the hour.

Grace Stevens, dressed formally but colourfully in a snug-fitting crimson shift dress and a pair of ridiculously high black patent heels, held firmly onto the hands of the beautiful dark-haired, dark-eyed five-year-old boy and the pretty little girl intent on waving and blowing kisses to those she recognised as they followed Harriet Westmoreland's brother, John, down the aisle to the very front of the nave where friends and family were already filling up the vacant pews. After the warm, bright autumn sunshine of the morning, the interior of the church was both dusky and yet, somewhat incongruously, filled with dancing dust motes where a shaft of light managed to penetrate the interior through one particularly high stained-glass window. Despite leaving the warmth and light behind her, Grace kept her dark glasses in place, releasing her son's hand in order to pat at her eyes behind them as well as, occasionally, consolingly at the arm of Harriet's brother now seated beside her. She made an attempt to pull Pietronella, her four-year-old, onto her lap in order that those still making their way down the aisle might have a seat, but the little girl wriggled from Grace's hands and, instead, wrapped her pudgy fingers through John Burton's arm in its navy suit, bending her head to his bowed face until they were touching, before glancing back in surprise at Grace at the wetness on John's face.

Grace's eyes behind the Fendi sunglasses followed Harriet's daughter, Libby – dressed all in black as befitted the occasion – as she made her way from the front of the church, her sleeping one-year-old son, Lysander, held firmly over one shoulder. Libby's partner, Sebastian Henderson, stopped briefly beside Grace and, with a simple nod, Grace allowed Seb to take Jonty from his seat beside her, clasp the little boy's hand in his own and continue his journey down the aisle to the back of the church where Libby now stood, head bowed, holding the hand of the older man at her side.

Grace looked at her watch then reached down to pull up Pietronella's white ankle socks before lifting her, bodily, onto her knee and patting Harriet's brother, somewhat ineffectually on *his* knee. She turned, frowning, towards the still-open heavy church doors at the back of the church where Westenbury's vicar, Ben Carey, stood ushering latecomers to any available seats before signalling to All Hallows' organist, Daphne Merton, to begin.

As the first haunting notes of Whitlock's 'Fidelis' rose and carried on up through the crowded church, an almost palpable collective sigh could be heard as the congregation stood, turning slightly to catch a first glimpse of the cortege now making its way behind Ben Carey to the front of the church. As it passed her, Grace felt the tears well and she let them fall, unhindered, from behind her glasses as her daughter looked up at her in wonder.

As the little procession reached its destination, Grace felt someone slip into the space beside her and reach for her hand.

'For God's sake, Harriet,' Grace whispered crossly as she moved everyone up along the pew, 'you'll be damned well late for your *own* funeral one of these days...'

'Can you believe this, Harriet?' Grace wiped her eyes once more as, forty minutes later, the cortege retraced its steps back up the nave towards the main entrance of the church, taking Mandy Henderson on her final journey to the churchyard. 'You know, that Mandy is actually... I can't even say the words... no longer *here* with us anymore?'

'No.' Harriet Westmoreland, Grace's best friend since school days, shook her head, for once short of words. 'How long have we known Mandy?' she finally asked. She paused to think, screwing up her eyes as she did the maths and answering her own question. 'Over thirty years. Do you remember your first glimpse of her at Midhope Grammar? I do.'

Grace tutted. 'Of course I do, Harriet. You know I do. I fell in love with her in our very first assembly as she sat with the other fifth and sixth-formers on that long bench in front of the teachers. God, *they* were a rum lot, weren't they?'

'Miss Clarke, the young PE teacher was OK,' Harriet mused, casting her mind back. 'I quite liked *her*, but how the pair of *us* ever became teachers with that motley crew as our only example, I'll never know.' Harriet shook her head again, reaching out a restraining hand to Pietronella who was eager to be off now she'd spotted David Henderson, Mandy's widowed husband and her own much adored adopted grandpa, before glancing round the church at the remaining mourners. 'Is Juno here? Or any other of the Sutherland sisters? I thought Pandora at least might have shown up?'

'I think I spotted Pandora briefly, sitting with Izzy and

Declan.' Grace smiled. 'You know Pandora – she'd have felt it her civic duty to be at the funeral of Westenbury's first lady. Anyway, she's on the governors at Little Acorns with David as well, isn't she? But I wouldn't have thought Juno would be here.' Grace frowned. 'She didn't know either David or Mandy as far as I know.' Grace and Harriet had become very friendly with all four Sutherland sisters when Pandora had put them through their paces in the village's production of Jesus Christ Superstar earlier that year, but it was Dr Juno Armstrong, the third of the sisters, who had become their mate.

'How *is* David?' Harriet asked. 'Do you know? How's he coping with losing Mandy? He obviously talks to Nick quite a bit over business, but you were always his mate. You know, his friend?'

'I honestly haven't seen much of him since the accident,' Grace said as, in turn, their pew filed off to join the end of the queue of slow-moving mourners.

'Really?'

Grace shook her head. 'He's obviously devastated, and I've not really liked to intrude on his grief. I called round with the kids soon after it happened and I've rung him a couple of times but he wasn't in a good place. Seb keeps me updated when he comes to collect Jonty when it's his turn to have him.'

'We're all going to have to get used to life without Mandy Henderson,' Harriet said, glancing at her brother, John behind them in the queue. 'It's going to be a lot harder for some than others...'

## 2

'Come on, Hat, let's get over to Clementine's, I'm desperate for a drink and to dump these heels.' Grace rubbed at the back of her lower leg and frowned.

'A drink?' Harriet Westmoreland glanced to her left where Libby, her eldest daughter, stood with her partner, Seb Henderson, David and Mandy's only son. 'It's not even eleven-thirty yet. And what about the committal? We can't just troll off down the road for a quick gin when she's not even been laid to rest.'

'Family only, apparently.' Grace looked slightly put out. 'As if we two aren't her oldest friends. You know, who here has known her the longest of all…? Who adored her, copied everything she did? Whose day was totally made by one single glance across the school assembly hall from her? I do feel, Harriet, we were more family than some of her *actual* family.'

'Grace,' Harriet said patiently, 'we couldn't stand her a lot of the time.'

'Shh, for heaven's sake, don't speak ill of the dead. OK, OK, I admit, over the years, you me and her have had our differences, but you know perfectly well Mandy's death has hit both of us like a ton of bricks. I still can't believe

I'm never going to see her again…' Grace broke off, openly wiping away tears that fell from behind her sunglasses before reaching down to pull up Pietronella's pristine white socks once more.

'She drove us both mad, Grace, you know she did, so let's not pretend otherwise.' Harriet raised an eyebrow. 'I still think if Nick had been the type of husband to be seduced by another woman, she'd have snared him when they were working together in Italy.'

'Talking about me?' Nick Westmoreland appeared at their side, putting an arm around each of them.

'No, Mandy.'

'Well, all nice stuff, I hope. You can't badmouth a person once they've gone, and especially at their own funeral.

'Oh God, Nick, don't. Just saying that, you know, that she's *gone*, I can't bear it.' Grace wiped her eyes again.

'Not like you, Grace.' Nick frowned in her direction before picking up Pietronella and throwing her up in the air. 'You and Mandy were always at daggers drawn with each other.'

'Do you think you should be doing that, Nick?' Harriet frowned at her husband. 'You know, playing at fairgrounds with Pietronella? We're at a funeral, not a party.'

For a split-second Nick looked contrite and then shook his head. 'Don't be daft. I bet Mandy wouldn't have wanted us to be miserable.'

'I bet she would,' Harriet muttered. 'She'll hate it if she's looking down on us now and we're having a good time without her.' She shivered slightly as she gazed up into the fortuitously forget-me-not blue sky, the very colour of Mandy's eyes. No one would *ever* be able to forget

Amanda Henderson, nee Goodners, only daughter of one of the largest mill-owning families in Yorkshire and wife of the very wealthy and charismatic David Henderson.

'Mandy just couldn't help herself; you know that. She needed the adoration of others whether it be man, woman or child, in order to live.'

'For heaven's sake, Hat, you're making poor old Mandy out to be the village vampire.' Nick was cross. 'Sucking the life out of the village peasants so she could bloom and live forever.'

'Well, I'm sorry, Nick, you only have to look at my brother John...' Harriet lowered her voice. 'In love with Mandy since he was a teenager. She dangled him on a string all his life. Where is John anyway?' She frowned, her eyes taking in every aspect of the room as they searched for her older brother.

'Have a little respect for the poor woman.' Nick broke off as Seb and Libby walked towards them. 'Especially in front of Seb. He's totally distraught.'

'Dad, could you take Lysander for me? And keep an eye on Jonty as well? A graveyard isn't the right place for children and David's asked that it's just himself, Seb and me...' Libby handed a sleeping Lysander over to her father who was already struggling to hang on to Jonty and Pietronella. 'And, as Mandy's oldest and dearest friends, David has asked that you and Mum join us at the committal, Grace.'

Mandy's dearest friends? Harriet and Grace exchanged glances but, without another word, dutifully followed Libby around the church path and down to the far end of the churchyard where Seb and David Henderson, Ben

Carey, the vicar, together with a strikingly handsome elderly woman they didn't know, stood waiting.

'Who's the woman with David?' Clementine Ahern, joint owner with David Henderson of the fabulously upmarket fine dining restaurant in the centre of Westenbury village, paused in the act of passing round a delectable array of her signature canapés and nodded towards David Henderson who was handing round drinks and, by the look of it, psyching himself up to make a speech to those gathering around him.

'Caroline Henderson, David's mother,' Harriet replied. 'She's very stylish, isn't she?' Harriet took one of the tiny morsels and ate with relish, but immediately felt guilty. 'I've never understood funerals,' she said to Clementine. 'The wake afterwards, I mean. Why do we drink and eat and make merry when we're feeling dreadful? Look at Seb over there. He looks really awful, doesn't he?'

'It can't be easy for Libby.' Clem smiled sympathetically. 'I mean, she's only… what? Twenty-one…?'

'Twenty-two at the end of the month.'

'And she's got a one-year-old and just started back at Leeds on her medical degree? Have they moved into Holly Close Farm yet?'

'Yes, but it's still a virtual building site and Seb is in Italy and Brazil a lot with work and so she's there a lot by herself with a young baby.'

'Isn't she frightened being down there on her own? At night, I mean?' Clem frowned, absentmindedly popping one of the tiny pastramis and guacamole wraps into her mouth.

'It's the most fabulous place to live, but very remote for a young girl when she's there by herself.'

'I know, I know. We were all a bit against it, as you know, but Seb and Libby were desperate for the place, determined to go ahead with its renovation and David obviously had the means to help them buy it.'

'This is all so surreal.' Grace walked over to join them, helping herself from Clem's tray and pointing her glass of champagne in Harriet's direction. 'Champagne makes me want to cry even when I'm celebrating something good, so if I have much more of this, with Mandy, you know, *gone...*' Grace broke off to blow her nose.

'Are you OK?' Clem asked glancing round The Orangery where more people were beginning to gather. 'Where's Dan?'

'Gone.'

'Gone? What do you mean, *gone*?'

'We've split up. Again.' Grace put down her champagne and fumbled for a tissue.

'Oh my goodness, Grace. I didn't know.' Clem looked stricken. 'When? What happened?'

'We'd just not been getting on. He's been brilliant with the kids, taking Jonty on as his own and adopting Pietronella two years ago. Can't have been easy for him, especially with *her* problems.'

'I sometimes forget she has Down's Syndrome,' Clementine said, squeezing Grace's arm, 'which is a pretty daft thing to say. Sorry.'

'Dan's always found Jonty going off to stay with Seb most weekends really difficult. Said he felt rejected; that even though Jonty's home is obviously with us, Jonty just couldn't wait for Seb to pick him up. Dan being made redundant from work last month really didn't help either and I suppose I'm not the most patient of people. He's just been sitting around the house watching bloody *Judge Judy* on TV… And then, when the accident happened, you know, when we found out that Mandy had died, he really broke down.'

'Over Mandy?' Harriet frowned. 'I didn't know those two were particularly close.'

'No, neither did I.' Grace raised an eyebrow. 'But after that, he just kind of closed in on himself and when I said he needed to sort himself out, he said the best way to do that was probably to go and live at his mother's house for a while. It's been let out as a holiday cottage since she died last year, so I suppose he saw it as a bolthole.'

'And are you OK with that?' Clem asked.

'To be honest, Clem, we'd not been getting on for ages. You do know that Dan left me before? Years ago? When I was desperately trying to get pregnant and he ended up having an affair with another woman? Yes, sorry, of course you know all this.'

'So, is it that you felt you couldn't trust him? You know, he might end up doing it again?'

'No, nothing like that. I don't think so anyway. I mean, I'd pretty much evened up the score by having my own affair with Seb and getting pregnant with Jonty. I don't know,' Grace sighed, holding out a hand to Pietronella who came sliding towards her on new black patent shoes. 'Perhaps it's that, once your husband strays, the trust is gone and it's easier to give up on the relationship. I actually think we're totally burned out. You know, you can't keep on flogging a dead horse, can you? I don't think I love him anymore. Goodness, I think I've only just admitted that to *myself*.' Grace's face was stricken as she downed a mouthful of the champagne.

'It's *not* going to be easy with the two children, you know, Grace.' Harriet bent down to Pietronella and pulled up her socks.

'Obviously. But Dan will, I'm assuming anyway, want to share childcare. He's just gone over to Heath Green, you know, not the other side of the world. And...' For a moment Grace looked excited. 'I've not said anything to anyone, and I've not agreed to it yet...'

'What? Agreed to what?' Harriet and Clementine leaned forward to hear.

'Cassandra Beresford at Little Acorns rang me this morning. The new teacher who's taken over the Y5 class came a real cropper on her bike last night. She's pretty sporty apparently and was doing some mad off-road biking up near the moors, fell twenty feet, broke her leg and pelvis very badly and had to be air-ambulanced off.'

'Gosh, the poor woman. And Cassie wants you to fill in?'

'She asked me, yes.'

'Not full-time, Grace?' Harriet pulled a face.

Grace nodded. 'Jonty's in Reception there already and Cassie says Pietronella can start in nursery a term before she was going to do anyway.'

'Blimey, you're mad. Full-time? With no Dan to help you at home?'

'It'll be fine. I'll drop Jonty and Pietronella off at Little Acorns. And then just stay. And teach.'

'And have all that marking and admin and meetings?' Harriet shook her head at the very thought.

'Come on, Hat, you know I've been itching to get back in the saddle again. What would I do all day by myself once the children were at school? Loads of mothers with two young kids have to work. And now Dan's out of work, and I'm technically a single mother I suppose, I really will have to work. And I want to.'

'Fair enough, but I think you'll find it hard. Shh, shh, David's about to say something.' Harriet turned from Grace and Clem towards the centre of the restaurant where David Henderson was tapping his glass to attract the guests' attention.

'Thank you all so much for coming here this morning to honour and to say goodbye to Amanda. None of us – Seb, Jonty, all who knew and loved Mandy and, of course, myself – could ever have envisaged this dreadful day. Although the terrible accident that took her away from us – her family and friends – was well over a month ago now, I still wake every morning expecting her to be there, laying the table for breakfast – always starched napkins, even for breakfast...' David broke off, unable to go on.

*Typical Mandy*, Grace thought. *Who the hell has napkins with their cornflakes, especially starched linen ones?*

'... I've been asking myself, what I'll do without Mandy. As I'm sure many of you know, we'd been together almost thirty years. The minute I saw her, on her first day as an undergraduate at Oxford, I was totally floored by everything about her. When Seb came along, completely unexpectedly, several months later, it meant her not completing her studies and her wanting to move back North to be near her parents, but I was more than happy to move with her. So, what will I do without her? Travel? Do good works? Get stuck into the garden? I really don't know...' Here he trailed off, seemingly unsure how to continue. 'I really don't...' He looked down as a little hand found its way into his own and he smiled down at Pietronella before bending down to lift her up. 'Grandchildren, whether my own or adopted...' He managed to smile at those around him. 'Mandy adored Jonty, Lysander and this gorgeous little thing here.' He stopped as Pietronella took hold of his tie and wiped at his eyes. 'There you go,' he said, 'grandchildren, that's the answer.'


'Oh God, don't look now...' Grace stopped in the middle of pouring milk into her coffee and turned her back on the woman making her way across the restaurant in their direction. 'I said, *don't look*, Harriet.'

'Oh, come on, if anyone says *don't look* the first thing you do is *look*... Vienna, how *are* you?' Harriet put down her own cup and smiled at the newcomer. 'I didn't see you in church.'

'Hello, Grace, hello Harriet, how very good to see you both. It must be, what, over two years since we were with you skiing in Cortina d'Ampezzo? Did you ever progress, Harriet? No? No. So, I assumed you'd both be here for poor Dave. No, you're right, I did tell Charles we should be setting off before we did, but would he listen? And then we found ourselves stuck on the M1 and I did so want to be here in plenty of time, you know, in order to give Dave our full support...'

'And how are...'

'... and, as I said to Charles last night when we heard the

news about poor Mandy, it's only right and proper that, as Dave and Mandy's oldest and dearest pals, we should be at his side throughout this whole dreadful business.'

Grace stared. 'You only found out last night? That Mandy had died I mean?'

'Yes. How awful is that? We've been away all of the summer, of course; we just *had* to get out of the country and away from all the damned Brexit issues. Anyway, it was Maxine Varsey-Drillington – do you know the Varsey-Drillingtons? – who rang me yesterday. She'd heard only that morning and of course I was *mortified* that, as Dave's very closest friends, we were totally unaware of the tragedy. I rang Dave straight away as you would expect but, according to his mother – charming woman – who answered the phone, he was down at the church with the vicar. She was able to fill me in with a few details.' Vienna Carrington broke off her monologue and Grace and Harriet, who found they'd both been holding their breath as her words hit them head on, relaxed slightly before she launched once more. 'Ah, Dave, you're here, you poor, poor man.' Vienna took one of his hands in both of hers in an overly dramatic hold. 'Why? Why on earth didn't you let us *know*? We only found out last night. And from Maxine VD of all people.' The manner in which Vienna said the latter's name left no doubt as to her feelings for the informant.

'Hello, Vienna, how are you?' David managed to release himself from Vienna's hold. 'Thank you for coming. I'm so sorry I've not been able to contact you. I knew you'd moved house again and I'm afraid the telephone numbers I had for you from when we were in Cortina appear to be no longer relevant and—'

'No, you're *right*, we did have to change them, there was a woman who was intent on stalking Charles. Had a *terrible* time with her.'

Grace, Harriet and David turned as one to look at Charles Carrington, and Grace wanted to giggle. Never in a million years would one anticipate the extremely large, doughy-looking man talking to Seb and Libby over by the bar, to be the recipient of untoward, unwelcome attention.

'Oh yes, fancied the pants off Charles, became quite obsessed with him. We had to change the house phone and mobile numbers.'

'Right, I see.' David looked mystified. 'Obviously, after what happened, I was particularly *desperate* to get hold of you and Charles…'

Vienna visibly preened. 'Of course, of course, Dave. As your closest friends, you would have wanted *us* to be one of the first to know of the tragedy.'

David hesitated for a second and frowned at this, but went on. 'Anyway, Mandy did have your new number but, unfortunately, she was in such a hurry when she left to stay with you, she wrote it up on the kitchen board wrongly. Well, I assume so. When I've tried to ring you on that number, I just draw a blank. End up with a taxi place in Dudley.'

'Left to stay with *me*? With *us*?' That little piece of information appeared to stop Vienna in her tracks like nothing had before. She stared at David.

'The day before the accident? Mandy said you'd invited her down to stay, Vienna. Some girly do near Birmingham? She was going to do some shopping in the city and then stay with you in Warwick. She was on her way back up the M1 the next day when it happened.'

Grace glanced across at Harriet who was staring intently at Vienna.

'I really don't know what you're talking about, Dave. I've not been in touch with any of you – including Mandy – since we all travelled back to the UK after our week together in Cortina two years ago.'

Grace felt her pulse begin to race as Vienna continued to speak, at first with some degree of concern before slowly morphing into righteous indignation at the realisation that Mandy Henderson had apparently been using her as some sort of unsolicited alibi. 'As I say, Dave,' Vienna went on stiffly, 'I've really no idea what makes you think Mandy had been staying with me.' She looked directly at Grace and then at Harriet who had gone quite pale, before fixing her large baby-blue eyes on David. 'Something's obviously been going on behind your back, Dave, but rest assured, neither Charles nor myself have any notion of – or involvement in – what that might eventually turn out to be.'

# 3

'I really can't imagine what's possessed you, Grace.'

'Possessed me?' Grace stepped neatly over a pile of tinned baked beans and tomatoes (chopped, with garlic and basil) and, taking a firm practised hold of her daughter's arm, placed it expertly into the Little Acorns navy sweatshirt along with the tin of tuna Pietronella's stubby fingers were intent on adding to her pile.

'Going back to work.' Katherine Greenwood tutted as she sat at the kitchen table drinking the coffee Grace had poured for her. 'And full-time for heaven's sake. You don't think it's total madness? Especially as Dan appears to have upped and left you once more.'

'It's one of the reasons I'm going back.' The gracious smile Grace offered up to her mother belied the thought that the older woman was probably quite correct in her prognosis regarding Grace's state of mind and that she was, in fact, *exceptionally* mad in returning to teaching when she had two young children to bring up singlehanded now that Dan appeared to be having yet another mid-life crisis and had buggered off to live by himself.

'What are you doing round here so early anyway, Mum?' Grace glanced up at the kitchen clock. Hell, this was when she needed two pairs of hands to get the kids up and ready and breakfasted, but she knew it would never occur to her mother to get stuck in. Especially with Pietronella who wasn't averse to sharing her soggy Weetabix with anyone who looked slightly interested in what was in her breakfast bowl. If she didn't get a move on, she was going to be late for her first day back at school. 'Jonty, for heaven's sake will you leave that iPad alone and come and sit down and eat your breakfast?'

'Not behaving?' Katherine sniffed, glancing over at Jonty who was still without a sock. 'It's all this toing and froing he does every weekend. One minute he's here and then he's over with Sebastian and Libby. And, for what's it's worth, Grace, I know Libby is your goddaughter, but she's only twenty-one...'

'Twenty-two.'

'Sorry?' Katherine reached for the cafetière and poured herself more coffee. Oh hell, she was obviously in for the duration.

'Libby's just gone twenty-two. Mum, do you think you could find Jonty's other sock. Jonty, will you put that damned thing down and eat?'

'Exactly.' Katherine sniffed again, this time at the milk in the little blue and white spotted jug Dan had bought Grace years ago on a weekend away in the Lake District. 'Exactly, Grace. Twenty-two and off back to university when Lysander – that really is a terribly *modern* name isn't it? – is so tiny and wanting his mummy at home with him. And, you know, Grace, I never once even *contemplated* childcare when you and your brother were little and I certainly never *swore* in front of you children when you were growing up.

'Modern?' Ignoring her mother's musings on what was appropriate language to use in front of her kids, Grace ferried both children to the table and poured cereal. She'd get up earlier in the morning, she promised herself. Make sure the kids had eggs of some sort. 'Lysander's as old as the hills, isn't it?'

'Oh, you know what I mean. Children today have such, such...' Katherine paused, searching for an appropriate adjective. 'Such *flowery* names, don't they? I mean, what's wrong with John or David? Talking of David...'

'I thought you were talking about Lysander?' Grace buttered a cold piece of toast, demolishing it in three bites.

'Well yes, I do think it's ridiculous that with all *their* money, Libby is going back to university instead of staying at home and looking after that little boy when he's only a year old. She'll miss out on so much. I mean, it's not as if she needs a career now, is it? With all that Henderson wealth behind her. All I'm saying, Grace, is you appear to have come out badly in all of this. Dan's decided, for whatever reason—'

'Mum!' Grace gave her mother a warning glance before bending to wipe Pietronella's mouth with a flannel and then, as the grey mush appeared to have multiplied like some alien being clinging parasitically, not only to Pietronella's forehead and school sweatshirt (one of Jonty's: with Mandy's funeral yesterday she'd not had a chance to pop into town to buy the requisite items for her) but also to Grace's best, let's-make-a-good-impression-on-my-first-day-back-at-school skirt, Grace closed her eyes and silently swore once more.

'Darling, I'm just saying.'

'Not in front of the kids, Mum.'

'To answer your question, I came round early to offer assistance. But, as I was *saying*, surely the Hendersons should be coughing up to help financially? Jonty *is* Sebastian's son after all. *And* David Henderson's grandson. Surely you don't have to go back to work, darling?'

'Mum, I want to go back to work. I *love* teaching and I'm suddenly been handed work at Little Acorns again without the palaver of applying, getting my CV up to date and going through interviews. You know all this. And of course, Seb pays for Jonty. You know *that*, too. So, don't make out we're starving in a garret. I just need to be a bit more organised. Whatever you might say about Dan, he did always help out with the kids.'

Katherine sniffed once more. 'And why wouldn't he?' She paused to ponder her own question. 'Although, I suppose, with these two not being, you know—' she lowered her voice '—his own flesh and blood...'

'Mum, for heaven's sake.'

'Where *is* Dandy?' Jonty, who'd obviously been taking in every little word between his mother and maternal grandmother, swirled the remains of his milk around three remaining soggy Rice Krispies until, with centrifugal force, the liquid shot over the rim of the bowl and onto Pietronella's school skirt.

'Naughty!' Pietronella grinned, sinking her fingers into the wetness of the navy material.

'Ridiculous name, *Dandy*,' Katherine Greenwood snorted. 'Sounds like that comic Simon used to love to read. Do you remember, Grace?' Katherine smiled nostalgically.

'Every Saturday morning he'd skip down to the newsagent in the village with me, holding on to my hand, desperate to get his hands on *Dennis the Menace*.'

'*Beano*,' Grace breathed under her breath as she stripped Pietronella of her skirt and sweatshirt and threw them towards the utility.

'Sorry? Oh, right. Desperate Dan then? And I bet *your* Daniel was feeling a bit desperate as well... I mean, no wonder he's left if he doesn't know whether he's Daddy or Daniel. The poor man obviously is having a crisis of identity.'

Grace found she was grinding her teeth. 'Jonty, you know Dandy isn't feeling too well at the moment and has gone to get better by staying at Granny Stevens's old house.'

Katherine snorted once more (years of practice in this particularly *equine* mode of disapproval had rendered her an expert in the field) before launching. 'Should have sold that house when Renee Stevens died last year. Give a man a bolthole and he will.'

'Will what?' Why on earth was she even getting into this conversation, Grace thought wearily, when she should be already in her new classroom, getting things sorted for the coming day's lessons?

'Bolt.' Katherine stood up, smoothed her Jaeger skirt and made to leave. 'If there's anything else I can do for you, darling, you know where I am.' She kissed Jonty on his head, frowned and nodded towards Pietronella – who, trying to help Grace, was now in the process of divesting herself of vest and pants – checked her watch and reached for her bag. 'I must dash, darling, I have a facial in the village booked in for nine.'

'What the fuck.' Pietronella was now standing, just in socks and shoes, reaching for something on the breakfast table but glancing back at Katherine.

'Did that child just say what I thought she said?' Katherine stopped in her tracks, staring in horror first at her adopted granddaughter and then at Grace. 'What did she say?'

'Want the fork,' Grace said calmly, handing Pietronella a white plastic fork from behind the butter dish. 'Ever since we took her to see *Toy Story* 4, she's been obsessed with white plastic forks. Go and see the film, Mum, and then you'll understand.'


'Oh, thank goodness, Grace. You're an absolute angel.' Cassie Beresford, headteacher of Westenbury's Little Acorns primary school, breathed a visible sigh of relief. 'If you hadn't agreed to cover, I'd have had to go in there again myself today while the supply agency came up with anyone half suitable. One day yesterday was enough and I've got so much admin to get on with today as well as a governors' meeting with David. How is he? I did pop over to the church for the funeral – you know, stood at the back to show my respects – but I didn't really know Mandy like you and Harriet did.'

'Enough?'

'Sorry?' Cassie smiled, obviously distracted by a commotion out in the corridor.

'You said one day was enough.'

'Well, they're not the easiest Y5 class I've ever taken, but you'll soon whip them into shape. You like them big and bolshy, don't you?'

*Not when I'm knackered already*, Grace thought idly, but said cheerily, 'You know me, Cassandra, I like a challenge.'

'Well, you'll certainly find this little lot challenging. April Harrison, their new teacher, appears to have had a somewhat shall we say *laissez-faire?* attitude to discipline. And she interviewed *so* well,' Cassie sighed, before marching towards the classroom door and the corridor to investigate and reprimand the bunch of Y6 pupils who appeared to feel it their prerogative, now they were in the top class with Mr Donnington, the deputy head, to be in when they should be out.

'Out,' Cassie barked at the four eleven-year-olds who were trying to make themselves invisible behind a mobile board displaying a selection of somewhat Picasso-esque Y2 self-portraits. 'You know the rules.' She glared at each one in turn as they trooped out into the playground before turning back to Grace. 'I don't know how long April's going to be off, Grace. It could be months. Oh, and watch out for Noah Haddon...'

By lunchtime, Grace was beginning to think April Harrison must have thrown herself off her bike and down that ravine purposely to get out of teaching this class. Three weeks with them had obviously been enough and she'd taken the easy way out. *Stop it, Grace*, she chastised herself as she headed for the staff room and her ham and cheese sandwich. *The poor woman has hurt herself badly and you, you're a professional with almost twenty years' teaching experience*. She wasn't going to let this bunch of kids get to her. They just needed a firm hand. She stopped in surprise as she saw Jonty outside the Reception classroom, a large galvanised bucket at his feet. It seemed strange seeing her own child in her place of work, and for a split-second Grace felt somewhat disorientated.

'What's the matter, Jonty, do you feel sick?' She turned in his direction rather than continuing down towards the staff room.

He shook his head but refused to look at her.

Grace frowned. 'What are you doing?'

Jonty looked at his feet, his face pale, but said nothing.

'What are you *doing*?' she repeated. 'Why aren't you outside with the rest of your class?'

'Miss O'Connor said I had to stand here and not play out.'

'But why?' Grace was mystified. 'Have you been sick? Do you feel ill?'

Jonty shook his head once more, indicating the bucket. 'I've got to spit into it until it's full.'

'Into the bucket? Spit into it?'

Jonty nodded. 'I did a spit at Mohammed, Mummy, and Miss O'Connor said if I liked spitting so much, I could stand here until I'd filled the bucket. But I can't.' He gave an ineffectual little spit in the direction of the enormous bucket (obviously commandeered from Stan, the caretaker's cleaning cupboard) and then started to giggle.

'Well, you can jolly well stop laughing, Jonty, it's not a laughing matter. You don't spit at the other children and then think it's funny.' Oh hell, this was all she needed: being a teacher in a school where her son was also a pupil, and where she was privy to all that he was up to, good or bad, was a whole new ball game. And she couldn't imagine Cassie being impressed by Jonty's punishment: it was a bit draconian – albeit pretty funny, she had to admit – and not what a modern headteacher, concerned with safeguarding would be encouraging in her school.

Grace dithered, glaring at Jonty as he tried a few more experimental spits into the bucket interspersed by giggles which made her want to laugh with him. Her heart melted: he was only five years old for heaven's sake. Well, he'd just have to take his punishment and hope Cassie saw him there and then have a word with Miss O'Connor. Grace didn't even know Miss O'Connor's first name. Both she and April Harrison had started at the school at the beginning of this new term and, whereas the former had apparently several years' experience under her belt (as well as, allegedly, a mountain bike constantly under her backside until her accident) this was Miss O'Connor's first teaching job and she was in her probationary year.

Grace glanced up at the huge, original Victorian clock that had methodically counted out the school's minutes, hours and years for well over a century and, swearing under her breath, realised that not only was she on playground duty but her uneaten and now somewhat squashed cheese and ham sandwich was still in her hand.

'We don't do it like that.'

'Are you talking to me, Noah?'

'Yeah.'

'Well, first of all you don't shout out in that rude manner, secondly, I have a name when you're addressing me, and third, I really don't need *you* to tell *me* how to do my job.' Grace felt herself bristle at the cocky ten-year-old slouched over his table. 'Oh, and sit up too when I'm talking to you.'

Noah Haddon turned round and grinned at his mates. 'But, Miss, it's not *your* job, it's Miss Harrison's. When's she coming back? We really miss her. *She's* a great teacher.' The implication, after a morning of teaching 5AH, that she, Grace, *wasn't*, hung in the air like a bad smell only to be replaced by a very real and noxious odour that wafted her way as she stood to stand in front of Noah, arms folded and eyebrows raised. 'Aw, Miss, Bradley's trumped.' Holding his nose in exaggerated offence, Noah and Bradley Armitage collapsed into loud guffaws.

Dismissing her first thought to send the pair of them out into the corridor with a galvanised bucket and instructions to stay there until they'd farted themselves silly into it, Grace rounded on the chief troublemaker. Rule number one of teaching: sort out the ringleader, go for the jugular and the rest will crumple. 'You and I, Noah, are in great danger of falling out. And believe me when I tell you, you don't want to fall out with me...'

By three-thirty, when the bell had rung for the end of afternoon school, Grace needed gin. 'Oh no, we're not having this. Come back and sit down right now,' she said with raised voice as there was a mass exodus for the door. '*I'll* tell you when you can leave. Pick that pencil up, Zane; put that book away, Rosie.' Grace barked orders while the class looked on, itching to be free for the day. 'I'm not clearing up after you.'

'But, Miss, we'll be late. Me mum gets cross if I'm late out.'

'Yes, Maisie, and *I* get cross if *I'm* late home because *I've* had to stay behind to clear up after you people. Right, stand behind your tables and let me see you leave this classroom in a civilised manner.'

This must be the worst class she'd ever experienced. Maybe it was her? Maybe the five years she'd been out of the classroom since having the children meant she no longer was able to handle a class?

'Staff meeting, Grace.' Josh Donnington, Little Acorns' deputy head waved across at her as he headed for the staff room.

Staff meeting? Oh, hell's bells, she'd forgotten the weekly Tuesday staff meeting. What was she supposed to do with Pietronella and Jonty? She couldn't do this. She couldn't be there for her own children while trying to manage and teach this unruly bunch she'd inherited. Her mum was right. It was madness. She'd go and tell Cassie right now it had been a mistake.

'Sorry, Mrs Stevens, I forgot my reading book.' Belle McKinley skipped back into the classroom. 'I really liked you being our teacher today,' she said as she rooted in her tray for her book. 'You will be here tomorrow, won't you?'

'Grace, how about if I take Pietronella and Jonty home with me for an hour?' David Henderson popped his head round her door as Belle gave them both a shy smile and continued to hunt for the book.

'Really?'

'Absolutely. If Mandy had been here, she'd have offered, you know she would.'

'Are you sure?' Grace smiled gratefully both at David and

then at Belle as she held up her missing book and headed for the classroom door.

Maybe, Grace thought as she shifted the pile of unmarked books into her bag, she could do this after all.

# 4

'What? What do you mean, Dad's coming back to live in Westenbury?' Ariadne Sutherland put down her untasted coffee and stared.

'I knew this would be how you'd react.' Dr Juno Armstrong, Ariadne's younger sister tutted.

'Who the hell does he think he is?' Ariadne scowled crossly. 'He ups and leaves Mum over sixteen years ago, marries some Russian tart—'

'He and Anichka never actually got around to getting married, Ariadne.'

'—has another child – our brother – who we've never even met for heaven's sake...'

'Er, actually, Ariadne, I have met him.' Juno pulled a face.

'You've *met* him? Our *brother*? This Boris boy?'

'Half-brother.' Juno was placating. 'And you know he's not called *Boris*. Arius is really rather lovely. He's an exceptionally bright kid about to start his A levels. Look, you might as well both know, I've never said anything, but I've been in touch with Dad quite a bit recently.'

'Same here.' Pandora, the third of the Sutherland sisters, bit her lip nervously. 'Not often though,' she quickly added as she saw Ariadne's face. 'It's just with Hugo and Arius being the same age, it seemed really rather silly not to get them together…' Pandora broke off, wilting under Ariadne's glare. The eldest of the four sisters, and exceptionally bright like her father, Professor Patrick Sutherland, the renowned classicist, Ariadne had the ability to cut one dead at forty paces.

'Oh, very cosy. The two of you have been playing Happy Families with Dad and this Arius kid all these months and you never thought to tell *me*? Did neither of you consider Mum in all this?' If Ariadne had been in a bad mood at the start of this conversation, she was now angry. 'How *could* you?'

'Because we knew we'd get just this reaction from you,' Pandora sniffed crossly.

'I could do with a drink,' Ariadne said mulishly, glancing at the half-full bottle of red by the sink.

'Well, you're not getting one here, Ari,' Juno retorted. 'It's only five o'clock and the kids will be home any minute. I don't want them reporting back to their father I'm already halfway down a bottle of wine again when they get in from school. I don't know how *you've* managed to get here so quickly, Ariadne. I thought you teachers never left your posts until midnight?'

'Heads of years have non-contact time for all the stress they're under,' Ariadne said somewhat loftily. 'I can work from home occasionally. So, Pandora, you've obviously been in touch with Dad more than anyone. What's the story? What's happened to make him want to come back to Westenbury? Where's he thinking of living? And, more importantly, how are we going to keep it from Mum?'

'Well, according to Dad, now he's long past retirement age – how old will he be now…?'

'I'm sure you two know exactly,' Ariadne snapped caustically. 'You know, with all the birthday cards you've sent him over the years.'

'He was seventy-two last June,' Juno said patiently. 'But he's still been working part-time at the university in Manchester. And he's still writing books.'

'I know,' Ariadne replied. 'I have them all.'

'You do?' Pandora raised an eyebrow at her eldest sister.

'Look, he may have been an adulterous, randy old dog all his life but he still is a brilliant classicist and, as a Classics teacher myself, I obviously have to keep up with current thinking.'

Pandora was about to put together a withering retort when Juno hastily jumped in between her elder sisters. 'So,' she went on, placatingly, 'Dad's just about retired; Anichka has now obviously realised she's ended up with an old man who probably wants looking after in his old age and has gone off with a much younger model; and Dad has been left with a sixteen-year-old to bring up. He feels all his family are over here in Yorkshire—'

'Family?' Ariadne snorted. 'He gave up all claims to *family* when he buggered off sixteen years ago.'

'—and, as you know, Midhope sixth-form college is one of the best in the country. Kids actually get the train across from Manchester on a daily basis. Did you know that?'

'Well, it's only thirty minutes on the train. Why wouldn't they if they can get a place there?'

'Anyway,' Juno went on, 'Arius won't *have* to get the

train from Manchester because he and Dad are going to be living back over here.'

'But where's Dad going to *live*?' Ariadne suddenly frowned. 'Is he buying somewhere? That last book of his that Channel 4 optioned must have paid pretty well. Oh, for heaven's sake, he doesn't think he can go back to living with Mum? After sixteen years away?'

'No of course not, don't be ridiculous.' Pandora frowned in turn. 'Lexia and Cillian are there with her anyway. I actually thought Lexia might be looking for somewhere herself now she and Theo have split up. But she says she's happy living with Mum.'

'God, just think of all that cake she's going to have to eat.' Juno grinned and the others laughed with her, easing the tension in the room somewhat. Helen Sutherland's obsession with *The Great British Bake Off* and all things cakey showed no sign of abating. Trouble was, with Helen, practice didn't make perfect.

'Dad's looking for somewhere to rent,' Pandora said, glancing up at the kitchen clock. 'I really must go and make Hugo's tea. It's so lovely having him at home all the time. Best thing we did letting him decide not to go back to boarding school. A lot cheaper too. Anyway, it's really good because Arius will be going to Midhope sixth-form college with Hugo.'

'Hasn't term started? We're heading towards the end of September now.'

'Hmm, Hugo's already done a week. Apparently, Arius is very bright and is going to do A level Russian – well, you would, wouldn't you, if your mum was Russian? The college has welcomed him with open arms and he's starting next week.'

'But where's Dad going to *live*?' Ariadne asked crossly once more. 'He can't be *anywhere* near Mum. It'll send her over the top knowing he's on her doorstep. And who's going to tell her he's moved back? *I'm* not doing it. I'm really worried that once she finds out, she'll think he's returning to her, not just to the village. You know what she's like: she'll end up stalking him, jumping out at him from behind the baked beans in the co-op.'

'I don't think she will. She says she doesn't want to be the one to keep us – and now the grandchildren – from seeing Dad. She is so much better than she was. You know she is.'

'I know that,' Ariadne nodded, 'but there's no way he can be allowed to be a part of her life. I am *not* picking up the pieces again.'

'Again? Ari, it was Lexia and myself who did all that at the time.' Pandora sniffed crossly and then paused. 'But I agree with you, Mum mustn't think there's any hope that he's coming back to her after all these years.'

'Yes, but...'

The banging of the kitchen door broke Ariadne off mid-rant and Pandora got up once more and again began to make tracks to leave. 'Your two are here now, Juno. I'm off.'

'Where's Tilda?' Juno turned as Gabriel, her thirteen-year-old walked into the kitchen.

'She's somewhere.'

'What do you mean, *somewhere*? Wasn't she on the school bus?'

'Yes, she's coming, she's somewhere. I'm starving. What

can I have?' Gabe headed for the fridge while Juno waited for the second bang of the outside door.

'*Where* is she? Why didn't you wait for her?' Juno tipped back on her chair to look through the kitchen window into the garden.

'I'm not walking with my *sister*. That would be so, like, *weird*. Can I have this pasta left over from supper last night?'

Juno didn't answer but stood to peer down the garden path through the open window. 'What's she *doing*? Tilda, what's the matter? What are you *doing*?' Without another word Juno left the kitchen and hurried down towards the bottom of the garden where Tilda was sat on the step underneath the Buddleia, the prolific purple flowers almost hiding her eleven-year-old. 'What's on earth's the matter, darling?'

Fat tears were rolling, seemingly unstoppable down Tilda's pale face. 'I hate it. I'm not going back.'

Juno sat down beside her and took her hand. 'Hate what, sweetie? School?'

'It's a *desperate* place, full of people who don't even know their square numbers. At eleven?' Tilda sobbed. 'Not to know your square numbers?'

Juno wanted to laugh at Tilda's use of the word *desperate* but, instead, did a quick trawl of her memory. Did *she* know them? She might be a doctor, and she supposed she must have known her square numbers at some point in her educational journey, but she couldn't, sitting here, in the warmth of a warm September afternoon with the scent of late summer flowers flooding her senses, recall seventeen squared.

'When Mrs Jamieson asked if we knew what square numbers were in maths, I stood up and went through them all right up to thirty squared... and I could have carried on...'

'Really? Seventeen and eighteen squared?' Juno tried a mental calculation but gave up as she saw Tilda's face.

'They all laughed at me. Even Mrs Jamieson laughed. And then Ethan Roberts said I was weird and Faye said... Faye said...' Tilda broke off, unable to continue.

'Faye?' Juno frowned. 'Faye from junior school? Best friend Faye?'

Tilda nodded. 'She said, "she's *always* been weird" and everybody laughed and now they've started calling me *Weirdo*.'

'It'll all be different tomorrow,' Juno soothed. 'Faye was probably just joining in a bit because, well, unfortunately that's what kids at your age do. They want to be on the right side.'

'You mean, not on the weirdo's side?' Tilda sobbed. 'And it *won't* be different tomorrow. I've not made any new friends at Westenbury Comp and all my old ones from Little Acorns are in different classes or they've suddenly got new best friends. I just want to go back to Little Acorns and be in Mr Donnington's class again.'

'The thing is, Tilda, you were a big fish in a little pond then. You were in the top class and form captain, and I know you and Mr Donnington got on really well, but—'

'I *loved* it there. Well, I'm not going back to that place tomorrow. You'll just have to sell my uniform and I'll be home-tutored.'

'Oh? And who's going to tutor you?' Juno smiled as Tilda wiped her eyes on her red and white striped tie.

'*You* can. You're a doctor. You're pretty intelligent. Not in Aunt Ariadne's league, I'll grant you...'

Oh, this daughter of hers. Such an old-fashioned little thing, as her grandmother, Helen, had once dubbed her. Too bright for her own good.

'... or Scott. Now you're almost officially divorced from Dad and finally admitted Scott is more than just someone at the surgery, well, I'm sure between the pair of you, you could take me on? And then I could have Classics tuition – I've always wanted to learn Greek and Latin – at weekends from Aunt Ariadne, singing lessons from Aunt Lexia, baking lessons from Granny...'

*God forbid*, Juno thought.

'... and then... then I could do like they do at Open University—'

'How do *you* know about what they do at the Open University?'

'—and go to summer school...'

'Summer school?'

'Hmm,' Tilda said, rubbing at her eyes once more but obviously perking up at the thought. 'I could do summer school with Dad in America and learn all my Physics and Chemistry there with him. I mean, for heaven's sake, in Science today we drew a Bunsen burner and then we were *allowed* to light it...' Tilda tutted in derision. 'So, I showed Mr Davis the old trick of running your finger through the yellow flame without it burning.'

'You put your fingers in the flame?' Juno tutted in turn.

'Of course. The hole is closed, there's no oxygen and so

wafting your finger through the yellow flame isn't going to burn it. Instead of being impressed at my knowledge, he got really cross and started going on about Health and Safety and listening to instructions and who did I think I was? I did explain my dad was a research chemist.'

'Oh Tilda.'

'And that I'd had a Bunsen burner for my *seventh* birthday and was totally aware of the dangers inherent in the oxygen-fuelled *blue* flame.'

Inherent? Juno stared. No wonder Tilda was, after just two weeks at Westenbury Comprehensive, beginning to get right up the noses of the teachers there. 'Come on, Tilda, go inside and get that uniform off—'

'I'm never putting it *on* again.'

'—and then go and see Harry Trotter before supper. He's needing some exercise. Go and ride him round the paddock. Oh, and see if there are any eggs from the hens.'

'Is she OK?' Ariadne and Pandora, making their way down the path towards their respective cars, stopped as Juno continued to sit in the sunshine, enjoying the last of the day's warmth.

'It's Tilda, being Tilda,' Juno said. 'She's finding it hard to settle into school. She'll be fine in a couple of weeks.'

'Well, I did warn you,' Ariadne replied. 'I'm really surprised you didn't go down the grammar school route when she passed the exam last year. Why you insisted she go to the local comp even though she was offered a place at the grammar is beyond me.'

'And you a socialist, Ari? Surely grammar schools don't have a place in your agenda?' Juno smarted under the hidden accusation that she'd not got Tilda's best interests at heart. 'I just wanted her and Gabe to be at the same school. I wanted her to be a normal little girl and go with the rest of her class; I didn't want her being hot-housed and thinking she was different from the others.'

'I hate to tell you this, Juno, but she *is* different. I know exactly how she's feeling because I loathed being at Westenbury Comprehensive myself all those years ago.' Ariadne paused and then went on. 'Making the right decisions re a child's education, even if doesn't quite fit in with what one believes, must surely come before one's own political agenda,' Ariadne said loftily.

'God, with you for an aunt, no wonder Tilda is how she is.'

'Have you thought about boarding?' Pandora asked. 'Hugo did so well up at St—'

'*Boarding?* No, absolutely not, Pan. For a start there's no way I'd want to be parted from her, especially now Fraser and I are about to get divorced. She'd think I wanted her out of the way.' Juno paused. 'You know, especially since she knows about Scott and me being an item. And, even if I wanted her to go away to school, I certainly couldn't afford it. She'll be absolutely fine in a few weeks. I know she will.'

# 5

Grace reckoned she'd give anything – even her much coveted Loro Piana cashmere sweater – for just one extra hour in bed this Saturday morning. She glanced at her phone on the bedside table – Jesus, it was only 6 a.m. – and tried playing dead, or at least fast asleep, while Pietronella, on her left, posted pieces of cold, hard Lego down her pyjama bottoms and Jonty, on her right, concentrated on employing her left arm, back and right arm as a makeshift Formula1 racetrack, zooming his car with a *brrrm brrrm* accompaniment that came to a crescendo every time it reached the vicinity of her ear.

David and Mandy had given her the beautiful navy sweater the Christmas after she'd had Jonty and was still with Seb, even though both she and Seb had known their somewhat brief relationship was already teetering. She didn't regret any of the past, Grace realised, as she wrapped one arm around each of her children and, roaring that she was Mr Sleep Monster, deprived of sleep, proceeded to tickle them unmercifully as punishment until they were breathless and hiccupping with giggles. No, she'd do it all again; she just wished at least one of the men she'd chosen to accompany her on this journey – her husband Dan and her ex-lover Seb – had been able to stay the course and would now take the kids down for breakfast and leave her to the extra sleep for which she so desperately yearned.

'Worms,' Pietronella said as she divested her chunky little frame of the ancient *Toy Story* pyjamas and, naked, headed back towards her own room for Willy, the stuffed soft-toy snake she was convinced was a worm. Despite her Down's Syndrome, Grace and Dan's adopted daughter was making really good progress with her speech and motor skills and Grace was determined to keep her at Little Acorns rather than having her educated at a school for children with special needs.

Grace's determination to keep *herself* at Little Acorns after the week she'd just endured at the hands of the class from hell was debateable, she mused, as she stroked Jonty's dark hair and breathed in his sleepy, musky little boy scent.

'Worms,' Pietronella pronounced again as she came back into the bedroom, now wearing her scarlet school sweatshirt – albeit back to front – and thrust Willy in Grace's direction.

'Darling, it's Saturday,' Grace said with a wry smile, accepting it would be the only willy heading her way that day. And probably in the near future too. Perhaps she should try Tinder? Or perhaps, she heard her mother's voice, she should try harder to mend the broken relationship with Dan. But she didn't think she wanted to. More and more, she was beginning to realise she actually didn't want to be with him. She didn't love him anymore. There, she'd acknowledged the fact once more, albeit only in her head. 'Pietronella, you don't need your school uniform on today.'

'Worms.' Pietronella frowned, wiggling Willy in Grace's face.

'Yes, it's worms. It's *worm* day,' Jonty shouted gleefully. 'Come on, Mummy, we've got to fish for worms.'

Jesus, that was all she needed. Grace had totally forgotten this bloody silly, money-raising, worm-divining caper she was expected, both as a parent and as a teacher, to attend at school. The last thing she needed on a Saturday morning was to be back at school, forced to watch Noah Haddon and his gang throwing worms in her direction. She'd ring Dan and tell him *he'd* have to take the kids. There was *no way* she was heading back to school herself on a Saturday morning. No way whatsoever.

'I thought you said Dan was bringing the kids?' Harriet, in the process of forking out the five-pound entry fee, which entitled her to a numbered patch of grass on the school playing field as well as a child's plastic watering can and a Tupperware box – presumably to hold the worms once divined – turned to Grace three places behind her in the queue.

'And I thought *you* said Nick was bringing your two and, as you were particularly *scoleciphobic*, there was no way on this planet you were having anything to do with this madness.'

'I have a phobia of worms, not *school*…' Harriet sniffed, shuddering and looking with distaste over to the main competition area where kids and their parents were already limbering up as if they were about to enter an Olympic event.

'Scoleciphobia *is* an irrational fear of worms, you daft thing,' Grace laughed. 'And you haven't got a *phobia*. You just don't like them. If you had an actual *phobia*, wild horses wouldn't have dragged you here, and you'd be trembling and sweating and about to have a panic attack.'

'Just what I told Nick on the phone last night when he said he was still in Milan and wouldn't be back in time.' Harriet tutted as Thea pulled her hand impatiently towards the playing field.

'We're going to *beat* you.' Thea, now joined by Jonty, was taunting a sandy haired, bespectacled little boy who had wandered hopefully in their direction. His mother glared at Thea in some distaste, raising an eyebrow in both Harriet and Grace's direction.

'These mothers who're also teachers at the school need to sort their own kids,' she said loudly for them to hear while glaring once more at Thea before grabbing hold of her own child's hand and marching off.

'Jesus, Thea is becoming insufferable,' Harriet said crossly to Grace. 'She's so bossy, so full of herself, totally different from Fin who wouldn't say boo to a goose. How they're twins is beyond me. Thea, back here *now*,' Harriet snapped, embarrassed. 'And it's not winning, it's the taking part that's important,' she added loudly for the benefit of the retreating indignant mother.

'Oh, that's just Monday morning assembly claptrap,' Grace whispered, grinning. 'We're in it to win aren't we, Pietronella?'

Pietronella grinned back, her dark eyes dancing behind the little rounded spectacles, Willy tucked under one arm, and a Tupperware box clutched determinedly in her hand.

'Oh, Juno, I didn't expect to see you here?' Harriet smiled. 'I thought Tilda had already left and gone on to the high school?' Harriet moved away from her designated patch of grass where Fin was hesitantly dribbling water from a small plastic watering can.

'Not like that, you need more water, Fin. Let *me* do it. *I* can do it.' Thea, red-faced and determined, snatched the can from Fin.

'Oy, Thea, not so bossy,' Harriet called, while her daughter, ignoring her censure, pounced triumphantly on her first worm, holding it aloft in the manner of a smug Little Jack Horner.

Juno laughed at Thea's feisty concentration and turned back to the others. 'Tilda *has* left, she left in the summer,' Juno smiled, 'but she insisted on coming back to see Mr Donnington. I'm afraid she's finding it hard at the comp.' Juno sighed. 'Anyway, my sister Lexia is here with Cillian somewhere; I said we'd share a pitch with her.' Juno stared at the little group of ex-pupils – now all in Y7 at Westenbury Comp – who had come back, mascaraed and highlighted, hair still in tight braids after two weeks on the Costa Del Sol, airing their nonchalance at this juvenile activity as well as flashing newly acquired braces on their teeth and bosoms that had magically appeared over the long summer break. They'd gone through the many rites of passage to high school and, while on Monday morning they'd be back in stiff shirt collars and the too long skirts bought by budget-conscious parents hoping for at least a couple of years wear in them, here, back at their old junior school they could show off their faux Michael Kors totes while pretending to ignore the teachers over whom, only ten weeks earlier, they'd cried as they handed final leaving presents and *Best Teacher in the World* cards.

Looking round, Juno couldn't see Tilda with any of these old mates of hers. Despite Tilda's determination to leave the house with some rather badly-applied glittery blue eyeshadow and too-black eyeliner (as well as without her glasses) she still seemed to have been left behind by the girls who'd once been her friends, but who were now either intent on ignoring the boys with whom they'd once played football, or were in the process of giving them and their older brothers surreptitious glances, eyeing them up with a new vision.

'God these girls don't half change during the summer break.' Juno frowned as she continued to scan the field for Tilda. 'They go from being little girls telling bad jokes, to braces, boyfriends and a chest to die for.' She paused. 'Who's the gorgeous girl serving pop and crisps?' She indicated, with a nod of her head, the makeshift bar at one end of the school field.

'Oh, of course,' Harriet said, 'she wasn't here last year when Tilda was in Y6, was she? That's Miss O'Connor, the new teacher in Reception. The twins and Jonty are in with her. She's from Dublin and I get the impression she's not finding these five-year-olds all that easy.' Harriet grimaced. 'Particularly Thea, who's becoming a real bossy little britches. I've told Miss O'Connor not to stand any nonsense from her.'

'She's like a young colt, isn't she?' Juno smiled as she and Harriet continued to admire the new teacher, her long black hair swinging in a ponytail at the top of her head as she dashed around trying to keep up with the demands of the refreshment queue. 'Gosh, wouldn't you just love to be her age once again?'

'Well, I hear you're having a pretty good time at *your age*?' Harriet said, giving Juno a sly grin. 'With the lovely Dr Butler?'

Blushing slightly, Juno nodded. 'We did try and keep it quiet for a while – you know while Fraser and I were in the process of separating – but gossip starts. You know how it is.'

'Well, I can't think of any reason you'd keep it quiet now. He is rather gorgeous; and he was most attentive when I presented him with my athlete's foot.' Harriet grinned. 'A bit embarrassing showing an extremely dishy doctor my manky toes.'

Juno laughed. 'I have to say, I keep on pinching myself that he's all mine; you know, that it's all worked out and that Gabe and Tilda really like him too. We've been together a good six months now,' she added, almost proudly.

'Good for you.' Harriet smiled. 'And brilliant that the kids get on with him as well.'

'I know. I can't believe my luck. Fraser didn't have a clue about any sport and Scott, like so many Antipodeans – or am I stereotyping? – is sports mad. Scott chats away to Gabe about motor racing and rugby and people I've never even heard of. He's even trying to get tickets for the rugby – don't ask me *which* rugby – down at Twickenham for the pair of them. Yes, it's all great.'

'So, any plans to move in together?'

'Oh gosh, early days yet, Harriet. And to be honest, I'm really enjoying being single – you know having the bed to myself when I want it. And, of course...' Juno broke off as an exceptionally attractive man arrived at Harriet's side, kissing her affectionately on both cheeks.

'Do you know David, Juno…? Put that worm down, Thea… *down*, away from me… David Henderson, Chair of Governors here at school?'

'Hello, David.' Juno held out her hand. 'We've never actually met although you're on our list at the surgery, I believe? I was so sorry to hear about your wife, really sorry for your loss.'

David held her hand, smiling down at her and Juno thought, as did every other woman to whom he was introduced, what a beautiful-looking man he was. His touch was warm, and the intelligent brown eyes that remained on her own for longer than was probably necessary, were kind and interested.

'Ah, Dr Armstrong I presume?' He smiled again. 'Yes, we are—' he quickly corrected himself '—*I am* a patient at the surgery but usually see Declan or, occasionally if I'm in need of gossip or a good laugh, Izzy.'

As David moved away, bending down to help Fin with a particularly tenacious worm, Harriet grinned across at Juno who was looking slightly flustered. 'So, is he as gorgeous as you'd heard?' she whispered knowingly. 'I've not known one woman who hasn't thought herself slightly in love with David Henderson on first meeting him.'

'What about on the second and third meeting?' Juno arched an eyebrow, still feeling slightly fluttery at David's touch.

'Still stands,' Harriet said. 'We've all been there with our little fantasies. Not that we'd ever admit to it, of course,' she added hastily. 'He's just one of those men. Charismatic I suppose you'd call him…Away with the *worm*, Thea…' She shuddered. 'God, I hate bloody worms… And of course, now that poor Mandy has died…'

'There's a vacancy in the village?' Juno smiled, both at Harriet's protracted dancing on the spot as she avoided worms escaping the underworld – Hades wouldn't be pleased, she thought idly – and her apparent enthusiasm for filling the vacancy left by Mandy's death. 'I thought Mandy Henderson was a big friend of yours?'

'Oh, it's all very incestuous – typical small town.' Harriet frowned. 'Grace and I were at school together with Mandy, although *she* was head girl when we were horrible adolescents – you know, smoking in the gym…'

'The *gym*?' Juno laughed.

'We didn't have a bike shed for some reason,' Harriet said seriously. 'It was the Girls' Grammar down in Midhope before it became a comp – they probably didn't think girls came to school on bikes. Anyway, Grace and I have had – obviously *had*, being the operative word now – a love-hate relationship with Mandy for nearly thirty years…' Harriet trailed off. 'Funny, isn't it? I never thought I'd miss Mandy as much as I do.'

'Poor David,' Juno sympathised. 'I can't imagine he'll even be *thinking* about anyone else but Mandy…' She broke off as David approached them once more and then, smiling at him – gosh he was rather gorgeous – set off to find Tilda, her sister, Lexia and her nephew, Cillian.

'You and Nick are coming over this evening, aren't you, Harriet?' David caught up with her as she and the twins headed back to the carpark, Thea triumphantly holding on to her third- prize box of Maltesers for twenty-three worms divined. 'You know, this birthday drinks-do my mother has insisted on giving for me? I could really do without it, to be honest.'

Harriet smiled. 'Would you rather we didn't turn up then? Say something's come up? Can't get a babysitter or something?'

'Oh God, no. Don't do that, and bring the kids anyway. My mother is determined to get me out and about and back into society.'

'Westenbury? Society?' Harriet started to laugh at the idea there was any society in this village of his and then was suddenly serious. 'How's Seb?' she asked. 'He's taken Mandy's death really hard, hasn't he?' She stroked David's arm through his dark-coloured shirt sleeve. Blimey, she thought, he might be a grandad – hell, she was a granny herself at the ridiculous age of forty-three – but at forty-seven, David Henderson looked ten years younger. There was a touch of grey at his temples but, when she thought about it, there always had been. He was tall and slim and those mesmerising dark eyes of his were bright and intelligent.

'Totally.' David frowned and then hesitated. 'My mother's helping me sort all Mandy's things at the moment. Heavens, she had some clothes, that wife of mine. You know, if you and Grace – and Libby of course – want to take anything when you're over this evening before we send it all off to the charity shops?'

'The charity shops? David, there must be thousands and thousands of pounds worth of stuff. Her Hermes bags for a start?'

'I know, but it's no good to me, is it? Pink was never my colour. And I might like to consider myself a modern man, but I'm afraid I've never fancied myself with a handbag.' David smiled at the thought.

'The thing is, I don't think Brenda and Barbara who run the hospice shop down in the village would have a clue what to do with all those gorgeous things. They'd have to totally up their insurance just to have the stuff there, don't you think?'

David frowned again. 'Bit of a liability, you mean? You know Mandy left all her jewellery to Libby and Pietronella?'

'Did she? Goodness.' Harriet was shocked at Mandy's thinking of her daughter. 'How kind of her.'

'She loved Libby, Hat.'

'I think she'd have loved anyone who wasn't Grace.' Harriet smiled. 'She hated the fact Seb was with Grace for a while.'

'No, you're wrong there, you know. OK, she didn't like that Grace was so much older than Seb and that she and Grace had been at odds with each other ever since they were kids, but she did have a certain affection for you two. Found you both a challenge – and you know how Mandy liked a challenge.'

Harriet nodded and then said in a low voice, 'Have you found out anything, David? You know, where Mandy'd been and who she'd been with, just before she died?'

David shook his head. 'All the police reports, and the crash investigation say she was by herself in the car. As far as *I* knew she'd been down to stay with Vienna in Warwickshire. She even texted me saying she'd arrived safely and Vienna and Charles sent their love. I really wouldn't have known any different if she hadn't had the accident and Vienna and Charles not been away all the summer – and the pair of them hadn't suddenly arrived at the funeral out of the blue like that.' David rubbed a hand over his eyes. 'Look, Harriet, you more than anyone knew what she was like. She dangled your poor brother, John, on a string for years. Do you think she was seeing *him* again? Could she have arranged to meet up with him for a clandestine couple of days?' When Harriet didn't reply, as she truly didn't know the answer, he went on, 'I mean, she was obviously up to her old tricks again. There was always *someone*.'

'How did you stand it?' Harriet was suddenly furious. 'How did you put up with it all these years?'

'Mandy, as I'm sure you know yourself, was a bit of an addiction.'

'Oh, rubbish, David. Surely there's only so much you can put up with? You're allowed one mistake in a marriage, but a whole string of them…?'

'Bloody little sod,' Grace interrupted their conversation, shaking her hair wildly as she appeared at their side.

'Who? Jonty?'

'No, of course not *Jonty*. I wouldn't say that about my own *son*. It's a kid in my class.' She turned to where a group of ten-year-old boys were giggling several hundred yards away as the ringleader, Noah Haddon, circled nonchalantly on his too-big bike, appearing totally innocent of the crime. 'I'll have him in class on Monday. He's not throwing worms in *my* hair and getting away with it.'

# 6

'Happy Birthday, darling.' Caroline Henderson raised her glass of champagne in a toast to her son. 'Here's to your next year being a lot, lot kinder than this last one turned out to be.'

'Happy Birthday, David.' Those gathered in David's garden, in the still warm, but fading light of the late September afternoon, dutifully raised their glasses in his direction. He hadn't changed from the navy shirt and chinos he'd put on that morning for his visit, as Chair of Governors, to the school and he appeared relaxed in a way he'd not been since the dreadful accident a month earlier. The heady scents from Mandy's carefully tended flower beds (she'd been a knowledgeable and highly competent gardener) drifted over to the patio where numerous outdoor chairs and sofas, laden and stuffed with expensive fabric cushions were an invitation to rest weary feet. Harriet, a keen but amateur gardener herself – when worms were not part of the equation – noted with pleasure the mushroom-shaped, vibrantly purple flowers of a mass of Trachelium next to the spikey cluster of white and pink Astilbe. Was there anything Mandy hadn't been a success at, once she'd put her mind to it?

'God, let me sit down.' Grace was the first to succumb, draining her glass as she kicked off her sandals and wiggled her bare toes in ecstasy. 'It'll be socks and boots again soon,' she said ruefully. 'We need to soak up the last of the summer while we can.'

Harriet and Clementine both made to join her on the upholstered garden swing. 'Shove up, Grace, there's room for three,' Harriet said. 'Is Dan coming?'

'He was invited—' Grace pulled a face '—but he's obviously decided not to.'

'Is he OK?' Clementine frowned. 'Rafe and I saw him a couple of evenings ago when we took the dogs out for a walk over the fields. He was just walking by himself, head down. Hardly acknowledged us at all.'

'Oh, don't ask me,' Grace snapped. 'He's driving me mad. He's beginning to look like someone on the streets. He didn't appear to have shaved or even had a shower when I called round at his mother's place with the kids after the ridiculous worm thing this morning.'

'Depression is a terrible thing, Grace.'

'Hey, don't lecture me, Clem,' Grace said tartly. 'I've been there, if you remember.'

'No, I *don't*, actually, Grace,' Clem replied, stung by the sharp retort. 'It was before I met you. Before I moved into the village.'

'Oh, I'm sorry, that was uncalled for.' Grace was contrite. 'I'm such a bad-tempered old boot at the moment. I'm *so* sorry, Clem,' she said again. 'I just don't know what to do about Dan. He's miserable, I know that, but he really appears to not want much to do with me and the kids at the moment. And yes, I know, if he's clinically depressed, he needs my help rather than my censure. He just keeps saying Mandy's death has affected him, knocked him sideways. And then, of course, he's been made redundant. But to be honest, Clem, before all this happened, we really weren't getting on at all. We were sort of tip-toeing round each other, almost making polite conversation. I don't think he'd hugged me for months, never mind, you know...' Grace lowered her voice. '... Actual *sex*.'

Clementine poured wine for her. 'Do you not think you've taken on too much? You know, Dan has taken off again and you've suddenly decided to go back to work full-time? That can't be easy with two kids. Do you really have to work?'

Grace shook her head. 'No, I suppose not. I could tell Cassie I'll cover just until she finds someone else to take over. Have to say, it's very tempting. Normally, I'd be loving being back in charge of a class again, but the kids I've inherited are really horrible. Actually, they can't be, can they? A whole class of thirty kids can't *all* be awful?'

'Is it the class above Allegra's?' Clem asked. 'They've always had a hell of a reputation. You'll sort them. That is, if you intend carrying on?'

'Well, I told Cassie I would, but I'm just so tired. And I *am* worried about Dan, even though, between you and me, things hadn't been right for ages. Part of me thinks we should never have given it another go once he'd left the first time. I just feel, oh, fed up that any relationship I've had hasn't worked out.' Grace glanced across at Seb who was stood talking to his father and grandmother. 'Seb's another one who's struggling. But *he* has a right to be miserable; he's grieving for Mandy and, knowing how close they were, he's going to have to take it day by day. But

I don't know what Dan's problem is.' Grace pulled a face. 'Probably me.'

'You're a very strong, independent woman, Grace.'

'Strong? What are you saying? That I must be hell to live with?'

Harriet, who'd been listening but not contributing to the conversation, gave a bark of laughter. 'I lived with her when we were students. Apart from her coming in drunk at three in the morning and waking us all up, singing Etta James's "I Just Wanna Make Love to You", pinching my best – my one and only – cashmere sweater and concocting revolting things to eat with tins of baked beans and spaghetti hoops, she was alright, really.'

'My culinary expertise has moved on,' Grace said seriously, 'and I now have my own cashmere – a Loro Piana jumper, no less. But I still *love* Etta James's "I Just Wanna Make Love to You."' She sang, slowly and convincingly, belting out each note so that David and Seb, stood chatting with Nick and Rafe – Harriet and Clem's husbands respectively – both turned as one and smiled. 'I miss singing. I really enjoyed being involved in *Jesus;* it was good fun, wasn't it?'

'Food for the soul.' Clem smiled. 'There, Seb's looking a lot better than he did a few days ago. He was over at the restaurant last week with David and Caroline and looked quite dreadful.'

'He'll be fine,' Harriet said hopefully. 'He's got Libby and the boys. And, although he and Libby have enough on their plates with the new house and Lysander as well as with them both working full-time, he often takes Pietronella as well back to the farm with him when he comes to pick up Jonty.'

'Look how he's looking at Libby now,' Clem said fondly. 'He really adores her, doesn't he?'

Grace felt a twinge of what she hoped wasn't envy, but had a horrible feeling was just that. She didn't ever recall Seb gazing in her direction with such love in his eyes as he was now looking towards Libby. OK, she and he had had a very intense physical relationship for a couple of months – Grace almost blushed remembering the amazing sex they'd shared – but she was sure that, had she not fallen very unexpectedly pregnant with Jonty after years of trying for a baby with Dan, she and Seb would surely have drifted apart, their age difference a huge factor in bringing the affair to an end, and they'd both have happily gone their own ways without any regrets. She watched as he bent down to say something to Jonty and then, swinging him up onto his shoulders, walked over to Libby who was in the process of preventing Lysander from falling into the pond with the Koi carp.

Clementine continued to smile across at Seb and Libby, who now had their arms wrapped around each other, when her phone rang. 'What, this evening? No, I'm not working in the restaurant tonight but... Leeds? ... Why over there? I'm here with Harriet and Grace... Well, I can ask them...' Clem held her mobile at arm's length. 'It's Izzy,' she whispered. 'Off to Leeds for a girls' night out with Juno, apparently, for some reason. Wants to know if we're up for it...?' She was shaking her head and pulling a face as she mouthed, 'I'll tell her we're here and we're all busy and can't get babysitters, shall I?'

Harriet was shaking her head in perfect synchronisation with Clem's. 'Yes, say that,' she mouthed back. 'No way do

I want to trail over to Leeds at such short notice.' She was looking forward to getting the twins into bed early and having a lazy evening with Nick over a cheese and ham sandwich, a glass of SB, and a catch up of *Killing Eve*. She could almost taste the combination of Wensleydale cheese with the York ham she'd bought from the deli in Sainsbury's yesterday. It didn't take much, she thought ruefully, to get her revved up and excited these days.

'That would have been *really* great, Izzy, but... oh right... *your* birthday too? It's David's today as well.' Clem held the phone away from her once more. 'It's Izzy's *birthday*,' she whispered to the others, a little moue of despair on her face.

'Oh, come on, let's go,' Grace suddenly said loudly. 'I've not had a good night out for months.'

'We went to that flower-arranging thing with Westenbury Young Wives,' Harriet said accusingly. 'You know, a couple of weeks ago.'

'Exactly,' Grace snorted. 'Well I'm up for it. Give me the phone, Clem. Izzy? It's Grace. *I'll* come with you. Just let me sort babysitters and get my glad rags on and then I'm with you.'


'How come it's a girls' night out on a Saturday and on your birthday?' Grace smiled at Izzy before pulling closed the door of the minibus taxi behind her and, sitting herself down on the somewhat grubby seat, proceeded to fasten herself in. 'God, I've not done the whole minibus thing with a gang of women for years. I'm a bit out of practice.'

'So am I,' Juno said, slightly nervous. 'We don't have to drink tons of cocktails with overtly sexual names, do we?'

'Oh, for heaven's sake you two,' Izzy shouted down the bus from where she'd bagged the back seat as a matter of course, obviously re-living her school-bus days. 'You sound like a pair of blue-rinsed old ladies on a Sunday afternoon church outing. I'm ordering Cock-Sucking Cowboys all round when we get there.'

Juno raised her eyes skywards as Grace laughed and asked, 'Get where? You haven't told us where we're going yet... hang on, this is Harriet's lane... down here.'

'Well,' Izzy explained, as Harriet appeared on the drive and waved, only to disappear back into the house with a sobbing Thea two seconds later, 'Declan *had* booked a table for the four of us – me, Declan, Juno and Scott – at *Clementine's* and, much as I adore going there, it does make you feel your age a bit.'

'Which is?' Grace asked, smiling as she peered out of the minibus window. 'What *is* Harriet doing?'

'You're *not* allowed to ask the age question, Grace,' Izzy sniffed, producing a bottle of Prosecco and a couple of plastic glasses, ignoring the STRICTLY NO ALCOHOL signs on every window. 'It's OK, really it is,' she called to the young Asian driver who was glaring at her through his rear-view mirror. 'We're doctors, responsible members of the community.' She popped the cork, poured two glasses and handed them to Grace and Juno. 'Ah, here's Harriet... oh, no, gone again...' Izzy took a mouthful of the gassy liquid and pulled a face. 'Never understood the mania for this stuff. So, as I was saying, Declan had booked a table for the four of us, totally forgetting, the pillock that he is, that he and Scott were already booked on a long weekend away together in Portugal.'

'So *Declan's* having an affair with Scott now, is he?' Grace laughed. 'And did you know about this, Juno?'

'We're always having to prise the pair of them apart,' Izzy said almost crossly. 'Juno and Scott, I mean, not Declan and Scott. God, I daren't go into Juno's practice room at the surgery for fear of finding them at it on the examining couch or over her desk.' Izzy sighed, pouring more alcohol. 'She's still in the throes of that wonderful feeling of being in love with a new man.'

Juno tutted, embarrassed. 'Do you mind, Izzy?' But she couldn't help grinning. 'OK, I am, I am. I admit it all and it's brilliant.'

'So how come Scott's gone away with Declan?' Grace asked.

'Golf, bloody golf.' Izzy pulled a face. 'Some annual doctors' competition. They were supposed to be back this afternoon, so my celebratory birthday dinner was still on for this evening. And then Declan phones at lunchtime to say the plane's been delayed by five hours.'

'Five hours?' Grace asked. 'Blimey, well at least they'll get some sort of compensation from the airline for that.'

'And *we* get to have a girls' night out,' Izzy laughed. 'Fair dos.' She belched discreetly, momentarily closing her eyes 'Goodness, this stuff makes one horribly flatulent.'

'Who sounds like a windy old woman now?' Juno raised an eyebrow. 'What *is* Harriet doing?'

They all peered out of the bus window to see Harriet calling for Nick as she attempted to peel a sobbing, pyjamaed Thea off her right leg, the tarnished silver tiara atop Thea's blonde curls hanging drunkenly over one eye. 'But *I* want to go out on a girls' night out,' she was sobbing. '*I'm* a *girl*. You're all old ladies.'

'That child will go far.' Izzy grinned as Harriet, slightly dishevelled, finally climbed the steps of the minibus.

'All the way to approved school – or boarding school at least – if she carries on like this.' Harriet ran a hand through her hair and took a vacant seat. 'I've already been hauled in to see Cassie at school this week about her behaviour, the little madam.'

'Have a drink,' Izzy laughed.

'Class A drugs will do,' Harriet said, straightening her skirt. 'God, I feel I've been dragged through a hedge backwards. Don't worry,' she shouted, as she caught the worried eye of the driver, 'I was only kidding. Right, we need to pick Clem up and then we can get off down the motorway. 'Where are we going in Leeds, Izzy?'

'All will be revealed,' Izzy said importantly. 'Trust me, I'm a doctor.'

'You *are* joking?' Grace, Harriet, Clementine and Juno followed Izzy into a large, draughty village hall in some fairly sleazy suburb of Leeds on the outskirts of the city. Even Izzy had the grace to look somewhat alarmed as they trooped in and stood at the back while what must have been around sixty women in front of them began to settle themselves at various tables, bottles of Prosecco and trendy gins at the ready.

'Izzy, what are we *doing*? Why are we *here*?' Clementine wasn't at all happy and spoke sharply as she glared at Izzy.

'Oh, it'll be fine,' Izzy said airily. 'I've been promising Leo I'd come to one of his shows for ages, and, with Declan and Scott standing us up, this suddenly seemed a good opportunity. So, I rang him this afternoon to find out where he was performing this evening and…' She trailed off, quailing somewhat at the others' stony faces.

'So,' Grace said, eyebrow raised, 'I'm assuming Leo isn't a lion? Or a lion *tamer*?'

'A comedian?' Harriet ventured hopefully. 'You know, practising in the sticks before he makes it at The Apollo? I like a good comedian.'

'A stripper,' Juno sighed, closing her eyes momentarily before turning back to the others. 'Leo Hutchinson or, to give him his Sunday-best name, "Big Leo – King of the Jungle", is on our list at the surgery.'

'I don't think you should be proclaiming that in public, Juno,' Izzy said primly.

'What?' Juno asked crossly. 'That Leo Hutchinson is a stripper? Or that he's *big*? I would imagine we'll be able to assess that for ourselves before too long, don't you?'

'No, I mean, that he's on our list.' Izzy lowered her voice to a whisper. 'At the surgery, I mean. You know, patient confidentiality and all that?'

'Oh, for heaven's sake, Izzy.'

'Well, I've always felt a bit sorry for him.' Izzy shrugged her shoulders, looking round for a vacant table. 'He's managed to get off the drugs; he's very proud of himself for that, and now he's trying to make it with this new business venture of his. As his GP, I think I should be giving him the moral support he's asking for.'

'Well, it can't be that you're here to see his bits and pieces,' Juno said grimly. 'He has them out for examination every time he's in the surgery. Half an hour, Izzy, I'll give him half an hour and then I want to go into Leeds itself for a decent drink and a dance. Which is what you promised us from the get-go.'

'With just a little diversion before we get there,' Izzy grinned. 'Oh, come on you lot, stop acting your age and think of it as something to cross off your bucket list.'

'A sighting of the Aurora Borealis heads *my* bucket list,' Harriet said resolutely, 'not a sighting of Big Leo's lurrrve tool.' She thought longingly of the cheese and ham sandwich she'd had to forego in order to comply with this little outing of Izzy's. God, could this day get any worse? Worms and now, apparently, willies.

'Shh, shh,' Izzy ordered as Grace managed to procure a couple of extra chairs in order that the five of them could sit down around a somewhat wobbly table at the edge of the hall. 'It's starting.'

A tinny sound system coughed out the first few notes of Bruno Mars' 'Uptown Funk' and the women in the room roared their approval, those at the back standing up and hollering in expectation of what might materialise from the billowing clouds of dry ice drifting from the stage.

'My goodness, look at that smoke,' Clem said, worried. 'Something's on fire…'

'I wish they'd sit down,' Harriet complained. 'I can't see.'

Grace laughed. 'And do you want to? Really?'

'Well, now we're here, and we've paid our tenners for the privilege, it would be rude not to, don't you think? It's dry ice, Clem, stop panicking.' Harriet patted Clementine's arm. 'Have a drink, it'll make it all seem less awful.'

'Pour me one and make it a big one,' Grace said grimly over the music hiccoughing round the hall. 'If I've got to be here, I might as well go for the whole experience.' She downed a glass of the cheap, warm Chardonnay from the makeshift bar – did they have a licence, she wondered? – and, wincing as the metallic-tasting liquid went down, stood and began to clap and cheer along with the young girls, mothers and grannies (possibly great-grannies, she grinned to herself, as she viewed the tiny shrunken woman on the next table, yelling and clapping with gusto) who had left husbands and partners at home to see King Leo get his kit off.

'Oh, for heaven's sake, do we *have* to join in?' Juno gave one final furious glance across at Izzy and then, picturing her soon-to-be-ex-husband Fraser's look of total disapproval if he were to see her now, stood up and, in order to help create some sort of atmosphere in the chilly room, gave a fairly inaudible 'Get 'em off.'

'You'll have to shout louder than that, love, if you want to see what he's got,' the granny on the next table cackled loudly in Juno's direction.

'I can't even see *him* in all that dry ice, never mind his tackle,' Juno laughed, beginning to enjoy herself. She was really happy, she thought to herself: she no longer had to think about Fraser; Scott would be home from Portugal later that evening and round to see her the following day and, once *this* farce was over, she and the girls could head into Leeds. She'd always loved clubbing, loved the sultry heat and heavy beat of a really good nightclub, but marriage to Fraser had put an end to all that. She'd suggest she and Scott go clubbing, she thought, hugging herself at the idea. She didn't even know if he'd be up for it; that was the beauty of a still fairly new relationship – there were always things to surprise and delight you about them. Did he like dancing? Was he any good at it? Or was he a dreadful dad-dancer? If his expertise at sex was anything to go by, she reckoned Scott must be a veritable Dirty Dancer. God she'd loved that film; still did, if she was honest. Patrick Swayze had been her first love and, although she must have been only a little girl when the film first came out, when she was around twelve she and her mate Jenny Cooper had sneaked into Jenny's sitting room one hot afternoon during the long boring six-week summer holiday from school when they should have been outside playing tennis and watched Mrs Cooper's video of the film. Something had happened to Juno that afternoon. She wasn't quite sure what it was, but she knew it felt really lovely and made her want to squirm on the brown moquette sofa she and Jenny were sitting on, one ear alert for Jenny's mum telling them to go outside – they shouldn't be watching films like that at their age.

The only worry Juno had, she realised as the dry ice drifted towards them, making her want to cough, was Tilda and her seeming inability to settle at the high school. Putting that from her mind and knowing her daughter was with her Aunt Ariadne until the following day, Juno beamed down at the others and gave another, this time much more audible, 'Show us what you've got!'

# 7

'What's he doing now?' Harriet peered through the dry ice swirling around their table. It reminded her of foggy November mornings when she'd feed the kids porridge with syrup and search out the previous winter's scarves, woolly hats and gloves before sending them off to school wrapped up against the cold. 'Do you not think he's overdoing the misty atmosphere just a bit?' She reached for her cardigan. 'I'm frozen.'

Grace and Izzy started laughing as Harriet wrapped the warm pink garment around her upper body. 'Jump up and down a bit and join in. Are you not feeling even *slightly* hot at the sight of the Jungle King's bronzed, gleaming body?' Grace was obviously enjoying herself.

'Bronzed, gleaming body?' Harriet tutted. 'He's a five-foot-three, seven-stone weakling and he'd have sand kicked in his face if he ever *attempted* to acquire a beach tan. Can we go yet? I'm starving.' She turned back to the stage. 'What the hell's he doing now? Is he simulating sex? Hang on, I need my glasses… Is that panting and heavy breathing supposed to be a turn-on?'

'Must be,' Grace laughed. 'Those women at the front are really going for it.'

'It's a bit excessive, isn't it? You know that noise he's making?'

Izzy suddenly grabbed Juno's arm, a look of determination on her face. 'Come on, Juno,' she urged as she set off towards the front.

Clementine turned to Grace and Harriet. 'Oh, please don't say they're off for a threesome with him. Izzy's had too much to drink. Oh, for heaven's sake, they're on the stage with him... they've got him on the floor...what are they *doing*?'

The music – Christina Aguilera's 'Dirty' – came to a sudden abrupt halt as the flimsy red velvet curtains swung drunkenly across the stage to meet each other, hiding King Leo, Izzy and Juno from view apart from one pale, skinny leg protruding from behind the moth-eaten material.

'I don't *think* it's a private threesome,' Grace ventured, frowning. 'Come on, let's see what's up.'

The lights in the hall flickered and then came on, revealing the harsh reality of sixty or so bewildered women rubber-necking and peering towards the stage. 'Is he alright, love?' one elderly woman in gold lurex asked, as Clementine, Harriet and Grace made their way down to the front. 'What time's he back on? Have I got time to spend a quick penny?'

'Do they think we're his managers?' Harriet said crossly and Grace laughed.

'Well, we've not had us money's worth tonight, have we?' Two skimpily dressed, heavily made-up girls glared at the three of them as they hurried past to join Izzy and Juno. 'I said we should have gone to Bingo. Have we still time to make the first house?'

'Clem, ring 999,' Izzy snapped. She'd obviously sobered up fast and was in the process of administering an EpiPen to Leo's thigh. 'He's a severe asthmatic,' she said grimly, 'and allergic to just about everything.' She held up the pen before plunging it heavily once more into his leg.

Harriet and Clementine looked away.

'The dry ice has obviously got to him,' Izzy panted, sitting back on her heels, 'but there's something else.' She moved back towards Leo's head, attempting to peel back his closed eyelids. 'Oh hell, I think he's back on the drugs; I think he's overdosed.'

Although Clementine had obviously almost immediately got through, she seemed unable to speak to the operator and Juno grabbed the mobile from her hands, speaking swiftly and authoritatively. 'Drug overdose... not conscious, no... I'm his GP... yes, at a strip club with him... well yes, his *GP*... well *two* of his GPs actually...'

'Not exactly a *club*, is it?' Grace murmured. 'A village hall, surely?'

'Clem, are you OK?' Harriet had turned to say something to Clementine but, taking in her white face and obvious distress, took her arm, leading her down the three steps and off the stage, sitting her down before handing her a bottle of abandoned water.

'Lucy,' Clementine sniffed, searching her pocket for a tissue and waving away the bottled water. 'Seeing Leo like that, you know in that state, just reminded me of how Lucy used to be when she was on the drugs. It all just came back. The minute we walked in, and I realised we were at a strip-do, I felt anxious. Do you remember years ago, when we were here in Leeds and realised it was Lucy pole-dancing?

I'm feeling the same as I felt then, Hat. I just want to go home to Rafe and the kids.'

'The first time you told us Lucy was your twin? I'll never forget it.'

'I used to love Leeds, loved it when I actually worked in the restaurants here, but after that night...' Clem blew her nose.

'Izzy should have known better than to bring you somewhere like this.' Harriet was cross.

'The thing is, Hat, you lot don't realise what's going on.'

'Us lot? What do you mean, *us lot*? Going on? What, here in Leeds?' Harriet frowned. 'There's drugs in all big cities.'

'And in the villages,' Clem said shortly.

'Villages?' Harriet stared.

'Oh, for heaven's sake, Harriet. How do you *think* Leo gets his drugs? He doesn't need to take himself off into Leeds or Manchester or Midhope anymore. Or into *any* city centre. If you want drugs, you can get your supplies anywhere.'

'But not round where we live?' Harriet shook her head. 'Not in Westenbury and the village I live in?'

'Sometimes I think you and Grace are *so* naïve, Harriet. You live in your cosy little middle-class white oasis, the pair of you.'

'Westenbury isn't like that. The Patels live up our lane,' Harriet protested, feeling slightly foolish as soon as the words left her mouth. 'And India's friend, Nareem, lives down in the village and often comes home with her.'

Clementine tutted. 'You don't know the half of what goes on. Guests at the restaurant regularly snort coke in the gents.'

'No? Really?'

'Really. You go to any middle-class dinner party these days and if you want to relax with a joint over your coffee and petits-fours at the end of the night, *someone* will more than likely have something for you.'

'I think you're making this up, Clem. You're ultra-sensitive because of what you've been through with Lucy.'

'Where do you think Leo's got his gear tonight?'

'His gear?'

'His stuff. His drugs,' Clementine continued crossly.

'I've no idea. I wouldn't have a clue.' Harriet gazed around at the women in the hall who were now – after the organiser of the evening's entertainment had appeared through the curtains to explain and apologise – gathering bags and half-drunk bottles of wine and making their way towards the exits. She couldn't imagine any of *these* women pushing drugs.

'County lines,' Clementine snapped.

'County lines?'

'Young people – kids as well – being used to bring drugs into the shires, into the villages round here from the drug gangs and dealers in Manchester and Leeds.'

Harriet shrugged. 'I suppose I have the image of drug pushers being heroin users themselves, you know hanging round doorways and nightclubs in the town centres.'

'What these people in their big houses and gated communities don't realise, when they're offering drugs at their trendy dinner parties, is the danger young kids who're persuaded into this life are in. Or, if they do, they don't appear to care. It could be *my* kids, *your* kids.'

Harriet was momentarily startled. Surely Thea and her little gang of friends weren't already drug-dealing?

'Max is eleven now, the same age as Juno's daughter, and just started at the high school. I can't be watching him every minute. I don't know what he's up to when he's at football practice or playing cricket.'

'Playing football and cricket, presumably.' Harriet smiled. 'Come on, Clem, you really are being over the top here. As if Max would be drug-dealing.'

Clementine tutted. 'I don't for one-minute think he's got anything to do with what's going on in the village, Harriet. But who knows? And these kids aren't drug-*dealing*. The *dealers* do that. No, the dealers just suck up kids by whatever means to hand and get them to *carry* for them. You know, take the drugs on trains into the outlying areas and villages for them. These kids are *mules* and no one suspects the cute kid on the train in his football gear or cricket whites of having anything else but a cricket ball, a Mars bar and a towel in his sports bag. But they're wrong.'

'I'm really glad you decided not to get the train back home and came out to eat with us instead,' Izzy said, squeezing Clementine's arm. 'And I apologise for dragging you into that den of iniquity. I should have thought, you know, about Lucy and everything…' She trailed off as the waiter placed their starters in front of them. 'And you'd have missed this fabulous food too.'

'I'm so hungry,' Juno moaned greedily as she reached for the bread basket. 'I need something to mop up all that cheap wine you made us drink, Izzy.'

'I think, all in all, it wasn't a bad start to my birthday evening,' Izzy said seriously. 'It could have been a lot worse.'

'I doubt it.' Grace raised an eyebrow. 'Izzy, it was *awful*.'

'*Terrible*.' Juno agreed, laughing.

'Something to tell your grandchildren when you're an old lady,' Izzy said patiently. 'We should *have* these experiences. They all add up to the minutiae of life.'

'They wouldn't believe you,' Harriet said through a mouthful of seafood. 'God, these prawns are divine. One minute, you're cheering King Leo on, and the next you're jabbing an EpiPen into him. Will he be OK, do you think?'

'Yes, he should be. I did wonder if I ought, you know, as his doctor, to go with him in the ambulance, but I draw the line at sitting for hours on end on a hard plastic chair with the rest of Leeds's Saturday night drunks and brawlers.'

'Thank goodness he had his EpiPen with him,' Juno said.

'He didn't,' Izzy said. 'Or at least he didn't have it with him on stage as far as I could see.'

'Bit difficult to have it on him when he was stark-bollock naked, apart from that dreadful, mangy leopard-skin pouch hiding his bits and pieces.' Harriet started to laugh.

'I always carry one with me,' Izzy said. 'You know, in my handbag.'

'What, a leopard-skin pouch?' Harriet stared.

Izzy tutted. 'No, you moron, an EpiPen.'

'Really?' Juno was impressed. 'I certainly don't.'

'Ever since I had a child die in front of me at a netball match when Emily was at junior school. The poor kid would more than likely have been OK if she'd carried an EpiPen.'

They were all silent as they digested this dreadful bit of information.

'I need to *dance*,' Juno said eventually. 'Once we've eaten, I vote we find somewhere to dance.'

'I'm up for it,' Izzy grinned. 'It is my birthday after all. Do you know, I think the last time I had a good bop was when we came into Leeds just before you married Peter, Clementine. Do you remember how funny Mandy was, taking us into that gay club – she had no idea that's what it was?'

'I miss her,' Grace said simply. 'She might have been an absolute pain in the neck—'

'In the backside,' Harriet nodded in agreement.

'—but I miss her. At least she always knew what things were on the menu. What the hell have I ordered here?' Grace poked about the plate with her fork.

'Did you ever hear that story about Mandy and the thank-you letter?' Harriet put down her drink, laughing.

The others leaned forwards, shaking their heads.

'Well,' Harriet said, 'you know what an absolute stickler for etiquette and thank-you letters Mandy was?'

'God, yes,' Grace frowned, 'you couldn't compliment her on a new dress without her sending one of her expensive little thank-you cards.'

'So, apparently, David and Mandy had been to some big, upmarket wedding near Harrogate. Big posh do. And afterwards, Mandy, as always, sends a card to the girl's mother, their host. "Thank you so much for a perfectly delightful reception," she writes, "the food was superb, the setting and flowers exceptional and, as for Naomi's dress, well, her dress was absolutely *minging*..."'

'No!' Grace, Clem and Juno stared open-mouthed while Izzy gave a bark of laughter. 'And was it? You know, *minging*? A revolting *meringue*?'

'No, of course it wasn't,' Harriet giggled. 'This was

Harrogate, for heaven's sake. No one wears over-the-top wedding dresses in Harrogate. No, typical Mandy, she liked to think she was up with common parlance. Unfortunately, this time she got it wrong, thinking minging meant ravishingly sublime. She was snubbed by half of Harrogate until someone let on why and she then had to grovel to get back into society. You're right, Grace, I do miss her. She always gave us something to talk about.'

'Like she is doing now.' Izzy leaned forward, always eager for gossip. 'So, I heard she was *with* someone when she died? And not David?'

'Don't know where you've heard that, Izzy,' Grace said shortly, obviously in protective mode. 'There was only Mandy in the car when it turned over on the M1.'

'I bet she'd been up to *something*,' Izzy insisted, waving her wine glass around so the last of its contents splashed onto the tablecloth. 'I know,' she grinned, 'I bet she was Mrs Big…'

'Mrs Big? What *are* you taking about, Izzy?'

'I bet anything she was running a drug cartel for all the middle-class recreational drug users in their big posh houses in the village and was down in Birmingham to restock her supplies. What about that, then? She was an extremely intelligent woman was our Mandy. Intelligent, bored housewife, running an international drug cartel…'

'Westenbury? International?' The others laughed. 'God, you do talk rubbish at times, Izzy. She was actually a lawyer at one point,' Grace added. 'You know, on the side of the good guys?'

'Great cover. You'd never suspect an ex-lawyer.' Izzy raised an eyebrow.

'She's a magistrate... *was* a magistrate, for heaven's sake.' Grace tutted and poured herself more wine.

Izzy's eyes gleamed. 'There you go: an ex-lawyer who's a magistrate. She'd have known what was going on: issuing search warrants, she'd have been able to warn the drug barons where the police were about to bash down doors. Oh, and fluent in Italian...' Izzy shook a knowing finger.

'What's speaking Italian got to do with it?'

Izzy lowered her voice. 'It's obvious. The Mafia... you know...'

'And I bet you think Man Never Landed on the Moon, either,' Juno laughed. 'God, you and your conspiracy theories, Izzy. Right, the night is for the living. Dancing after we've eaten?'

'We don't actually need to leave the restaurant,' Juno interrupted, looking around. 'Look, it's actually a drinking club upstairs with a dance floor.'

Things were looking up, Grace thought. Whatever she'd ordered to eat – some sort of pea, mint and halloumi fritter – was ambrosial, the wine after the disgusting stuff at the village hall was going down very nicely indeed (too nicely really but, what the hell, she didn't get out often) and the distant beat from her favourite Ed Sheeran song was drifting down from the bar on the floor above.

And a rather delicious man two tables away whose eye – accidentally or otherwise – had held her own, very briefly but more than once, was most definitely in her line of vision.

It had been a long time since she'd actually felt that wonderful stirring of lust, anticipation and expectation at first glimpse of a man she didn't know (you couldn't count their rather gorgeous shorts-wearing postman whose golden-haired, muscularly-tanned legs had been a regular feature of any fantasies in which, after a day with two kids under five, she'd had the time or energy to indulge) and it was pleasingly gratifying to realise she might now be over forty, but the connection between eye, brain and nether regions was still, although rusty, in fairly good working order.

She'd felt like this, she mused, when she first saw Sebastian Henderson at that nightclub down in Midhope. Gosh, that had hit her like a ton of bricks. Maybe she'd just been particularly vulnerable at the time, with Dan having left her for another woman. Was that what she was feeling now? Some vulnerability at once again being without a man? Not one bit, she smiled to herself. She didn't – she was now admitting for the first time even to herself – *want* Dan to come back home. They should never have got back together in the first place.

'What are you smiling at?' Harriet leaned over in her direction.

'This heavenly food.' Grace lied. 'And the whole evening. Totally bonkers wasn't it?'

'Hmm, I'll be glad to get home. I'm tired.'

'Oh no, come on, Hat, we must have a dance before we go back. It's not—' Grace glanced at her watch '—eleven yet. I never get out these days; don't let's cut it short.'

'Do you know that man over there?' Juno, on Grace's left, nudged her arm.

'No, do you?' (*The problem with you, Grace*, Dan always used to say, *is that you turn every question back into a question*.) 'No, I've never seen him before,' she amended, pouring water for them all and, in the process, catching his eye once more.

'Oh, he just seems to be looking over here quite a bit. I wondered if you knew him.'

'Get used to it,' Harriet laughed. 'Men always fall in love with Grace across rooms. *I've* had to get used to it since we were thirteen with all the boys at youth club staring across the ping-pong table wanting to snog her.'

'Oh, don't be ridiculous.' Grace was embarrassed. 'I seem to remember the night you met Nick, gazing across at each other in the union bar, no one else got a look in.'

The man in question *this* particular night was sat on a table of all men. (A men's night out? On a Saturday night? Did men do such things? Men's night out? Grace mused. *Lads'* night out, she supposed. But these six men didn't appear particularly laddish.) He was tall, and let's face it, she liked *tall* men. He was dark-haired, and again, let's face it, she always went for dark men. Dan was dark. Seb was dark. Yep, she'd always been a fancier of tall, dark and handsome men.

But then again, who wasn't?

The wine she'd drunk had definitely gone to her head. Grace smiled to herself once more as, an hour later, the five of them, eschewing pudding, screwed up their napkins and headed upstairs where Bruno Mars (for the second time that evening, she mused) was belting out, advising the room, '*I think I wanna marry you.*'

Grace hadn't been in a club like this for years (she'd actually thought they didn't exist anymore: surely it was all now *Electro House* and *Trap music* and other stuff she didn't understand and which made her feel old and out of touch) and she could see that, although it was the usual beer-sodden men leering unapologetically over the women dancing together in packs for safety on the tiny wooden floor, something was making her want to get onto the floor and join them. Maybe it was simply because she *hadn't* been out like this for years – over five years, she supposed, seeing Jonty was now five. She'd spent most of the time in the first year after Jonty's birth recovering from the dreadful postnatal depression that had descended when he was just a few weeks old. And, when she was back with Dan and they had then adopted Pietronella, neither she nor Dan had, it now seemed, either the time, energy or even the desire to get their glad rags on and give themselves up to the music and simply dance.

'Come on, Grace,' Juno was saying as the others moved towards the bar. 'Put your stuff down and let's *dance*.'

It was probably too much wine, Grace realised, but as she took to the floor, loving the beat of Sia's *Chandelier*, her limbs felt fluid, almost possessed by the music, while any thoughts she'd been harbouring about work, about Jonty's behaviour at school, about Dan and about Mandy's death disappeared into the ether; the only thing that mattered was dancing and moving to the music.

She must have been dancing for a good three records, moving through the music of Lewis Capaldi to Pixie Lott and on to Avicii, she and Juno singing the words loudly as they raised their arms in the air, when she looked up and realised that the man from the restaurant downstairs was standing very near to her, arms folded and nursing a bottled beer while his eyes never left her face.

'I need the loo, Grace,' Juno whispered in her ear. 'And, anyway, I think you've pulled.'

# 8

Grace knew she'd had too much to drink, recognised that if she drank any more she was in danger of taking to the dance floor by herself and, with limbs that felt wonderfully fluid as well as a brain that was becoming pleasantly woolly, she was possibly going to make a complete idiot of herself. Once Juno had left to go to the loo, Grace looked round for the others and saw that Izzy, Harriet and Clem had managed to find a table and were deep in conversation over something.

She didn't want to sit down, she'd been sitting down all evening and, although she was physically tired after her difficult week at school, her head was still telling her to make the most of her evening out.

Water, she needed water.

Picking up her bag, Grace made her way over to the bar in the far corner of the room, waiting her turn to be served. The man from the restaurant downstairs, the one who'd also been standing at the edge of the dance floor while she and Juno danced, was waiting his turn to be served and he turned and smiled at her approach. He continued to look and hold her eye and Grace wondered if, after all, she did know him.

She half-smiled and turned away, concentrating on finding her purse in her bag.

'You dance well.' He was at her side and Grace looked up, knowing that there was some inevitability in his being next to her.

'The drink,' she said. 'Anyone can dance with alcohol inside them.'

'Can I get you another? And then dance some more?' He smiled down at her and she was immediately struck by the beauty of his eyes. Green, long eyelashes, and the kindness you might see in a dog's or horse's eye but rarely, on first glance, in a fellow human being. Not that she knew much about either dogs *or* horses, but the way this man continued to look down at her reminded her of her Granny's old Labrador. God, she really had had too much wine if the first thing she thought of was Bingo who'd been dead these past twenty years.

'Water?'

'Please.' Grace allowed the man to push through to the bar in order to buy her a drink and five minutes later he surfaced from the melee with a bottle of sparkling water for her and a bottled lager for himself. *How often*, Grace mused, *does one meet someone for whom one feels an instant attraction?* She knew Harriet, who had been married to Nick for well over twenty years, had felt it, and she certainly had fallen instantly in love – in lust, she corrected herself as the man handed her the drink and she drank long and gratefully – with Seb Henderson.

'Is it always the eyes?' Grace asked as she drained the bottle of water and placed it with deliberate care on a table already sticky and overloaded with glasses, and half-drunk bottles of beer.

'Is what always the eyes?' he asked, his own quite mesmerising eyes never leaving her own.

'You *know*,' she frowned. 'I've had far too much to drink, and yet I'm trying to work out what it is that makes one person stand out from another. What it is that has made you catch my eye…' Grace paused. 'I'm sorry, I'm not making any sense. I'd better get back to the others, they'll be wondering where I am.'

'They can see you. They know you're safe.'

'And am I?'

'Safe, you mean?' He laughed down at her. 'As houses.' He held up his bottle of lager. 'Non-alcoholic: I'm driving.'

'I really could do with some air.' Grace was beginning to feel slightly spaced out. Not sick, not drunk, but warm and in need of fresh air rather than the alcohol, perfume and sweat-tainted air that she'd been breathing for the last hour or so.

'Do you need your friend to go out with you?'

'No, I'll be fine.'

'Come on, I'll walk downstairs with you. There's a garden at the back, very unusual for the centre of Leeds, but you shouldn't be there by yourself at this time of night.'

'There's no need. Really.'

'Up to you.'

'Thank you then.'

Grace picked up her bag, caught Juno's eye to indicate she was having five minutes' fresh air outside, and walked towards the door, the man's hand lightly on her arm as he guided her forward. At the far end of the room, she paused and then went through the door that led down the stairs and outside onto the square. They were in one of the older parts of the city where a large stone-faced alleyway led to a beer garden at the back of the club.

'Used to be a pub and this was where the dray horses went through with the barrels of beer,' he said.

'You seem to know its history?'

'I was at university here: my stomping ground for several years. You feeling OK?'

'Yes, better now I've had some air.'

'You really shouldn't leave clubs with strange men, you know. Did your mother never tell you that?' He glanced down at her ring finger. 'Or your husband?'

'I no longer have one,' Grace said sadly. 'We've separated again.'

'I'm sorry.'

'Don't be. It's fine.' Grace smiled. And, maybe it was her intoxicated state of mind, but she knew it was. If she still loved Dan, if she and her husband had any feelings whatsoever left for each other apart from him being the father of her children, no way would she have been flirting with this man. 'I'm still thirsty.'

The man handed Grace his still almost-full bottle of lager and she drank gratefully, wiping her mouth with her hand before handing it back to him.

'Come with me,' he said with a smile, leading her across the garden, its mowed lawn damp and springy beneath her flimsy heels. 'Look.'

'Goodness.'

'A harvest moon. I knew there was going to be one this evening.'

Grace gazed in wonder at the huge amber sphere that hung, motionless, ahead of them as they leaned, side by side against the high wall that separated this little oasis from the night-time city street on the other side. 'I wouldn't know a thing about moons,' she said eventually. 'You know, their names or all that waxing and waning stuff. The only thing I remember is my granny being almost frightened if she happened to spot the new moon through the window. Thought it terribly unlucky, apparently.'

He laughed. 'In reality, you can't actually see a new moon. What one considers to be a new moon is actually a day – or night – old.'

'Right.'

'Sorry, I'm boring you. Bit of a hobby of mine, sky-watching at night.'

Grace shivered, wrapping her jacket around herself.

'Are you cold? You should go back in. Your friends will be getting worried.'

Grace shook her head. She wasn't cold, but she knew without either of them saying a word that if she stayed, didn't go back to the others as he suggested, that there *was* no going back. Grace reached a hand towards him, placing it inside his jacket and then, by moving her hand, found a shirt button and unfastened it. And the next. And a third. His skin was warm and smooth apart from a small collection of soft hair as she moved her hand lower.

He made the next move, holding Grace's head in both hands before lowering his mouth to her own and kissing her deeply. It was the perfect kiss, not wet with an unwelcome beery tongue, but firm and dry and incredibly sensual and Grace recognised she'd wanted this from the very first moment his eyes had met her own in the restaurant.

It felt, Grace realised, absolutely thrilling to be kissing someone she didn't know. She didn't even know his name and he'd made no enquiry after her own. She knew nothing about him; his mouth and skin, his hands and scent were totally alien to her and yet she felt safe there, totally absorbed and involved in the kiss.

His hands moved under the back of her silk top, lifting it from the anchorage of her skirt and Grace felt herself breathe out slowly at the wonderfully heady feeling of large warm masculine hands firm on her bare back, her skin almost calling out in anticipation of more to come.

'I don't usually do this sort of thing,' Grace whispered into the man's neck, loving the feel of warm skin against warm skin, the ridiculous ease with which this was happening and the recognition that she, probably more than him, was instigating what was happening.

'I'm sure you don't,' he smiled into her hair, lifting its chestnut length in his hands before turning her round to kiss the nape of her neck. 'Blame the moon, it's always the moon.'


'What the hell were you thinking of?' Harriet said crossly once they were all back in the waiting taxi and heading for the M62 and home. 'Going into a dark pub garden all by yourself in the dead of night?'

'I wasn't by myself,' Grace answered quietly. 'And it wasn't dark. There was a full harvest moon.'

'Harvest moon?' Clem said, frowning. 'Oh gosh, that reminds me, it's Harvest Festival at church in the morning and I haven't sorted anything out for Allegra to take.'

'A tin of fruit salad will do,' Izzy said comfortably, her eyes closed and near sleep as the taxi purred along the almost empty motorway. 'You know, that tin at the back of your kitchen cupboard that's been there years because nobody likes those horrible slimy little bits of pear.' She shuddered.

'I can't see Clem having any truck with tinned anything,' Juno yawned. 'God, I'm knackered. 'So, what *were* you up to, Grace?' she went on, as she lost the fight to keep her own eyes open and leaned her head into the window. 'Why were you moon-watching anyway?'

'First time I've heard it called that,' Izzy drawled sleepily.

'You could have been murdered,' Harriet snapped crossly.

'What are you now, my mother?' Grace tutted, embarrassment at what she'd just done, making her speak sharply.

'He looked like a drug-dealer to me,' Harriet went on. 'Is that why he knew about the garden at the back of the pub? Did he try to sell you something?'

'What was it, Grace?' Izzy was laughing at Harriet's censure. 'Come and see the moon, darling? Oh, and how about a wrap of Mcat while you're at it?'

'Does Mcat come in wraps?' Juno asked doubtfully.

'Oh, for heaven's sake, the lot of you.' Grace tutted again. 'You sound like a load of middle-aged busybodies.'

'Hey, we lead such boring, urban lives,' Izzy said, half-asleep, 'we have to get our kicks from somewhere. Gossiping about what you've been up to with the only attractive man in that dive back there is right up our street.'

'He *was* incredibly attractive,' Clem conceded, patting Grace's hand. 'But you don't think he looked a bit, you know, a bit suspicious? I mean, what was he doing in a place like that all by himself?'

'He wasn't by himself,' Grace said in some exasperation. 'He was out with some mates from his uni days.'

'But not drinking? Out on the razz with his mates on a Saturday night and not drinking?' I agree with you, Clementine. Sounds *very* suspicious to me.' Izzy opened her eyes briefly to wink at Clem.

'He was *driving*. Obviously, he wasn't *drinking*.'

'Ah,' Izzy said sagely. 'Working. Making a quick getaway once he'd offloaded all the drugs. Big black BMW with blacked out windows and a couple of burners in the glove compartment?'

'Burners?' Juno and Harriet spoke as one. 'What are *burners*?'

'Oh, you are such little innocents,' Izzy said loftily. 'I bet Mandy Henderson knew *all* about burners.'

'Drug dealers will have several phones,' Clem explained. 'They're called burners and they can be chucked away to avoid being tracked by the police.'

'So,' Juno said, feeling sorry for Grace, 'he looked very nice. What did he *really* do? Where was he from? What was he called and, more importantly, have you arranged to see him again?'

Grace shook her head and closed her eyes. 'In answer to your questions, Juno: Don't know, don't know, don't know. And no.

# 9

'Darling, what on earth's the matter?'

Tilda sat at the end of Juno's bed, fat tears rolling down her pale cheeks. Juno glanced at her bedside clock: 6.30 a.m. and a Sunday morning. There was absolutely no reason whatsoever to get out of bed, and she longed to turn over, bury her face back in the pillow and try to get back into the rather wonderful dream involving Scott and his incredibly talented hands and mouth. Juno felt herself blush slightly as the full extent of what she'd been up to with Scott suddenly appeared like a picture in her mind's eye and she shook her head, making a big effort to sit up and concentrate on what Tilda was saying.

Tilda thrust her hand in her mother's direction and, as her eyes focused, Juno simultaneously felt her heart sink. God, this was all Tilda needed when, after an awful week at school where, according to Gabe, more and more of even the older kids who'd only just met her, were laughing at her little eccentricities, she'd cried for a good deal of the weekend. 'Oh darling, she *was* getting on a bit you know. And she did have a great life, always setting off on yet another adventure.' Juno tried to jolly Tilda along as Lady

Gaga's stiff little form lay on Tilda's palm. 'She was the Amelia Earhart or... or Mary Kingsley of the gerbil world.'

'Or Jeanne Baret,' Tilda sniffed, stroking the soft brown fur of the dead gerbil.

'Who?'

'Jeanne Baret, 1740 to 1807, recognised as the first woman to circumnavigate the globe.'

'Right,' Juno said faintly, closing her eyes once more in an effort to hold on to Scott's sensual mouth and lips on her neck moving downwards.

'Of course, she had to do it disguised as a man,' Tilda went on somewhat scornfully, warming to her theme. 'She was on the world expedition of the French Navy – Admiral Louis-Antoine de Bouganville was in charge – and she had to bind her breasts with linen and become Jean Baret instead of Jeanne... Mum, now that I no longer have a gerbil can I have some peacocks?'

Oh Jesus, Juno thought, she could see herself agreeing to anything not to have a French history (or was it geography?) lesson thrust down her throat before it was even light on a Sunday morning.

'Look, how about you go and find a shoebox to put Lady Gaga in and then we can bury her later at one end of the paddock? We can have a proper funeral; you know, sing a hymn and say a prayer.'

'Mum I'm not five years old. Anyway, after the few weeks I've had at school, I don't believe in God; God wouldn't let me *suffer* like I am doing at the moment. And Aunt Ariadne doesn't believe in him either. We had a really good philosophical discussion last night while you were out *drinking*.' Tilda was obviously getting into her stride.

'Anyway, she's coming round later on this morning.' Tilda hesitated but only for a fraction of a second. 'And with peacocks, if you give her the go ahead and tell her it's OK.'

'Don't the pair of you bamboozle me into this,' Juno said crossly. 'I agreed to the hens. You got your own way there.'

'Exactly,' Tilda agreed. 'We're halfway there. Peacock chicks are not much different from chicken chicks. They have to be in an aviary for the first six weeks and the coop we've got for the hens—'

'Is *not* an aviary, Tilda.'

'No, but Brian says it's fine to begin with until he can extend the coop for the peacocks. You know, make it into an aviary. He says it wouldn't take him long at all.'

Brian Goodall was the gardener-come-handyman Juno and Fraser had inherited once they'd been foolish enough to buy this house with its acres of vegetable and fruit garden as well as the paddock for Harry Trotter – Tilda's somewhat malevolent pony – and the hens. Juno knew, particularly once Fraser had left her and the kids to live in America, she couldn't do without Brian although, to be fair, it was nothing to do with Fraser's leaving, as her soon-to-be-ex-husband had been even more useless than her when it came down to anything horticultural or connected with Tilda's growing pack of livestock. Thinking about Fraser reminded Juno they must do something about starting divorce proceedings. She supposed she'd have to set the ball rolling although, with Laura, Fraser's new girlfriend, now in situ, perhaps it was up to him rather than herself to make the first move.

'So, what do you think? You know, about the peacocks?' She obviously wasn't going to give it a rest. 'Tilda, this place is becoming more like Chester Zoo every day. You've absolutely no right to be talking either to Brian or Aunt Ariadne about more animals.'

'Well,' Tilda said logically, 'now Lady Gaga is no more—' she bent down to kiss the gerbil's little head and Juno gave an involuntary shudder '—then there's room for *one* more, isn't there? You know, one out and one in as it were. And if we're having one peacock, just one *tiny* little peacock chick, then we may as well as have *two* because one would be very lonely, don't you agree?'

Juno turned over, burying her face into the pillow. She had, she realised, the beginning of a headache.

'Ooh, I've missed you.' Juno reached up her hands, winding her fingers through Scott's dark hair as he wrapped his arms round her before bending to kiss her open mouth.

'I'll take myself off on more golfing trips if this is how you greet me on my return,' he grinned. 'Come here, you little hussy.' The ensuing kiss was long and deep and, as Juno was just considering the possibility of extending it even further by taking Scott upstairs, Gabriel arrived back from his sleepover at his mate Zak's house down in the village. Not possible at all, she reminded herself as she unwrapped herself quickly from Scott's arms, with one pubescent daughter and one adolescent son in the house.

''Lo,' Gabe grunted, heading for the fridge. Embarrassed at being caught snogging at nine-thirty on a Sunday morning, (why this should be more embarrassing than, say, ten-thirty on a Saturday evening, Juno wasn't quite sure) Juno heard herself going into twittery, jolly, *breakfast everybody?*

mode and, nudging Gabe out of the way, reached for eggs, bacon and a loaf of bread. She supposed she'd eventually get used to having her lover sitting at the breakfast table (the kids, being modern kids, certainly didn't appear to have any issue with Scott being there) but Juno still wasn't at ease with the whole situation. Scott, on the other hand, always appeared totally relaxed with her children and he now reached for the jacket she'd managed to divest him of five minutes earlier, saying he'd go out and help Tilda with Harry Trotter while Juno was preparing breakfast.

'You alright, Gabe?' Juno looked up from cracking and whisking eggs.

'Suppose.'

'What does that mean?'

'Nothing.'

'Are you off to football?'

Gabe shook his head. 'Not been picked. Even for reserve.'

'You should still turn up, Gabe. You know, show team spirit. Do you want a lift down?' The club Gabe played football for was a good fifteen-minute walk away and, glancing up at the kitchen clock, she realised she'd have to get a move on feeding him if he was to be there for kick-off at eleven.

Gabriel shook his head as, table mat in hand, he concentrated on separating the image of a dour-looking stag from its cork backing.

'Don't do that, you little vandal,' Juno snapped. 'Your Grandma Armstrong gave your dad and me those when we got married.' *Actually*, Juno thought, *peel away*: she'd always disliked those table mats. Almost as much as Jean Armstrong, her mother-in-law, herself.

'Well, it doesn't matter then, does it? Seeing as you'll never have to see her again?' Juno looked up in surprise but, before she could say anything, Gabe said, without looking at her, 'Tilda's a right pain now she's at school with me. Mum, she's so embarrassing. How come I've ended up with a sister like her?'

'Oy, stop right there, Mister,' Juno said crossly. 'She's your sister and she's younger than you. You should be protecting her, helping her.'

'Protecting her? Mum, it's me and the other kids that need protection. She's *weird*. She was telling some of the Year 8 girls they should stand up for themselves on the school bus. You know, when Scarlett Benson and her gang had chucked them off the back seat? You don't mess with Scarlett Benson and live.'

Juno wanted to laugh. Typical Tilda, she thought, new to the school and already standing up for the underdog as well as to the infamous Scarlett Benson. Just like her Aunt Ariadne had always done.

'And then Scarlett shouts down the bus for me to get Tilda in order, you know, sort her, because if *I* didn't, *she* would.'

'OK, OK, I get it,' Juno said, tickling Gabe where his short reddish hair sprouted out at a rather comical angle. 'Have you washed your neck recently?' He might be thirteen, but he was still her little boy. 'Come on, man up,' she laughed, thumping him lightly on the shoulder in an attempt to humour him. 'Breakfast is just about ready.'

'You alright, mate?' Scott, coming back into the kitchen bringing with him a scent of autumn as well as a more pungent whiff of horse, frowned in their direction as he moved to the sink to wash his hands.

'A bit fed up with being a big brother,' Juno mouthed above her son's bent head as he continued to pick morosely at the table mat.

'Fancy a kick-about after breakfast?' Scott asked as he dried his hands.

Gabriel lifted his head and stared in Scott's direction. 'Football? I didn't know you knew anything about football? I thought you lot were just into rugby?'

'Gabriel,' Juno admonished, embarrassed at his tone. 'You can't talk about people from New Zealand as *you lot.*'

'Football? Me?' Scott emphasised his New Zealand twang, ignoring Gabriel's uncustomary rudeness. 'Auckland under-thirteen champions, my team were, mate.'

'Really?' Gabe stared.

'Too right. You fill your boots with your mum's breakfast and then we'll get out there. Teach you all Skipper Delaney taught me.'


'I didn't know you were a footballer when you were a kid?' Juno broke off from clearing away the breakfast things to wrap her arms round Scott as Gabe went off to find his boots and Tilda searched for a shoe box. Despite her protestations not to be treated as a five-year-old, she wanted a decent burial for Lady Gaga. 'Not my Jimmy Choo box,' Juno shouted after her as she disappeared upstairs. 'They're the only posh shoes I've got,' she explained to Scott. 'So, football? Auckland champion?'

'Well, I might have exaggerated slightly there.' He grinned, moving his hand over her jeaned bottom as Juno turned to the sink, gazing out of the window at Brian Goodall who was already down the bottom of the paddock, doing something gardenerish. Harry Trotter watched, somewhat balefully, knowing Brian was the one person he couldn't put the wind up. Juno loved the burgeoning hues of carmine and rust that the season was giving the garden and, with Scott nuzzling at her neck and the whole glorious day ahead of them, she breathed a sigh of contentment.

'So, not an Auckland champion then? And *Skipper Delaney*?' Juno raised an eyebrow, wanting to laugh.

'Figments of my imagination,' Scott said. 'Nah, rugby was my game. But the kid's lost his confidence somewhere down the line. Probably with his dad going. He needs to get that back and he'll be right.'

'Psychologist now, are you?'

'Well, yes, I've always been interested in the mind as well as the body. I did think about majoring in Psychology at one point. But then…' He broke off, reaching down to cup her bottom with his hands once more before assuming an exaggeratedly lascivious whisper and adding, 'my love of bodies got in the way.'

Juno laughed but slapped at his roving hands. Having been married to a cold, undemonstrative man like Fraser for the past fourteen years, she still wasn't used to Scott's public shows of affection. 'I don't remember Fraser ever showing the slightest interest in football,' she said, delighted at Scott's wanting to build a relationship with Gabe. 'And he was even more frightened of Harry Trotter than I am.' She laughed again. 'I don't know what the hell we were thinking of buying this house with such a big garden.' She turned back to the window. 'Oh hell, look at those plums. The little buggers have been having sex again. The minute

I turn my back, they're at it again. We're overrun with the damned things.'

'Give me a bowl,' Scott laughed. 'I'll soon put a stop to their little games. I'll pick a load while you're having your funeral for the hamster. As long as you make a plum crumble with them. God, I love the crumbles you English make.'

'Gerbil actually. And yes, that's a good idea. Are you staying to eat later on?'

'Depends what time you're eating.'

'Oh?'

Scott hesitated and then sighed, not looking at Juno as he took up the place mat peeling Gabe had abandoned. 'Look, for some reason Esme has decided she's thinking of moving into the village. I said I'd show her round a bit.'

Juno stared. 'Esme as in your ex, Esme?'

Scott laughed. 'Hardly my ex, you daft thing.'

'You don't call the mother of your child your *ex*?' 'Maya is hardly a child. She's twenty-two...' He broke off as Tilda appeared, shoebox to hand.

'Tilda, that's my best Jimmy Choo box,' Juno tutted. 'I don't have much but what I do have I like to keep nice.'

'You're being very *materialistic*, Mum,' Tilda returned loftily.

'Too right I am,' Juno snapped, grabbing the box from Tilda's hands. 'If you're having a Humanist ceremony, seeing as you don't believe in God, you just need the equivalent of a wicker casket. Here...' Juno delved into the recycling bin and found an egg carton. 'Squash the sticky-out bits down and use this.'

'So, Esme is Maya's mum?' Tilda now asked with some

interest as she turned to Scott. 'And you didn't even *know* you had a daughter until a few months ago? That must be so, like, weird?'

'Weirder than you can imagine, Tilda.' Scott smiled. 'But wonderful. You know, to suddenly find out I'm a dad.'

'And you had an affair, *a liaison*, with your *landlady* when you were an eighteen-year-old medical student newly arrived in Sheffield?' Tilda's arms were folded as she questioned Scott intently.

'*Tilda!*' Juno frowned. Scott was beginning to look slightly uncomfortable under Tilda's direct gaze.

'Well yes…'

'But she must have been incredibly *old* if she was your landlady. And didn't she have a husband? What did *he* think about all this?'

'Enough, Tilda. You're being very personal.' Juno was embarrassed.

'I'm just interested,' Tilda sniffed. 'If I'm to be home-educated, this could be this week's PSHE lesson.'

'You are *not* being home-educated, Matilda. You've only done a few weeks at Westenbury Comp.'

'Yes, and in those weeks, it's not getting any more congenial and I've learned absolutely *nothing*. In fact, I'd go so far as to say my education is steadily regressing.' Tilda assumed a caring, sharing face. 'So, Scott, tell me more. How did it feel to suddenly become a father of a twenty-two-year old? And what is your relationship with her mother now? This Esme…?'

'OK, enough, out. And take the gerbil with you,' Juno said.

Scott started to laugh. 'Hey, you're a one-off, you, Matilda Armstrong.'

'No, actually I'm very likely a clone of my Aunt Ariadne. She's coming round later with peacocks.'

'No damned *peacocks*, Tilda.'

Still laughing, Scott sat down and faced Tilda. 'I was a very young and somewhat silly medical student, Tilda. My parents wanted me to stay in New Zealand, but I had big ideas of coming to England. By the time I got here, all the student accommodation was gone and I was given temporary digs with Esme Burkinshaw in Sheffield. She was a very lovely lady and I was very lonely, missing home and my parents. She mothered me…'

*As if*, Juno thought. What randy eighteen-year-old doesn't fancy the idea of sex with a thirty-eight-year old exceptionally attractive – and experienced – older woman.

'… and one thing, erm, one thing led to another as it were.'

'It's OK, Scott,' Tilda said almost kindly. 'I know what you're trying to tell me here. You couldn't help yourself? And Maya was the result? I understand.'

'Out, now Matilda, go on. You're embarrassing Scott.'

'I honestly wasn't embarrassed, Juno,' Scott said, obviously highly amused, once Tilda was out of earshot. 'Tilda met Esme that time she dropped Maya off here. I think it's good she now understands who everyone is.' He hesitated. 'Especially as Esme's decided Westenbury is where she wants to be.'

Juno made a quick decision. 'Right, I'm going to do a proper Sunday lunch – with plum crumble if you pick those plums. Ariadne is coming over. Why don't you invite Esme and Maya as well?'

Scott frowned. 'Are you sure?'

'Absolutely. If Esme moves over from Sheffield, will Maya come with her?'

'Possibly, I don't know.' Scott frowned. 'She's just about to start her master's at Sheffield Uni so I doubt she'll be wanting to drive over there every day. I have to say, it would be so wonderful if Maya was here as well. You know, now I've discovered I have a daughter, I want to try and be a dad to her.'

'Honestly, invite them over.' Juno smiled, reaching up to kiss Scott's mouth before handing him a bowl to collect the last of the late summer plums.

# IO

'It's so *lovely* to meet you at last, Juno. I'm so sorry I missed you when I dropped Maya off here for the first time last month. I met your two *gorgeous* children when I was here. They were so polite and welcoming.'

'Yes, I'm really sorry about that too. I got held up at my mother's that afternoon. My sister, Lexia, and my nephew Cillian are living over there at the moment and we ended up chatting and eating cake and the time just passed.'

'Of *course*, you're Lexia Sutherland's sister, aren't you?' Esme Burkinshaw affected a dramatic little movement with her hands, fanning her face with the most incredibly perfect nails Juno had ever seen. 'Oh, goodness me, I'm *such* a fan of hers. When Maya told me Scott was living with Lexia Sutherland's sister—'

'Not living with exactly,' Juno murmured.

'—I was *so* excited. I remember going to see her when she played at Sheffield Arena years ago. I'm *such* a fan. Is there any chance she's coming over this afternoon? Scott did say your sister was eating with us?'

'Sorry, it's my big sister, Ariadne, who's coming round.' Juno gave a tight little smile.

'Oh really? *How* disappointing. You couldn't just *ring*

her, could you? You know, invite her as well? I've been *such* a fan for years?'

Did this woman emphasise at least one word in every single sentence? Juno was beginning to feel quite overwhelmed by Esme's demonstrative enthusiasm. 'Erm no, I think she and my mother are going to my other sister, Pandora's, for lunch.'

Esme made a little moue of disappointment, her outlined red mouth a perfect match for the red nails she was still intent on fluttering around like some exotically scarlet spider. If spiders had ten legs, Juno thought idly, hiding her own plain, sensibly cut nails.

'Where's Maya?' Juno peered over Esme's shoulder. 'Is she not with you?'

'Hopefully coming over later. She had a bit of a hard night last night. You know what these young things are like.' Esme nudged Juno pointedly with her elbow. 'A chip off the old block if ever I saw one. Hmm?'

Juno stared. Did Esme mean herself or Scott, Maya's only recently discovered biological father. 'So,' Juno asked, unable to work out to whom Esme referred, 'what's made you think of moving over to this neck of the woods?' She poured wine and handed one to Esme who took the proffered glass with a slim tanned hand. How old must she be? Scott had said he'd been seduced at the age of eighteen by a woman nearly forty, so – Juno did a quick calculation – she must be nearly sixty. Juno gave her a surreptitious glance as she stood, took her glass and walked ahead of her to join the others in the garden. A good six or seven inches taller than Esme Burkinshaw's tiny five-foot frame, Juno felt almost giant-like in comparison to this woman who now squeezed herself onto the garden swing in between Tilda and Gabe. Despite it being the end of September, it was still beautifully mellow and warm, a real Indian summer.

'Hello, darlings,' Esme cooed. 'You're both back at school now?' She patted Gabe's knee absentmindedly and he stiffened, glaring at Juno before jumping up and retreating into the house and the safety of his PlayStation.

'Is he alright?' Esme looked concerned.

'Typical adolescent,' Tilda opined. 'He's not overly communicative at the moment.'

'And this is my eldest sister, Ariadne.' Juno smiled as Ari made her way up from the paddock where she'd been chatting to Brian. 'Blimey, is Brian still here? Doreen'll be after him if he's not sitting down to his Sunday dinner for half past one.' She looked at Ariadne suspiciously. 'What are you up to? With Brian?'

'Up to with the *gardener*? Goodness me, it *all* goes on in the sticks, doesn't it?' Esme gave a girlish giggle.

Ariadne gave her such a look in return, Juno began to laugh.

'And do *you* sing too, Hadirane?'

'Too, Emsey?' Ari kept an amazingly straight face as she deliberately mispronounced the woman's name.

'Like your *very* famous sister, *Lexia Sutherland*?' Esme twinkled in Ari's direction, announcing the name with great fervour and reverence in case, it appeared, Ariadne might need reminding of their sorority.

''Fraid not, Emsey,' Ari smiled, helping herself to a handful of nuts from the bowl in front of her and chewing methodically.

'Don't believe her,' Tilda scoffed. 'They all sing: Mum, all my aunts and my Grandma Helen. I can hold a tune myself if requested.'

'So,' Juno repeated, ignoring Tilda and re-filling Esme's glass, jumping in before Ariadne gave the woman short thrift as she was wont to do with anyone she found silly, racist or bigoted. Juno had no idea if Esme Burkinshaw was the latter two, but she certainly appeared jolly silly. 'Scott says you're thinking of moving over here from Sheffield?'

'Not *thinking* about it, love, it's all underway.'

'Oh?'

'I'm moving over properly next week.'

'Oh?' Juno heard herself repeat. 'That was quick. Have you sold your house in Sheffield then?'

'Oh no, no.' Esme shook her head, her earrings jangling as she did so. 'I have a *lovely* place out towards Hathersage – the Peak District, of course. But I'm going to rent a most amazing place not far from here for six months and see how it goes.'

'See how what goes?' Despite recognising Ariadne's first impression of Esme Burkinshaw as a total lightweight, she was, Juno could see, wanting to know more.

'Well, when I've been over here with Maya – you know, coming with her to see Scott once we realised he was back in England – I totally fell in love with this little village of yours. Of course, it's not a patch on the Peak District, but I know a *business opportunity* when I see one.' Esme put down her glass and smiled smugly at the others.

Scott, who'd been sitting back in his garden chair, saying very little up until then, now leaned forwards. 'Business opportunity?'

'The hardware shop down in Westenbury,' Esme explained.

The hardware shop? Juno stared. She couldn't see Esme Burkinshaw, with her long red nails and streak-free perma-tan, behind the counter of Fred Horsforth's hardware store in a long brown overall dispensing screws, plastic buckets and bird food. Fred had been there for ever, selling an eclectic mix of stuff which people could now buy much cheaper in town or in Sainsbury's.

'I heard he was selling up.' Ariadne nodded. 'Off to spend most of the year in Benidorm, he told me when I was last in.'

'So, you're taking Fred's place on?' Tilda asked with some animation. 'Oh good, I'll still be able to buy gerbil food from you.' And then, as she immediately remembered she'd just helped Lady Gaga back to her maker, as well as the realisation that it was Sunday and tomorrow was Monday and school, she sat back on the garden swing and closed her eyes in a parody of despair.

'Gerbil food?' Esme was momentarily nonplussed. 'Oh goodness me, *no*, Tilda,' she trilled. 'I've bought Horsforth's for a much more exciting venture than gerbils.'

'I can't envisage *anything* that could exceed the stimulation and excitement value of gerbils,' Tilda said from the depths of the cushion on which she was laid. 'Unless it was peacock chicks, of course.' She glanced from under her eyelashes at her mother and, despite Juno's first reaction being to laugh out loud, both at Tilda's excessive verbosity as well as Esme's raised eyebrow at the interruption to her announcement, she felt her daughter's underlying unhappiness and reached over to pat her hand.

'So, yes, *really* exciting.' Esme was soon back on track. 'The shop-fitters have been in there all last week as well as working all weekend to get it up and running.' She paused for effect, twinkling once more at her audience.

'And?' Ariadne was obviously getting impatient.

'Blush and Blow,' Esme announced proudly.

'Right.' Ariadne glanced across at Juno. Had her eleven-year-old niece not been present, Ariadne would have said more, particularly with regards the last word of the handle of Esme's new venture. 'A beauty salon, I assume?'

'Absolutely,' Esme said. 'It's what I *do*. I have *three* hair and beauty salons in Sheffield, and, when I saw Horsforth's place up for sale last spring, I made enquiries and have been working on the project ever since. We should be up and running in a couple of weeks.'

'How on earth have you got planning permission so quickly? I thought it took forever?'

'Depends who you know, love.' Esme gave a dirty laugh that was almost priapic.

'Aren't there enough hair salons in the village?' Ariadne asked, slightly flustered at the other woman's response. 'I bet there are at least four or five? There's already one next to Horsforth's, you know. What's it called?'

'Curl Up and Dye,' Esme said with some disdain. 'A quite dreadful name, don't you think?'

'I've always thought it rather amusing,' Juno ventured.

'Really? Well, I've bought that as well and I'm knocking through and incorporating it into Blush and Blow. It was a second-rate little place.'

'Oh, I used to get a good, cheap haircut there.' Ariadne smiled.

'Yes, I can see that.' Esme's own smile didn't quite belie what she thought of Ari's appearance, and Juno glanced at her big sister to gauge her reaction. Never one for the latest fashion or cosmetics, Ariadne's beauty routine was, she knew, a face wash with an eco-soap, a quick moisturise with a tub of Nivea and a slick of pink lippy when she remembered. Her thick blonde hair had been cut in the same, short style as long as Juno could remember. 'You come down to Blush and Blow in a couple of weeks and we'll transform you,' Esme now added. 'You won't know yourself.'

'So,' Scott frowned, 'that's a hell of a big place you're going to have down there. It'll be a huge footage once you put the two places together, won't it?'

'Well, this is the exciting bit. Westenbury – Midhope even – will have its first Turkish barber and...' She paused dramatically. '... Turkish baths.'

'Turkish barber?' The others all stared.

'Absolutely. They're all the *thing*. You go down any street in any town and you'll see two things these days: Starbucks and a Turkish barber.'

'Actually, Esme, Midhope still hasn't *got* a Starbucks,' Juno was quick to point out. She loved Starbucks – she'd often treated herself to a cappuccino and blueberry muffin sitting in Guild Square when she and Fraser had lived in Aberdeen.

'Oh Starbucks, *shmarbucks*,' Esme interrupted impatiently, flapping her red talons once more in Juno's direction. 'Once you've experienced the heady pleasure of a Turkish bath, you won't be wanting *coffee*.'

'Do you not think a Turkish bath and a Turkish barber a bit exotic for a village like Westenbury?' Ariadne looked doubtful. 'Do we actually have any Turks living round here? I mean,' she went on, 'the co-op has only just started selling Turkish Delight and thinking they've gone international.'

'That's all in place.' Esme smiled almost smugly. 'I have two *very* gorgeous young men from Istanbul who will be helping with the Turkish bath side of things. They're students at Midhope University but will be able to work part-time at the salon and there are several Turkish barbers and hairdressers who have settled in one area of Midhope with whom I'm in negotiation. And then I have Tracy.'

'Tracy?'

'Tracy works for me in Sheffield. She went out to Bodrum for a week's all-inclusive years ago – you know, the usual story: fell in love with one of the Turkish waiters and never came back. She and Hakan ended up running the family Turkish baths there. Anyway, she's back now – pummels like a dream. Once you've had Tracy, you never want anyone else.'

'Right,' Juno said faintly. There didn't seem to be anything else to say to that. 'So where are you going to be living, Esme?'

'I don't know if you know it, but there's an incredibly beautiful place called Holly Close Farm a couple of miles from here?'

'Yes.' Juno frowned. 'A friend of mine, Harriet, her daughter bought it last year. They've spent ages, and must be thousands, doing it up. Libby's not moving out, is she?'

'Oh no, no, well not as far as I know. I really don't know anything about the actual farm and who lives there but, on the same site, an old cottage was renovated into two separate smaller places at the same time.'

'But that's the Madison sisters' place.' Scott frowned and turned to Juno. 'You know, Juno, Graham Madison, the vet in the village who was Pontius Pilate in *Jesus Christ Superstar*? I chatted to him a lot in rehearsals and he told me all about Holly Close Farm. Really interesting family history there, apparently. Anyway, his daughter Charlie's an architect and did the whole site up. I'm sure Graham said Charlie and her sister, Daisy, live there. You know in the converted cottage?'

'Well, yes, I believe they do. Own it, I mean,' Esme continued. 'But they're both not living there at the moment. As far as I know, Charlie's back in London again for twelve months and the other sister – Daisy, is it? – has gone travelling somewhere. Could be Australia, I don't really know. Anyway, the two cottages were up for rent and I've taken one for six months. I'm moving my things over next week as I need to be here to run the place in the village until it's making a profit and I can put in a manager.'

'Well, that's very interesting,' Ariadne said slowly.

'The new beauty salon?' Esme smirked. 'It is, isn't it? I do hope you'll tell all your friends? Although, to be honest, there's already been so much interest, I'm sure I'm on to another winner. If my other places are anything to go by.'

'No,' Ariadne interrupted almost crossly. 'I didn't mean your beauty *parlour*.'

'Oh?'

'The whole concept of beauty parlours charging exorbitant prices in order to persuade mainly women that they need ridiculous treatments such as fillers, chemical skin peels and Botox in order to make themselves more attractive to men—'

'I bet Jeanne Baret didn't go and have a face lift before she set off on her mission to show she was as good as a man,' Tilda piped up.

Scott caught Juno's eye and she had to bite her lip to stop herself laughing out loud.

'—to make women more attractive to *men*.' Ariadne repeated crossly.

'I think you'll find, Hadirane, I have a number of *very* pleasant *lesbian* clients—'

'There you go, Aunt Ari, you're sorted,' Tilda said gravely while Juno gave her daughter a furious look.

'—who most certainly do not visit my beauty *salons* – parlour is such an outmoded word – to make themselves more attractive to *men*!'

Two tiny pinpricks of colour were now visible through Esme's carefully highlighted and bronzed cheeks and Juno immediately felt contrite. Her sister and daughter were being exceptionally rude to someone who was not only her guest but who was about to move into the village. They should be welcoming her with open arms. 'Well, I'll be one of your first clients, Esme.' Juno smiled. 'I had a Turkish bath in Aberdeen once and I absolutely loved it.'

'I'm sorry, Esme, that was terribly impolite of me.' Ariadne frowned. 'But, as I was saying, it's really very interesting that you should have rented one of the cottages down at Holly Close Farm.'

'Oh?' Esme smiled sweetly, gracious in her acceptance of Ari's apology.

'Our father, it appears, is going to be renting the other one.'

'What?' Juno and Tilda spoke as one.

'Grandpa Sutherland?' Tilda sat up straight, smiling for perhaps the first time that afternoon. 'He's coming to live near Westenbury?' She turned to Esme and confided, 'I've never really had a grandpa, you know.'

'I've only just found out myself,' Ariadne said, moving towards Juno. 'Pandora rang me just as I was leaving the house to come over here. I'd have told you straight away, Juno, but you know… with Esme here…' She trailed off.

'Well, we did know it was on the cards, Ari.' Juno turned towards Esme. 'Our parents are divorced, you see. Quite acrimoniously, really. But a long time ago.'

'Oh, goodness me.' Esme fanned herself once more with the ubiquitous red talons. 'Goodness me. Patrick is your father? He's Patrick… what… Sutherland? I met him over there just now. And he's Lexia Sutherland's father?'

'Yes, and *ours*,' Ariadne said irritably.

'Oh, but he's *such* a charming man. And terribly attractive too. How fortuitous is all this?'

'You won't believe this, Esme, but I've only met him a couple of times.' Tilda had perked up quite dramatically. 'He's a terribly *clever man*, you know. Mum, I bet *he'd* home-educate me?' She turned back to Esme and Scott. 'He's a professor, you know,' she boasted. 'Professor of Classics: Professor Patrick Sutherland. He's often on TV.'

'I think we need more wine,' Scott said. 'Anything else to announce, to celebrate? Anyone getting married? Engaged? Moving in, moving on, moving out? Pregnant?' He reached for the second bottle of wine in its Perspex cooler.

'Well, OK then.' Ariadne appeared embarrassed, refusing to meet Juno's eyes. 'Just one thing.'

'Can lesbians *get* pregnant?' Tilda mused.

'For heaven's sake, Tilda.' Juno rolled her eyes, tutting, part of her wanting to laugh at her daughter's question.

'So, Aunt Ari,' Tilda asked, in the manner of a roving reporter. 'Tell us what you've been up to now?'

All eyes turned back to Ariadne.

'OK, so, erm…' Ariadne looked decidedly shifty. 'Peacock chicks? Four of them? Settling down nicely in your hen coop…?'

# 11

Would there be enough on that leg of lamb sitting in the fridge to feed her lot later that day, along with Grace and her two if she were to invite them round too? Harriet felt she'd not had a good chat with Grace for ages. Whenever they were about to get down to a really good natter about what was going on in their lives, a child would pop up demanding a drink, or a wee or a biscuit. She'd still not really got to the bottom of why Dan had moved out almost two months earlier, and what on earth had Grace been thinking of last night? Going outside with some strange man as if she was a teenager once again? Harriet hadn't been kidding when she'd said Grace could have been murdered, for heaven's sake.

Grace had always been the naughty one. Harriet smiled to herself as Nick rolled over and pulled her into his arms. Always the one who'd got them into trouble at grammar school with her blatant disregard for its petty rules, especially those policed by the over-confident sixth-former who became David's wife, Mandy Henderson, when she was their head girl.

'You awake?' Nick asked sleepily, stroking her hair.

'Hmm.' Harriet reached for his hand, moving her legs across his. 'Grace met someone last night.'

'Well, I suppose there's absolutely no reason why Grace shouldn't meet someone new,' Nick said. 'I mean, Dan's a waste of space. He has an affair, years ago, and then comes crawling back to Grace and now he's buggered off again. I saw him the other day down in the Jolly Sailor. He was looking really rough; you know, down at heel, unshaven, uninterested in anything we were talking about really.'

'Grace reckons he's very depressed, which is under-standable now he's lost his job and can't find another. Grace didn't ask him to leave, you know.'

'No, I realise that. Dan said as much.'

'Grace said he was so much worse after Mandy died. He sort of went downhill after that and decided he'd be better off on his own for a while.' Harriet paused. 'You don't think he was the one, you know…?'

'Who'd been with Mandy before she died? I can't see it, can you? David is convinced she'd been with *someone* though.'

'I'm amazed, knowing David, that he's not had a private detective on the job. I'd have thought he'd have thrown any amount of money at it, you know, just to find out.'

'Funnily enough, I had exactly the same conversation with him last night after you lot had all gone off on your girly night out.' Nick frowned, stroking Harriet's bottom through her pyjamas. *His* pyjamas, actually. 'Why do you insist on wearing these things?' he grumbled, one hand burrowing – rather pleasantly, Harriet realised – down one leg.

'And?' Harriet leaned into Nick's hand.

'And what?'

'David? What did he say to that?'

'Oh, that I must have been aware of what Mandy was like when the fancy took her. He thought very probably it was John she was seeing again. I mean, you only had to see what a state your brother was in, sitting in the church at the funeral.'

'Hmm, she ruined his life, really.'

'Rubbish, Hat, and you know it. Your John has ruined – if that's what you want to call it – his *own* life running after Mandy for the past thirty years. He should have grown up and realised she'd never leave David for him. Anyway, David says he's not opening any cans of worms—'

'Ooh, don't.'

'Don't what? This?' Nick's fingers had now reached, and was stroking, the soft skin at the top of Harriet's leg.

'Ooh, no, *do*. *Do* do that, I mean.' Harriet sighed appreciatively. 'Just don't mention bloody *worms*.'

'Alright, David said he was going to let sleeping dogs lie? Are you OK with *dogs* or do I have to search for more metaphors? This is getting hard work, Hat. Just lie back and appreciate my undivided attention. How often do we get five minutes to ourselves?'

'Mummy?'

'Fin, darling, it's not quite time to be *up* yet.'

'Well, it *was*,' Nick sighed, covering himself before resolutely sitting up and squinting at his youngest son who was standing over on Harriet's side of the bed.

'But, Mummy, I need to tell you something.'

'Do you, darling? You don't think it could wait?'

Fin shook his head firmly. 'Mummy, I've just seen Miss O'Connor in my bedroom.'

Harriet leaned over the side of the bed and looked at Fin before feeling his forehead. Was he ill? Did he have a fever and had been dreaming? 'No, Fin, don't be silly. Miss O'Connor is at school. Well, no,' Harriet corrected herself, 'it's Sunday, so she won't be at school, obviously. You've had a dream, Fin, that's all.'

'No, honestly, Mummy, she opened my bedroom door and when she saw me in bed she went "oooh" and ran away.'

'Why on earth would Miss O'Connor be in your bedroom on a Sunday morning, running away when she saw you? Where did she *run* to?' Harriet ruffled Fin's blond hair and, leaning over, kissed his cheek. He didn't appear hot or feverish.

'I think she must have had dirty knees because she'd just had a bath.'

Nick, who had closed his eyes in the hope of going back to sleep opened his right one and said in a jolly voice. 'Well, I hope she didn't use all the water, Fin, because I'd quite like a shower myself in the next hour or so.' He lowered his voice. 'Is this the age when kids have imaginary friends, Hat?'

Harriet shrugged. 'Dunno. Isn't that when they're quite a bit younger? Fin,' she went on, 'I don't think Miss O'Connor would want to be having a bath at *this* time of the morning in, you know, in *our* house, do you?' She started to laugh. Honestly, these kids of hers. What would they come up with next?

'Well, *I* think she'd just had a bath because when I opened my door to see where she'd gone, she was running away in one of your best pink towels. You know, the ones you say we can't use. She was running away up the stairs to Kit's bedroom in one of your *best* pink towels.' Fin was slightly indignant.

'Miss O'Connor?' Nick asked. 'Isn't she that ninety-year-old harridan teacher who used to terrify Kit when he was little? You know, when he and Libby were at the village school?'

Harriet closed her eyes and, sighing deeply, said, 'No, Nicholas, Miss O'Connor is the twins' newly qualified, very, very gorgeous *young* teacher who appears—' she lowered her voice '—to be upstairs in your *other* son's attic bedroom, where, I assume, she's been all night.'


'Kit, this is *not* on. It's not a...' Harriet struggled for the right words. 'It's not a *knocking shop* for heaven's sake.'

'Bloody hell, Mum,' Kit said. 'Where d'you come up with such phrases?' Not in the least embarrassed at being caught, literally, Harriet assumed, with his pants down, her twenty-year-old son stood at the fridge in his navy towelling bathrobe, searching for orange juice. Oh, but he was such a good-looking boy, this boy of hers. Over six-foot-two with the same blond hair and brown eyes as his father, Kit Westmoreland had every girl in the area (as well as outside it) falling for him.

'But that girl you've had upstairs in your bed is the twins' *teacher* for heaven's sake. Did she know? When she came back here with you last night? Who you were?'

Kit laughed. 'From the way she shot back up to the attic

after trying to find the loo, I presume not. She was like a terrified rabbit. I'd no idea what she was going on about until she managed to calm down and I realised she'd gone into Fin's room thinking it was the bathroom. I'd obviously given her the wrong directions.' He started to laugh again. 'I bet poor old Fin thought he was dreaming.'

'This is not funny, Kit. For heaven's sake, don't let Thea see her.'

'Thea? Why not? I'm sure she'd like to show Niamh her Barbies.'

'You know as well as I do, Thea has never once been interested in dolls and prams and the like. Look, Thea's a bit of a gang leader in her class…'

Kit really did laugh out loud at that. 'Gangs in Reception?'

'… and Miss O'Connor's not finding her easy to handle.'

Kit frowned. 'Miss O'Connor? Who's Miss O'Connor? Oh, is that her name?'

'You are incorrigible, Christopher Westmoreland.' Harriet slammed marmalade and Marmite onto the kitchen table and glared at Kit.

'Well, maybe Thea and Niamh can bond over breakfast. You know, on the gang leader's turf as it were.' Kit was about to laugh again but then, as he saw Harriet wasn't in the least amused, said, 'Look, Mum, can I remind you I've saved you and Dad a fortune by not going to university like Libby.'

'Oh, don't tell me you were being altruistic when you decided to finish your education at eighteen?'

'If I knew what altruistic meant, I could tell you if I was being it. All I'm saying is, if I'd gone away to university, I'd have had any number of girls in my bedroom in my student digs and you wouldn't have batted an eye.'

'Of course we wouldn't.' Harriet glared again, passing Kit cutlery and mugs. Should she think about napkins like Mandy had always insisted on? You know, if they were having a guest for breakfast. 'We wouldn't have *known* about it.'

'My point exactly. Look at Libby. She was younger than me when she started sleeping with Seb. And here in her bedroom as well. He was always here.'

'Yes, but Libby was in a serious relationship with Seb. You…' Harriet fought for the right words. 'You, Kit are being promiscuous, sleeping around, picking up girls and sleeping with them when you don't even know their full name. I'm assuming you are practising safe sex?'

'Don't need to *practise*, Mum…' Kit grinned.

Jesus, could she ever have spoken to her own mother like Kit was speaking to her now?

'And don't tell me you didn't sleep with Dad before you got married,' Kit went on.

Harriet felt herself flush. 'Again, that was different. I was in a serious relationship too. I was married by the time I was your age. Well, almost.'

'Mum, the minute I can afford a place of my own, I'll be off.'

'But you don't know where Dad and David want you to be.' Kit had gone straight from finishing A Levels, to working for David Henderson and his father. 'I thought there was some talk of you being based in London? Or even Milan, so Dad doesn't have to be away so much?'

'Possibly. You know, I went to look at a couple of places up for rent yesterday.'

'Oh?' Even though he drove her mad, the thought of this son of hers – any of her children she supposed – leaving her, made Harriet's heart miss a beat.

'You know the cottages Charlie Madison renovated next to Libby and Seb's place down at Holly Close Farm? They were both up for rent.'

'They *were* up for rent? Aren't Charlie and her sister living there?'

'Apparently Charlie's gone back to London with that new boyfriend of hers and Daisy's gone travelling. Libby told me the other day when she was here for tea.'

'But they're already taken?'

'Hmm.'

'Expensive, I bet.'

'Hmm.'

'Look, Kit…' Harriet stopped laying the table and turned, folding her arms as she did so. 'How are you affording all this? That fabulous Audi you bought last week, and now thinking of renting an upmarket place like the Holly Farm cottages?' She picked up the beautifully cut jacket he'd obviously abandoned round a chair when he and Miss O'Connor had finally come back in the early hours of the morning and examined the label. 'Brunello Cucinelli, Kit?' Harriet stroked the soft, fine wool fabric. 'Don't tell me you bought this on the Monday market down in town?'

'Mum, I sell fabulous Italian textiles and clothing. That's my job. I'm not going to see clients dressed in a shiny polyester suit from Primark, am I?'

'Well, does Dad give you a clothing allowance?'

Kit shook his head. 'You know he doesn't,' he said almost irritably.

'And he and David said you had to start at the bottom like any other of their reps. Work your way up in the company. So I don't believe they're paying you enough to be buying expensive stuff like this or that car out on the drive? Kit?'

Ignoring Harriet, Kit picked up glasses and the juice carton. 'Need to take this upstairs, Mum. Obviously need to work out a plan to get Miss O'Connor past Al Capone.'

Grace, when she arrived with the kids later on that Sunday, looked fabulous. The day was much colder than the week just gone and had brought with it a real sense of the winter days ahead. She appeared to have put away the casual light-coloured summer clothes she'd been wearing at David's birthday drinks do the previous afternoon and was dressed in the tan and aubergine shades that so suited her dark eyes and long chestnut-coloured hair. A pair of beautiful ox-blood flat leather boots only emphasised her shapely legs, while a tight-fitting woollen skirt in the same shade showed off her slim figure. Grace Stevens, at forty-two, was still an exceptionally attractive woman, Harriet conceded as she herself, sweating and shiny-faced, grappled with a couple of enormous legs of lamb.

'Feeding the five thousand?' Grace smiled as Harriet wiped her face on her pinny before launching into a bag of carrots.

'More, I think,' Harriet frowned. 'I seem to be gathering extra people by the minute. I had to send Nick out to the farm shop for another leg of lamb. Could probably have done with all four of the poor creature's limbs.'

'Throw those potatoes over,' Grace said. 'Jonty's gone to find your two and Pietronella's gone to watch *Love Island* with India. 'So, who've you got coming?'

'Twelve of us.' Harriet reached for a second bag of carrots.

'Twelve? It's not Christmas already, is it?' Grace laughed. She appeared remarkably jolly this morning, Harriet thought, considering the amount of alcohol she'd put away the night before. Harriet threw a surreptitious sideways glance at Grace who was already getting stuck in, peeling potatoes with gusto.

'Just sort of multiplied. My plan was to get you and the kids here so you could tell me all about last night.'

'Last night?' Grace didn't miss a beat.

'Hey, don't give me that innocent, butter wouldn't melt, look of yours. Last night? With the drug dealer?'

'He's not a *drug dealer*.'

'Oh, what is he, then?'

Grace shrugged gaily. 'No idea.'

'Well, what was he called?'

'No idea.'

'Blimey. Do you know anything about him?'

'Only that he kisses like an angel.'

'And the rest?'

'The rest?'

'You know? Was there more...?'

'Mum, who's coming for lunch? How many do I have to lay the table for? 'Lo, Aunty Grace.' India, yawning widely and rubbing sleep from her eyes as only a twelve-year-old can, was being doggedly followed, step by step, by Pietronella and was obviously not impressed at having to leave the comfort of TV and sofa to lay the table or babysit a four-year-old.

'OK,' Harriet said, counting on her fingers: 'us six Aunty Grace and her two, Grandad, Lilian...'

'Oh good, is Lilian coming?' Grace smiled. 'I've not seen her for ages.' Lilian Brennan, who lived in the village, had helped Harriet with the children when they were little and was still on hand to babysit both the twins and Grace's two if needed.

'And er, it looks like Miss O'Connor as well.'

'Miss O'Connor?' Both Grace and India stared.

'Miss O'Connor as in the kids' teacher?' Grace put down her potato peeler. 'Since when have the kids' teachers been invited for Sunday lunch? Reception teachers live in the stock cupboard, don't they? You know, occasionally popping out for a quick mug of tea and a custard cream before heading back to where they belong. They're not real people who eat roast lamb and...' Grace broke off to see what Harriet was preparing 'Chocolate mousse?'

'India, leave that and take Pietronella out to the other kids, will you? They're playing in the garden.'

'What, and miss what you're about to tell Aunty Grace? It's Kit, isn't it? I bet it's Kit who's brought her home.'

'Miss O'Connor is a friend of Kit's, yes, you're right.' Harriet concentrated on whipping cream, refusing to meet India's raised eyebrow. 'And any friend of Kit's is welcome to stay and eat with us.'

'Friend?' India scoffed, taking Pietronella's hand somewhat grudgingly. 'With benefits, more like.'

'Out,' Harriet, raise her cream-laden whisk in India's direction and, once she'd left the kitchen turned back to Grace. 'Did *we* know about such things when we were twelve?'

'I'm sure we did. But it was just snogging behind the bike shed.'

'We didn't *have* a bike shed, remember?'

'OK, snogging behind the metaphorical bike shed, rather than, you know, having sex with someone we've only just met.'

'Goodness, I should think not, at twelve... at *any* age...' Harriet glanced across at Grace and raised her own eyebrow.

Grace's scarlet face told her everything she needed to know.

## 12

'You didn't say Granny Sylvia and Colin were coming too,' India said accusingly, striding back into the kitchen and putting a stop to any further questioning of Grace on Harriet's part.

'Well, because they're *not*.'

'They *are*. They've just pulled up and are taking their cases out of the car.' India looked at her mother. 'Didn't you know?'

'The last weekend in September, Sylvia said. Surely that's *next* weekend?' Harriet looked at the calendar hanging above the fridge, showing different kids from Little Acorns involved in a variety of activities and poses, and closed her eyes as she saw the ring around the present day's date. She closed her eyes in disbelief. 'Bloody hell,' she snapped. 'Where's September gone? Is there a fatted calf to hand somewhere?'

'Well at least you're in the middle of preparing a big lunch.' Grace picked up her knife and re-opened the bag of potatoes she'd just closed, obviously relieved that attention was no longer on her and her alleged gymnastics of the previous evening. 'Just think how awful if you'd all trolled off somewhere and it was *obvious* you'd forgotten they were coming.'

'I hadn't *forgotten*,' Harriet said crossly.

'What do *you* call it, then?' India asked.

'Misappropriating the date... Sylvia, how lovely to see you.' Harriet quickly rearranged her face while, behind her, India sniggered. 'And what good time you've made. Colin, you're looking well too. Obviously been on the golf course.'

'If only.' Nick's stepfather, Sir Colin Fitzgerald QC, harrumphed and cleared his throat as he kissed Harriet's cheek.

'And he's working flat out at the moment,' Sylvia tutted. 'I was actually afraid we were going to have to cancel this week up North with you.'

'A week?' Harriet quailed slightly. 'How lovely... Now I'm just going to give Nick a shout – he's out in the garden somewhere, you know how he loves his bonfires at this time of year – and he'll get you both a drink while I just check your room hasn't been invaded by the kids and their toys. In fact, Grace, would you mind taking over here – you know where the sherry is – and then India will take you to find Nick while I just...'

Grinning inanely, Harriet fled upstairs. Clean sheets and towels. Please God, let there be some in the airing cupboard... and then off to India's room with the double bed... and quickly shift her stuff down the landing to Thea's bottom bunk bed. India would object at being on the bottom but, as Thea had decided that as she was 'top girl' in every sense of the word, she'd assured Harriet the top bunk was the rightful pace to rest her head. They'd just have to fight it out between themselves.

Jesus, what a mess. How could one adolescent make so much bloody *mess*?

Gathering an armful of dirty jeans, sweatshirts, tights and knickers, as well as a couple of soaking wet towels, she dumped the lot in the laundry basket and noted, with a few choice words, India's PE kit and school uniform she'd be needing in the morning, still unwashed.

'Bugger, blast and bugger,' she snapped. 'Oh, Lilian, thank God.' Harriet was stopped in her tracks by the sight of Lilian Brennan, appearing at the bedroom door like the proverbial fairy godmother.

'Sure, Harriet, you go back down and get on with your dinner and I'll sort up here. I know where everything is, although you might want to get me the cleaning yoke – you can't put Nick's mammy and himself in there without me giving it a bit of a fettle first.'

'You are a godsend, Lilian. Listen, before I go back down, you don't fancy having a lodger, do you?'

'You're thinking of leaving?' Lilian was startled.

'Ooh, there's a thought. No, not me, it's a friend of Kit's. Actually, she's the twins' and Jonty's teacher, would you believe? And, you'll like this, she's called Niamh O'Connor and she's from Dublin, not far at all from where you lived.'

'Oh, really?' Lilian looked up with interest from where she was sorting clean bedlinen.

'I had a long chat with her this morning. She was terribly embarrassed at being here, you know, being the kids' teacher – she'd no idea Kit was their big brother – and desperately tried to slide out the back door when no one was looking. I stopped her going and made her come into the kitchen and at least have a coffee. Anyway, the story is she met some boy from Manchester while she was on holiday in Spain last year and once she qualified as a teacher decided to follow him over here. Unfortunately, by the time she got the job at Little Acorns, the boy had changed his mind…'

'Sure, and don't we know that can happen?' Lilian had already thumped pillows into clean cases and was reaching for the duvet.

'And so she's been left in limbo somewhat, not knowing *anyone* here and sharing a house down in Midhope with some horrible-sounding people. She's not enjoying the teaching, is really lonely and is about to jack it in and go back home to her mum. I just thought if she had someone nice to live with, she could at least do her NQT year and be fully qualified before she goes back to Dublin?'

'Well, I need to think about it, Harriet. I do like living by myself as you know. I'm becoming a bit of a creature of habit. I like to have my tea at a certain time and with my particular plate and mug, and so on.'

'Oh, I know that, Lilian.' Harriet reached for a pair of India's knickers that had somehow landed behind the curtains and rubbed, ineffectually, at a splodge of dried foundation on the dressing table with them. 'As I say, we had a long chat. She's so young; I mean, she's about Libby's age, but whereas Libby could always stand up for herself, this poor girl seems to be out of her depth. And Kit's not helped. You know, bringing her home like this.'

'Ah, come on now, Harriet, what young girl wouldn't be tempted into having a ride with that gorgeous son of yours. You know, a ride even on a goat, is better by far than having to walk.'

'Right.' Harriet frowned, lost as she often was, with Lilian's misplaced sayings.

Lilian stepped back to survey her handiwork with the freshly made bed. 'There now, nearly done. You go back down and sort the food and tell India to bring up the hoover thing. She's big enough and daft enough to do it herself now, so she is.'


'You do know, Thea, that Mrs Beresford, Miss O'Connor and myself haven't been too happy with some of your behaviour at school?' Harriet thought she'd better try and cook up something to explain Niamh's presence to this youngest daughter of hers. 'Sometimes we don't think you're as nice to the other children at school as you could be. And so, erm, so Daddy and I invited Miss O'Connor to have lunch with us today so that she can see what a *good* girl you *really* are.'

Thea pouted, shaking back her blonde curls. 'I can tell everyone in Show and Tell tomorrow that Miss O'Connor's been to *my* house for lunch. She hasn't been to *anyone* else's house.'

'No, no, no,' Harriet quickly jumped in. 'No, Thea. You see it's a sort of a… a *secret* mission. You know, like erm…' Harriet racked her brains as she put a tentative finger into her pudding to see if it had set. 'Like Danger Mousse…'

'Danger *Mousse?*' Thea's raised eyebrow gave every indication that, even at the age of five, she had inherited her paternal grandmother's facial expressions.

'*Mouse. Mouse.* Miss O'Connor is like Danger *Mouse.* Mrs Beresford doesn't want anyone to *know* about it.' Oh

God, that's all she needed, the schoolground Mafia getting to hear that their kids' teacher had been having it off with that naughty Thea Westmoreland's big brother.

'Jonty,' Thea said importantly as Grace's son wandered into the kitchen looking for his leader. 'This is a *big* secret, and you mustn't tell Fin or Pietronella because *they* can't keep secrets. You mustn't tell *anyone*, but Miss O'Connor isn't really a teacher. She's a spy. You know, like James Bond.'

'Who's James Bond?' Jonty raised his big eyes – Mandy's eyes, Harriet saw with a pang of realisation – and stared.

'I'm not really quite *sure*,' Thea said importantly. 'But Daddy and Kit said he was a spy on a mission – like Miss O'Connor is – and they really like him. They were watching him last week on Sky. He drives very fast cars and kills people and there was a *lot* of explosions. Boom!'

'So, is that lovely sports car out on the drive Miss O'Connor's?' Jonty was impressed.

'No, silly, that's Kit's. Kit is very rich now, you know.' Thea adored her big brother.

Jonty looked worried. 'And does Miss O'Connor kill people and make explosions?'

Nick, who, unbeknown to Harriet, was taking off his wellingtons in the utility, gave a bark of laughter.

'Well, you see if you can do any better,' Harriet shouted back crossly. 'And next time you're watching unsuitable films, will you check that the microdots aren't in there with you?'

'So *does* Miss O'Connor drive fast cars and make explosions?' Thea asked doubtfully.

*Oh, for the love of God, no,* Harriet wanted to say to

Thea who was still very suspicious of her little fabrication. *She's just a lovely young girl from Dublin who's been daft enough to follow some man over to England, and then get into bed with your big brother.* Instead she said, 'It's part of Miss O'Connor's job to spend some time with her pupils at the weekend. Just to see how they behave at home. So, young lady, your very best behaviour please, now and especially at school next week or Mrs Beresford will be after you. And then *I* will, at home, as well. Now, why don't you see if Kit is out of bed and showered yet, oh and let Grandad in – he's just arrived – and then ask everyone what they would like to drink? Daddy can pour and you three can serve.'

'Oh, I don't think Pietronella—'

'Shut it, Thea, we're not having this. Now do as you're told, we're eating in ten minutes.'


'Aw, Hat, you haven't sat me next to the judgemental Judge, have you?' Grace pulled a face. 'Last time I sat down at dinner with him, his hand was clamped permanently on my knee. It was a bit like having a clammy hot water bottle strapped to my leg. And he's actually quite bigoted, you know.'

'Yes, Grace, I do know. Put the dog under the table,' Harriet advised. 'With any luck Sam'll see him off. Nick, earn your keep, tell everyone where to sit,' she shouted through the open dining room door.

'I'm decanting this fabulous red Colin brought with him!' Nick shouted back irritably, obviously frightened of corking Judge Sir Colin Fitzgerald's ridiculously expensive wine that always accompanied him on his sojourn up North. India, earn your keep, tell everyone where to sit.'

'Me? I don't know where everyone should go. Kit, you do it.'

'*I'll* do it.' Thea began to herd everyone like a particularly tenacious sheepdog. 'Miss O'Connor, do you want to come and sit next to me?'

'Don't be daft, Thea, she wants to sit next to Kit.' India pulled a silly face and Harriet shot her a look.

'Oh, for heaven's sake, just sit down everybody. Wherever you want.' *But don't let Dad sit next to Sylvia*, Harriet thought. Her father insisted on addressing Sylvia with her full handle of Lady Sylvia (Harriet was never sure if he was being reverent or taking the piss) and, being deaf, Kenneth could never understand what Sylvia was saying, while her mother-in-law, trying to work her way through Kenneth's broad Yorkshire accent, usually ended up nodding politely and smiling, 'Really? How wonderful,' in her clipped Surrey tones (which, Harriet noted, had achieved even more clippiness since marrying the Judge) regardless of whether Kenneth had just told her his rhubarb had failed that year or his last mate from the British Legion had been hospitalised and finally died a particularly long and lingering death.

'Dad,' Harriet called desperately as he headed for Lady Sylvia, 'would you mind carving?'

Kenneth retraced his steps back to where the two huge legs of lamb were resting on the side after being cooked – Harriet sent up a prayer to that great butcher in the sky – to perfection, and took the proffered carving knife while Grace and Lilian helped bring in dishes from the kitchen. 'Eh love, you could ride bare-arsed to London on this,'

Kenneth complained, holding up the knife for her inspection. 'Haven't you got a better one?'

'Kit, earn your keep, get the two other knives from the kitchen and help Grandad carve. Oh, and bring in the mint sauce too; the mint is from Grandad's allotment.'

Five minutes later and, Harriet observed almost smugly, everyone was tucking in. It was bloody hard work all this feeding of guests, expected or otherwise, but there was something quite wonderful in having all your family round the table at once. She really should have asked Libby, she thought. And Seb. And then Jonty would have had both his parents here. She did hope Seb was going to be OK and climb out of the unhappiness he was going through after Mandy's death. He'd appeared much more like himself at David's party the previous afternoon. But then, she supposed, she'd have felt obliged to ask David as well. And Caroline, David's mother was still there. Twenty round the table was really just too many.

Appreciative murmurs, clinking of glasses and the pouring of wine were the only sounds made for the first few minutes. There was a tricky moment when Niamh, sitting next to Judge Colin, gave a surprised 'Ooh,' as Colin reached an exploratory hand in the direction of her knee but, with combined glares in his direction from Sylvia, Lilian and Harriet herself, together with Grace asking loudly and pertinently, 'Colin, have you had any dealings with the #MeToo Movement in one of your courts?' Colin harrumphed loudly and got on with his lunch.

'So, Colin,' Nick addressed his stepfather as he poured more of the coveted Merlot, 'you say you've been having a stressful time in court?'

'It's about time he retired,' Sylvia said tartly. 'He's *quite* exhausted with it all.'

'Hmm, terrible case last week of a murdered homosexual,' Colin began, clearing his throat loudly and putting down his knife and fork.

'Did you know, Harriet,' Kenneth said knowingly, leaning forwards in her direction and silencing everyone with his sudden pronouncement, 'it came as a *big* surprise to me to learn that Albert Hall were a homosexual...' He paused for a few seconds. 'Actually, I tell a lie, he were *bifocal* apparently.'

'Albert Hall? That's in London, Grandad,' India said kindly.

'Aye well, that's as might be, but the Albert Hall I used to go to school with lived down by t'cut. He were married, you know, but apparently a bit bifocal on t'side.'

'I've always thought,' Sylvia put in, 'George Michael was much maligned. I mean, it's quite feasible that when he was constantly visiting the Gents', the poor man was suffering some sort of urinary tract problem. I loved "Careless Whisper"; your father and I danced to it, Nicholas, on our fifteenth wedding anniversary.'

'County lines,' Judge Colin suddenly barked, obviously not wanting to talk of Sylvia's first husband. 'Having to sit on a lot of these cases.'

'Now, tell me, Judge Fitzpatrick...' Lilian leaned forward. 'I've been hearing and reading *such* a lot about these, but I'm not quite sure what it's all about. It was actually on the radio this morning that they've got as far as *Harrogate*.' Lilian spoke as if it were the Germans invading during WW2.

'Dreadful carry on,' Colin tutted. 'Basically, it's organised crime: the distribution of drugs from the big cities into smaller towns – like Midhope and Harrogate – but now moving into the rural areas like your lovely villages round here. Children and vulnerable people are sucked in to carry the stuff. There's different lines and they all have names.'

'Names?' Harriet frowned. 'What sort of names?'

'Gucci Line, Nike Line, Itching and Scratching Line. Give it any name you want, really.' Judge Colin paused as Nick refilled his glass. 'The line goes usually from one of the big four areas – London, the Midlands, Manchester, West Yorkshire – with drugs being delivered by young kids who've been recruited, usually because of some vulnerability. It could be a broken home, abuse at home, social deprivation, you know, the usual stuff. Once a child is sucked in, it's very difficult for him to get out of it. And, also, the homes of vulnerable adults – you know those with mental health issues – are often taken over as a sort of headquarters—'

'Oh, sure and I know this one,' Lilian interrupted, almost proudly. '*Cuckooing*, it's called, I believe?'

'—then once the drugs are actually down the line and in the outlying areas, in the villages, the dealer will advertise—'

'Advertise?' Nick frowned. 'How do you advertise you're a dealer?'

'Snapchat is one way. I'm not really up on social media stuff but I believe something you put on Snapchat actually disappears after a while? Is that right, Kit?'

Kit nodded, as did Niamh.

'Dealers will have a Ring and Bring service, so you just ring and the drugs are delivered to your door.'

'A bit like Tesco's?' Harriet stared. 'Fancy.'

'Cannabis?' Lilian asked, obviously fascinated with the whole concept. 'I did try it once, you know—'

'Right,' Harriet said jumping in and glancing over at India and the younger children. 'Pudding time, I think, don't you?'

'Not usually,' Colin shook his head at Lilian. 'It's the harder stuff that provides the focus: heroin, cocaine and amphetamines. The gang's security is obviously paramount to the whole business and each young runner they groom and take on only know one other phone number along the delivery chain. Terrible scourge on our society, terrible.'

Harriet looked across at Kit who was giving the conversation between Lilian and Judge Colin his full concentration, and she felt her heart skip a beat. Where *was* Kit getting his money from? Had David or Seb offered him a loan to buy the Audi? Not knowing anything about cars – a black car was a black car was a black car in her eyes – she'd assumed at first the car Kit had arrived home with was the usual rep's run-around. Now she wasn't so sure and she made the decision to have another conversation with Nick about it as well as a good root around Kit's room when he was next away. See what she could find.

'I really like having you as my teacher,' Fin was saying to Miss O'Connor, gazing up with some reverence as plates were finally cleared and collected.

'So do I,' Jonty joined in. 'You're the best teacher I've *ever* had.'

'How many has he had?' Grace giggled, as she helped Harriet and Lilian clear plates. 'He's only been in Reception.'

'Oh, do let me help,' Niamh said, jumping up and knocking Colin's red wine into his lap in her eagerness to show willing. She blushed scarlet to the roots of her long dark hair. 'I'm so sorry…'

'It's alright, Miss O'Connor,' Thea said kindly as Niamh attempted to dab at Judge Colin's trousers with her napkin and Kit started to laugh.

'But he's *soaked*,' Niamh said, biting her lip as she continued to scrabble around in Colin's crotch.

'Really,' Thea reassured her loudly, 'I don't think Grandpa Colin will mind a bit. Mummy's always telling Aunty Grace he's just an *old soak*.'

# 13

Monday morning, another start to a full week at school and Grace wasn't looking forward to it at all. After the excitement of Sunday lunch with the twins at Harriet's yesterday, plus a surfeit of sugar (Sylvia and Judge Colin had brought a bounty of goodies with them and, with a couple of glasses of wine fuelling the grown-ups as well as the heated discussion that ensued over whether cannabis should be legalised, the kids had had free rein to indulge unhindered) both Jonty and Pietronella were now bad-tempered and sleepy.

To be honest, Grace was feeling the same way herself: her period had just started which always made her grumpy, and she heard herself being unusually ratty with the children as she chivvied them into the clean uniforms she'd still been ironing at midnight. Maybe she needed a tonic. Her own mother had regularly dosed herself and her younger brother, Simon with some rather lovely green, orange-tasting liquid in a big brown bottle at the very first sign of tears or tiredness or not wanting to go to school for some reason. Minadex, that was it. Gosh, she hadn't thought about that stuff for years. She had a sudden need to be a child again, to have her mother sort her life out for her with a bottle of tonic.

Grace knew what was really behind this feeling of wanting to curl up in a ball and make the world go away: Saturday night. How could she have done what she did with a total stranger? At the time, and yesterday as well, it had all seemed quite liberating, daring and almost jolly when Harriet had wanted her to spill the beans and tell her exactly what had happened. Now, in the miserable grey light of a late-September Monday morning, with the kids complaining of being cold at the re-appearance of chilly, dark mornings after the heat of summer, it all just seemed horribly embarrassing.

Sordid even.

*You daft bint*, Grace chastised herself crossly. *What the hell got into you?*

*Too much alcohol*, she answered herself. *Get over it. Move on.*

'Dandy!' Grace looked up from pouring cereal, juice and milk as Jonty scrambled down from his chair at the kitchen table and ran to Dan who had suddenly appeared at her side.

'Dan? Gosh I wasn't expecting *you*. You're looking a lot better.' Grace was surprised to see her husband showered, shaved and wearing his best suit. He'd had a haircut too and, although he'd put some weight on and his face was pasty, he was looking more like the man she'd married. And separated from. And got back together with. And now, separated from again. Blimey, it was one big rollercoaster, their marriage. Was he here to tell her he'd got over his depression and wanted to give it all another go?

But did she want him back at home? He'd been gone almost two months, leaving not much longer after David had rung them with the terrible news that Mandy had died. Dan had been behaving somewhat erratically for a couple of months before that, not sleeping too well, either not interested in socialising or then suddenly wanting her to go out and, almost frenziedly, partying. She'd been convinced Dan was seeing another woman – Grace recognised the signs from before: one minute up and the next down as he swung from the euphoria to the guilt, of an adulterous affair.

While Grace had grappled with the situation, she'd not actually said anything to Dan, both because she wasn't convinced that another woman *was* the problem this time round and also knowing, to her shame, she'd taken Dan back primarily because she wanted a father figure for Jonty and not because she truly loved him as she once had. The trust and love she'd had when she married Dan Stevens had gone into the ether when he'd left her for another woman while she was trying desperately hard to get pregnant. All she'd wanted was the chance to have a baby of her own and what had Dan been up to at the time? Swinging from the chandelier with a girl nearly half his age. Once Pietronella had come into their lives, Grace accepted they were really now a proper family, and she'd done her best to create a loving, stable unit for her children, as well as trying hard to be the wife she'd once been to Dan. Jonty and Pietronella were the only important things in her life and, if their happiness depended on Dan's coming back, so be it.

'Dandy looking lovely.' Pietronella was more interested in her breakfast than seeing her father, but she gave him a friendly wave with her white plastic fork before determinedly fishing out cornflakes from the milk once more, her brown eyes screwed up in concentrated effort behind her little round spectacles as the milk dripped through the prongs of the plastic.

'You *are* looking lovely.' Grace looked him up and down. 'Well, better anyhow.'

'Look, Grace, can I have a word? You know...' He indicated with his head the privacy of the hallway.

'Pas devant les enfants?' Grace raised an eyebrow and then, ensuring both children were actually eating something, glanced at the clock before heading out of the door. 'I really am going to have to leave in fifteen minutes, Dan.'

'I know, I know,' he apologised. 'That's why I came round now, so I could catch you all before I go.'

'Go where?'

'Look, things haven't been good between us for ages, Grace. Probably my fault. Being made redundant hasn't been easy.'

'I'm sure it hasn't, but it didn't need you to abandon us and go and live at your mother's place. Surely?'

'We've discussed this, Grace, and I'm sorry. I'm sorry that, despite really trying on both our parts, especially now that we have the children, we really don't seem able to make a go of this marriage. My fault mainly, I guess...'

Grace sighed. 'No, I'm as much to blame, I suppose.'

'I *am* sorry, you know.' When Grace didn't say anything he went on, 'Bit of a waste of space really, aren't I? Anyway, I've got an interview for a new job.'

'Hence the suit and haircut?' Grace smiled. 'That's great. Well done. Where is it?'

'Exeter.'

'Exeter? But that's miles away, isn't it?' Geography had

never been her strong point, but even she knew it wasn't in Yorkshire.

'Nearly 300.' He glanced at his watch. 'And I need to be off or I won't make the appointment with the boss on time.'

'But why Exeter, for heaven's sake? What about *me*? What about the *kids*?'

'Grace, come on.' Dan paused, stroking Grace's arm, but refusing to look her in the eye. 'We both know it's not working between us. I blew it when I messed up with Camilla. We've tried, for the kids' sake, to make it work, but I know your heart isn't in it.'

'*My* heart? What about Jonty and Pietronella's hearts? You're their dad.'

'Come on, Grace,' Dan said once again, this time accompanied by an almost irritable sigh. 'I'm just *Dandy* to Jonty.'

'Stop it, Dan. Jonty has *two* dads.'

'And Seb is the important dad. I know that, I've accepted that.'

'Well, you obviously have if you've applied for a job in Exeter, for heaven's sake. But you are Pietronella's *only* dad. You and I adopted Pietronella, and you promised to be her dad like I promised to be her mum. She's *ours*. You're her *dad*.'

'I know, I'm sorry.'

'I mean, even if you don't want to live with *me* anymore, at least stay round here, in your mum's place, so that the children know where you are and can see you all the time.'

'There are no jobs round here.'

'Manchester? Leeds? Sheffield? There must be loads of jobs...? Hang on...' Grace heard the proverbial penny drop – actually clang – loud and clearly. 'There's someone else. In Exeter, isn't there? You've got some woman down there.'

Dan actually laughed at that. Hollow, Grace conceded, but still a laugh. 'Don't be daft, Grace. Look at me. I'm overweight, unfit, getting over a bad bout of depression. You know, when have I had the time or inclination to run after some woman in the South of England?'

'It's possible. You could have met her online.'

'I didn't and I haven't. Look, I might not get this job, but I would really like it. I'm going to keep Mum's house on. Airbnb it perhaps, and then I can come up some weekends... *most* weekends,' he amended when he saw Grace's face, 'so that I can see Jonty and Pietronella. I actually need to get away from here.'

'Here? What do you mean, *here*?'

'This area. Midhope. The North. I need to be away from it.'

'Right. Fine. Great. You go off to Exeter. We'll be *fine* here. Pietronella, come and give Daddy a big kiss. You might not see him for a while.' Immediately the words were out of her mouth, Grace was contrite; she was being a total dog in the manger. She didn't love Dan anymore; didn't want him back, so why was she was making out that she did? It was the kids, Jonty and Pietronella, she was worried for. Not herself. Not Dan. The kids. 'Jonty, Dandy's going to be away for a while.' Grace softened her voice. 'Looking for a new job. Isn't that lovely? We'll see him *very* soon.'

'Maybe Grandpa David and my *daddy* can give Dandy a job? Why can't he work for *them*?'

Grace winced at Jonty's words and Dan raised an eyebrow. 'I'm always going to be up against this,' he said sadly as he left.

'I'm sorry, Dan, I'm so sorry.' She felt tears start and went over to hug him fiercely. He kissed her cheek before walking over to the children, patting them briefly on the head and kissing each of their cheeks in turn.

'We'll see you very soon, Dan. Good luck with the interview,' Grace said to his departing back and then, pasting a big smile on her face, rallied the kids into action.

Monday morning was not shaping up well and, effing hell, she was damned-well late *again* now.

'Grace, you do know Deimante is in with you this morning?' Josh Donnington, Little Acorns' deputy stopped her as she dropped Jonty with Niamh O'Connor, and Pietronella in Nursery.

'That's fine. Really good actually.' Deimante Miniauskiene was the school's lollipop lady, cleaner and dinner lady and was desperate to get onto a PGCE course in order to train to be an actual teacher. Unfortunately, although she was obviously very bright – she had a degree in astrophysics from a university in her native Lithuania – she continued to find both spoken and written English difficult and had, in the summer, been turned down once again by those universities in the area offering the training course she so badly needed in order to be able to teach primary-aged children. In addition to her other duties in the school, Cassie Beresford had managed to get Deimante two days' work as a teaching assistant where she was assigned to different classes to work alongside the teacher, taking individual children and small groups as required.

'That's great,' Grace reiterated. 'She can help me set up the Light experiments in Science.'

Josh Donnington frowned. 'Light? Why are you teaching Light, Grace?'

'Why? Because I spent all Saturday afternoon – after being pelted with worms by that little sod, Noah Haddon – planning it. That's *why*, Josh.' Grace knew she was being offhand, but, after Dan's visit that morning, she was that way out.

'But they've done Light, Grace,' Josh said calmly. 'We changed all the Science topics round last year so that we'd be one step ahead when the proposed new Sex and Relationships Education syllabus comes into Science next September.'

'But it's only *this* September now,' Grace said crossly.

'I know that, Grace,' Josh said patiently, 'but you know Cassie likes to be up and running with new initiatives before we legally have to. The Governors have passed it all, and the letter to parents informing them of the content as well as their choice to remove their child if they so wish – none do – were sent out in the first week. The new syllabus and what you should be covering is in Planning. You need to be teaching it now.'

'And nobody thought to tell *me* this?'

'Grace, you've taught Sex Education before.' Cassie, on the way down to Reception had overheard the conversation and joined her and Josh. 'You taught it to Y6 when you were here two years ago.'

'Yes, but with a very *nice* class. Not with this lot.' Grace sighed heavily. 'Fine, fine, no problem,' she snapped. 'It'll be fine.'

'Of course it will,' Cassie soothed. 'And with Deimante in with you, I bet you'll have a bit of fun too.'

Was Sex Education supposed to be *fun*, Grace wondered as she went about preparing for the morning. Sex itself wasn't always *fun*, Grace conceded as she hunted for what she needed online. Oh, but *Saturday night's* sex had been something else: dangerous, potent, incredible. Sordid? Grace felt her nether regions respond as she remembered the man's touch, his clever hands, his beautiful mouth. She'd woven her fingers through his long dark curls as he'd lifted her onto the wall in the darkest corner of the garden, parting her legs gently as his mouth…

'Hey, Grace, I's wis yous sis mornings. Sat's good.' Deimante, on the way back in from her road traffic duty, brandished her lollipop in Grace's direction and grinned, showing a mouth of immaculate white teeth. 'What's we doing?'

'English first,' Grace smiled.

'Jolly goods show.' Deimante had taken to coming out with terribly English phrases; she'd obviously been watching Jacob Rees Mogg on TV. 'Every little helps.' Or adverts for Tesco.

'Then Sex.'

'Sex?' Deimante frowned, her smile immediately gone. 'What you means, sex?'

'Sex Education. I *thought* we were doing Light and I was going to ask you set the little experiments up while I took the register.'

'I sink we betters doing Light. Much more appropriates for sis ages.'

'I agree, but the man in charge has spoken.'
'Boris Johnsons?'
'Josh Donnington.'

Oh *good*, Grace thought, as she completed and saved the online *Sims* register. Noah Haddon was absent. With any luck he'd got some terribly infectious disease and would be off for months. Or, even better, he'd moved house. Done a flit as her granny used to say. As far as she knew he lived with *his* granny – she'd spotted an older woman, who appeared to have little control over her grandson, at the Worm Divining on Saturday, but maybe that had been temporary and he'd gone to live with his parents now elsewhere.

She could always live in hope, Grace thought, turning to the class and making the decision, now that the pack leader wasn't in situ, to set out her stall with a few choice words. She wasn't prepared to have another week like the previous one.

'Last week,' she addressed the twenty-eight ten-year-olds in her care, 'I wasn't at all impressed with the behaviour of this class. Now, this is a new week and *I'm* in charge here for as long as it takes... put your hand down, Molly, I'm talking. You will put up your hand if you want to speak to me... when *I've* stopped speaking, Molly... and the shouting out you appear to think appropriate in my classroom, is not...'

Grace was getting into her stride, enjoying herself almost. This was what they needed: to know who was in charge round here. Kids needed parameters, needed to know how far they could go. Once they'd gelled as a group, once they were aware of what was acceptable in her class, then she could take her foot of the gas as it were and form a good working relationship with the children.

'Molly, *what*? What is it?'

'Miss, Noah's out there in t'playground.'

Grace knew it had been too good to last: the most hard-work kids *never* got ill, *never* missed a day at school, but were determinedly sent out of the house each morning with relief by mothers – and grannies – struggling with their offspring's behaviour at home as well. Grace knew she was being horribly prejudiced, stereotyping kids like this, and that every child was different but, after almost twenty years at the chalk face, she'd come to recognise certain patterns of behaviour. And once they got to high school that was a different story again: attendance rates of kids with real behavioural issues would plummet as they kicked against authority, often ending up in the PRU – the Pupil Referral Unit – and, particularly if they then found themselves in trouble with the police and in the Youth Courts, by the age of thirteen or fourteen their formal education was often over. Their education in the university of life however, with its lessons in drugs, alcohol, petty and more serious crime issues, together with the mental health problems for which drugs were often turned to, or were a result of, was already well under way.

All this went through Grace's head as she waited for Noah to appear in the classroom. When he didn't, and Molly called out, 'He's still there, Miss,' Grace walked over to the window. Noah was sat in the playground, arms wrapped around himself, head on his knees. 'And he's got his bike with him, Miss. We're not allowed to come to school on our bikes, Miss. Mrs Beresford says—'

'Thank you, Molly, I do know the school rules. OK, reading books out. No one gets out of their seat.'

'Miss, I need to change mine.'

'Mrs Miniauskiene will come and sit with you and hear some readers. This is silent reading, and I mean *silent*.' The last thing she – and presumably Noah – needed was twenty-eight kids with their noses pressed to the window to see what was going on.

Grace let herself out of the side door and walked across to the boy sitting with his back against the wall of the school's Victorian entrance. 'What's up, Noah?'

'Nowt.'

'Well, something must be.' Grace sat herself down beside the boy who moved himself slightly as her arm touched his own, refusing to say anything further.

'You know,' Grace said, 'sometimes it's good to talk about things if there's something worrying you.'

'There's nothing worrying me. I just don't want to come in to school with *you* teaching us.'

'Right.'

'I liked Miss Harrison. She didn't tell me what to do like you do. She didn't boss me around like you do and get cross like you do.'

'OK. So, maybe you didn't want to come into school because you knew I wasn't happy when you threw worms into my hair on Saturday?'

Noah didn't say anything but Grace could tell she was probably on the right track. She glanced down at his arm, still wrapped protectively around his knees, his navy school sweatshirt pulled up slightly so that Grace was able to see a purplish mark near his wrist.

'That's a nasty bruise,' she said gently. 'Has someone hurt you?'

'My dad's coming down to school to see *you*,' he said suddenly. 'I told him you were mean to me all last week. He's coming down to see you.'

'Is that right? When's this then?'

'After school sometime. He said he's coming in. And he'll have you.'

'Oh, right? So, this dad of yours. What does he do?'

Noah didn't say anything for a while, obviously considering the question, and then he turned and looked at Grace. 'He's an arms dealer. And a drug dealer. And if you carry on being mean to me, he'll get one of his gang to finish you off.' At this final riposte, he jumped up, grabbed his school bag and stalked into school leaving Grace to move his abandoned bike into the cloakroom and follow on behind.

Obviously embarrassed and cross at being escorted in from the playground, Noah marched angrily to his table under Deimante's narrowed eye, scowled ferociously at a couple of the girls who shot inquisitive glances in his direction and then, with his hands stuck into his trouser pockets, slumped with much muttering onto his chair.


'Cassie, can I have a word?' At break, Grace popped her head around the head's office door. The morning had turned out relatively quiet and productive under Grace's determined plan for a calmer classroom. And Deimante, on full alert, had jumped in like a Rottweiler on any child who wandered out of its seat or interrupted by shouting out as Grace was teaching.

'Come in, Grace, I was just coming to find you. Close the door, would you? I've had a phone call from Noah Haddon's father; he's made an appointment to see me and asked to see you as well. He's coming in straight after school as he seems to think you and Noah are having your differences?'

'You know we are. I told you that at the end of last week.'

'Hmm.' Cassie frowned. 'Noah was bloody hard work the day I taught Y5, you know, before you took over. You do know he's new to the school?'

'Yes, of course. I got his file out to see what his issues are, but there's very little in there.'

'That's his last school's fault: I'm so cross with them for not sending on his details. Apparently, his dad decided only a couple of days before term started that he wanted to move him over here so that he was near to his granny who lives in Westenbury. I've been ringing and ringing his last school, but both the head and deputy are new and didn't seem to know anything about him. It really isn't on, you know. Anyway, the head finally emailed me this morning to say she's posted his file over. She didn't want to send too much detail by email – confidentiality and safeguarding and all that – and that I'd understand once I read the file on Noah. What she did say was there's some physical abuse.'

'I guessed as much.' Grace frowned. 'Poor kid. He was upset this morning, didn't want to come into school and he's got some bruising on his arm.'

'Right,' Cassie said. 'I'm going to have to tread carefully

with his dad then. I wish I'd been able to read his file before seeing Mr Haddon this afternoon.'

'Especially as he's a drug dealer.'

'Is he?' Cassie looked worried. 'How do you know?'

'Noah's just told me. Actually, he said his dad was an arms dealer too.'

'Can you *be* both at once?' Cassie and Grace stared at one another. 'I think we'd better have Josh in with us, don't you?'

'Armed Response might be better,' Grace laughed nervously. 'I'm not sure Josh is up to it.'

# 14

After leaving Cassie's office, Grace sought out Niamh O'Connor who not only seemed much happier with her class but confided that she'd had a *special* little talk with Thea. Obviously bursting with the news that Miss O'Connor had been to her house for lunch, Niamh had had to sit Thea down and, inform her 'in no uncertain terms, Grace, you know?' that it was a *special* secret and not to be repeated in Show and Tell or *anywhere* or to *anyone*. Full of importance at being endowed with such a secret, Thea had promised that she wouldn't tell anyone about Miss O'Connor's secret mission.

'I'm not really sure what secret mission she was talking about, Grace,' Niamh frowned, obviously slightly puzzled, 'but I tell you what, she's been on her best behaviour all morning and not stepped out of line once. Oh, and I'm going over to Lilian's this evening. You know, to look at the room she has to rent?' Grace loved listening to this girl's melodious Dublin accent, the way her sentences almost always appeared to end with a questioning intonation. Niamh frowned again as she ate her way through a packet of ginger biscuits. (How could anyone so beautifully slim eat so many biscuits, Grace wondered in admiration) 'It'll probably be a bit like being back at home again with my mammy, but at least I'll be a lot nearer to school and I won't have to put up any longer living down in the town centre and with people I don't like.'

Grace decided that launching into an unprepared Sex Education session on a Monday morning wasn't the most sensible of options and, instead, after break, brought her planned lesson on English proverbs and sayings forward from the afternoon.

'Oh good, I never very understandings sese,' Deimante said in an aside to Grace as she helped give out the required stationery. 'Jean in se office was tellings me yesterday something about her grandmas and teaching her to suck eggs. Your English language is so hards.' She looked glum for several seconds, aware it was her lack of comprehension of English, with all its nuances, that was keeping her from training to be a primary school teacher.

Armed with large sheets of paper and felt-tipped pens, the children worked in groups, drawing the literal interpretation of the proverb Grace issued to their group, acting it out for the others to guess before attempting to explain the metaphorical meaning.

Working co-operatively in teams was something these kids weren't good at, but there was much concentrated effort over the illustrations, and hilarity when acting out their proverb. The grinning, vomiting cat who'd over-indulged the cream and the snarling leopard whose spots remained tenaciously in situ despite much frantic washing and rubbing of his coat were received with gales of laughter, and Grace began to relax and enjoy herself, knowing this was why she loved teaching and had never, until taking on this particular Y5 class, wanted to do anything different.

'That were right good, Miss,' Polly Meadowcroft laughed as Grace brought them back to her on the carpet and raised a hand for quiet.

'I thought it were rubbish,' Noah sneered – just loud enough for Grace to hear – to one of his followers who'd been enthusiastically acting out a stereotypical old man with a stick while pushing Deimante – whose fluffed-up hair and pouting lips were a parody of the drag queen Grace had once seen on TV – in front of him.

'Age before beauty, Mrs Miniauskiene,' Stacey Maynard had guessed as they all finally came to sit at Grace's feet. 'Cos you're really pretty.'

'Sat's right,' Deimante grinned, about to sit on the carpet herself before remembering she was actually the other adult in the room and moving, instead, to stand by Grace.

'OK.' Grace smiled, pleased at the success of the lesson and the class's improved behaviour; she was finally getting somewhere with them. Sex that afternoon was looking a definite possibility. 'Now, in your group, you need to work together and you have just ten minutes to brainstorm any sayings or proverbs you might know or have heard yourselves. Grannies are often good at coming out with these (bit granny-ist, that, Grace, she silently admonished herself) and Mrs Barlow in the office has a whole repertoire of them... No, Molly, you can't go down to the office and interview her... And then, if you have time, you can use your dictionaries to look up the meaning of both repertoire...'

Grace wrote the word on her smart board. 'And the word *cliché*.'

'Miss...'

'Mrs Stevens,' Grace corrected.

'Mrs Stevens,' Noah corrected politely. 'I've got a good one. Well, I've got two.'

'Well done, Noah.' Grace smiled, pleased to see some latent enthusiasm. 'Would you like to share them with us?'

'Confucius, he say, boy with hole in pocket feeling cocky all day.'

'Right OK, thank you very much, Noah for that... Anyone else?'

'And,' Noah went on with a puzzled face, 'a man rushing through the airport door is obviously going to Bangkok. I don't really understand that, Miss. Do you?'

The little sod, Grace thought grimly.

'I's not sure *I* do.' Deimante shook her head, looking to Grace for explanation.

'Do you know, Mrs Miniauskiene,' Grace assumed a puzzled face of her own, 'I'm not sure about that one either. I tell you what, Noah, Mrs Barlow in the office is brilliant at knowing the meaning of these. No, no, hang on, Mrs Barlow isn't to be disturbed when she's on reception. You pop down to Mrs Beresford and ask her if *she* knows the meaning. She's in her office at the moment with Reverend Carey, the vicar. Headteachers and vicars know *everything*.' Grace smiled sweetly, ushering Noah determinedly out of the door before closing it firmly behind him.

By three-thirty Grace had a headache and the last thing

she needed was a confrontation with Noah Haddon's dad.

'Grace, *Grace.*' Deimante had obviously been waiting for her to come down from her classroom and hissed with some agitation as she walked towards reception. 'I's seen him – Noah's daddy. He's already in wis Mrs Head. Grace, he's big mans. Big, big fearsome mans. Lots of tattoos all down his necks and ACAB on his fingers...' She paused, puzzled. 'Is he tries to remember his alphabets?'

'All Coppers Are Bastards,' Grace explained, her heart plummeting. Oh hell, this wasn't going to be easy.

The door opened and Cassie came out with the man, shaking his hand and smiling. 'That's great, Mr Mulhall, thank you so much for your offer of help in the classroom. And you'll be able to help with readers when it's raining and you can't be up on the roof...? You'll just need to pass a basic DBS check – have a word with Mrs Barlow before you pick Rhiannon up, and she'll tell you how to go about it – and we'll be in touch.'

'Never judge a book by its cover, Grace.' Cassie laughed at Grace's surprised face. 'Which is a damned sight easier to explain than the one you sent Noah Haddon with this morning. I thought the vicar was going to fall off his chair he was laughing so much. Mr Mulhall has offered to join our parent helpers in the classroom, but he has a roofing company and can only come in when it's raining.'

'Right.' Grace didn't know what else to say.

'Mr Haddon's late.' Cassie frowned, looking at her watch. 'I've just seen Noah walk past with his granny...' She stopped talking as Jean Barlow popped her head round the door.

'Mr Haddon to see you, Mrs Beresford.'

Grace wondered if she was having an actual heart attack, and the ridiculous question of who would look after her kids if she died spun crazily through her head as her pulse raced and her heart tried its best to exit her chest. The last time she'd seen the man Jean Barlow was ushering into the office, and who was now staring at Grace with total and utter incomprehension, was Saturday night, in the dark of a Leeds nightclub garden.

## 15

'Do have a seat, Mr Haddon.' Cassie smiled at the man. 'Hopefully we can work through some of the issues we seem to be having with Noah.' She turned to Grace, giving her a searching look. 'This is Grace Stevens who's taken over as Noah's class teacher—' she openly frowned at Grace who felt herself almost turned to stone '—while Miss Harrison is recovering from the very bad fall from her bike over on the moors.'

'Mrs Stevens?' Mr Haddon raised an eyebrow and Grace saw very little of the kindness she'd obviously imagined in his eyes, and which she'd likened to her granny's dog, Bingo on Saturday night. Obviously too much Sauvignon Blanc knocked back in too short a time, Grace thought, dreadfully embarrassed as she sat squirming in her chair unable, it seemed, to get an intelligent – let alone intelligible – word out.

'And when will Miss Harrison be returning? Noah liked her very much and was just beginning to build up a good relationship with her and was starting to make real progress.'

*As if*, Grace thought, as cynicism at the man's words began to bring her out of her shocked, almost catatonic state and focus her mind on the reason why they were actually having this meeting. Noah Haddon, from what she could see, had been running rings round April Harrison, doing very little work and getting away with murder.

'It could be quite some time, Mr Haddon, but I can assure you Mrs Stevens is an extremely professional and experienced member of my staff who will be doing everything in her power to bring out the very best in Noah, as well as addressing any issues which I hope, now you're here, you'll be able to tell us about.'

'And does that include Mrs Stevens grabbing hold of Noah so hard to contain him that he's left with a badly bruised wrist?'

'What?' Grace stared at Noah's father and felt her pulse race. 'What *are* you talking about?'

'Hang on, hang on.' Cassie raised a hand and leaned forward over her desk. 'Are you making an accusation against a member of my staff, Mr Haddon? If so, I need my deputy here. I think it best if we have him here, anyway.' Cassie strode over to the door, barked a request that Jean go and find Josh Donnington and then returned to her seat. 'No...' Cassie held up her hand once more. 'Please don't say another word, Mr Haddon, until Mr Donnington has joined us.'

A thick silence that was almost palpable ensued and, apart from the loud and angry buzz of a flailing wasp on the office window, no other sound was made until the deputy head knocked briefly and let himself in.

'Ah, here he is now,' Cassie said with obvious relief.

Josh Donnington slid into the chair Cassie pulled out for him before handing him a notepad and pen. 'I need this to be written down, Mr Donnington,' Cassie said. 'OK, Mr Haddon, what are you saying?'

Mr Haddon sat back, his face pale. 'I'm not saying for a moment that Noah is an angel – I'm sure you're aware, Mrs Beresford, that Noah has some behavioural issues.'

'Well, to be honest, Mr Haddon,' Cassie said almost crossly, 'we've not been kept in the loop at all. Noah's former school has been totally derelict in its duty in not passing on all the information we require both of your son's educational progress as well as his behaviour.' Cassie paused and Grace could see she was cross. 'And, to be blunt, I would have assumed, seeing as you've moved Noah *because* of his problems at his previous school, *you'd* have been in touch yourself over the summer holiday, before Noah even started with us, to give us some background and to what we might expect from him.'

'But that's just what I didn't want to happen. I didn't want the school to have any pre-conceived ideas about Noah. This was to be a fresh start with a fresh teacher. And now—'

'And now *what*, Mr Haddon?' Grace was suddenly furious. 'What exactly has Noah told you I've done to him?'

'Mrs Stevens,' Cassie was in professional mode. 'I think it might be better if you were to leave this meeting.'

'I don't *think* so.' Grace folded her arms indicating she was going nowhere. 'If Mr Haddon is accusing me of something, I want to hear this. What I will say, Mr Haddon, is that Noah was very upset this morning about something and I had to actually persuade him into school from the playground. I noticed a bruise on his wrist and asked him if someone had been hurting him.'

'Exactly. He said *you* had, Mrs Stevens. He said you appeared to have taken a dislike to him from the minute you met him last week and on Friday you were so cross with him you grabbed his wrist and twisted it.'

'I think there may be a safeguarding issue here,' Cassie started, but broke off at a brief knock on the door followed by Jean putting her head round it once more. 'Mrs Haddon's here, Mrs Beresford.'

'*Mrs* Haddon?' Cassie pulled a face at Grace before glancing at Noah's father. 'Show her in, Jean.'

A tall, willowy, exceptionally attractive woman, probably Grace's own age, walked into the office, holding out her hand first to Cassie and then to Grace.

Bloody hell, Grace thought. He had a wife. She'd done what she'd done on Saturday night with a man who had a wife. The woman was immaculately dressed in expensive-looking black leather boots, a black knee-length, beautifully-cut, fine wool skirt to the knee and a Sarah Pacini (Grace recognised it at once, having coveted the exact same one in the upmarket dress shop in the village) grey sweater. Her chestnut hair – the same colour as hers, Grace noticed – fell in a perfect curtain to beyond her shoulder but there was something about her eyes, the way that she was looking at her husband, Grace couldn't quite work out.

'Do come in and have a…' Cassie started to say, but was stopped in her tracks by Mr Haddon immediately jumping from his seat.

'Excuse me,' he growled, taking his wife's arm roughly and manhandling her out of the room, their raised voices drifting back to the others left sitting in a state of some confusion.

'What the hell's going on?' Cassie stood up. 'Josh, do you think you should go out there?'

'Me? He's bigger than me.'

'Hey, what's goings on here?' Deimante's voice could be heard loud and strident from the reception area. 'You no do sats. Sats not on at all... Out, go on, get outs or I calls the fuzz.'

'I'll get Mrs Beresford.' Jean Barlow's excited voice joined Deimante's angry one as Grace and Cassie, with a somewhat reluctant Josh Donnington following slowly in their wake, both dashed for the open door of Cassie's office.

'What the hell is going on?' Cassie repeated as Deimante, holding on to Mr Haddon's arm, began pushing him, none too gently, on to one of the three red cushioned armchairs in reception while Jean hovered nervously at her side.

'Do I need to call the police?' Cassie asked calmly. 'Where is *Mrs* Haddon now? Is she hurt?'

'*She* hurt?' Deimante almost glared at Cassie. 'She not se ones hurting round heres,' she snapped indignantly. 'She *doings* the hurting to sis poor mans here. Bang, wallops...' Deimante demonstrated a near-miss thump in the direction of Cassie who jumped back in alarm, tottering slightly in her three-inch heels – she always liked to appear taller than her five-foot-nothing when meeting parents for the first time – and onto Josh's big toe.

'Ow, *Cassie*...'

Ignoring Josh, Cassie went to crouch down at Mr Haddon's side while Grace just stared. Here was the man from Saturday night in Leeds, the exceptionally attractive man who'd pointed out that amazing harvest moon – and done other things Grace preferred, at this moment in time, not to think about as he sat in front of her (in *school*, for heaven's sake) – his head in his hands and an air of total desolation in his stance.

'Mr Haddon, won't you please come back into my office and I'll get Jean to make us some tea?'

'Gin,' Deimante sniffed disparagingly. 'Se poor mans need gin, not tea…'

'Thank you, Deimante. Are *you* alright?'

'Of course. I was about to goes for her with my lollipops.' Deimante indicated her red and yellow lollipop stick which had fallen drunkenly from its usual place by the school's entrance and now lay slewed across the first of the red chairs. 'She doesn't scaredy cats me.'

'Mr Haddon, would you prefer to come back in and just talk with myself? You know, without any other members of my staff being in the room?'

Mr Haddon raised his face from his hands, looking directly at Grace. An angry red mark stood out below the man's eye which was already looking puffy. 'It's fine,' he said, sighing as he tentatively touched the affected area. 'As Noah's class teacher, you need to know some history…' He paused as he stood, brushing a tired hand through his longish dark hair and then, as Cassie frowned, offered his hand to Grace. 'It's Ross.' He gave an almost imperceptible smile. 'Ross Haddon.'

'My wife shouldn't have *been* here,' Ross Haddon sighed as soon as he'd sat himself down once more. 'Either my mother-in-law or Noah himself must have said something about my being here this afternoon.' He paused as Jean Barlow bustled in importantly with the icepack usually reserved for kids' banged heads, giving it to Ross with a solicitous pat of her hand.

'Thank you so much, that's so kind.' Once Jean had left the room, closing the door gently behind her, Ross placed the ice pack to one side and leaned forward. 'My wife, Natasha, shouldn't have come,' he repeated. 'She's not *allowed*. There's a… oh heavens, this is not easy to say… There's a six-month restraining order against her. There's supposed to be no contact whatsoever between us without a third party being present, and when she sees Noah.'

'She's hurt Noah?'

'No, no,' Ross exclaimed. 'Natasha wouldn't do that; she'd never hurt him. It's me, I'm afraid, she takes her anger out on. That's why I needed to get her out of your office. I apologise, I felt so angry when I saw her, and my first reaction was just to make sure she wasn't breaking the order; she's not supposed to be anywhere near me. I was shocked when I saw her because, as far as I knew, she was shooting in France…'

'Shooting?' Josh shot a nervous glance first towards Ross and then at Cassie.

'*On* a shoot,' Ross explained. 'My wife is a model.'

Hence the height, gorgeous face and clothes that hung on her like a, well like a model, Grace thought to herself.

'If the police know she's breached the order – and hit me once more into the bargain – she'll be arrested and taken back to court. And I really don't want that for her. Natasha's already on a community order with Leeds probation for assault.'

'Against yourself?' Cassie asked gently.

'Hmm.'

'Mr Haddon,' Grace started, trying hard not to give any indication to Cassie and Josh that this afternoon wasn't the first time she'd met Noah's father. (*Met him*? Jesus, that was some explosive *meeting*...) 'I can assure you that the marks on Noah's wrist were not made by myself or any other adult here.'

'Have you any idea why Noah might have taken against you so much, Mrs Stevens? He's been quite forceful in his opinion of you. I know he can be hard work – Natasha and I were constantly in to see the heads of the other schools.'

'Schools?' Cassie frowned. 'How many has he been to?'

'We started him off just outside Leeds where we were living at the time. And then Natasha needed to be nearer to London for work, and she just disappeared with him one day. This was a couple of years ago, and the poor kid ended up with a series of au pairs looking after him whenever Natasha had to fly off at a moment's notice. I fought for shared custody for Noah but, in the end, Natasha agreed to come back North to Leeds to the family home. Everything was fine to begin with and Noah was fairly settled, but within a month or two Natasha's anger issues came to the fore once again...' He paused, obviously finding the conversation difficult. 'Natasha was charged with assault and the restraining order put in place and her mother – Noah's granny, who's lived here in Westenbury the past five years or so – suggested Noah and I move near to her so that she could be around for him when I'm not. I'm often away myself with work. When the cottage next door to my mother-in-law came up for rent at the beginning of the summer it all seemed a bit fortuitous and I made the decision to move myself and Noah over here.'

Drug running? Arms dealing? Grace took a surreptitious glance at Ross who was, in turn, looking directly at her with those incredible green eyes of his. What did a drug baron look like? Surely not like Ross Haddon?

'Natasha is still living in Leeds and has to have permission from her supervisor at probation if she needs to change her Rehabilitation Activity Requirement appointment in order to travel for work. She wants to have Noah living with her permanently, which she can't have at the moment.'

'Noah obviously wants to be with his mum?' Cassie asked gently.

'Hmm. He doesn't understand why she can't live with us, and gets angry with her for not being with him permanently and with me too because he thinks it's me dictating the situation and keeping her away from living with us. It's really hard for Jill, my mother-in-law, as well. Natasha's her only daughter, but she's only too aware of Natasha's issues, and that we have to abide by the order of the Family Court who decided in my favour and directed that for the time being Noah must live with me...' Ross Haddon trailed off, appearing uncertain how to continue.

Grace jumped into the ensuing silence. 'You know, Mr Haddon, I truly believe children aren't born naughty. You know, they're not *naturally* that way. Most kids want to please, and when they don't behave, it's usually a sign of misplaced worry and anxiety. Fear even. I think probably Noah has taken a dislike to me because he did get on so well with Miss Harrison and then, within a couple of weeks he's had to get used to a new teacher again.' Grace frowned. 'I'm afraid I'm a bit of a stickler for good behaviour in my class, Mr Haddon, and I may have come down on him rather more heavily than I might, had I known his background.' Grace, who'd always prided herself in bringing round the most recalcitrant child to her way of thinking, felt uncomfortable. She had, perhaps, tried to rein Noah Haddon in rather too tightly, jumping on any little misdemeanour of his, however small, in order to show the rest of the class she'd stand no nonsense from them. Going for the ringleader... She'd always hated teachers who were guilty of what could be seen as victimisation, and now, it appeared, she was as bad as them.

'I think, Mrs Stevens, there's possibly a reason Noah hasn't taken to you, and appears, from what you say, to be taking his anger out on you.'

'Oh?' Grace frowned.

'You mean, Grace bears a quite striking resemblance to your wife?' Cassie interrupted, her head to one side as she considered.

Ross Haddon nodded. 'Yes. I thought so the minute I first saw Mrs Stevens.'

Grace felt herself flush. Oh, great stuff, she thought, crossly. When Ross Haddon had been staring at her in the nightclub on Saturday evening, he'd obviously been looking for a substitute for Natasha. He was clearly still in love with the angry bint, despite her tendency for thumping him one. Maybe, he got off on it? Maybe, she should have thumped him herself under the light of that bloody harvest moon, instead of reaching her hand into his shirt and starting the series of events that, although incredibly sensuous at the time, was now having her wanting to squirm with embarrassment?

'But that doesn't explain the bruising on Noah's arm,'

Josh Donnington now said. 'If Mrs Stevens here *wasn't* to blame...'

*Of course I wasn't, you pillock, Josh*, Grace thought angrily. Did he, for even one second, consider her capable of such an act?

'Do you think your wife *could* have inflicted the bruise, Mr Haddon?' Cassie spoke quietly.

When Ross Haddon didn't answer, Grace said gently, 'You know, Noah was terribly upset this morning. As I said, I had to go out into the playground once school had started to persuade him to come inside. If your wife is around at the moment, you know, when you weren't expecting her to be, do you think Noah had already seen her this weekend and you didn't know about it? Do you think...?' Grace trailed off, not quite sure how to suggest it might have been Noah's mother herself who'd hurt her child.

'Would your wife have found an opportunity to talk to him over the weekend?' Josh asked, almost accusingly. 'You know, were you with Noah *all* the time?'

'Noah spends a lot of time on his own playing football both in our garden and his granny's where we've put up nets for him.' Ross frowned. 'He had been picked to play football with Leeds United Academy when we were living over there but, unfortunately, I just can't get him over there several evenings a week and Jill, my mother-in-law, has had breast surgery and is unable to drive at the moment. Noah, understandably, is very resentful that I've moved him over here and he can't play for Leeds. Anyway, that's by the by. I *was* working Saturday *morning*.'

And discussing the moon with me on Saturday *evening*, Grace thought, not daring to meet Ross Haddon's eyes.

'I think, Mr Haddon, you're going to have to go home, pick up Noah from your mother-in-law's and then, very gently, try to get to the bottom of all this. Please, rest assured that despite Noah saying Mrs Stevens here was the one to hurt him, that clearly isn't the case. And then, we're going to have to work very closely together on what is going to be best for Noah. I'm assuming social services have had some input re Noah himself? You know, with what's been going on with your wife? As well as with Leeds Probation? I hope they're putting strategies into place to enable Noah to see his mother while you yourself are not allowed any contact with her?'

Ross Haddon nodded briefly in Cassie's direction before standing and placing his teacup on the table to his right as he did so. He shook Cassie's and Josh Donnington's hand before moving to the door where he turned slightly in order to catch Grace's eye. Oh hell, she thought, as her pulse began to race and her heart did that horribly wonderful flippy thing she recognised from old: *I fancy him like mad. I really, really fancy him.*

'So, *what* are you saying?' Harriet frowned as she helped Grace fold clothes, still warm from the drier, interspersed with drinking the glass of wine she'd poured for herself. 'That bloke you spent some time with – well, quite a *lot* of time with, actually, Grace...'

'Alright, alright,' Grace snapped irritably. 'I asked you over here for tea and sympathy not wine and a telling off. This has been the Monday from hell: my husband and I have now *officially* split up, I've been accused of physically abusing a child in my class and – bloody hell, Hat, sod the tea, pour me some of that wine, would you? – the man I seduced in a Leeds pub garden only two nights ago turns out to be said child's father. Oh, and I've got a period pain from hell.' She clutched her abdomen as a cramp tightened its grip on her insides. 'You couldn't make it up, could you?'

'Well, at least you're not pregnant from your little encounter,' Harriet soothed, pushing the glass of wine towards her. 'Although, you know, Grace, you didn't know where, you know... where he'd *been...*'

'Give me some credit, Harriet.' Grace sighed deeply, totally embarrassed. 'I might be a total novice when it comes to one-night stands, but I do have some notion of safe sex.'

Grace downed the half glass of white wine Harriet had poured for her then, massaging her stomach, put her head down onto the kitchen table and, sighing loudly once more, closed her eyes.

# 16

He loved having these new friends. They were much older than him, of course, but that didn't seem to matter; they really liked him, wanted him for their mate and, whenever he could get away from home, they'd be waiting for him, making him feel like one of their gang. He didn't even mind them having a go on the brand-new bike his mum had bought him for his birthday. It was a Diamondback Line 24 and still too big really, but now he wasn't going off to play football anymore, it had taken over his life and he was getting really good on it and it was really useful for setting off to meet Liam and Spider.

He hated this new class he was in where he was having to make friends all over again. He knew the other kids in the class didn't like him much and he had to pretend to be tougher than he really was just to survive, but it was becoming increasingly hard, especially with the new class teacher who was an absolute bully and put him down whenever she could.

It was all his dad's fault, of course.

He frowned at his distorted reflection in the bike's shiny handlebar and, without a backward glance, set off to meet them once again.

## 17

'I can't believe we're already into October.' Juno frowned, glancing towards the date proudly and exuberantly displayed in red on the brand-new surgery LED display board above Marian, the receptionist's head in Westenbury Surgery.

'Season of mellow fruitfulness or something, isn't it?' Dr Declan Stanford murmured vaguely, signing the forms Marian had thrust in his direction as he'd attempted, unsuccessfully, to slip past her unnoticed.

'Season of black woolly tights and a whole load of bloody coughs and colds,' Izzy shouted from her own room. She thrust a black tights-clad leg around her door in a strange parody of either a stripper or exotic dancer, Juno couldn't quite work out which. *'First of October, come what may, legs won't see the light of day.* I just made that up,' she added proudly as the rest of her appeared in reception. Izzy stopped short as Marian, intent on her computer, added more information to the display board and then burst out laughing. 'Beast Clinic? What the hell's our *Beast Clinic*? I know Dr Scott Butler might be referred to as a bit of a *sexual* beast by some round here—' she shot a lascivious look towards Juno who tutted crossly '—but I'm not sure you should be advertising this to all our patients, Marian or they might all want a look in.'

'Oh, for heaven's sake,' Marian tutted crossly before correcting her error. Just missed out the "r". It's your breast clinic this afternoon, Izzy.'

'I've been thinking,' Izzy went on.

'Are you sure that's wise?' Declan called over his shoulder. 'Your *thinking* usually leads to something *I* end up having to *think* about too. And usually in the middle of the night when I should be sleeping and instead, am lying, wide awake, *thinking*.'

'So, as I said,' Izzy went on, totally ignoring her husband, 'I've been *thinking*. Now we've got our brand-new LED display in place...'

'And at great expense,' Declan added gloomily. '*That* was as a result of some of your *thinking*.'

'... I think we should be putting up there, details about our new clinics.'

'What new clinics?' Juno, Declan and Marian turned as one towards Izzy.

'Well, you know the Government's latest strategy is all about taking preventative action? You know, sort the cause rather than the cure? Well,' Izzy was warming to her theme,' I think Westenbury Surgery should have a reputation...'

'I think it probably already has, Izzy, with you at the helm.' Dr Scott Butler, hurrying in and late for his surgery, smiled winningly in Izzy's direction, winked at Juno and carried on walking to the safety of his practice room.

'You're late, as usual, Dr Butler,' Izzy snapped. 'And don't go wandering off. I need *you* to head up one of these new clinics. Now, what was I saying? Ah yes, this practice should have a reputation as being at the forefront, the *vanguard* as it were, of preventative procedures particularly with alcohol, smoking and drugs. Anyone…'

Oh hell, Juno thought, checking the LED display and seeing it was almost eight-thirty and a queue of patients was already forming at the locked door, Izzy was off on one. Juno's new year's resolution back in January – when Fraser had first left her and gone off to the States – to be on time, ready and waiting for her first patient, computer fired up and raring to go had rarely, she thought somewhat ruefully, been realised. Not helped these days, she knew, by increasingly having Scott in her bed these chilly autumn mornings. Oh, but her life had changed so much for the better since Scott Butler had come into it. After rather more years that she liked to admit, even to herself, of living with Fraser in what could only be described as a sexually arid desert, Scott had burst into her life, awakening all sorts of rampant desires she'd never thought she'd harboured. He was bloody good in bed, Juno smiled to herself, recalling her state of passion just two hours earlier. A sexual *beast* indeed.

'Juno, are you listening?' Izzy was glaring at her. 'New clinics? Anyone who saw the state of Leo Hutchinson in that strip joint—'

'Village hall,' Juno murmured, glancing hopefully towards the stairs that led down to her own tiny practice room.

'—that *den of iniquity*,' Izzy added pompously, conveniently forgetting it was herself who'd organised and rallied them along to that particular outing, 'will realise we have a professional *duty* to the village and beyond, to get behind the pernicious and increasing problem of drug addiction in all its forms.'

'Put me down for an alcohol clinic,' Scott nodded towards Izzy as he headed for his room. 'I'll call it *Fifty ways to lose your liver*. Oh, and mine's a gin and tonic – and make it a large one.' He was still chortling to himself as he closed his door behind him.

'Actually, you know, I think, for once, he's right.' Izzy nodded her head sagely. 'We don't *want* to come over as if we're preaching from the pulpit. If people want that, if people want to feel guilty after knocking back a bottle of vodka, or – women particularly – realising they're downing more than a bottle of SB an evening – they can head on to the village church and listen to Ben Carey's sermons.'

'I don't think Ben Carey ever preaches about alcohol, does he?' Juno asked doubtfully. 'Particularly when he's been down in the Jolly Sailor knocking back a couple of pints himself the night before?'

'Exactly.' Izzy's eyes gleamed. 'When folks can't rely on the village vicar to put them on the road to redemption, they'll have to rely on *us*. And we mustn't appear to be doing a John Wesley on them or no one will want to take part.' She closed her eyes momentarily, obviously thinking. 'My clinic will be called *Do smokers contribute to Government Coffers?* Yes, that will look good up on the LED display.' Izzy frowned. 'But do we write coffers or coughers? Would this lot understand the pun? Give it a practice run up there for me, would you, Marian? So I can see what it looks like?'

'No, I won't,' Marian snapped crossly. 'I've got better things to do than put up information *I* don't understand either. Mr Bellamy's prostate is waiting, Izzy and you're cluttering up my reception.

Juno dealt with the usual Monday morning complaints: everything from an infected toenail to a dislocated kneecap and the more unusual, if not downright suspicious, complaint of a misplaced carrot (I'm not rightly sure *how* it got up there, Dr) which she immediately and fastidiously referred on to A and E.

Taking a quick breather for a coffee and a biscuit, Juno actually kicked off her shoes, lay down on her examining couch and closed her eyes for two minutes. This early morning sex (and the late-night stuff too, she grinned to herself as she stretched luxuriously and munched contentedly on her Garibaldi) was robbing her of her beauty sleep. 'Oh, but it's all rather *erotic*,' she said out loud to the empty room as she felt for and shoved another biscuit into her mouth. (What was she always telling her kids about not eating stuff when they were lying down?)

'Erm, are you alright, Dr Armstrong? The receptionist said it was OK for me to come straight in...'

Juno shot up at ninety degrees, coughing and spraying biscuit crumbs towards the man who was standing at the side of the couch, not quite sure whether to sit or wait until Juno found her shoes before assuming the mantle of the caring family doctor she liked to portray, once more.

'Gari... baldi...' Juno coughed, her eyes watering as she abandoned the search for one recalcitrant loafer.

'Sorry? No, no, it's Gary *Davidson*.'

'Garibaldi... biscuit?' Juno spluttered, unable to dislodge

a crumb that seemed to have descended and was tenaciously hanging on in there in her left lung. Oh heavens. She reached for a bottle of water but that simply made her cough more.

'Should I wait outside?' Mr Davidson asked nervously. 'You appear to be in a bit of a state?'

'No, no, I'm fine, I was just, just er expounding on the deliciousness of a Garibaldi biscuit, er, Gary. I do sometimes get a bit carried away. Must be the currants...' Juno ran a hand through her blonde curls, catching sight of her red-faced, mascara-streaked reflection in the mirror above her sink. She rubbed quickly at the black beneath her eyes. 'Right, Gary,' Juno eventually wheezed. 'I'm all ears now. What can I do for you?'

'Well, to be honest, Doctor, last night my wife thought I was perhaps having a stroke because my heart was racing and my eyes became terribly sensitive to light. I kept having to close them as they really hurt. Eventually I went to lay down in the dark but my heart was still racing.'

'How old are you now?'

'Sixty-eight.'

'I think we should get you checked out up at Midhope General. I'm surprised your wife didn't take you straight up to A and E. You know, if she thought you were having a stroke. Sixty-eight is not an atypical age for having one.' Juno coughed, still trying to release the trapped biscuit crumb. 'Right, let's send you—'

'No, no, Doctor. I'm almost sure it wasn't a stroke. I'm totally embarrassed...'

'Embarrassed?' Surely not another misplaced carrot? Juno coughed some more before turning questioningly to the man.

'I've been over-indulging the Coke.'

'Oh, I've been *there*,' Juno said placatingly. 'Couldn't get enough of the stuff when I was doing my finals.' She gave him a sympathetic smile.

'Really?' The man looked shocked.

'Really,' Juno confirmed, nodding. 'And not good for you, not good for you at all. But, to be honest, Gary, it was probably better than turning to the bottle, which, at the time, I could so easily have done. Red Bull and Coke – or Pepsi…' She trailed off, embarrassed. 'Wrong Coke? Right?'

'Right.' He paused for a while, obviously unsure what to say next. 'OK, look, I'm going to be up front with you, Doctor. My wife doesn't know about my little habit and I reckon I need some help. I've been indulging, you know, taking coke – cocaine – for a while now. Got a bit of a habit going.'

'Right, OK.' Embarrassment at getting hold of the wrong end of the stick, plus relief that she wasn't having to send yet another patient of hers with a misplaced object up to A and E, was rendering Juno solicitous in the extreme. 'We don't often get—' Juno scanned her screen for a clue to his work '—professionals in their sixties admitting to being a cocaine user,' she said gently. 'How much of a habit is your er, your actual *habit*, if you get my meaning?'

'I obviously can't take it like I used to,' he said, not smiling. 'You know, I'm a child of the Sixties and early Seventies; it's what we did back then, getting stoned as we listened to Led Zep and Rory Gallagher.'

'Heard of Led Zep, but not the other one,' Juno said, glancing at the clock on the wall; she needed to get a move on.

'Irish Blues singer,' Gary said.

'So, why do you think you've got yourself into this state?' Juno asked.

'Stress at work, mainly, I guess. You know, when it all seems too much, it's dead easy just to have a quick line. No one can tell what you've been up to.' He gave a short laugh. 'Unlike one of my managers who, we *all* know, has vodka in his water bottle. I really must have a word with him,' he went on, almost to himself, 'but it seems a bit hypocritical knowing what *I'm* up to.'

Juno stared. 'At work? Goodness me, that's not good.' She glanced at her computer once more. 'Maybe you should be thinking of retiring? You know, a spot of golf, an allotment? Growing a few carrots?' (No, maybe not *carrots*.) 'Taking it a bit easier?'

'Come on, Doctor, we're all having to work until we're seventy these days. You know, to pay off the massive mortgage we took out to buy the house we felt we had to have?' Gary Davidson shrugged. 'What else can you do, hmm?'

'Right, we need to help you out of this habit,' Juno said, trying to think who to refer him to. There was the drug rehabilitation place down in the town centre, but she wasn't sure if that was appropriate for this well-dressed professional sitting in front of her. She turned and folded her arms, curious. 'How do you actually get the stuff?'

'Dead easy, Doctor. No hanging round dark corners of pubs these days, waiting for someone to ask if you want to score. Oh no, just one text and it's delivered smartly to your door, faster than a takeaway Pizza, by a well-dressed young man in an upmarket Audi.'

'I thought it was black BMWs with tinted windows?' Juno raised an eyebrow.

'Moved on, Doctor,' Gary sniffed, almost comfortably. 'Sign of the times, you know?'

'So, would you class yourself as an addict?' Juno, who, she was ashamed to admit, knew only rudimentary stuff about drugs, wondered if she should pass Gary Davidson over to Izzy for help. This was ridiculous, she chastised herself as she scrolled down her computer looking for the address of the local drug helpline. If he were on heroin and wanting help, she'd be suggesting and writing a prescription for methadone substitute and making an appointment for him with the local drug rehab place. But, apart from advising Mr Davidson to give up his cocaine habit as, at worst he'd end up having a stroke or, at best, his nose would eventually drop off, she wasn't quite sure.

'An addict?' Mr Davidson paused to consider. 'No, I'd say I was dependent, rather than addicted. But then, no more than my wife is dependent on the fancy gins she turns to every night at six, or my gardener who wheezes his way through his forty-a-day fag habit or my secretary who can't get through the day without her Valium. And, you only have to look at the huge number of bottles put out for the glass-recycling truck every Monday morning, to realise half the village is dependent on alcohol.'

He wasn't wrong, Juno thought a tad guiltily. How much wine had she and Scott knocked back the other Sunday with Ariadne and Esme? *Because* Esme was there, Juno told herself. The other three had had to up their alcohol consumption to anaesthetise themselves against the woman's relentless banal chatter. How *could* Scott have been seduced by her all those years ago? Juno's first impression of Esme Burkinshaw was not terribly complimentary.

'So, what do you think, Doctor?'

'Oh, sorry, Gary.' Guiltily, Juno brought herself back to the present. 'This is what we're going to do.'

Izzy was right, Juno mused as she drove out through the village and towards Westenbury Comprehensive where she'd arranged to pick up Tilda. Izzy's idea about running drug clinics, whether it be for class A drugs or alcohol and fags, was a good one as well as, it appeared, a necessary one.

Tilda flung her bag onto the back seat of the Mini and hunted in the glove compartment for chocolate.

'There's a banana in my bag, better for you than sweets.' Juno glanced over at Tilda. 'How's it gone today? Any better, darling?'

Tilda shrugged. 'Suppose. I asked if I could join the lunchtime Latin Club – it's on every Monday for Year 10.'

'Year 10?' Juno glanced across at Tilda who was demolishing the banana without finesse.

'Hmm,' Tilda nodded. 'There are some rather *intelligent* Year 10s who're wanting to learn Latin because they're thinking of becoming lawyers and doctors.' Tilda rammed in the rest of the banana and, while she chewed, Juno wondered had she herself ever needed the Latin Patrick had tried to teach her when she was little? Certainly the medical terminology, rooted in Latin as well as Greek, had been easier to comprehend at med school because of Patrick's sporadic insistence his daughters speak Latin with him at home, before he got bored with the whole idea and was off, either in his study writing his current tome or making love to the latest in the long line of the many affairs that eventually drove Helen, their mother, to succumb to the mental illness for which she'd been sectioned.

'Anyway, Mr Tovey, the Latin teacher, was just telling me to go away and come back in another three years – such ageism, Mum, it's not on you know – when the Year 10 lot all said, "Aw, Mr Tovey, let her stay if she wants. She's a right weirdo, this Year 7 kid…" I wasn't happy with *that*, Mum… "but she's dead clever…" *that* was alright, and so I stayed and it was so good… *Salve, mihi nomen est Matilda.*'

'Right,' Juno said faintly. 'Good, well done, but you know, Tilda, you should be out in the sunshine at lunchtime, making friends with the kids in your class, with kids your own age.'

'Oh, they just talk about *Love Island* and the boys they fancy in Year 8.' Tilda reached forwards for another root in the glove compartment.

'And Year 10s don't?' Juno frowned. 'I've told you, Tilda, there's no chocolate in there.'

'What, fancy boys in Year 8?'

'You know what I mean,' Juno tutted. This was not a good idea, Tilda's having lessons at lunchtime with the older kids. She'd have to ring school and forbid it: Tilda needed to make friends her own age, and watching *Love Island* and fancying Year 8 boys, not declining Latin nouns and conjugating Latin verbs.

'So, why've you picked me up from school?' Tilda lay back, mouthing Latin vocabulary to herself. 'And why haven't you picked up Gabe as well?'

'Well, I know how you don't like the school bus, and when I called Gabe at lunchtime, and told him I'd be waiting at the school gate to take you both down to see Grandpa's new place, he said no way was he being picked up by his mum like a five-year-old. The other kids would think he was a real mummy's boy. He's got a key; he can let himself in and make some toast or something to keep him going until we get back.'

'What if he puts the knife in the toaster again, you know to get those little crumpets out…?'

Juno, who'd been thinking exactly the same thing, frowned. 'He's thirteen, Tilda, he doesn't need his mother breathing down his neck all the time. So, as I say, I thought we'd go over and see Grandpa Patrick's new place. I have to say, Harriet's told me so much about Holly Close Farm and the two cottages there, I'm really looking forward to seeing them.'

'And your dad, too?' Tilda gave Juno a sideways glance as her mother pulled onto the main road that led to the outlying village of Heath Green.

'Well yes, of course. But you know, Tilda, I've only seen him a handful of times in the last sixteen years or so. Ever since he left Granny Helen for Anichka and had Arius. It just didn't seem fair to Granny. Anyway, Aunt Ariadne and Aunt Pandora are meeting us there too. Your Grandpa Patrick is trying hard to get us all together and be a family.'

'Why?'

'Why? Well, I suppose because he and Anichka are no longer together and he's been left to look after Arius. I suppose he thinks all Arius's – gosh that's hard to say:

*Arius's* – family are over here in Yorkshire and he should get to know us.'

'Are you sure it's down here?' Tilda asked, frowning as they appeared to be driving into a dead-end. 'Don't get the car stuck, will you?'

'Yes, it's fine, we're right. Oh look, Tilda, what a beautiful place to live. That's the farmhouse Harriet's daughter, Libby, and her boyfriend are doing up.'

'Boyfriend?' Tilda frowned. 'Isn't she married?'

'Libby and her partner, Seb have just about finished renovating,' Juno repeated. 'And you can just see the roof of the two cottages down below that your grandfather and Esme are renting.'

'Not together?' Tilda looked shocked.

'No, of course not *together*,' Juno tutted.

'Well, they all look to be having a bit of a jolly time *together*,' Tilda said peering through the windscreen at the newly turfed lawn in front of the beautiful farmhouse as Juno pulled up and cut the engine. 'There's loads of them there – I think they're having a party.'

Tilda jumped out and, without waiting for Juno, set off towards the grandfather she'd only met on a couple of previous occasions. '*Salve*,' Tilda's voice drifted back towards Juno, '*Salve, avus. Salve et grata.*'

# 18

'You do know,' Tilda was saying to the tall, very attractive blond boy she'd almost pinned up against the wall of the ivy-covered farm cottages, 'you're my uncle? Well, my half-uncle, I suppose. You wouldn't be interested in teaching me to speak Russian, would you?'

'Hello, Arius.' Juno elbowed Tilda out of the way before smiling up at her half-brother. Juno and her three sisters were all tall, but this sixteen-year-old half-brother of theirs whom they'd only recently got to know, was already a good head and shoulders above her. 'How are you settling in here and at the sixth-form college?'

'It's a bit quiet down here,' he said seriously, indicating with a sweep of his arm the golden, autumn fields that stretched seemingly forever into the distance. A large red combine-harvester was obviously taking advantage of the afternoon's balmy weather, determinedly bringing in the last of the summer grass, now mown and rolled into huge yellow wheels. 'I mean, we actually lived in an apartment in Didsbury – I'm a real city boy at heart. I'll need to escape back there at the weekend to see my mates and smell some petrol fumes.'

Juno laughed as Ariadne and Pandora walked over to

stand with them. 'You'll get used to it,' she said. 'This has to be one of the most glorious views in Yorkshire.'

'I actually find it all a bit scary,' Arius admitted. 'There's just so much, you know, fresh air and *space*. And at night, it's so quiet; it's so quiet, I can't sleep.'

'Now then,' Pandora trilled, 'isn't this lovely? It's a shame Lexia couldn't make it so Dad would have *all* his children here.'

'I bet there's a few more scattered round the British Isles we don't know about,' Ariadne said scathingly as Arius quickly walked off down towards the field to answer his phone.

'Shh.' Pandora frowned. 'For heaven's sake, Ariadne, not in front of Arius, Tilda and Hugo. Dad's here now, with Arius, and we all need to act like adults, enjoy having them around and make the best of the situation. It's not ideal, I know, but the alternative is to pretend he's not back and have nothing to do with them. I talked to Mum, told her we're down here and that we're seeing Dad—'

'Oh, you didn't, did you? What did you do *that* for?' Ariadne scowled. 'That's all we need, Mum arriving on the scene with a gun, finally getting her revenge on her husband for leaving her sixteen years ago.'

'Don't be ridiculous, Ari,' Juno tutted, but nevertheless checking the lane for any more visitors who might include Helen Sutherland. 'Mum wouldn't know how to fire a gun.'

'And *you've* changed your tune, Pandora,' Ariadne interrupted crossly. '*You* didn't have a good word to say about Dad until you went over to Manchester to see him six months ago.'

'We need to move on and be adult about this,' Pandora repeated firmly. 'And you're here, yourself, Ariadne. If you were so against it, you'd have refused to be here this afternoon. Oh look, good, Dad's got champagne...' She broke off as a group of people began making their way down towards them from the actual farm house – Holly Close Farm – at the same time as Esme Burkinshaw with Pandora's son Hugo, whom Esme had obviously commandeered to help, appeared from her side of the pair of semi-detached cottages. She was carrying what appeared to be a trayful of canapés, making her way gingerly, in heels, towards Patrick Sutherland who'd stationed himself at an old stone table in front of his cottage, and was now intent on pouring glasses of fizz for everyone.

'Now,' Esme was saying loudly, 'Patrick and I got together this morning to organise this little drinks-do of ours so that we could all be introduced to one another and get to know Liberty and Sebastian as well. 'It's so lovely that we can actually catch the last of the afternoon sunshine. Yoo-hoo, down here, Liberty, we're all down here!' she turned and called importantly before handing round rather stodgy-looking salmon and cream cheese blinis. 'Do have a serviette, Hadirane.'

'Thank you so much, Emsey, I *will* take a *napkin*,' Ariadne said pointedly, while Juno kicked her. 'The woman's *common*,' Ariadne hissed as Esme moved away to welcome the others, 'and don't tell me she's not after Dad.'

'And you're a snob, Ari,' Juno hissed back. 'For all your political idealism, your ranting about social conscience and... and gender issues, you're still a *snob*.'

'Since when has my political leaning and stance on gender

issues got anything to do with me not being able to stand the word *serviette*?' Ariadne appeared genuinely puzzled.

'You know exactly what I'm saying, Ari,' Juno said irritably. 'And, why it would bother you that anyone might be after Dad is beyond me. Why should *you* care?'

'I just don't fancy Emsey as a stepmother.' Ariadne began to laugh at the very thought.

'I wouldn't worry, I think our Mrs Burkinshaw has far bigger fish to fry than Dad. Just look at her now.'

Esme had dumped her blinis on Hugo and, with outstretched hands, tottered on her four-inch heels towards the newcomers. 'Welcome, welcome, to our little *soirée*,' she trilled, 'I'm so pleased you were able to make it.'

David Henderson, with Lysander on his shoulders, Harriet, Libby and, somewhat surprisingly at this time of day, Kit Westmoreland, Libby's brother, were met by Esme with effusive words and ushered towards Patrick who had just opened another bottle of champagne.

'David, how lovely to meet you at last.' Esme immediately took David's arm possessively, hanging on as if, now she had it, she wasn't ever going to let it go. 'So, we have champagne: none of that gassy Prosecco stuff you young people like to think is the real McCoy.' She tutted girlishly towards Libby and Kit. '*We* know the difference, don't we, David?'

Harriet, joining Juno and Ariadne over by the boundary fence, pulled a face. 'Who the hell is that?'

'That, Harriet, is Libby and Seb's new neighbour. Well, one of them at least.' Juno wanted to laugh as she watched David's face turn from one of polite welcome to one of a need for escape while held captive by Esme. 'Dad's renting one half of the cottages and Esme has moved over from

Sheffield – sorry, *the Peak District* – and is renting the other while she oversees her new business down in Westenbury village. You remember Scott suddenly found out he had a twenty-two-year-old daughter while we were rehearsing *Superstar* in the spring?'

'Oh gosh, is that her? The landlady who seduced Scott when he was a poor innocent student newly arrived from the colonies?' Harriet stared and then began to laugh. 'Blimey, I mean, she's a bit of a looker now, isn't she? Twenty years or so ago, she must have been a real goer. Every eighteen-year-old's fantasy.'

'Well, she's going to be in her element now with David dropping round at the farm to see Seb and Lysander. He'll be right up her street being almost twenty years younger.' Juno smiled as the three of them continued to watch Esme cling tenaciously to David's arm.

'David's going to come down one full day a week to look after Lysander while Libby's at med school, and I'm going to have him the other day that Mandy was supposed to have been on childcare duty,' Harriet now said. 'Oh, so is that your *dad*, Juno? He looks a handsome bloke as well.'

'Watch out for him, Hat.' Ariadne gave a little smile. 'He'll try and charm you.'

'Well, I don't mind being charmed and flirted with.' Harriet grinned. 'Have to brighten up my somewhat mundane existence somehow.'

'Where are the twins and India?' Juno asked. 'Are they not with you?'

'No. I've been looking after Lysander all day – I'd just brought him back. David was already here – he'd brought something round for Seb – and next thing we know, we're all invited down here for champagne. Lilian has picked the twins up from school and she'll be at home when India gets off the school bus.' Harriet smiled, turning to face the fabulous view in front of the farm and two cottages, breathing in the mellow late-afternoon autumn air. 'I wasn't expecting a welcome committee like this – you know, champagne on a Monday afternoon? Seems quite sybaritic.' She went on, 'And Kit decided to come with me because he got back early from his meeting in Birmingham and wanted to have another look at the cottages even though he knew they'd both already been snapped up. He'd loved to have rented one of them, but they were already taken.'

'Expensive though,' Ariadne mused. 'You know, for a young kid like Kit?'

'Tell me about it, although, to be fair, he's pretty canny with his money.' Harriet stopped herself: why on earth was she telling someone she didn't know that well that Kit appeared to have more money than he should have at his age? 'Anyway,' she went on, 'he'd be far better buying somewhere than renting, but, at the end of the day, he doesn't really know where David and Nick want him to be with regards the business; it's a strong possibility they'll have him based in Milan rather than in this country. I think Kit feels he's missed out by not going to university at eighteen like all his mates did – you know, he's never left to live away from home and, now he's twenty, he's champing at the bit somewhat.'

'I suppose he doesn't want to be still living at home with his mum and dad?' Ariadne pulled a face. 'I can understand that; I couldn't wait to leave once I was eighteen and off to uni. And the last thing I wanted was to return, either home to my parents' house or actually back up to Yorkshire.'

Harriet nodded. 'It doesn't help that the twins are only five, racing round the house and always in his room, and India is already eyeing up his attic bedroom, ready to move in there. He's a grown man, he doesn't want to be living with his parents and a whole load of kids.'

'Cramping his style on the romance front too, I would imagine?' Ariadne laughed. 'He's a very good-looking boy, Harriet. I bet the girls are queuing up?'

'Literally,' Harriet sighed, lowering her voice. 'He actually had the twins' teacher in his bed this weekend.'

Ariadne stared. 'Really? Blimey? How old is she?'

Harriet laughed at Ariadne's shocked face. 'Oh, just a couple of years older than Kit – newly qualified – and then, once *she'd* left, another one called round last night, and his phone *never* stops ringing.'

'He's twenty. Let him enjoy it all. Mind you, I can see why he'd be better off with a place of his own.'

Harriet sighed. 'It's just that *I* have to pick up the pieces. I have to take the twins into Miss O'Connor's class and I know, poor girl, she'll be wanting to know what Kit's up to, dying to ask if he's at home and is he going to ring her? I've seen it all before.'

'What, with Kit you mean?' Juno, who had wandered down to look at the glorious view, was back at their side and joining in the conversation.

'No – well, yes, I've already had to mop up several girls broken-hearted over Kit – but it's a bit like history repeating itself. My brother, John, was just the same at his age. My poor mother used to be beside herself when there was yet another girl crying on the doorstep. I suppose I just constantly worry that Kit might end up unhappy, you know, like my brother, John.'

'Well, he looks happy enough now.' Ariadne nodded towards the perimeter fence where Kit, still dressed in his navy work suit, was leaning, chatting and smiling with a dark-haired girl.

'Who's that?' Harriet frowned, squinting to see if she knew the girl.

'Maya,' Juno said, immediately recognising who Kit was talking to.

'Maya?'

'Scott's daughter,' Juno said somewhat shortly.

'Ah, and Esme's daughter? Right...' Harriet continued to stare. 'She's very lovely.'

'Well, Scott isn't exactly unattractive, is he?' Ariadne smiled. 'Good-looking men do tend to have good-looking kids, I suppose?'

The three of them continued to look over at the pair, taking in the very obvious fire that was being kindled between Kit and Maya.

'Stop staring,' Juno eventually said, 'we're behaving like three nosy old biddies.'

'Nothing wrong with being an old biddy,' Ariadne said comfortably. 'I reckon...' She broke off as David Henderson joined the three of them.

'Juno,' Harriet said, finally turning away from Kit, 'I know *you* already know David, but Ariadne, have you met David Henderson?'

Ariadne held out her hand, and as David smiled down at her, Juno, not for the first time, wondered fleetingly whether the immediate physical attraction her eldest sister was obviously feeling for this rather gorgeous man questioned her conviction that she preferred women. As far as Juno knew, Ariadne had certainly had relationships with men in the past, before meeting and falling in love with Gina, her senior fellow at Berkeley that is. After three years together, the relationship had ended and Ariadne, crushed, had returned to England, and eventually back to Yorkshire, vowing never again to give herself so completely to any other human being, man or woman. Juno now stared as Ariadne, like so many other women before her, leaned into David slightly, obviously falling under the spell of this charismatic man. Juno knew Ariadne's irritability, her often pugnacious approach to her family and those she worked with, was not just a result of being a product of her parents' dysfunctional marriage, but had quite a lot to do with being unable to come to terms with losing Gina. Or maybe, Juno thought, as David Henderson continued to smile at Ariadne with questioning, intelligent eyes, it was all down to her sister's genes and there was absolutely nothing she could do about being born an irascible, bad-tempered old termagant.

'Ari?' Juno finally nudged her. 'David's talking to you.'

'I'm so sorry, David,' Ariadne said, reddening, 'lovely to meet you.' She gave David one of her rare, beautiful smiles before turning and heading off to find her father.

As the shadows lengthened and the early evening began to turn chilly, Juno realised she needed to get Tilda home and start thinking about what she and the kids were going to eat. After several of Esme's stodgy canapés, the last thing she felt like doing was setting-to in the kitchen, but she knew Gabriel would be starving even if he'd managed to evade electrocution with the toaster. Her father, champagne glass in hand, had joined her and the others and he and David were soon immersed in discussing Patrick's latest biography of Aristotle, *The Father of Western Philosophy* which, apparently, David had already bought and read. Their talk was soon interrupted by Esme bustling into their midst, champagne bottle at the ready.

'I think everyone's driving, Esme, thank you. One small glass is my limit if I don't want to end up in court.' David upended the remains of his champagne onto the grass.

'Or having to stay the night, David,' Esme pouted, winking at Juno.

David, Juno assumed, was too well-mannered to say what everyone else was most likely thinking and, smiling politely at Esme, he offered his hand instead. 'Must be going, Esme. Lovely to meet you and thank you for the drink.'

'Oh, you ridiculous man,' Esme giggled girlishly and, ignoring David's hand, reached up instead and kissed his cheek. 'We're best friends now. I do hope we're going to see lots of you down here, David. And—' she reached into her mauve silk cardigan pocket bringing out some sort of flyer which she proceeded to hand round '—also down at Blush and Blow. We'll be opening very soon and I know you'll all want to take advantage of the opening offer of two for one at my new Turkish Hammam. Westenbury won't know what's hit it once we're up and running.'

Very likely, Juno thought, while Harriet, staring at Esme, was obviously of the same opinion.

As they all made their goodbyes, Juno turned to look for Arius and Hugo. 'Where's Arius, Dad? Is Hugo with him?'

'They decided to go over to Manchester,' Pandora said, almost proudly. 'I gave them money for a taxi down to the station half an hour ago. It's so lovely that the two of them have become such pals.'

'Manchester?' Ariadne frowned. 'On a Monday evening?'

'Why ever not?' Pandora tutted, smiling. 'They're sixteen, they're wanting to have a bit of fun. Arius obviously has all his pals still over there and apparently there's some club that he usually goes to on a Monday night. I'm so pleased he's taken Hugo under his wing a bit. Being away at boarding school until recently,' she turned to explain to David, 'means Hugo doesn't really know many people here in Midhope.'

'Well, I'm amazed at your letting him go, Pandora,' Ariadne said, frowning. 'He's only just started his A level course. Doesn't he have a whole load of college work to do?'

'I'm sure he does,' Pandora answered, narrowing her eyes at what she perceived to be Ariadne's criticism of her as a mother, 'but I trust him implicitly to catch up tomorrow. I'm sorry, Ariadne, *you've* never had a child of your own and certainly not an almost-seventeen-year-old. You have to know when to loosen the reins somewhat. Don't you agree, Esme?'

'Oh absolutely. Maya was a nightmare at sixteen.'

'I wasn't suggesting Hugo is a nightmare,' Pandora said stiffly. 'He's never been a moment's trouble.'

'Well, there you go then,' Esme said, turning back to David and Patrick, obviously having heard quite enough of Pandora's views on how to handle teenagers.

# 19

A couple of weeks on from the excruciatingly embarrassing discovery of knowing she'd been up to no good with Noah Haddon's dad – his *dad* for heaven's sake – Grace was beginning to settle into the workaday routine of not only being a single mother with responsibility for two kids under five, but of being back full-time as a class teacher of ten-year-olds – with all that that entailed – into the bargain.

She could do this, Grace told herself. And she could. The way to do it was to set the alarm for five-thirty, having set out everything she and the kids needed for the morning, before allowing herself to fall exhausted into bed not long after the children themselves were asleep. Her own clothes, down to matching bra and knickers and whichever shoes went best with her outfit, were meticulously laid out on the chair at the bottom of her bed, and clean uniforms for Jonty and Pietronella were ready in order of their putting on in their bedrooms. The breakfast table was laid with juice and cereal or, now that the mornings were chilly, porridge oats already steeping in milk in the fridge ready to blast in the microwave once the children were up and running.

Grace was, she knew, luckier than a lot of single mothers

having to work full-time. For a start, let's face it, she didn't *have* to work; this was her choice. Seb was more than generous in the allowance he paid regularly into her account for Jonty; the mortgage wasn't huge and Dan and she were still sharing the repayments so she could afford to have Lilian Brennan come in a couple of mornings to do some housework and, if she'd wanted to go out in the evening (which she didn't,) Lilian was on hand to babysit. However, she was aware Dan might not pay the mortgage forever. Who knew how the two of them would end up? At the moment happy ever after didn't seem to be on the cards.

A couple of days after Dan had left for the job interview, he rang her from Exeter to say he'd been called back for a second grilling and then, after a couple of nail-biting hours, been offered the job down there to start the following week. How did she feel about it all, he'd tentatively probed? Did she think, he asked, he was doing the right thing? At the end of the day, he said, he needed to work and this was a great opportunity, but he was going to miss the kids so much. He didn't, she noticed, say the same about herself. Grace had sat on the stairs, phone in hand, and given her blessing for Dan to relocate to Exeter. The alternative, she reckoned, was his coming back, being unemployed and miserable with her or being miserable in his mother's place. Once she gave her opinion that yes, the children would miss him dreadfully, but it was probably the right thing to do, he appeared to perk up and become quite animated about his new life. He was, he said, going to leave his car there and hire a van to drive back North before packing his things and quite a bit of his mother's furniture, ready to move down South to the flat he'd already found to rent.

After the call, Grace was tempted to ring Harriet (*Your husband of twelve years has left you with two kids under five in order to relocate four-hundred miles away: discuss*) but, instead, made herself a strong coffee, which she knew would probably keep her awake half the night, sat herself down on the stairs once more which, for some reason, she'd found over the past few months to be a great place to think, and tried to work out just what she was feeling. She'd been married to Dan for twelve years and, while she'd often seen him 'givin t'glad eye' as her granny called it, to other women, it had still been a huge shock when he'd moved out six years ago to be with Camilla, the young Australian girl who'd come to work in his office. Life was strange, Grace thought as she felt the caffeine hit her nervous system and wondered whether to enhance it further by smoking a cigarette as well. (Dan had been an occasional smoker which she'd not minded too much, but she doubted there was a packet left in the house.) After Dan had moved out to be with Camilla, she'd thought her world had ended, but it hadn't: it was merely the beginning. On a night out with Mandy Henderson, she'd met Mandy and David's beautiful – and terribly *young* – son, Seb. Jonty had been the result and then, after she and Seb had parted (really, it had only been a matter of time, she and Seb had both acknowledged) she'd agreed that she and Dan should give their marriage another go and they'd adopted Pietronella. Now that Dan had gone once more, this then was her world: Jonty and Pietronella were everything to her, and anyone else was superfluous to requirements.

Grace had drained her coffee cup and, feeling slightly guilty at acknowledging Dan as *superfluous to requirements*, gone to check the kids were asleep before attacking the pile of marking she'd brought home from school.

She and Dan had taken Jonty and Pietronella out for a kids' movie and pizza on the Saturday teatime, before Dan had driven himself and the white van (*white van man, superfluous to requirements*) down to his newly rented flat in Exeter the following day.

'Am I doing the right thing, Grace?' Dan had asked again as she and the kids had dropped him back at his mother's place after the pizza and, although terribly sad, knowing her marriage was over, probably *really* over this time, she'd nodded. It was no one's fault; maybe the pair of them should have fought harder for their marriage and their kids, but Grace knew they didn't make each other happy and it was a relief to leave him there, knowing he had a new job and would still be in touch with her and the children.

'No, darling, he most certainly *isn't* doing the right thing.' Grace's mother was *not* happy, when Grace had, rather rashly, given in to the pressure of her probing and filled her in about her husband's state of mind. 'Why does Dan think it's all alright to relocate to the other end of the country, leaving you to fend for yourself? Your father would never have *considered* doing such a thing to me when you and your brother were little, never mind him actually packing up his things and leaving me in the lurch as Dan appears to have done to you. *Again.*' Katherine Greenwood was on one of her unannounced visits, arriving ten minutes after

Grace and the children, tired and hungry, had let themselves into the house after another day at school.

'Not now, Mum,' Grace frowned. 'If you want to make yourself useful, there's a bag of potatoes in the kitchen need peeling.'

'Oh darling, I would, but I've just been up in Westenbury village… Look…' Katherine flapped her hands in Grace's direction. 'There's a fabulous new place just about to open where that funny little hardware shop used to be. Blush and Blow, it's called. The girl there has done such a good job on my nails.'

'If it's not open yet how come you got your nails done already?' Grace was only half-listening, more concerned now with what Pietronella was up to as she sat, glued, in front of a cartoon on TV.

'Should that child be watching so much TV?' Katherine asked, frowning.

'Probably not,' Grace said shortly.

'Anyway, yes, the place isn't officially open until next week – can you imagine, darling, a Turkish baths in your little village – but the beauty side is up and running and I had one of the first appointments… Should that child be scratching her head like that?'

'Again, Mum, probably not.' Grace went to stand in front of Pietronella who batted her affectionately out of her line of vision. 'Nits,' Grace said cheerfully. 'It had to happen sometime, I suppose.'

'I don't recall you or your brother *ever* bringing home such things.' Katherine visibly shuddered. 'Mind you, I don't think Mrs Kerrigan at Daisy Mount would have allowed them anywhere *near* her school. Such a lovely, *select* little school, it was; you used to look so sweet in your little striped blazer and straw boater.' Katherine glanced with some disdain at Pietronella's Little Acorns' navy sweatshirt on which something indeterminate – it could have been glue, her lunch or snot (or probably all three) – was emblazoned. 'It's such a shame the school died when she did.'

Grace laughed at that. 'The cemetery's the best place for the pair of them. Right, Mum, if you're not going to help me with supper and, I guess, you don't fancy being the Nit Nurse, maybe you'd like to listen to Jonty read?'

Ignoring Grace's suggestion, Katherine frowned and said, 'I know I've said this before, Grace, but I'll say it again: I'm surprised that David allows his grandson to go to a, you know, a *state school*.' Katherine lowered her voice as if discussing something gynaecological.

'*Allows* Jonty? What *are* you talking about, Mum?' Grace felt growing irritation. 'Where Jonty goes to school is mine and Seb's decision. Nothing whatsoever to do with David.'

'But surely, darling, he wants the best for Jonty?'

'Mum, at the moment, Little Acorns is most certainly the best place for both my kids. Seb went there himself when it was Westenbury C of E, you know.'

Katherine sniffed. 'Yes, that's as maybe. But Seb soon ended up going private. It wasn't long before David and Mandy sent him off to King Edward's.'

'Mum, I don't know why we're having this conversation now. Seb was eleven when he went to King Edward's. Jonty is five. When he's eleven, I'll consider have this conversation with you then.'

'Fine, fine.' Katherine put up her hands with their

red-painted nails in an impatient gesture of acquiescence. 'I'll shut up—'

'Good.'

'—except, you know, I was talking to your father over supper last night. And it suddenly occurred to me.'

'What did, Mum?' Grace was already at Pietronella's hair with a comb. 'Oh, God, the little blighters. Look at the size of these, Mum.'

'I really have no intention of coming anywhere near.'

'Where, Mummy? Let me see.' Jonty jumped on the back of the sofa, peering down at Pietronella who was straining round Grace to watch Dumbo.

'Out of the way. I don't want you catching them too.' Grace pushed Jonty gently off the sofa where he rolled onto the carpet, giggling. 'Mind you,' she added, for the benefit of Katherine who'd removed herself further away from any infestation, 'he's probably already got them.'

'It's not fair,' Jonty continued to giggle while climbing back on board the sofa and attempting to hug Pietronella. 'I want nits too. I can keep them in a matchbox and feed them cheese and Branston pickle sandwiches.' This idea amused him so much he fell, giggling, off the arm of the sofa, crash landed onto his Tonka truck, cutting his lip on the yellow metal.

'Blood,' Pietronella said in delight. 'Jonty, blood.'

'Mum, throw me that box of tissues, would you,' Grace said calmly, picking Jonty up and examining his mouth and tooth.

'I don't how you stay so relaxed, Grace, really I don't.' Katherine sighed, throwing the tissues in her direction. 'This is what I was saying to your father last night.'

'What?' Grace raised an eyebrow. 'You and Dad were discussing how you were both going to come over and help me? Hmm?'

'Well no, darling, you appear to be in total control without any help from myself or Daddy. No, it suddenly occurred to me that now poor David is by himself, now that poor Mandy is—' she lowered her voice again, once more in gynaecological mode '—you know, *no more*, and *you* are all alone as well…'

'Forget it, Mum,' Grace said firmly, arranging Jonty well away from his sister and handing both him and Pietronella a bowl of carrot sticks and hummus each ('how *modern*,' Katherine sniffed) she'd prepared the previous evening.

Katherine followed Grace into the kitchen. 'So, I was having lunch at *Clementine's* the other day with the girls – we had such a lovely lunch; Clementine is so clever – and David happened to pop in… keeping his eye on another of his little businesses, no doubt… Anyway, Pamela Bailey… you remember Pamela, darling? Had a terrible time when she went in for a hysterectomy and hitching up of everything, you know, *down below*? Butchered, absolutely *butchered* apparently. I've told her she needs to get in touch with one of those no win, no fee claims against the surgeon. Some young girl from China apparently. Or was it Ceylon?'

'Sri Lanka,' Grace murmured, reaching into the fridge for a pack of sausages.

Katherine frowned. 'No, I don't think so, darling, I'm sure she said Ceylon. Anyway, Pamela is *convinced* that Mandy was up to no good when she died.'

'What do you mean *up to no good*?' Grace snapped crossly, knowing full well what her mother was implying.

Hadn't she, Grace, been *up to no good*, herself, with Mr Haddon (she couldn't think of him as Ross) only a few weeks earlier and knew exactly what was behind Katherine's implication.

'Pamela said that Mandy Henderson had always had, you know, *liaisons* throughout her marriage to David. I have to say, Grace, although I believe there was maybe a little *something* with Harriet's brother in the past, I was really quite taken aback and I immediately jumped in to poor Mandy's defence. I did say that, with the strong connection between our family and the Hendersons, *I* would surely have been one of the *first* to hear about any such gossip and I put Pamela right in her place there and then.' Katherine stopped to gauge Grace's reaction and when Grace carried on, calmly chopping carrots, went on, 'Total rubbish, isn't it?'

'Total,' Grace replied firmly, moving to lay the kitchen table.

'Only,' Katherine wasn't letting it go, 'if the poor man *has* been led a merry dance all these years, then I'm sure he'd be only too happy to find someone who would, you know, make him feel better. Someone to start again with? So, what about you and David?'

'Euan David, Mum? Isn't he that Welsh cricketer? You want me to take up with some Welsh international now?'

'Oh pishpots, stop pretending you don't know what I'm saying, Grace. And just think about it, Grace: what a catch David is.'

'Mum, enough already,' Grace finally snapped. 'Now, if you want to stay for bangers and mash with me and the kids, you're more than welcome. Otherwise, please get it into your head that David and I are mates. Just mates. And always will be, just that. Nothing more. Right?'

Things were settling down at school. Jonty was enjoying being in Miss O'Connor's class, and Cassie had done as she'd promised with regards the statement of Special Educational Needs for Pietronella and, after a minor battle with local authority funding, Pietronella now had one to one support every morning in order to assist with the development of her fine motor skills.

Unfortunately, Grace hadn't been able to report a huge improvement in Noah Haddon's behaviour or attitude. A parental visit to a child's head and class teacher doesn't always prompt an instant change in said child's behaviour and Noah was no exception. He continued to try to wind Grace up but, with the rest of the class accepting that she was in charge and would be with them for the foreseeable future, there was a much better atmosphere in her Y5 classroom and Grace felt herself relax and start to build a good relationship with the majority of the children.

After the meeting with Ross Haddon, Cassie Beresford had obviously recognised a potential safeguarding issue with Noah and his parents and, as the school's Designated Safeguarding Lead, had immediately contacted the relevant agencies for, in her words, some 'co-operative working and joined up thinking'. Grace had to hand it to Cassie: if she said she was going to do something it was done at once.

Cassie apparently had had a long chat with Noah the morning after the meeting with his father, trying to gauge Noah's emotional response when challenged about his accusation that it had been Grace who had caused the bruising on his arm. Noah, she'd reported back to Grace, had initially struggled to take responsibility for his behaviour but, with some gentle probing had begun to show some remorse and even empathy as to how Grace, as his teacher, might have felt at being accused of hurting him. Despite all this, Noah refused to say how he'd got the bruise and Grace had been advised to keep a covert watch for any further signs of abuse, particularly when Noah was getting changed for Games and PE. And be accused by the little sod of her watching him as he got changed, she'd almost remonstrated with Cassie, but then thought better of it.

Noah was a superb little footballer – apparently, he'd been chosen to train with Leeds United Academy, but now he and Ross Haddon had moved into the village to be near his granny, and Ross was often working until much later in the evening (Grace still had no idea what he did for a living, despite a sneaky look at Noah's admission forms) it just wasn't feasible to enable him to continue. This was something else Noah, perhaps understandably, had been kicking off about.

'OK, Noah, let's strike a bit of a bargain, you and me, shall we?' After one particularly confrontational morning, Grace had taken Noah to one side.

'A bargain?' Noah had glared angrily up at her as Grace motioned him to stay behind while the rest of the class went out for break. 'I don't do bargains.'

'So,' Grace had countered, ignoring his rudeness. 'You scratch my back and I'll scratch yours, Noah. I want a calm, hard-working class. You want to play football.'

In the end Grace had succeeded in coming to some

sort of compromise with Noah, using football as a bit of a bargaining tool: if he could manage to stay in his seat when required, as well as not calling out, as was his wont, Grace allowed him five minutes before break and before lunch when he could choose one member of the class to go with him and Deimante out onto the playing field and let off steam.

'I's playing for Man U pretty soon,' Deimante puffed after one of these sessions, wiping a sheen of sweat from her pretty face. 'Sat boy, Noahs is good. I was only ables to stops one goals off hims today.'

'You've actually been in goal?' Grace started laughing as Deimante continued to rub herself down.

'Too rights,' Deimante sniffed. 'Of course.'

'And you can, you know, save goals…?'

Deimante tutted. 'I was abouts to join *Lietuvos nacionaline moteru futbola komanda.*'

'The what?' Grace was still laughing as Deimante glared at her.

'Lithuanian National Women's footballs team,' Deimante said, shrugging her shoulders nonchalantly at Grace. 'As goalie. I's good goalie, but Gatis – my mans – say we must come to Englands. To this back of beyonds.'

'But you're happy here, aren't you Deimante?' Grace had stopped laughing and was feeling a bit ashamed of her derision. Deimante Miniauskiene never ceased to amaze her: she had, apparently, a degree in astrophysics from some university in Lithuania and now, she was telling Grace, she was a women's international goalkeeper too?

'Yes, I's very happy heres. Even betters if sey let me trains to be teacher.' Deimante sighed again, folded the towel and began to make her way to the hall and her stint as dinnertime supervisor. 'But,' she turned at the door, 'with sis bloody Brexits, who knows where Gatis – my man – and I's ending up?'

'You might be forced to go back to Lithuania?' Grace frowned.

Deimante shrugged. 'Who knows? We keeps our eye peeleds on Boris and whoever comes after him. You knows whats sey say: *even a clocks that is broken is right twice a days*.' She gave Grace a knowing look, a wink and headed importantly to her next task.

Grace went to sit at her computer, trying to work out the relevance – if any – of Deimante's departing little homily to the state of the nation, and hit her email button. The usual stuff: a message from Molly's mother to say she was taking her to a dental appointment the following day, an email from Josh Donnington to all the staff requesting the week's planning and one from another parent: R. Haddon.

Grace opened the email and, with a slightly raised heartbeat, read its content:

Dear Mrs Stevens

I wonder if you'd be good enough to speak with me on a personal matter, rather than with regards Noah? I'd very much appreciate it if you'd call me on the number below this evening, after ten? If I don't hear from you, I totally respect your decision and I give you full assurance of my not contacting you again on this matter in the future.

Ross Haddon

## 20

Why she'd put her lippy on to speak on the phone with Ross Haddon, Grace couldn't quite work out. She wasn't even sure, as she toyed with a glass of white wine later that evening, if she was actually going to ring him anyway. Who did she think she was kidding? Of course she was going to ring him. If only to find out what he wanted, Grace argued with herself. *Well of course to find that out, you daft woman.* She tutted, picking up the TV remote and immediately putting it down once more on the arm of the sofa, her thoughts drifting to David Henderson rather than Mr Haddon.

She'd left school that afternoon and immediately bumped into David in the carpark on his way to see Cassie in his capacity as Chair of Governors at Little Acorns.

'You're always here.' Grace had smiled as David reached into his pocket for two packets of chocolate buttons, handing them to Jonty and Pietronella with the usual warnings not to eat them until Mummy said so. 'Haven't you got a home to go to?'

'Not much there for me at the moment, Grace.' David smiled back, and Grace wanted to kick herself for her insensitivity. 'Anyway, Cassie has asked me in to go over some safeguarding issues with her and Josh.'

'Oh, God, David, I'm so sorry. Look, you know you're welcome to come round anytime. Come for lunch on Sunday,' she added. 'I'll ask Libby and Seb and then you can have all your grandchildren round you at once.'

'I'm fine.' David smiled again. 'I really am. But you know, what with my mother trying to fix me up—' (and *my* mother as well, Grace nearly added, but thought better of it) '—with her friends' divorced daughters as well as that dreadful woman who's living down at the Holly Close cottages—'

'What dreadful woman?'

'Esme somebody? She's the owner of the new Turkish Hamman where Horsforth's hardware store was. Ridiculous idea in a rural village like Westenbury.'

Grace grinned. 'Stop it, David. You're sounding like Victor Meldrew. And you're only mad because you didn't think of it first.'

'Not at all,' David protested. 'I really think a rural village should be just that: you know, rural. How on earth did the woman get planning permission to turn a perfectly good little hardware store into a Turkish bath for heaven's sake?'

'David, stop it,' Grace said once more. 'You, more than anyone, should know the excitement of starting up a new business. *I'm* off for a damned good pummelling as soon as it's up and running. Give this Esme woman a chance.'

David started to laugh, his brown eyes dancing with the mirth much absent since Mandy's death.

'Tinder.' Grace laughed in turn.

'Sorry?'

'Get yourself on Tinder. Just for a bit of fun.'

'Hell no, I might meet Esme on there.' He paused and, stroking Grace's arm briefly, laughed. 'Tell you what, Grace. If you do it, I'll do it. We could do it together,' and, grinning down at her, he patted the kids on the head before heading for reception.

Grace had stared after him, very conscious of the brief touch of his hand on her arm and wondered at herself as she conjured up a ridiculous – but rather exciting – scenario of herself and David, both on Tinder, both looking for someone and ending up, by mistake (like on some daft rom com film) out on a date together.

'You silly woman,' Grace censured herself now, as she recalled again both the touch of his warm hand on her arm as well as the ensuing little fantasy she'd conjured up as, laughing, David had walked off to his meeting with Cassie. She looked down at her watch for the umpteenth time, mindlessly flicking through the channels on the TV and, once again recalling this conversation with David, let her mind dwell on her mother's ridiculous notion that she, Grace, might be the one to fill the vacancy created by Mandy's death. Maybe there was a bit of a vacancy in her own life too – dangerous liaisons with the likes of Ross Haddon really weren't the way to fill them, were they?

She recalled the very first time she'd met David Henderson. She'd been dressed as a German Nazi officer, with Harriet as a nun in full habit and wimple, for a trip to the theatre to see, and get involved in, a production of *Sing-along-a-sound-of-music*. On their return to Harriet's place, she'd jumped on David, thinking he was Nick, Harriet's husband. She could clearly recall Harriet's asking: 'So, what did you think of David Henderson? and her reply: 'I think he's probably the type of man I would find extremely attractive had I not been too embarrassed to take a second look. Once I'd nibbled his ear and to all intents and purposes rotated my bum in his groin, the last thing I was going to do was actually meet his eyes…'

'For heaven's sake, you daft bint,' Grace muttered aloud, unsure whether she was addressing herself or her mother, 'Mandy's not been dead three months yet. And you, Grace, have only been officially separated two days. Take up knitting. Or macramé – what the hell is macramé anyway? And why are you talking to yourself? First sign of madness…'

It was nerves, that's what it was, sitting here, waiting for the hands of the grandmother clock in the corner of the sitting room to reach ten o'clock.

At quarter to ten she went upstairs to check on Jonty and Pietronella.

At ten to ten she went into the kitchen to make a coffee she didn't want.

At five to ten she went to the loo once again.

At ten o'clock she reached for her phone and then, not wanting to appear too eager, put it down and picked up last Sunday's *Times*.

At five past ten she could stand the tension no longer, grabbed her phone and had nervously jabbed in half the number Ross Haddon had given her when Jonty appeared at the door, said, 'Mummy, Mummy, I feel…' and promptly and very profusely vomited onto the sitting room carpet, himself and, as Grace dashed forwards to reach him, over her bare feet.

'You poor little button. What's made you so poorly?' Oh hell, which first? A bucket or the loo? The downstairs loo being nearer than the utility, Grace manoeuvred him in there and stood holding Jonty's head while he retched once more.

It was going up to eleven by the time Grace had put Jonty in the shower, found clean pyjamas and tucked him into her own bed with a bucket at its side. She found another bucket, cleaned and disinfected the carpet, sprayed several squirts of Dior's *J'adore* around the sitting room to purge the smell from her nostrils and, after peeling off her own stinking tracksuit bottoms, wearily turned the shower on herself.

What now? Go to bed and forget Ross Haddon? Grace knew she couldn't, she'd never sleep. She'd ring him and, if he wasn't here, leave a message with her apologies. Without any further ado, she pulled on her own pyjamas and dressing gown and went to sit on her favourite stair where she'd be able to hear Jonty if he needed her, together with the added benefit of not having to sit in the noxious combination of sick, disinfectant and perfume fumes.

He answered instantly. 'Hello, Ross Haddon speaking.'

'Mr Haddon, it's Grace Stevens. You asked that I call you.'

'Grace, thank you so much for getting back to me.'

'I would have rung at ten as you asked, but my little boy decided to throw up all over me.'

'Is he OK?'

'I think so. He's no fever or anything. I'll see how he is in the morning.'

'Grace, look, can we meet up?' Ross sounded nervous.

'Meet up?'

'A drink? A meal maybe?'

'Why?' Grace knew she was coming over as defensive and wasn't quite sure why.

'Why?' He sounded amused. 'I thought that was pretty obvious.'

'You mean to talk more about Noah? Well, if you want to make an appointment, message me through my school email and we can arrange something.'

'No, not to talk about Noah, although, yes, there are things I think it's best you know. I'd like to see you, Grace.'

There was a silence as Grace tried to think what to do. Was there some moral code she'd be breaking by going for a drink with the father of a child in her class. A married man. But hell, hadn't she already broken any moral code by her actions a few Saturday evenings ago?

'You're married, Mr Haddon.'

'I'm separated from my wife, Mrs Stevens...' He paused. 'As the embarrassing incident at school last week surely indicated?'

'I'm really not sure *what* all of that indicated,' Grace retorted. 'And, to be honest, I'm not sure it's any of my business.'

'But that's why I'd really like to sit down with you and explain some more. You see...'

Grace was saved from answering by the reappearance of Jonty at her side, now looking decidedly perky. 'Sorry, I missed that. My little boy's out of bed once again.'

'Grace, I'll be in the Coach and Horses at Upper Clawson on Thursday evening. Do you know it? Look, I know it's quite a way out up there, but it should be fairly quiet during the week. I'll book a table for two. Say 8 p.m.? That gives you two days to decide whether you'll meet up with me or not. Don't text me or anything – I'll be there anyway. If you decide to be there, that will be wonderful. If not, I really understand and I promise you I won't contact you again – anything to do with Noah and I'll go through Mrs Beresford or your deputy head chap.'

Grace heard, in the background, 'Dad, who are you talking to?' (What on earth was Noah Haddon doing up at eleven o'clock at night?) and the phone went dead as Ross hung up.

Very presumptuous, Grace thought, almost crossly. Did Ross Haddon think he was in some sort of romantic novel, setting up cosy little dinners *à deux* without the foggiest idea whether she would be free, or able to get a babysitter? For all he knew, she might *already* be out on some hot date, or off with friends to watch the – allegedly – unmissable John Godber at the theatre, or out at the opening of that new Turkish Hamman in the village or… or… eating poached eggs on toast (she was, she admitted to herself, becoming quite *addicted* to poached eggs at the moment) in front of a catch up of *Eastenders*.

'Mummy, you're looking a bit pink.' Jonty, sat patiently at Grace's side on the stairs, put up his hand to her cheek.

Grace smiled down at his serious face. 'So are you now, thank goodness; you were as white as a sheet an hour ago. 'You feeling OK now?'

'I'm a bit hungry actually.' He frowned.

'Really?' He did look remarkably better, Grace thought, as she felt his forehead.

'I'd like some toast.'

'Do you know, darling, so would I.'

## 21

'Get a grip,' Grace admonished herself out loud to her empty bedroom as she rifled nervously through her wardrobe, unable to decide what to wear. She really must stop this talking to herself: was it a symptom of potentially going round the bend? 'No,' she answered herself, deliberately speaking aloud and at a higher volume than usual, 'it's a symptom of there being no one else here to talk to and tell me what the hell I'm doing sneaking off to some back of the beyond pub out on the Pennines to meet a married man. 'Who I fancy like mad,' she added to her reflection in the mirror. 'Don't forget that, Gracey girl.'

'Who Gwacey Girl?' Pietronella reached stubby fingers for Grace's new Charlotte Tilbury lipstick sitting on her dressing table, still in its carrier bag from Harvey Nicks in Leeds.

'That's your mama,' Grace laughed, planting a kiss on Pietronella's short black shiny bob. 'Come here.' Grace smiled, showing her daughter how to purse her lips before applying the bright red lipstick first onto her own mouth and then onto her daughter's. 'Don't you look gorgeous?' And, Grace thought, stroking Pietronella's hair and watching them both in the mirror, she really was. She had the dark hair and eyes of her Italian birth mother and, while she'd been born with Down's Syndrome, she was already surpassing what Grace and Dan had been told they might expect with regards both her fine motor development and intellectual progression.

Pietronella reached into Grace's wardrobe, pulling at something on a hanger and retreating bottom first with the long, elegantly beautiful scarlet dress Grace had bought for some do years ago but which, for some reason she couldn't now recall, she and Dan had not actually gone to. 'Wear this, Gwacey Girl,' Pietronella commanded.

'I don't think I can get into *that* anymore,' Grace laughed. What the hell, she'd give it a jolly good go. Divesting herself of jeans, jumper and bra she pulled on the slinky little number, the silk caressing her smooth bare skin as she endeavoured to turn and pull up the zip.

'Have a go, Nella,' Grace puffed, proffering her back to Pietronella.

'Fat botty, Gwacey Girl,' Pietronella said sagely, her little fingers unable to pull the zip up above Grace's backside.

'Thanks for that, darling.' Grace sighed. What the hell was she doing having her own personal little fashion parade anyway when she should be getting ready to head off to the Coach and Horses? Her insides did that little flippy thing they'd learned to do whenever she thought of Ross Haddon. What the hell *was* she going to wear?

'Lilly here now.' Pietronella's head came up in delight as the front door banged below. 'Lilly help with red dress,' she added, setting off for the stairs.

'Oh no, really, don't bring Lilian up,' Grace protested, but Pietronella was off.

This was such a beautiful dress, Grace thought, recalling, with a pang, former, and now gone forever, youthful and carefree days. She saw in the mirror the much-younger woman she'd once been, when she was still single; when she could stay out dancing most of the night and still be up at the crack of dawn with the boundless energy needed for a full day's teaching in front of her. She pulled up her chestnut hair on top of her head before assuming a model's pose, pouting and pursing her rouged lips until her eyes met the reflection of an amused David Henderson behind her.

'Pietronella said you were stuck and to come up with her to help.' He grinned, obviously slightly embarrassed at Grace's semi-naked state and finding himself in her bedroom. 'I thought you must be locked in the bathroom or something.'

'Oh, we're just playing dressing-up.' Grace laughed, feeling equally awkward.

'I popped round to bring Jonty's coat he left when he was with me the other day,' David said by way of explanation. 'Thought you might be wondering where it was. Gorgeous dress,' he added, smiling as he moved towards her. 'Is the zip stuck going up or coming down?'

'Can't actually *get* it up,' Grace tutted, breathing in the faint tang of David's aftershave as his hand reached behind her, leaving her, for some unfathomable reason, with a strange fluttery feeling in the pit of her stomach. What on earth was matter with her? His hand on her back was cool and, as he bent slightly, concentrating on the task, his face made contact with her naked skin and they both jumped slightly.

With one practised move, David pulled the zip and stood

to one side, catching her eye once more in the mirror, both seemingly unable to look away from the other.

'Thank you.' Grace dropped her eyes first, her face flushed.

'My pleasure.' David smiled.

The dress fitted perfectly.

Grace drove herself the ten miles or so out to the Coach and Horses at Upper Clawson, the October vista turning increasingly dark as the street lights petered out, her wheels spinning wetly on the moorland road once the drizzle turned to heavier rain. God, you wouldn't turn a dog out in this, Grace tutted to herself as she peered through the non-stop rivulets of rain which accompanied the metronome beating of time executed by the wipers against her windscreen. Part of her wished she was back at the house with Lilian, but then, she thought, if she was back at home Lilian wouldn't be babysitting.

Why on earth had she felt unsettled at David's hand on her bare back? This was David, for heaven's sake: her *almost* father-in-law; the children's grandfather. David Henderson, her mate; Mandy's husband. Mandy's widower, she corrected herself, before turning all her attention to crossing the dark moorland road where several hardy sheep were still, despite the dark and the rain, nonchalantly grazing at the kerbside grass, manoeuvring the car through the narrow entrance and into the pub carpark.

Grace didn't see him at first and for a few seconds wondered if he'd thought better of wanting to meet up with her. Maybe his wife, his mother-in-law, Cassie, Noah himself had got wind of his intention and advised him that meeting his son's teacher was just not cricket. Grace felt slightly embarrassed as she walked up to the bar, looking round for Ross Haddon who didn't appear to be waiting for her. She checked her watch. She'd deliberately arrived ten minutes late in order not to appear too eager and now regretted this little game-playing she'd instigated: he'd probably waited ten minutes and then assumed she wasn't coming and headed back home.

'Grace.' Just one word and, as she'd later tell Harriet, he had her at her name. He placed a hand on the sleeve of her trench coat. 'You're wet.' He smiled, holding her gaze until she felt herself grow warm and had to look away, because she didn't know what else to do. 'I've a table over here.'

He turned and led the way towards the very back of the pub restaurant where she could see he'd already laid claim to a table and where a novel and a pair of spectacles were sat with a half-drunk glass of white wine.

'I'm glad you came,' he said simply. 'What will you have to drink?'

'Just a small glass of wine please. I'm driving.'

'This is my limit too,' he said, holding up the glass while rubbing ruefully at his beard. Grace had never been one for beards – she couldn't bear big bushy lumberjack-type specimens – but Ross Haddon's was merely one step on from designer stubble and she realised it was one of the things that had attracted her to him in the first place.

In the end, Grace had opted for a short black skirt and long black over-the-knee suede boots with a simple cream cashmere polo-necked sweater and, as she sat down at the table, while Ross went off once more to the bar, she knew she'd made the right decision. She was curious to know what he was reading and moved the glass so she could see properly: *Great Expectations*. Well, she wasn't anticipating *that*, although, to be honest, she didn't know what she'd had him down for on the book front.

'So,' Grace said, half-jokingly, but with the lingering thought that quite possibly this was no laughing matter, 'Noah tells me you're a drug dealer?'

'Oh, did he tell you?'

'Sorry?' Grace felt her eyes widen as Ross placed a small glass of New Zealand Marlborough in front of her before sitting down opposite.

'Noah likes to shock people.' Ross gave an amused shake of his head.

'So, is it true?' Grace's eyes sought her coat which was hanging on the back of another chair. It was looking like she might need a quick getaway.

'Well, yes.'

'Yes? You're kidding me? I think I'd better leave right now...'

'I lead a research team at RTS.'

'RTS Pharmaceuticals?' Grace stared.

'That's the one.' Ross Haddon appeared slightly embarrassed.

'The largest drugs company in Europe?'

'In the world, I believe.' Ross gave a half smile. 'I'm involved in a joint project for the government at the moment, working with our opposite numbers in the States and Germany endeavouring to find a solution...'

'A solution?' Grace was fascinated.

'Oh, you know, a solution to the widespread abuse of

recreational drugs in society.' He stopped suddenly. 'Sorry, this is all a bit boring for you.'

'Boring? Gosh, no, I find it fascinating.'

'When you've been going round and round in circles for the best part of five years, flying off to yet *another* conference, meeting *more* governmental drug tsars but knowing, deep down, there *is* no solution, then there is a tendency to despondency.'

'So, you read to escape reality?' Grace picked up the Dickens.

'I tend to run ten miles or so to do that.' He began to laugh. 'Hence, Noah thinks it highly amusing to inform people I'm a drug *runner* as well.' He held up his Charles Dickens and went on, 'And thanks to audiobooks and modern technology, I now find I can combine the two. A twenty-mile run and I can listen to half a book...'

Ross trailed off as his eyes caught her own and, not knowing what to say, both he and Grace reached for their glass, jumping slightly as hand met hand.

'Look, Grace, the other night. You know, in Leeds...'

Grace felt her face flush. 'I'm really sorry,' she said stiffly. 'I don't *normally* behave like that. You know,' she stuttered, 'do that sort of thing with someone I've just met. If you must know, I'm totally and utterly embarrassed. I was very drunk.'

Ross reached for her hand, gently stroking the base of her thumb with his own and Grace had an almost unstoppable urge to reach up her own hand, just to feel his skin beneath her fingers.

Instead she sat back and said, 'So tell me what that was all about at school the other evening. You know, with your wife? Things are obviously not as they should be.'

Ross sighed and sat back and, for a moment, appeared unable to speak.

'You know, Grace, if you're in an abusive relationship, the last thing you want to do is actually admit to yourself that you are in such a relationship, never mind tell others that that's the case.'

'I'm sorry,' Grace said awkwardly. 'I shouldn't have brought it up.'

'I'm able to talk about it now.' Ross paused. 'Well, at least I think I am. But you know, there's a great sense of shame in knowing that, for a bloke like me – a six-foot, thirteen-stone bloke – he's unable to stand up for himself or has somehow failed in his role as a husband. As a father. You know,' he grimaced, lifting his hands to air-quote the next words, 'as a *man*.'

'Was it always the same?' Grace asked. 'I mean, from when you first met… I'm sorry, I can't remember your wife's name.'

'Natasha. No not at all. We actually met on a scuba-diving course. One of those ridiculous freezing cold dives you have to do in the middle of January in some godforsaken flooded quarry near Morecambe in order to pass your Padi open-water qualification.' Ross actually shivered and then laughed at the memory. 'Can you imagine?'

Grace couldn't.

'We hit it off straight away. One of those relationships where you know almost instantly they're the one for you.' Ross smiled and held Grace's eye. 'Do you know what I mean?'

Grace did.

'So, it came as a tremendous shock when, as we were

driving down the motorway – the M1 on the way to London – she said she really didn't want to stop off at Meadow Hall as we'd planned, and when I said I really needed to pick up a suit I'd ordered and it would only take five minutes, Natasha just launched.'

'What do you mean, *just launched*?' Grace frowned. 'Shouting at you? That must have been dangerous when you were in the fast lane? Mind you, I can understand her not wanting to go to Meadow Hell. Especially if it was a Saturday.' Grace knew she was twittering, attempting levity, which was ridiculous when it was obviously painful for Ross and he was taking her into his confidence.

'So, out of the blue Natasha started yelling, doing her best to belittle and humiliate me. At first, I started to laugh because I thought it was all some sort of act, a joke, you know because neither of us really wanted to go to an overheated, noisy shopping centre on a Saturday lunchtime.'

'Not very funny, I wouldn't have thought.' Grace was serious now and leaned forward as he continued.

'No, it wasn't. Especially when I was in the fast lane of the motorway and she starts thumping me.'

Grace stared. 'Thumping you? Oh, you poor thing. How utterly dreadful.'

Ross nodded. 'I stopped the car at the next service station, got out and bought us coffee. By the time I came back to the car, she'd calmed down,'

'I bet she felt silly.'

'She just said she was extremely stressed with the amount of modelling work coming in and the places she had to fly off to.'

'Sounds a wonderful life to me.' Grace smiled, thinking

of her badly behaved Y5 class and all the marking and other admin piling up back at home.

'It *was* a great life for Natasha. For both of us really because I sometimes managed to arrange it so that our overseas trips coincided. Usually to New York or Germany.'

'And were you married at this point?'

Ross nodded. 'Yes. We were actually married in New York just six months or so after we met. We moved down to London and then back to Leeds for my work. I'm originally from Manchester – well, Cheshire really but, I think I said, I was at university at Leeds – love the city – and it was easy to get the train or drive over to Manchester when I was in the office or fly out from Leeds or Manchester airports. I almost forgot about the little incident on the motorway – you know, didn't want to admit even to myself what had happened.'

'Until?' Grace could tell there was definitely an *until*.

'Almost straight away, once we were married, Natasha became convinced I was having affairs.'

'And were you?' Grace stared at Ross, casting her mind back uncomfortably to a few Saturday evenings ago in Leeds. Was this man a serial letch then, taking every chance possible to show harvest moons to unsuspecting women who'd had too much to drink and who should have known better at their age?

'Grace, believe it or not, you are the only other woman I've looked at since meeting Natasha eleven years ago.'

Bit more than *looked at*, Grace wanted to say but, instead, said, 'Why on earth would she think that then?'

Ross shrugged. 'I honestly don't know. She became possessive, wanting to know where I'd been and who with.

She tried to control how much money I was spending – she'd go through my cheque book – and once, just before we separated, rang me when I was in JB Sports, for heaven's sake, shouting and demanding to know why I'd just bought another pair of running shoes.'

Grace stared. 'But how did she know? Had she followed you?'

'Oh, she certainly did that on a few occasions,' Ross said, shaking his head as he remembered. 'But no, once we had Apple Pay, she constantly checked our joint account, knew immediately where I was and what I'd been buying.'

Grace exhaled deeply. 'You poor, poor thing. I couldn't have stood it. I hate anyone telling me what I can or cannot do, checking up on me, watching my every move. How did you stand it? Why did you stay?'

'Because, despite everything, I still loved her. Most of the time she was kind, generous, funny, the woman I'd first met and fallen in love with. And, because we had Noah between us. He wasn't actually planned, you see. Well, not on my part, anyway. I certainly didn't feel, a year after we married, that we were in a stable enough relationship to bring a child into it, so I kept putting off the "let's have a baby" chat. Unbeknown to me, Natasha took it upon herself to come off the pill and the next thing I knew, she was cooking a celebratory supper with champagne and candles as she had 'something wonderful' to tell me.

'Goodness,' said Grace. 'What did you say?'

'Do you know, at the time, as she sat there, all Madonna-like, already dressed in some floaty smock thing, I was absolutely thrilled. One does have an amazing capability to believe what one wants to believe and I *honestly* believed that this was a new beginning for us, and how she'd been in the past was just a blip and she'd overcome her temper and possessiveness.'

'And was it?' Grace remembered how she'd adored being pregnant with Jonty. How she'd found the pregnancy so easy, had loved getting big and cumbersome knowing there was going to be the baby she'd never thought she was able to have at the end of it all.

'Well, being pregnant suited her. Natasha even patched up the rift she'd had over the years with her mother, going to see her each week.'

'Noah's granny? The lady who picks him up from school?'

Ross nodded. 'Natasha fell out with her years ago. Blamed her, apparently, for leaving her father when Natasha was in her teens. All turns out he'd been physically abusive to Jill, my mother-in-law, all her married life, but Natasha adored him and when Jill finally managed to escape…'

'Escape?' Grace stared. 'The poor woman had to *escape*? From her home? Her family?'

'Grace,' Ross said patiently, 'until you've been in a toxic relationship yourself, you can have no idea how dreadful, how… how frighteningly *appalling* it can all get. When all you want to do is, yes, *escape*.'

'I'm sorry, I guess I'm being a bit naïve here. I suppose, because my parents have always loved each other – I mean, I know my mother nags my father until he just gets up and wanders off to the golf course, but they have a huge amount of respect for each other – and because I never ever felt afraid of my husband or Jonty's father…'

'Your husband isn't your son's father?'

'No.' Grace shook her head. 'Long story.'

'I'm sorry, I've only talked about myself.' Ross looked contrite.

'But that's why we're here, isn't it? To talk about you and Noah?'

'Actually, I invited you here to eat if you remember?' Ross smiled.

'I'm really not hungry,' Grace said. 'What I'd really like to do is have another glass of wine but one, when I'm driving, is my absolute limit.'

'Sensible.' Ross nodded.

Grace didn't respond to this but, instead, asked, 'What about when Natasha actually had the baby? How was she then?'

'Fine to begin with, but then the reality of being at home with a crying baby all day while I was often away, really sunk in.'

'You see, I can sympathise to some extent.' Grace found herself struggling to get the words out but, for some reason, felt she needed to tell this man everything. 'As I said, I loved being pregnant with Jonty, loved being a mum. But after a couple of weeks the most awful postnatal depression set in.' She looked up to see Ross watching her carefully as she spoke. 'I don't know why on earth I'm telling you all this. I think it was probably talking about drinking and driving. Anyway, with Jonty only a few months old, I drank far too much at a dinner party and then got in the car and drove. I was done for drink driving. I was suffering very badly from postnatal depression at the time. It was the worst time of my life; no one who's not experienced postnatal depression can ever know the absolute horror of it.' Grace paused.

'You don't think Natasha was going through something the same?'

'As far as I know, Natasha never experienced postnatal depression,' Ross said. 'I mean, I know it exists – my cousin's wife suffered terribly after their second child was born – but I honestly don't believe this was the problem here. Natasha just hated the fact that I was, as she called it, swanning off around the world, while she was at home with a tiny baby, totally convinced that every woman I met and worked with would lead potentially to an affair.' He paused. 'She once even sent an anonymous letter to my boss saying I was having an affair with my PA and that she should be warned I was a sexual predator.'

'No! Oh, my goodness. But why?' Grace reached out a hand to touch Ross's arm in a gesture of sympathy.

'Oh, Grace, I've read up so much on abusive, controlling relationships. Making false allegations against a partner, particularly to their place of work, is just another way of asserting control in an attempt to manipulate and isolate them.'

'And did you feel manipulated?' Grace asked, wanting suddenly to make it all better for him.

'I certainly felt isolated. You know, there's very little sympathy to be had for a bloke who appears to have everything – a happy home, a young child, a particularly attractive, intelligent and sociable wife…' He laughed shortly. 'Try telling the guys you play rugby with you daren't go home because you're frightened of a beating from your wife.'

'I can't imagine.' Grace frowned. 'I really can't. But why stay? Surely you wanted to get out of such an abusive relationship?'

'I had Noah.' Ross smiled. 'You know yourself what it's like when you adore your own child: there's no way you can just leave them. And, when things were fine, I still loved Tash. We actually had really good years together when Noah was a little boy. Part of me wondered if I'd imagined it all when the three of us were out having a great time doing things together, or we were on holiday or just at home laughing at some daft thing on TV. Natasha could go for weeks, months, without any sign of anger and then, suddenly, something would set her off.'

'Something?' Grace frowned. 'What like?'

'It was usually when something had gone wrong with one of her modelling jobs. Maybe one of the other girls had been assigned the outfit Natasha had particularly coveted or... or...' Ross shook his head at the memory. 'Or when the job she'd been promised actually ended up going to someone else. It's like something begins to fester in her mind that just gets bigger and bigger until she can't control herself and lashes out. I was always on tenterhooks waiting for the next accusation, the next angry outburst, the next thumping... Yes, Grace, my wife regularly thumped me... until twelve months ago when the arguments and physical abuse got so bad that the neighbours heard and called the police.' Ross pulled a face. 'There was a broken window, the argument spilled out into the garden as I tried to get out of there. The neighbours obviously assumed it was me that was the problem. I was arrested because Natasha said it was me, hurting her. I've *never*, Grace, not *once* hurt Natasha. Anyway, my mother-in-law, who was there at the time – as was, I'm terribly ashamed to say, Noah – was a witness in my defence and Natasha was charged and it all ended up in court.'

'You went along with it?'

'What do you mean, *went along with it*?' Ross frowned. 'You think I *encouraged* it?'

'No, no, I didn't mean that,' Grace interrupted hastily. 'What I'm asking is, you didn't try and stop the court hearing? You know, as a witness, not turn up?'

Ross didn't speak for a while. 'It was actually very tempting to do that,' he eventually said. 'You know, to not have all your dirty washing aired in public. Not have everyone at work, all your mates, know what's been going on.'

'But?'

'But when your ten-year-old has seen it all, when there's a broken kitchen window because your wife has thrown the kettle through it when she's aiming it at you, it suddenly hits you enough is enough. And, you know, even if I *had* tried to stop it all ending up in the magistrates' court and withdrawn the complaint, the police would still have charged her because they'd been called out, a child was in the house and they had a perfectly reliable witness in Jill, my mother-in-law. Domestic abuse, in all its many manifestations, is something that, these days, the police are legally bound to see through to some sort of conclusion. There's been a total and utter turnaround from, even twenty years ago, when the police would shrug and say, "Domestic, nothing to do with us, mate."'

'I'm not sure what to say, apart from I'm so sorry.' Grace shook her head. 'You've been through such a terrible time.'

Ross pulled a wry face. 'I'm fine. The physical scars have gone, and the mental scars are healing. My only concern now is Noah, obviously; you know, he's been through so much. There have been a string of nannies and au pairs who he's become really attached to and then become cross when they've left because we've moved or because Natasha became jealous of them; he misses his mum living with us – can't understand why she's not allowed near me – and he's had to start yet another new school. That's why I was so angry when I saw the bruise on his wrist, why I rang your head and demanded an explanation.'

'You don't still think *I* caused it, do you?' Grace stared. 'I'd hate it if you thought I could ever be capable of hurting a child. Hurting anyone…'

'No, no, absolutely not,' Ross said hurriedly. 'I'm totally embarrassed that I jumped in like that. And, obviously, totally worried that Noah made up such a story: I'm now convinced he got it playing football and made it all up to get back at you for not being Miss Harrison. I'm so sorry, Grace, I really am, that he told lies about you like that.'

'Oh, don't worry.' Grace shook her head. 'I've been accused of far worse things in my years as a teacher.'

'Have you?' Ross looked worried.

'Actually, no I haven't. I don't know why I said that. To make you feel better probably.' She stopped as Ross took her hand, listening intently to what she was saying.

'You know, Ross, I've never once had a one-night stand before—' Grace felt herself flush with embarrassment '—which to all intents and purposes was what the other Saturday night was.'

'Grace, I wanted it to be so much more.'

'You never asked my name. You never asked for my number.' It was only now, actually putting it into words, that Grace allowed herself to realise it was what she'd wanted all along. For Ross to want to see her again. She'd tried to convince herself, since it happened, that she was a newly-separated and, as such, a liberated woman and she had every *right* to have a one-off sexual fling in a garden in the centre of Leeds if that's what floated her boat at the time. Her argument, now, didn't seem to stack up, and it all seemed terribly sordid.

Ross didn't say anything for a while and eventually drained his glass. 'Christ, I could down a bottle,' he eventually said, running a hand through his long, dark hair. 'Grace,' he sighed, 'I didn't want you – didn't want anyone – dragged into this toxic part of my life. I was at the club because a mate of mine from uni was having a bit of a reunion. First time in a while I'd been out to socialise really – I don't like to leave Noah with Jill too often, not fair on either of them –and I wasn't drinking because I wanted to be able to drive straight home if there was a problem. I certainly wasn't on the lookout for a quick fumble in the dark.'

'I don't recall it being overly *quick*,' Grace said, immediately regretting it. What the hell was the matter with her?

'Grace, it was one of the most sensuous, unbelievably lovely…' He paused and looked at his watch, smiling at her embarrassment. '… Thirty minutes of my life, which I, for one certainly don't regret.'

'You're right about the alcohol.' Grace felt a sense of exhilaration start somewhere in the region of her toes, and wiggled them experimentally in her boots. 'Next time we have a conversation anything like this, can I have more than one small glass of wine inside me?'

Ross smiled and, reaching a hand to the back of her head, bent his mouth to hers, briefly kissing the corner of her mouth. 'And, after all I've told you, Grace,' he asked, 'will there *be* a next time?'

Grace nodded, unable to speak, and instead, reached up to kiss Ross right back.

## 22

'Blimey O'Reilly, the mortuary slab meets the Ibiza foam party,' Juno whooped before giving herself up totally to the administrations of Tracy, the four-foot-eleven bikini-clad masseuse with the bulging biceps of an Olympic bodybuilder. Who was it said most masseurs are people of few words but many pounds, Juno mused. Completely out of control, as her naked body was pummelled, washed and then spun every which way on the suds slopping off the marble slab, Juno managed, at one point, to glance across at Izzy who was undergoing the same treatment on the slab next to her.

'Izzy how are…?'

'Sh, shush,' Tracy admonished, pummelling Juno's backside as punishment. 'You'll ger all t'bloody soap in yer mouth.'

'Hell, I need to lose some weight,' Izzy tutted. 'She's just spun *you* round like something off *Strictly*, while poor old Ufuk here has had *me* bumping round like the glass plate in my microwave when it's gone off course.'

'For heaven's sake, Izzy…' Juno's eyes snapped open at the F-word. Since being accused by her ex-husband, Fraser, of being too fond of profanity (unlike the saintly Laura

238

McAskill who had replaced herself both in Fraser's bed and in his new life in Boston) Juno had found herself somewhat overly sensitive to its utterance in her hearing.

'Don't worry, love,' Tracy said, massaging the soles of Juno's bare feet until she wanted to titter and pull them away. 'It's 'is name. We've all 'ad to get used to it 'ere.'

'Ufuk is very good Turkish name for both men and women.' Ufuk smiled politely, while concentrating on Izzy's legs.

Goodness, Juno thought, he must have taken some stick over his name from the other students at Midhope University where, apparently, he was studying English Literature.

'It's actually a unisex name, derived from the Arabic word meaning *horizon*,' Ufuk went on. 'There are lots of Ufuks in Turkey: Ufuk Bayraktar, the actor and, of course, Ufuk Ceylan, the footballer.'

'Of course,' Izzy murmured sagely as, with the aid of copious amounts of suds, Ufuk finally managed to spin her naked body in one smooth, continuous one-hundred-and-eighty-degree turn.

'Esme thought it better I call myself Marcus or Nigel while I'm working in her new Blush and Blow, but I say I'm sorry, I have no intention of adopting one of your ridiculous English names just to pander to the sensibilities of your customers.'

'Too right, er, *Ufuk*.' Juno practised saying his name. 'You speak excellent English, *Ufuk*.' Once she'd said the name out loud a couple of times, Juno realised it didn't sound quite as vulgar as she'd anticipated. Suck *that* up, Fraser Armstrong, you moron, she thought comfortably, relaxing once more into Tracy's accomplished hands.

'He speaks much better than me.' Tracy grinned. 'Am gonna ger him to teach me proper,' she added as her thick fingers probed and prodded deliciously into Juno's shoulders.

It didn't take Juno long to realise that trying to make conversation while being pummelled resulted not only in a mouthful of foamy soap but a retributory slap on the buttocks from Tracy. So, instead, she found herself relaxing into a lovely little dream about what she might wear for her celebratory birthday dinner at Clementine's Scott had booked for them that evening, but was rudely brought back to the present when Tracy's hands were replaced by sandpaper.

'F… or heaven's sake,' Juno corrected herself at the last minute, her eyes snapping open once more.

Izzy obviously harboured no similar sensibilities with regards her own reaction to the next step in the Hamman process. 'Fuck, Ufuk!' she yelled, trying to escape the scrubber in his hand. 'Are you trying to take my entire skin off? I scrub my kitchen floor more gently than that.'

'Since when have you started scrubbing your… your… kitchen floor?' Juno managed to elicit as Tracy moved in for the kill. 'Holy moly, Tracy, are you on a mission or what?'

'No pain, no gain, lady.' Tracy grinned. 'You want to see the dirt that's come off you?' 'That gorgeous doctor of yours won't be able to keep his hands off your silky, smooth body tonight.'

'How do *you* know about Scott? And me?' Juno asked, slightly put out.

Tracy poured more suds over Juno, washing away the debris resulting from the intense scrubbing, before answering. ''E was 'ere yesterday, love. That's one 'ot man you've got yourself there, lady.'

Juno didn't know which she hated the most – being called *lady*, the fact that Tracy had seen, and had her hands on, Scott's naked body, or the masseuse knowing her business.

'Hot?' Izzy cackled, before erupting into more profanity as Ufuk threw a bucketful of freezing water over her to clear the final soapsuds. 'I suppose that's our Antipodean doctor for you; the surgery has never been so busy since Dr Butler arrived. Mind you,' she sniffed, sitting up and wiping cold water from her eyes, 'don't know what all the fuss is about myself. Now, if you're looking at gorgeous men in the village, there's only one.'

'Declan?' Juno asked.

'Declan?' Izzy snorted as she wrapped the proffered bathrobe around herself. 'Don't be daft. He's my *husband*, not the object of my *fantasies*.'

'Ooh, I bet *I* know who you mean.' Tracy's eyes gleamed as she headed for the changing room. 'That gorgeous David 'Enderson bloke? I had to actually fight Ufuk for who was going to get their hands on *him* yesterday.' She gave her colleague a knowing look before winking lasciviously at Juno and Izzy. 'Esme's got her sights firmly set on *him* too. I wouldn't have put it past her to strip off and start massaging the lovely Mr 'Enderson herself yesterday.'

'There's no *way* Esme would have come in here and ruined her hair and makeup in front of David Henderson.' Juno frowned, catching sight of her own scrubbed red face and hair, now a mass of blonde corkscrew curls, in the steamed-up mirror.

'But she must be twenty years old than David.' Izzy

frowned. 'What would a man in his forties want with a… a *pensioner* like Esme?'

'Ooh, meow.' Tracy grinned. 'Sixty's the new forty, you know. And you have to admit, Dr Izzy, Esme looks good for her age.' She glanced slyly across at Juno who was in the process of tying herself into her own robe. 'It didn't stop your Scott doing the deed, did it, Dr Juno? You know with Esme, twenty years ago? She must have been a real looker in those days.'

For heaven's sake, did Tracy know everything? Juno was beginning to feel distinctly uncomfortable with the way the conversation was going.

'So, did you two know David's wife?' Tracy went on. 'What was she like?'

'I knew her quite well actually. *Very* gorgeous,' Izzy said firmly. 'The most stylish, attractive woman you'll probably ever come across.' She paused. 'Well, in Westenbury, anyway. There *may* be a vacancy in the village, but I can't see it ever being filled. OK, lead me to a couch, some Turkish delight and a glass of something lovely now, please. I reckon I deserve it.'


Trussed up like a Christmas turkey in a startlingly white bathrobe and turban, Juno found herself tucked, pupa-like, into a huge chair with a plethora of even more eye-stoppingly brilliant white towels, and a glass of hot, sweet Turkish tea at her side.

'Not PG Tips this, is it?' Izzy whispered and then, to Ufuk's departing back, called, 'I think you've forgotten the milk.'

'Don't be such a pleb,' Juno tutted, laying back in her cloud of white and sighing contentedly. 'That was so good. I've never felt so clean in all my life. We must be pretty dirty creatures, we human beings.'

'Speak for yourself,' Izzy sniffed, pulling a face at the tea in her hand. 'And why a glass? Glasses are for *gin*, not hot tea. I like my tea in a mug. With milk.' She gazed around at the tasteful neutral decorations of this holding room, stroking and sniffing at the brand-new leather beneath her nest of towels. 'This must have all cost a bob or two,' Izzy lowered her voice. 'Where's she got all her money from, do you reckon?'

'Who?'

'You know, the merry widow.'

'I've no idea, Izzy. Does it matter?' Juno closed her eyes once more, revelling in the unusual and delightful situation of having absolutely nothing to do except lie back and relax. She could sense Izzy mentally hovering and gave in. 'Her husband died last year – that's when she told Maya the truth about Scott being her real father – and I gather she inherited some life insurance or something. Although, when she was over for lunch the other day, I got the impression she's a bit of a businesswoman, always on the lookout for something new to invest in. I think she's on to a winner with this place. Maya was saying she's booked up for months ahead – even thinking of expanding into the fish and chip shop next door if she can buy them out. She's wanting to do alternative therapies as well as the Hamman and beauty.'

'I hope *not*,' Izzy said, sitting up indignantly. 'It's one of the few pleasures I have left in life. I look forward to a bag of chips on Monday evenings after my alcohol clinic. It used to be a big gin and tonic to celebrate I'd got Monday over and done with, and it was all downhill to the weekend, but it seems a bit hypocritical now, after telling all the alkies to cut back on the booze, to then go home and pour the gin. Chips are almost as good an *alternative* therapy to gin.' Izzy clutched ruefully at her flesh beneath the towels. 'Well, perhaps not.'

'I'm not sure *alkies* is overly appropriate, Izzy,' Juno murmured.

'Neither is turning the chippy into a place for Qigong or Bowen Technique.' Izzy sighed heavily at the very idea. 'Even Declan has gone a bit, you know, alternative.'

'Oh?'

'Given up his occasional fag for vaping.'

'I noticed.' Juno nodded sleepily.

'Tshh,' Izzy snorted crossly. 'Aromatherapy for the lungs. It's like kissing a bowl of pot-pourri now.'

'Better than an old ashtray, surely?'

'It's what you get used to. So,' Izzy went on, '*you're* obviously getting, you know, used to it.'

Giving up all pretence of drifting off, Juno sat up. 'Used to what, exactly?'

'You know, with Scott. You really are quite an item now, aren't you?'

Juno smiled. 'I hope so. Do you know, Izzy, I don't think I've ever been as happy as I am at this moment? Poor old Tilda's still not enjoying school but, apart from that, there don't seem to be any great problems on the horizon.'

'And Gabriel's enjoying having a father figure around?'

'Hmm. Gabe doesn't say much, he never did – he's his father's son – but he and Scott are often out in the garden having a kick-about. And Gabe's asking about maybe going over to the States to see his father at Christmas.'

'Really?' Izzy looked doubtful.

'Yes. I'd obviously miss him. You know, it would be the first time I'd not have him at home for his Christmas dinner. I'd find that strange of course, but there you go, I'm always trying to get him to grow up a bit, you know become a bit more independent. It would do him good. And yes, I'm even enjoying having my dad living in the village again. When I was a kid, there was *always* Mum to worry about when Dad was off again, sniffing round his students. I think that's why I married Fraser: I wanted a happy, secure family of my own.'

'I thought you married Fraser because you were pregnant?'

'Well yes, that as well, obviously…'

'And he ended up going off to the States with the mad scientist woman.'

Juno tutted. 'Alright, alright, you don't need to remind me of all this. 'Yes, that's what I'm saying: I'm so happy now with Scott. I think, well I *know*, I love him. There, I've said it for the first time out loud. I *love* Dr Scott Butler. And he loves me.'


Almost three hours later, Juno finally left Blush and Blow, her hair straightened and coiffed to within an inch of its life and her usually short, sensible nails now red talons thanks to Esme's skills with gel. Wincing, both at the final cost as well as at the eye-watering thought of any rectal examination she might have to perform in the surgery on the following Monday morning, Juno made the decision to totally blow her bank account and head into Midhope town centre in the hope of finding a flirty little number to accompany her new hair and nails.

She was so looking forward to an evening totally alone with Scott. She'd only ever been to Clementine's on two previous occasions and had absolutely adored the food and ambiance there. With Scott sitting across the table from her, and a glass – alright, a bottle – of champagne on hand to celebrate her birthday, she reckoned she'd be in heaven. How long had she and Scott officially been together now? She'd fancied him like mad almost from the first day he'd arrived as locum at Westenbury surgery – let's face it, who wouldn't? – and that was at the start of the new year. So, here they were now, in November, and they were a definite item, with Scott spending probably the same number of nights in her bed as his own in the house he was renting in Rushdale Avenue. Juno mentally counted the months as she drove the twenty-five minutes' journey into Midhope town centre: seven or eight once they'd got together and she and Fraser had agreed to divorce.

Juno spotted the dress at once. A simple black shift that, she persuaded herself after coming up for air once she'd found the price ticket, could even be worn for work when she'd worn it to death for going out in. With Scott at the surgery, she'd eschewed her old down-at-heel flatties and greying mismatched underwear as well as thrown out a whole load of sweaters and skirts that should have bitten the dust years ago. One never knew, she smiled to herself as the assistant handed over the stiff carrier crackling with tissue and promise, just when Scott might suddenly appear in her practice room on the pretext of handing her a file only to feel a cool, practised hand under the back of her sweater or stroking her neck. She shivered deliciously at the thought and headed for the carpark and home.

'You look lovely, Mum.' Tilda looked up from her *Teach Yourself Russian* library book, swallowed what she'd been chewing and, squinting over her newly acquired reading spectacles, gazed properly as Juno came into the kitchen executing a little twirl. Still dressed in her horse-mucking-out clothes, Tilda turned back to the kitchen table, continuing to devour the towering pile of toast and Marmite as if her life depended on it.

'Is Harry Trotter safely away for the night?' Juno asked, admiring her new long red nails as she went to empty the dishwasher.

'Hmm.'

'And the chicks locked up?'

Tilda nodded. 'We should be able to let them wander round the garden in a couple of days without worrying that they'll fly off.'

'And you'll be alright?'

'Hmm.'

'Grandpa should be here to babysit soon.'

'Babysit?' Tilda scoffed. 'Patrick and I are going to converse in Latin.'

'Do you not think you should call him *Grandpa*?'

'Nope,' Tilda said firmly. 'He's not really *been* a grandfather these past twelve years, has he? I don't think either of us are going to pretend otherwise. It was he who suggested I call him Patrick rather than *Grandpa*: he says *Grandpa* makes him feel old.'

'Well, he is getting on, you know.' Juno smiled. 'He had his seventy-second birthday in June.'

'Where's Gabe?' Tilda shoved another mouthful of toast in her mouth without waiting for an answer.

'Over at Ethan's. His mum's going to drop him back later, so listen out for him.' Juno frowned. 'Oh, and remind him he's got that maths homework to do again.'

'I did it for him,' Tilda said nonchalantly.

'Tilda!' Juno turned as she removed the last of the cutlery from the dishwasher. 'You can't do that.'

'Yes, I can. Honestly, I *can*. It was dead easy. Gabe finds quadratic equations hard.'

'How on earth do *you* know how to do quadratic equations at twelve?'

'I asked Aunt Ariadne and she showed me. I knew *you* wouldn't approve.'

'Wouldn't approve? Oh, for heaven's sake, Tilda, I...' Juno frowned and broke off when she heard the front door open and voices filtering down the hall as both Scott and Patrick arrived together. 'Look, Tilda, you are *not* to do Gabe's homework even if he promises to pay you. I'm going to have to go. Hello, Dad, we're off. Watch *Strictly* or something daft on TV, will you, rather than teaching her Latin?'

'Happy Birthday, Juno.' Scott smiled that heart-stopping smile of his, placing a beautifully wrapped and beribboned box in front of Juno as one of Clementine's waiters, dressed in the livery of black T-shirt and orange apron, attempted to open the bottle of Dom Perignon Scott had asked to be brought to their table.

'Oh, Scott.' He was looking at her with such love in his eyes, Juno felt herself flush.

'Well open it then. Go on.' He was laughing at her. 'You look absolutely gorgeous tonight, Juno... You alright, mate?' Scott glanced at the waiter who didn't appear much older than Gabe, Juno mused, and who appeared to be struggling with releasing the wire cage surrounding the bottle's cork. 'Shall I try?' he asked kindly.

That's what Juno loved so much about Scott: his ability to muck in and help, regardless. Fraser, her ex-husband would, she knew, have just sat there pompously waiting for the poor kid to serve him his drink. Not that Fraser would ever have ordered anything so ridiculously expensive as the champagne. Had he ever even *remembered* her birthday? There'd once been, she recalled, a somewhat crumpled box of Milk Tray left on her pillow in the early years of their marriage, but her hopes of something rather more exciting hidden among the strawberry and orange creams were dashed as she encountered nothing more thrilling than squashed, sickly milk chocolate.

The waiter tried once more, obviously embarrassed at his fingers' inability to twist the wire and, as Juno looked from the bottle to the kid's face, she saw a thin film of sweat appear on his pale forehead, and his breathing begin to accelerate at his exertion.

'It's OK.' She smiled. 'Is this your first time? I bet I'd be the same. Don't worry...' Juno trailed off as she saw the waiter's pupils were hugely enlarged in his white face. 'I don't think you're very well, sweetheart.'

The boy placed the unopened bottle onto the table, wiping his face with the clean black tea towel all Clementine's waiters carried neatly folded in the back waistband of their apron. 'It's fine, it's fine, I can do it,' he muttered anxiously, wiping at his face once more before reaching for the bottle again.

'Kyle, go and sit down in the restroom.' David Henderson appeared at their table and opened the bottle of champagne in one fluid movement, expertly pouring two glasses of the foaming liquid. 'Sorry about that,' David said with a smile. 'I hope that's not spoiled your celebration? I hear it's your birthday, Dr Armstrong?'

'I always forget you're a partner in the restaurant, David.' Juno smiled back thinking, as she always did whenever she saw David Henderson, what a beautiful face and what kind eyes the man had. 'Have you met Scott? Dr Scott Butler?'

'I don't call in here too often these days,' David said. 'Clem is more than able to get on with it herself. I suppose I'm what's called a sleeping partner.' He grinned at the thought. 'I just wanted to check something with Clem and saw Kyle struggling.' David held out his hand to Scott. 'No, I don't think we've met. Nice to meet you. I did see your performance in *Superstar* in the spring. And Declan tells me you're a golfer?'

'For my sins.'

'Well, I'm always looking for someone who fancies a round—' David broke off, looking up in surprise as a small, rather fat little man almost ran up to their table, hand outstretched.

'David, I'm *so* glad I've found you here. I had an appointment in Leeds this afternoon and decided to come over to Midhope in the hope of finding you so I could tell you in person how very, very sorry I was to hear of Mandy's accident.'

Something wasn't right here, Juno thought in some confusion. The man, effusive in his sympathy, was totally ignoring David who was still standing beside them at their table. Instead, he had taken Scott's hand and was pressing it between his own chubby fingers while Scott, his face drained of all colour to an almost deathly white, appeared unable to speak.

## 23

After the evening spent with him up at the pub at Upper Clawson, Grace knew she wanted to see more and more of Ross Haddon. It was very, very strange, she acknowledged both to herself and to Harriet – who was always eager for gossip – spending time with Ross of an evening and then having his son in front of her in the classroom the very next morning. She couldn't imagine what Noah's reaction would be if he were to find out she'd been out on several dates with his father and Ross, she knew, was certainly not letting him in on the secret.

It was a *hell* of a secret really. Grace wasn't sure what Cassie would say either if she knew one of her teachers was seeing – secretly – the father of one of the children in her own class. It wouldn't have been so bad, Grace thought, if Noah was in a different class, lower down the school maybe, but there he was, every morning, lounging at his table, very often confrontational if not downright rude. He'd inherited Ross's beautiful green eyes, but whereas Ross's were kind and loving, Noah's would often flash with anger as he stared at her with dislike, distaste even, when she had to take him to task and even, on a couple of occasions, when he was really kicking off, escorting him from the classroom. And then, out of the blue, Grace would be reading a humorous poem or short story to the class, and Noah would be in thrall and, letting down his guard, laugh loudly and with delight. Or, on the occasion when she'd got to the bit where Bess, the landlord's beautiful daughter, in Noyes' *The Highwayman*, manages to shoot herself in order to warn her lover of the Redcoats' presence, she'd glanced up at Noah and tears were actually rolling down his cheeks. He'd rubbed them away of course, said the poem was absolute rubbish and Bess, if she'd had any sense, would have shot the redcoats fuzz themselves rather than *herself*, but Grace had seen a very different side to Noah Haddon and, teacher that she was, she felt encouraged. Exultant almost.

The previous Friday, Seb had called her during her school lunch break to say he'd been able to take an earlier flight than expected from his meeting in Milan and would it be OK if he picked up Jonty at three-thirty and took him for a pizza? Would Pietronella like to come with them too? Do one-legged ducks swim in a circle? Pietronella was *always* up for socialising, particularly if it involved Seb, who she adored, and a stuffed-crust pizza. It was not always easy trying to explain to her daughter why Jonty appeared to be in line for all the treats with his 'other daddy' (his only daddy now, Grace thought, ruefully) while she, Pietronella, was left at home with Grace.

Realising she had a couple of hours to herself, and having overheard the boys in the class excitedly discussing Jasper Middleton's Laser Quest birthday party to which all the lads were invited straight from school (good luck with *that*, Mrs Middleton) Grace, on impulse, had texted Ross. He'd rung her straight back. Why didn't she drive over to meet him at a hotel he knew near Holmfirth that did the most wonderful afternoon-tea?

'Afternoon-tea?' Grace had laughed. 'I won't be able to get there until after five.' (*And I've got my school flatties on and a shirt covered in glue and paint.*)

'That's fine. They serve it until six.'

'I've got a bit of a thing about afternoon tea,' Ross had explained, almost apologetically, once she was sitting opposite him. 'It's my dirty little secret – I've been known to call in and indulge all by myself if no one will come with me. Must be the egg and cress finger sandwiches.'

There was a bad moment when the smiling little Italian waiter had produced a starched white napkin, snapping it theatrically onto her school skirt like a magician, with 'Ah, *Mrs* Haddon, I can't mistake you and your so beautiful hair (he obviously could). Mr Haddon has persuaded you to come back with him again? *Molto bene, molto bene.*'

'Sorry about that,' Ross had said, obviously embarrassed, once the waiter had stopped fussing and left them alone with their glass of champagne and a stand of various sandwiches, scones and cakes. 'Natasha did come here with me once, more than a year ago now when we'd first discovered this place when we were over at her mother's for the weekend. But she wouldn't indulge in anything except the champagne. Too many carbs apparently.'

'It's fine, Ross, really.' Grace had stroked his arm. 'And *I'm* more than happy to indulge in *everything*.' She'd reached over and helped herself to a cucumber sandwich before blushing furiously. *Oh hell, what a stupid thing to say.*

Ross had looked at her with those wonderful green eyes

of his and held up his glass of champagne before indicating the pot of tea steaming fragrantly to his right. 'Here's to *everything*.' He'd smiled. 'Shall I be mother?'

A week after the afternoon-tea outing (which had been just that: tea and chat, mainly about Ross's work – which Grace found fascinating – Noah and literature) Grace concentrated on not spoiling both her newly applied makeup or the garment itself, as she carefully pulled on the rather lovely cream fine-wool sweater dress she'd been saving for a special occasion, admiring the way it clung to her curves in all the right places and imagining Ross's hands on her body. She completed the look with a pair of sheer holdups, tan suede heels and by cinching in her waist with a matching suede belt.

David had picked up both Jonty and Pietronella straight from school and was taking them out for tea to their usual family-friendly Italian down in Midhope before taking them home to sleep in the bedrooms her kids had commandeered when Mandy was alive. It had once been a fairly regular thing, especially when she and Dan had been splitting up once again, for Mandy to whisk the pair of them off for a sleepover; any tiny sliver of resentment Grace might just occasionally harbour at Mandy's peremptory demand that she take her grandchildren home with her for the night, was soon countered by the chance to recover her sense of self as she soaked in a bath with a particularly large and delicious gin and tonic.

David, it seemed, had deemed it his duty to carry on the tradition of the occasional picking up the children from school and for that, particularly tonight, Grace could be nothing but grateful.

There, she was dressed and ready and, although she shouldn't be the one to say it, was looking good. More than good. It was, Grace admitted to her reflection, as she saw her pupils overly large and dark and her cheeks slightly flushed, the anticipation of seeing Ross again that evening.

He was late. He'd been held up at work, and then in an accident that had closed the M62 to the late Friday evening traffic from Manchester. Once back in Westenbury, he explained, Noah hadn't been happy that he was going out again and had had a mighty sulk at having to stay on with Granny rather than being taken home as expected. It was going up to ten o'clock before she was with him in the Friday-evening-crowded bar in the middle of town.

'Gosh I've not been down into a town centre pub for years,' Grace managed to say as they pushed their way through to the bar area where a mass of humanity was jostling for service. Bank cards and Apple Pay, rather than the desperately waved fivers she remembered from when she and Harriet used to come into town were, it appeared, de rigueur.

'You won't get much for a fiver these days.' Ross smiled, handing her a huge fishbowl of white wine and replacing his phone in his jacket pocket.

'Do I drink this or do backstroke in it?' Grace asked as they simultaneously spotted a table about to be vacated and headed directly for it.

Ross grinned back at her, taking her hand but saying

nothing until they were seated. 'Grace, you look absolutely gorgeous tonight. That dress suits you.' He reached a hand, stroking her arm through the soft, cream woollen fabric. 'It goes with your hair.'

'Thank you.' It had been such a long time since anyone had paid her a compliment, had told her she was looking good, that Grace didn't quite know how to reply. How silly, she thought, to have forgotten how to react to a man's obvious pleasure in both her company and her appearance. 'I'm not used to compliments,' she added.

'Aren't you? Why?' Ross looked almost taken aback and Grace actually laughed at his expression.

'Being a single mum with two kids under five, and teaching every day, doesn't give me much time for myself,' she said. 'I can't remember the last time I had my hair cut.'

'Don't.'

'Don't what?' Grace smiled at his intense expression.

Ross leaned over and took a lock of her chestnut hair, winding it round and slowly, almost languorously, pulling it through his fingers. 'Cut your hair. Don't. It's far too beautiful to end up on the barber's floor.' He brought a lock of her hair to his face, almost burying his nose into it and, embarrassed, Grace laughed and pulled away, reaching for her wine and taking a too-large glug of wine that made her cough.

'What would you like to do this evening?'

'I thought we were doing it?'

'It's not too crowded and noisy in here for you?'

'Not at all. It reminds me of my youth.' Grace glanced around at the kids – mainly students from Midhope University – and felt a sudden pang for lost opportunity, for all the things she'd wanted to do and never achieved. Was she too old, now, to travel overland to Kathmandu? To go and work on a Kibbutz? To have a career change? To work in London or Paris as she'd always fancied doing until she met Dan and they'd both ended up staying in the town in which they'd both grown up? She hadn't, Grace knew, done half the stuff she'd promised her sixteen-year-old self she just *had* to have achieved by the time she would be past it at forty. At sixteen, one never thinks one will ever get to forty; it's years into the future. Too far ahead to even contemplate, really. And yet, here she was, at forty-two and her sixteen-year-old self couldn't quite believe it.

'You OK?' Ross was stroking her stockinged leg in a way that not only brought her back to the present, but reiterated the thought that, if her body had the ability to react as it was doing now, at this man's slightest touch to her leg, then, surely, she'd achieved something?

'I'm absolutely fine.' She smiled up at Ross and, as she leaned forward, putting her mouth to his face above the black stubble of his beard, the sixteen-year-old Grace winked in her direction and slid back into the past where she belonged. Blimey, Grace conceded, this wine must be stronger than she thought if not only was she having a conversation with her younger self but was openly kissing this beautiful man in public. He smelled of an unknown, but deliciously spicy aftershave and tasted of wine and something minty. Grace felt her insides do a sudden backflip as Ross reached a hand to her hair once more (what was it about Ross and her hair?) pulling her closer to him and teasing the corner of her mouth with his own. She really should have eaten something before she left home, she thought dizzily, no longer caring that she was a forty-something teacher, an upstanding member of the community with two kids but was, nevertheless, openly snogging some man in a crowded pub in the centre of town.

'Get a room, Aunty Grace.'

Grace sat back in her seat as though she'd been shot. 'Kit? Ah, Kit, what are *you* doing here?' Grace ran a hand through her hair and plastered a sober aunty smile (rather than the wanton floozy version he'd obviously already caught sight of) beatifically on her face.

'What am *I* doing here?' Kit grinned down at her from his six-foot height. 'This is where I always hang out; my local, I suppose you could call it. Wouldn't have thought *you'd* ever be seen in this den of iniquity, Aunty Grace.'

(Den of Iniquity? Grace thought tipsily. She must remember to tell Hat that Kit had apparently grasped the notion of imagery – or, was it cliché? – in his English Language lessons at that rugger-bugger, all boys, fee-paying school in the next town where his father had persuaded Harriet to send him when he was eleven.) 'Just having a quiet drink, Kit, with my friend Ross here.' She knew she was twittering, her words too high-pitched and, actively lowering her tone of voice, turned to Ross and said, with an exaggerated calm she didn't really feel, 'Ross, my friend Harriet's son, Kit Westmoreland. Kit this is Ross Haddon.'

The two men (goodness, when had that recalcitrant boy, Kit, become a man?) shook hands but, apart from the brief touching of his hand and a slight nod of acknowledgment in Kit's direction, Ross said nothing.

'Do you want to join us?' Grace finally asked in some

desperation when none of them appeared to know what to say next.

'No, no,' Kit replied heartily, himself now, it appeared, somewhat embarrassed at finding his mum's best friend – his Aunty Grace – in flagrante. 'You get back to what you were doing.'

Grace, her sense of humour coming to the fore (she was already exaggerating the story to tell to Harriet as soon as she could) actually laughed out loud at that, patting Kit's hand as she did so. 'Come on, come and have a drink with your Aunty Grace.'

'No, no, it's fine,' Kit repeated. 'I'm with a friend over there.'

Grace glanced towards the bar where a very beautiful (could there ever be any other where Kit was concerned?) dark-haired girl stood waiting for Kit's return. 'Hmm, not Miss O'Connor then?'

'Miss O'Connor?' Kit frowned momentarily. 'Oh Niamh? No, Aunty Grace, not Miss O'Connor's turn this evening, I'm afraid. She's called Maya and I need to get back to her or she's so gorgeous someone is bound to run off with her.' He grinned, showing perfectly white straight teeth which seemed to Grace very unfair considering the cache of forbidden sweets she knew he'd eaten as a child, but, she supposed, at the same time justified the hours Harriet had invested in nagging her elder son to actually look after said gnashers.

'You are incorrigible, Kit Westmoreland.' Grace grinned back.

'If I knew what it meant, I could perhaps agree with you,' he laughed. 'Nice to meet you, Ross. Enjoy the rest of your evening.'

Once he'd gone, Grace turned back to Ross, a smile still on her face. 'I love that boy,' she said.

'Yes, I can see that.' Ross appeared unamused.

'What's the matter?' Grace stared.

'Oh nothing. I'm being silly.' He took her hand but there was no warmth in the gesture.

'Come on, what is it?'

'I just hate being the centre of attention, hate anyone knowing my business.'

'Centre of attention?' Grace laughed. 'Kit came over to speak to me, not you. I don't think anyone here is taking any notice whatsoever of us, unless to think we're a bit old for this joint.' She laughed again, trying to jolly Ross out of his introspection.

'You know,' Ross still sounded cross, as if it were Grace's fault they were in this place he'd chosen, 'I'm here with you: my son's *teacher*.'

'And is that a problem?' When Ross continued to brood, Grace went on, 'Well, I'm *sorry*, but if you choose the busiest, most crowded pub in the very centre of town, you can't seriously be in pursuit of anonymity, can you? And what business are you talking about that makes you an object of such interest anyway?'

'I just assumed that in a student and young kids' dive like this, there would have been a bit more chance of achieving some sense of anonymity than anywhere else—'

'Should I have put a paper bag over my head?' Grace almost laughed.

'—and I didn't for one-minute assume you would actually be *acquainted* with anyone in here.' The cold manner in which he almost spat the word left Grace in no doubt as to his incredibly swift change of mood.

'Well,' she said, trying to lighten the atmosphere, 'you know what assume always does.'

'Sorry?' Ross snapped.

'Assume? Makes an ass out of you and me?'

'Really?' Ross glared in Grace's direction, and for a split-second she saw the same look of anger that had come her way at school in Cassie's study when he'd accused her of hurting Noah.

'I've obviously spoiled the evening,' Grace said stiffly, reaching for her coat. 'I'll get a taxi.'

'Oh God, Grace, I'm so sorry. Forgive me? I've had a stressful couple of days at work.' Ross took Grace's hand, stopping her from putting on her coat. 'Which I know is absolutely no excuse. God, I'm behaving like a pompous idiot. Please don't go. I can't tell you how much I've been looking forward all week to seeing you again.'

Grace hesitated, upset by his previously sharp words. Ross was looking up at her as she reached for her coat once more, his eyes so full of remorse she immediately capitulated. 'Why don't we both go? We do appear to be a couple of fish out of water in this place.' She raised her voice as the live band that had been warming up at the far end of the pub suddenly broke into their first session. 'It's a beautiful evening. Let's walk and get a taxi back. We can have a drink at home.'

Ross immediately stood, reaching for his own coat and scarf. 'Are you sure?' he asked. 'I really was behaving like a pillock.'

'Yes, you were actually, but I forgive you. I know how

worry and stress at work can make one react.' Grace reached up to kiss his cheek.

'Just give me a second while I check my phone. Just need to see if Noah has been in touch.'

Grace walked towards the entrance, eager to be out of the pulsating racket from the band that was now reverberating and bouncing off every wall as the first number reached its climax. She was getting old. She smiled to herself, before glancing at the very pretty girl – Maya – who was once more standing alone at the bar. Where was Kit?

She didn't have long to wonder. Grace pulled the heavy pub door towards her and immediately spotted him, laughing and talking to a group of similar-aged young men in one corner of the carpark. As she watched, one of the men, black hoody pulled up over his head, passed Kit something and Kit, grinning and totally unaware of Grace's scrutiny, patted his shoulder. 'Thanks, mate,' Kit said, loud enough for her to hear. 'I *need* this.' He slipped whatever it was into his jeans' back pocket and she watched him as he headed off into the night towards the black Audi she could see parked two streets away.

Ross caught up with her at the front of the pub and, taking her gloved hand and putting it into his navy overcoat pocket with his own, set off in the direction of the quieter part of town.

'Shall I ring for an Uber?' Grace asked, stopping to reach for the bag on her shoulder.

'Let's just walk,' he said. 'I need some quiet after the noise and crowd in that pub.'

'Didn't you realise what it was going to be like?' Grace asked. 'I could have told you it would be noisy and crowded.'

'You have to remember Noah and I have only been in the area three months. If that. I really don't know Midhope town centre and its pubs at all.' Ross walked quickly, seeming distracted, almost as if he were looking for something.

'Not the most salubrious of areas,' Grace said, shivering in the frosty November night air. 'If you don't know the town centre, I can give you a guided tour; you know show you the bus station, the train station, Sainsbury's, the red light area down on Emerald Street…' She broke off, laughing at the very thought that Ross might actually take her up on her offer.

Ross turned suddenly and they walked down the cobbled avenue Grace remembered as being the one which, when she was a schoolgirl, had the school uniform shop. It was here her mother brought herself and her brother, Simon, at the end of the six weeks' summer holiday to be re-kitted out with the Midhope Grammar School uniform for herself and the King William Grammar School uniform for Simon. How she'd hated that place: the rows of folded polyester aertex, the smell of new leather satchels and the too-long skirts her mother insisted they bought and which, Grace knew, would be rolled up as high as was physically possible once she was on the school bus with Harriet.

'Golly, I've not been down here for years,' Grace said almost to herself. 'I bet the uniform shop doesn't even exist anymore. The school was so strict about having to buy every single item from here, as if they were bespoke tailors.' She laughed at the thought and then stopped. 'I knew it. Look, a pound shop now.'

That used to be the linen shop, she thought, selling the Stars and Stripes duvet cover she'd coveted but which her mother refused to have in the house. 'We're English, not American,' Katherine Greenwood had snapped. 'Have the Union Jack if you really *must* have such garish frivolity on your bed that you'll be tired of by next week.'

And this was... oh, she remembered this one: The Dolls' Hospital. Of course it was. She'd brought Milly down here when Simon, in a fit of revenge at her accidentally breaking something of his, had yanked off both the doll's arms and one of her legs. Poor old shops, she thought. Victims of online shopping and Amazon. Not even the charity shops appeared interested in taking on the premises.

Ross suddenly stopped walking and Grace bumped into him. He put his arms round her so that her own arms were pinned at her side and without a word bent his head and kissed her so thoroughly she felt herself in danger of drowning.

'Wow,' she finally said, coming up for air and looking into those amazing green eyes of his. He took a handful of her long chestnut hair in each fist, wrapping the locks around his hands so that her face was within inches of his own. He was staring down at her with such intensity she didn't know if to laugh or be frightened.

'Grace,' was all he said before gently releasing her hair and, taking her hand, led her into the fourth empty shop doorway in a row of now-closed-down shops. The doorway led to a closed passageway that ran parallel to the totally deserted avenue and, pushing Grace against the wall, Ross brought a warm, firm hand against the silky smoothness of her stockinged leg, inching it deliberately and slowly upwards until it met bare flesh. Grace heard herself give a little 'oh' of surprise and longing and, parting her legs slightly, allowed Ross the access they both desired.

## 24

'I'm really sorry, I don't think you remember me, David?' The man, red-faced and sweating profusely, totally ignored David and, smiling sympathetically at Scott, delved into his jacket pocket, retrieving a folded handkerchief with which he dabbed at his face gratefully. 'Birmingham? At the Crow and Crocodile? The weekend Mandy died? I bumped into the pair of you while you were having dinner?' Realising David was still standing, totally immobile but obviously listening intently, the man turned to include him and Juno in the conversation. 'I do apologise.' He thrust a meaty paw at David and then towards Juno. 'George Crowther. I don't know if you knew Mandy? Mandy's grandfather and mine were cousins. Both in the textile trade when this area was famous for just that. Shame it all fell apart – bloody foreigners bringing their inferior stuff in. Tenuous link, I know, and until I bumped into her in Birmingham, I hadn't seen Mandy since just before she went to Oxford and I moved down to Warwickshire.'

George Crowther turned back to Scott. 'My sister told me she thought you had something to do with a restaurant in this neck of the woods so I Googled your name, David, and up this place popped. You've done well, haven't you?

Getting quite a reputation for fine dining? I told Lucinda – that's my sister – next time I was back in the area I'd pop over and offer mine and Lucinda's condolences and try this place out.' His eyes gleamed greedily and he openly licked his lips as his small porcine eyes followed the plates of food a waiter was about to serve at the next table. 'I don't get back up North too often – it's going a bit downhill these days isn't it? – but I can see you're trying to keep up with the South when it comes to fine dining.' He smiled somewhat condescendingly before helping himself to an olive from the dish at Juno's side. Crowther smacked his lips together appreciatively and Juno watched in fascination as a snail-trail of chilli oil escaped his mouth and descended into an orange pool in the cleft of his smooth, hairless chin.

'I was hoping to catch you here, David,' he continued to address Scott, ignoring David who still hadn't said a word, 'but most fortuitous to find you actually *dining* here this evening.' He gave a short bark of laughter before scooping up another couple of olives. 'Do you often sit and eat the profits instead of being front of house?' he asked, the remains of the olives glistening blackly between his front teeth. 'Do you think I could join you at your table? I've not eaten since lunchtime and I'm getting rather hungry.'

Juno stood up and reached for her bag. 'Mr Crowther, do have my seat here. I shan't be needing it any longer.' With as much dignity as she could muster, although her legs felt horribly trembly, she stepped past David, patted his arm sympathetically and headed for the door.

'Juno, get in the car. Please get in the car, you're going to get soaked.' Scott drew up at Juno's side as she walked through the village.

'Thank you, but I prefer to walk.' Juno carried on up the main street almost blindly, her one and only aim to get herself home, her makeup off and hide under the bed covers for the rest of eternity.

'You can't walk all the way in this rain and those heels.'

'Watch me.'

'I don't intend watching you. Just get in and let me—'

'Don't you dare say, "let me explain!"' Juno howled. 'It was *you* all along. Harriet thought it was her brother John who was with Mandy when she died. Grace even thought it could have been Dan, her husband.'

'I wasn't with Mandy when she died. I wasn't in the car. Please, Juno...'

Hope flared in Juno's heart, but quickly died when he was unable to reply to her shouting, 'But you'd *been* with her? You'd been in Birmingham with her? You were having an effing *affair* with her?'

'Evening, Dr Armstrong.' One of the elderly patients at the surgery, Mr Pickles, stopped in surprise, pulling on the lead of his white toy poodle and bringing it to an abrupt halt as he saw the state Juno was in. 'You alright, love?' He bent down slightly to peer through Scott's open car window. 'Is this chap hassling you?'

'I'm not a chap,' Scott snapped crossly and somewhat ambiguously. 'I'm your *doctor*. Of course I'm not hassling Dr Armstrong. I work with her.'

'Having a bit of a thing with her, *I* heard,' Mr Pickles cackled before turning back to Juno. 'Come on Pepsi, they're having a bit of a tiff. Leave 'em to it.' He pulled the poodle from its tree, mid-cocked-leg and walked off, chuckling to himself.

'Please Juno…'

Juno knew she couldn't walk the three miles or so out of the village on the ridiculous heels that were already turning her Hallux Rigidus to a burning, pulsating ball of fire. She wiped the rain from her eyes – or was it tears? – searching up the street in the hope of finding a passing taxi. *This is Westenbury Church Street, you daft bint*, she scolded herself, *not Piccadilly circus*. Kicking off the instruments of torture, she set off determinedly in the direction of home once more.

'Juno? What the hell are you *doing*?' Juno had never been quite so relieved to see her sister. Ariadne had overtaken the relentlessly kerb-crawling Scott, and had now pulled up beside her and was speaking through the open car window.

'Oh, thank God, Ariadne. Can you take me home?'

'Home? Yes, I was just off to your place for a takeaway pizza with the kids. Where's Scott? I thought you were going to Clementine's for a birthday meal?'

'I'm here, Ariadne.' Scott had jumped from his car, leaving it slewed to one side in the middle of the street. 'Just let me…'

'If you say "Let me explain" just once more, *Dr* Butler,' Juno spat the word, 'I will seriously take your stethoscope and shove it right where the sun don't shine. And with these new nails of mine—' Juno brandished her scarlet-red nail extensions in his direction '—you won't know if you're on this earth or Fuller's.'

'I think she's serious, Scott,' Ariadne said placatingly.

'I suggest I take her home and, whatever you've argued about probably won't seem as bad in the morning.'

'I wouldn't bet on it,' Juno snarled, throwing her sodden shoes in Scott's direction and catching him successfully on the side of his head before limping across to open the passenger door of Ariadne's beat up old Fiesta.

'Darling girl, what on earth's the matter?' Patrick Sutherland was in the kitchen making a pot of tea when Juno and Ariadne arrived back home.

'Where are the kids, Dad?' Juno had made an effort with her face in the car, rubbing at the streaked mascara and pulling tense fingers through Esme's ruined hairstyle before using a shaking hand to administer a slick of the lipstick she always kept in the inside pocket of her bag. The last thing she wanted was for Gabe and Tilda to see her like this. Although Fraser's moving out permanently to America didn't seem to have upset them too much – he'd been a particularly *absent* father even when he was present – deep down who knew what psychological damage their father's leaving had created? She, Juno, was the one constant in their lives and no way was she going to allow them to see her upset by the fact she'd been taken in by a philanderer. A two-timing philanderer who hadn't had the decency to put David Henderson in the picture. To tell him he'd been the last person to see Mandy before she died. But then of course he wouldn't, would he?

Upset? She was devastated.

'The kids, Dad?' Juno repeated.

'Gabriel's in his room being as uncommunicative as ever,'

Patrick said. 'I have to say, I thought I'd seen it all with adolescence when you four girls were growing up but—'

'Dad, I hate to remind you,' Juno interrupted tiredly, her fury at Scott beginning to abate as a slow-spreading depression began to reach its pernicious fingers to every cell in her body, 'you were very rarely around when we were teenagers.'

'Oh, I'm not sure that's quite right.' Patrick frowned. 'I think you may be harbouring some false memories there…'

A snort of derision from the depths of the drinks' cupboard as Ariadne hunted for the last of Fraser's Scotch put an end to that little fantasy of her father's.

'And Matilda is somewhere doing some maths homework I believe. She is a *very* clever girl, Juno. You know, darling, there was a girl from this area, Ruth someone—' Patrick closed his eyes as he tried to remember '—who went up to Oxford when she was just ten…'

'Ruth Lawrence, Dad. And don't even think about it. Matilda is not, and I repeat, *not* going to Oxford University at the age of twelve.'

'But she's not happy at Westenbury Comp.'

'Neither was I.' Ariadne handed Juno an exceptionally large glass of amber liquid. 'Here, get this down you, Juno… But you weren't overly interested in *me* at the time if I remember, Dad.'

'You girls are painting a very bleak picture of your growing-up years.' Patrick folded his arms. 'You've turned out very well, haven't you? All of you?'

'Despite being left to clear up the mess every time you left Mum,' Ariadne scowled.

'Oh, come on, you two,' Juno snapped, 'stop getting at each other. I'll tell you one thing, Dad. Seeing Mum cave in every time you were off with other women has made me determined not to end up the same.'

'What's happened?' Patrick frowned.

'What's happened is that I've been had and I'm not going to sit here and cry…' Juno broke off as fat tears ran down her face. 'Not going to cry…'

*No way, Juno. You are not your mother*, she told herself.

'The door was open.' The three of them turned to stare at Scott as he came into the kitchen and stood, arms by his side, unsure, it appeared, what to do next.

'That doesn't give you the right to walk *through* it,' Juno snapped, wiping at her face before folding her arms protectively around her middle.

'Come on, Dad, let's go.' Ariadne threw Patrick's coat towards him. 'Are we too late for Pizza Express?'

'Pizza Express?' Patrick shot a pained look in Ariadne's direction.

'Pizza Express,' Ari repeated firmly. 'Gabe, Tilda!' She moved from the kitchen and shouted up the stairs. 'Come on, your grandfather is treating us all to pizza.'

'So, you'd better start at the beginning,' Juno said, once the kitchen door had banged shut on the others. 'Great birthday this has turned out to be.'

'I'm sorry, Juno.'

'Yes, you said. I'm just very interested to know how you were supposed to be with me and were able to conduct a clandestine affair with Lady Mandy at the same time.'

'*Lady* Mandy?' For a split-second Scott looked shocked. 'He's not *Sir* David Henderson, is he?'

'Oh, for heaven's sake, does it make any difference?' Juno snapped. 'Are you trying to tell me if she'd been married to a peer of the realm, you'd have left her alone? Or would that have egged you on further? Do you Australasians get a kick from knocking off the hoi-polloi? Does it go back to your convict roots? You know, once felons but now getting it on with the upper classes?'

'My grandparents were Ten Pound Poms from Ramsbottom in Lancashire.'

'Exactly!'

'Sorry?'

'You will be. Leading me on with your F type and your fancy stethoscope.' Juno paused to take a breath and down the huge glass of alcohol Ariadne had pressed into her hand and which seemed to be going straight to her head. 'And me, bolivious... lobivious... vobilious...'

'Oblivious?'

'Yes, absolutely, that as well, to your sneaky, dirty little secret with another woman.' Juno stared at Scott, her eyes filling with tears. 'How could you? How could you *do* that to me?'

'I can't tell you how much I regret it. How sorry I am, Juno.'

'Oh no you don't,' she snapped, as Scott reached for the bottle of whiskey. 'Don't you even *think* about pouring yourself some of my husband's Scotch.'

'I am so sorry, Juno. Mandy came on to me, flirted with me, and yes, I had a bit of a thing with her.'

'A bit of a thing? A bit of a *thing*, you moron?'

'It wasn't serious. Not like with you.'

'Oh, don't give me that. You just can't keep it in your pants, can you?' Juno felt her heart pounding with fury. She wanted to hit him. Pummel him into the floor until he was strawberry jam she could spread on her toast.

'I met her in the artisan bakery in the village. You'd asked me to go and fetch you a loaf and she was in there buying the same one. We just got chatting.'

'So, it was love at first sight over a Nutty Walnut Cob, was it?'

'I wasn't in love with her. She's far too high-maintenance to have a proper relationship with.'

'Was.'

'Sorry?'

'*Was*,' Juno repeated, furiously. She's *dead*, for heaven's sake. You were the last person to see her. To be with her. How do you think that makes David feel?'

Scott sighed, running a hand through his dark hair. 'Are you sure I can't have some of that Scotch?'

Juno passed her glass over and he drained what was left. 'So how did you end up having a dirty weekend away with her?' she demanded.

'We'd been for a drink a couple of times.'

'How many times?'

'Does it matter?'

'It certainly does.'

'I don't know, Ju, two or three. She said David was off somewhere – Milan, I think it was – and she said she wanted to visit the James Watt Bicentenary exhibition at the Library of Birmingham...'

'What?'

'Yes, *James* Watt. You know, he invented the light bulb?'

'I know who James bloody Watt is, for fuck's sake, Scott. You fell for that?'

'Mandy was very interested in science,' he said, slightly huffily, 'and, being a doctor, she thought I might be too.'

'The only thing you were interested in was getting her into bed,' Juno snapped. 'Don't wrap it up as some sort of cultural outing.'

'You'd gone off somewhere with Tilda.'

Juno frowned. 'Had I? Where?'

'Some horse trial thing you were taking Tilda to watch for a treat during the summer holidays.'

'We were away one night.'

'So were we,' Scott sighed. 'One night. That's all it was.'

'Is that supposed to make me feel better?'

'I never wanted to hurt you.' Scott sighed again. 'We were in the Crow and Crocodile having dinner somewhere in Warwickshire. I don't actually know where we were – Mandy organised it all. I just met her there. And then, as luck would have it, the little fat guy you met this evening turned up at the next table. Some distant relative of Mandy's she'd not seen for thirty years or more. Mandy obviously didn't want to admit to being there with another man and thought it great fun to pretend I was David.'

'Great fun?' Juno stared.

'I'm sorry, Juno.'

'You said.'

'I don't want to lose you.' Scott moved over to where Juno was sitting on the battered old sofa and took her hand, stroking her fingers. 'I've ruined your birthday.'

'Did you not feel terrible every time you saw David?

Knowing things about his wife he didn't? Were you not worried that the police would want to come and talk to you?'

'I'd never actually met David Henderson until this evening. I'd heard of him of course. Who hasn't? And why would the police be interested in *me*?' Scott shook his head. 'We were in separate cars and I actually set off back to Westenbury the next morning. Mandy stayed until the following day, said she was going to do some shopping. She died coming home on the Monday morning.'

Juno looked at this man who'd swept her off her feet, the man she'd fallen in love with after twelve years in a loveless marriage with the pedantic, humourless Fraser Armstrong. Oh, but he was gorgeous. Wasn't everyone allowed one mistake? It wasn't as if they were married or anything, was it?

'Juno, I don't want to lose you,' he repeated, stroking her hair and looking down at her with that wonderful smile of his that was enough to have her toes curl in lustful anticipation.

She stood up, leaned forward to stroke his face in turn and then walked to the kitchen door, opening it fully before turning back to him and saying, 'You already have.'

## 25

'Cock porn!'

    'Sorry?'

'I want cock porn.'

'I'm sure you do, sweetie, but we can't always have just what we want when we want it.'

'Mumma, I *want* cock porn.'

'Pietronella, you had a big breakfast, you managed to find the bar of chocolate Grandpa David brought over for you and wolfed that when you thought I wasn't looking and when we get home, you'll be having lunch.' Grace glared at the elderly woman in front of her in the queue for the till at Sainsbury's who was eyeing Pietronella with some disdain.

Pietronella reached up on tippy toes for the bags of sweets on display at the till – wasn't there some new law against enticing kids with sugar? – hanging on to a bag of Werther's Originals like a drowning man until Grace took away her hand.

''Weeties,' Pietronella was on a roll. 'I want 'weeties,' she wailed, up on her toes once more and going in for a second attempt, this time with a bright yellow bag of humbugs.

'Oh, let her have them,' the woman in front snapped. 'I don't suppose with her condition it matters.'

'Excuse me?' Grace stopped dead, the bag of flour (self-raising super sponge) arrested in mid-air between the shopping trolley and the conveyer belt trundling slowly towards the till.

'Nothing, it's fine.' The woman turned her back on Grace and Pietronella, concentrating on the single item of (reduced to £1.99) tinned stewing-steak that was obviously her catch of the day.

'But you were saying?' Grace, in protective mode, refused to let it go.

'Well, these little Downies put weight on dead easy, don't they? It's a fact. You can't deny it. You only have to look at 'em to—'

Grace slammed the flour onto the conveyer belt watching, with some satisfaction, the puff of white escaping from the top of the paper bag. Downies! For heaven's sake, what century was the woman living in? *Calm down, Grace*, she told herself. *She can't help being an ignorant old woman.* And, to be fair, she did have to watch what Pietronella ate. Her daughter adored all food and would happily sit at the table and eat whatever was put in front of her as well as anything left in the serving dishes.

'Cock porn!' Once through the till and out the other side, Pietronella took up the clarion call once more, but this time with renewed energy.

'Darling, the word is *popcorn* and look, I bought some.' Grace held up the bag of yellow kernels. 'We can make popcorn after lunch.'

Pietronella, who was usually so calm, so biddable and even-tempered was having none of it. 'Tat *not* cock porn,' she cried, looking at the bag with derision. 'Cock porn white and big,' she yelled loudly to the amusement of a large Afro-Caribbean woman packing her shopping at the next till.

'Nat aways white, and unfortunately nat aways big neither, darlin'.' She started laughing at her own wit and Grace joined in, despite herself.

Unfortunately, their laughter did nothing but accelerate Pietronella to further frustration and, flinging herself onto the floor in fury, she proceeded to a full-blown tantrum, her arms and legs flailing as she brought the narrow walkway between the tills and a veritable mountain of empty cartons to a standstill.

'Can't you stop her?' the young manager asked as trolleys began to back up, not dissimilar to the Leeds-bound M62 on a Monday morning.

'You find her off-switch,' Grace said, no longer laughing, 'and I'll turn it off and stop her.' She reached down to grab Pietronella firmly by the wrist but her daughter was having none of it, kicking out and catching Grace squarely on the shin. 'Pietronella, enough now.'

'Hey, Pietronella, how about you stop this noise and we share this chocolate?' A tall, willowy figure, immaculately dressed in cream leather jeans tucked into tan flat leather boots, crouched beside the squirming, sobbing mess that was Pietronella.

Bribery with chocolate was not the answer, Grace thought crossly. 'I really don't think…' she began, and then stopped in some confusion. Not only had Pietronella immediately halted her tantrum, her little blue spectacles askew on her tear and snot-stained cheek as she gazed up at the woman in some adoration, but Grace knew immediately who the woman was.

'There now, that's better, isn't it?' the woman soothed, stroking Pietronella's dark bob and breaking off two pieces of milk chocolate before handing one to Pietronella and popping the other into her own mouth. 'Sorry about that,' she finally turned to Grace. 'I know chocolate probably isn't the answer, but at least we've got the traffic moving once more.' She paused and put her head to one side, her hair – the exact colour of Grace's own, Grace noted once more – swinging beautifully into place and smiled. 'It's Mrs Stevens, isn't it? My son, Noah's teacher?'

Red-faced and thankful that Natasha Haddon hadn't added to her list of introductions, *and my husband Ross's lover?* Grace could only nod. How awful would that have been, to be outed among the baked beans and spaghetti hoops in Sainsbury's on a crowded Saturday morning?

Gathering her wits as well as her shopping, Grace nodded again, smiled in embarrassment and turned back to Pietronella who was munching happily while staring hopefully at this giver of all good things. 'Come on, Nella, time to go home. Say thank you very much to the kind lady and let's go and make some lunch.'

'I do hope Noah has settled down more readily with you now?' Mrs Haddon asked, placing a leather-gloved hand on Grace's arm. 'I know he can be a bit of a handful and I'd hate him to be the cause of any disruption in your lives.'

'In our lives?' Grace stared, while Pietronella bumped the back of her mother's thighs with her head, eager, now lunch had been mentioned, to be off.

'I'd hate it if Noah's behaviour was affecting your family life, outside of school,' she said. 'Husbands are not always sympathetic to problems we may be having at work, are they? I do hope *your* husband is?' Natasha Haddon's smile was genuine and sympathetic. 'And I didn't realise you had a little girl with Down's Syndrome.'

*Why would you?* Grace was about to reply, but stopped herself in the same way she'd deigned not to answer the other woman's question about Dan. Instead she smiled, hoisted Pietronella, who was really too big for it, into the child seat of the trolley and said, 'Everything's absolutely fine at school and at home, Mrs Haddon. Thank you so much for your help with Pietronella. It's very much appreciated.'

'Not at all, she's a gorgeous little thing, isn't she?' She bent down to Pietronella and whispered something that Grace didn't catch in her ear, patted her head and watched as Grace headed for the door.

Instead of going straight home as she'd planned, Grace drove the couple of miles out of Westenbury and on to the village where Harriet and Nick lived. Much as she loved the country lane that led down to Harriet's old farmhouse, and couldn't help but look at and admire, today, the reds and burnished oranges of the last of the autumn leaves hanging tenaciously to the mighty oaks and sycamores that bordered the lane, there was always the bittersweet reminder that she, too, had once lived down here. Pregnant with Jonty, she and Seb Henderson had immediately put in a ridiculous offer for West Lane Farm, the dilapidated house and barn at the end of Harriet's lane. Oh, but she'd been so happy to be pregnant after trying and unable to be so while married to Dan. The ensuing postnatal depression she'd endured while living in a virtual building site, together with the realisation that she and Seb had really very little in common, had ended the reality of living happily ever after down the road from Harriet.

More than five years on, Grace found herself still unable to look properly down the valley at the ivy-covered farmhouse she'd once assumed would be her home for ever. David had bought West Lane Farm from Seb and herself and it was furnished and used to accommodate those doing business with David and Nick's textile clothing company, Luomo, as well, David had informed her only the other day, as being rented out as a luxurious holiday cottage and for Airbnb.

Thea and Sam, Harriet's dog, both running towards Grace's car as she pulled up in the drive and parked, brought Grace firmly back into the present. Absolutely no point in looking back, she told herself. She and Seb would never have survived as an item, she knew, and she had Jonty and Pietronella now and adored the pair of them. She gave a little shiver of delight as she remembered the evening with Ross the previous week. Life was good, she told herself firmly. Life was very good.

'Where's Jonty?' Thea demanded bossily as, totally ignoring Pietronella in the back seat, she peered through the open door of Grace's car.

'He's with his daddy and Libby.' Grace smiled, helping Pietronella, who'd fallen asleep after her tantrum, out of the car.

'Is my big sister, Libby, Jonty's *proper* mummy at the weekend?' Thea frowned.

'No, Thea,' Grace said patiently as she acknowledged, not for the first time, and only ever to herself, that Harriet's youngest daughter was beginning to get right up her nose. 'I'm *always* Jonty's mummy. Pietronella's here to play with you now for a while.'

'Pietronella's not *big* enough to play with *me*,' Thea retorted loftily, wandering off in the direction of the house, nose in the air.

*Little bitch*, thought Grace as she carried a sleepy Pietronella and followed in Thea's wake.

'Do you fancy adopting another?' Harriet said immediately she saw Grace at the door. 'Thea is a little so and so. I don't know what I've done wrong to produce that one.'

'Wasn't Libby a bit the same at her age, I seem to recall?' Any guilt at harbouring unpleasant thoughts about Thea disappeared with the knowledge Harriet felt the same about her own daughter.

'Possibly. Probably. Actually, absolutely,' Harriet conceded. 'I suppose, the difference being, with your first you'd never admit you've spawned a child from hell while, by the time you're on your fifth, you're more than up for handing her back to the devil. Anyway, I'm glad you're here. I've been trying to ring you all morning.'

'Oh? My phone had no charge so I set off to the supermarket without it. What's up?'

'I know who Mandy had been with when she died.'

'Oh my God. So she *had* actually been with someone?'

Harriet nodded. 'David's known a week or so, but kept it to himself.'

'John? Was it your brother John again?'

Harriet shook her head.

'Dan? You can tell me if it was Dan.' Grace felt her heart

pound and her pulse race the same way it always did if she was opening an envelope telling her she'd passed an exam or not. 'I mean, I'm not with him anymore, and that's absolutely fine, but—'

'It wasn't Dan.'

'Right. Good.'

'Excuse me, Thea, do you *mind*? I'm having a conversation with Aunty Grace. A *private* conversation. Go and take Pietronella back into the garden. Now!'

The minute the door had closed once more behind a sulking Thea, and Pietronella, who was more than happy to trail after her, Harriet said, 'Dr Butler.'

'Scott? Juno's Scott? No, I don't believe it.'

'You better had. It's true. David was in Clementine's last Saturday night chatting to Scott and Juno when it all came out.'

'Oh, poor Juno. She's so in love with him. They looked so right for each other. Are you sure?'

'According to David, yes.'

'And how was David? Absolutely devastated?'

Harriet frowned. 'Very down, yes of course. Not only has he lost the love of his life, but she'd been up to her old tricks again.'

'Goodness.'

'Hmm, little bombshell, that, isn't it?' Harriet paused. 'Were you coming over for anything particular?'

'No, I'm not staying. It's just something really strange I needed to talk to someone about.'

'Oh?'

'Well, I was in Sainsbury's…'

'Thea, for heaven's sake, out in the garden. Go—'

'But Mummy, you need to know—'

'Out—'

'There's a policeman in the garden.'

'A policeman?' Harriet and Grace exchanged glances before simultaneously jumping up as a loud knock came on the open door and a uniformed constable stood on the threshold.

'Hello, love. Police.'

'Gosh, is everything alright?'

'Just routine, love. Christopher Westmoreland? Is he in?'

'Kit?' Harriet had gone pale, while even Thea had been silenced by the officer's presence and was hiding behind Harriet's skirt. 'He's still in bed.'

The constable looked at the kitchen clock and raised an eyebrow, 'Well, do us a favour, love, and get him up. We need a quick word with him.'

# 26

'Oh, Mr Henderson?' Flustered, Juno stood up from her computer, smoothing down her skirt as she saw how it had creased from sitting. 'Come in. I didn't think I had you down on my list for an appointment?'

'I'm sorry, Dr Armstrong, I called in on the off chance that you'd be doing the Saturday morning surgery. I could have asked Grace or Harriet for your phone number but I was passing and dropped in... I'm here under false pretences... I just wanted to have a chat with you about... you know...'

'You managed to get past Marian on reception?' Juno smiled, but her pulse was racing. Why the hell did she feel as though she'd done something wrong? That she was as guilty as Scott for ruining this lovely man's marriage? That she was almost guilty of the murder – manslaughter anyhow – of Mandy Henderson? She'd never even met the woman, but maybe if she, Juno, had been more attractive, sexier, better in bed, been able to hang on to a man once she'd got him, then surely Scott wouldn't have strayed? He wouldn't have felt the need to have a fling and go off for the weekend, and David Henderson wouldn't be sitting here in front of her, his dark brown eyes looking deep into her own, but would be at home in that heavenly house of his, with his beautiful wife, dead-heading roses, organising surprise treats and games for their grandchildren...

These thoughts flashed like a speedway through her mind, and then another one: had David Henderson popped in on the off chance that it was Scott taking the Saturday morning surgery? Had he come in looking for trouble?

'I have no *intention* of discussing what happened with Dr Butler,' David said, appearing to read her mind, 'so don't panic that I've got a gun in here and am on a mission to avenge my cuckolding.' David patted the voluminous pocket of his navy Burberry mac and Juno couldn't help but take a look to see if there was any suspicious bulge that might contradict what he was actually saying, hiding in there. A shootout over Scott's examining couch was the last thing she wanted, even though she could have willingly sent him to his maker herself, several times over, during the past week.

'Only one doctor and Marian on duty each Saturday morning.' Juno smiled. 'Right OK. So, why *are* you here then if not a bad back, migraine or athlete's foot...?'

'I wanted to make sure *you* were alright, Juno.'

'Me?'

'The other Saturday night was obviously a huge shock to you. You know, when that dreadful little man, that distant cousin of my wife, came in looking for a free dinner, and instead, got more than he bargained for.' David gave a faint smile.

'I think we all got more than we bargained for,' Juno murmured, before looking at David with some surprise 'But it wasn't to you, then? A shock, I mean?' She examined his face, looking for clues. 'That your wife had been somewhere with another man?'

David shook his head. 'I knew she'd been off for the night with someone.'

'Did you?' Juno stared.

'Not immediately.' David paused and then went on, 'but I'd learned to have my suspicions whenever she said she was off to stay with friends. It wasn't the first time, you see.' David smiled once again. 'And, if she hadn't died, it wouldn't have been the last. Her alibi – who didn't have any idea she was such – let the cat out of the bag at my wife's funeral.'

'I'm so sorry,' Juno said again. 'You were married for a long time?'

'We were, but to be honest, Juno, and I don't know why I'm telling you this, I really don't know how much longer we'd have carried on. Being married, I mean.'

'Do you think some counselling might help?' Juno glanced towards her computer, prepared to look up private counselling services if David agreed that might be a way forward.

'Do *you*?'

'Do I what?' Juno wasn't quite sure who they were talking about anymore.

'Feel that you would benefit from some counselling?'

'Me? Goodness, no, I'm a doctor. You know, *physician, heal thyself…*'

'Hmm, I'm not sure that's a good enough argument… but, you know, I feel the same. I most certainly don't need professional counselling. What I do need is to know that you're OK and you're not blaming yourself in any way… Oh, Juno, I'm sorry, I didn't mean to upset you.' David reached for, and handed over, one of the tissues on Juno's desk and she wiped her eyes and blew hard, trumpeting loudly in her determination not to become the patient and he her doctor. 'I shouldn't have come…' He stood up and then paused, obviously thinking. 'Listen, Juno, you missed out on your birthday dinner at Clementine's. Come and have dinner with me one night? We can chat about this if you want. Or not. We can be each other's counsellors…?'

Juno gave her nose another exploratory trumpet and smiled. 'Thank you,' she said, 'I'd like that.'

'I'll be in touch.' He wound his burgundy woollen scarf around his neck and held up a hand in farewell before heading for the door and the Saturday lunchtime traffic.

# 27

Surely Kit wasn't involved in this county lines business Clementine was always going on about? Grace shook her head slightly, frowning as she passed the contents of the shopping bags, one by one, to Pietronella who was back to her sunny-natured self and wanting to help. It did mean the task took three times as long, Pietronella wrapping her stubby little fingers round the tins of beans and chopped tomatoes before trundling off in the direction of the fridge and kitchen cupboards, her breathing stertorous with the effort.

'Close your mouth, darling and breathe through your nose,' Grace automatically advised, her mind still on Kit. Funny how siblings could be so different. Libby had always been a bit of a madam, particularly when she was sixteen or so, and five-year-old Thea appeared to be heading in the same direction as her eldest sister. India and Fin, on the other hand, had been nothing but total sweeties, although, now India was hitting adolescence, Grace conceded, it could all change.

She smiled as she remembered how she and Harriet had themselves been such good little girls in their new grammar school uniforms, constantly trying, in assembly, to catch the eye of the totally gorgeous and charismatic Amanda Goodners five years above them. Once they'd hit fourteen or so, and Mandy was head girl, it was all change, and badly behaved enough, she recalled, for her and Hat to be suspended from school for a week. In those days, being suspended was the most dreadful thing to happen to a grammar-school girl.

Apart from being caught underage drinking in The Albert pub down in Midhope town centre, of course. The heady thrill of an illicit vodka and lime was probably only heightened by the flurry of fear executed by the possibility of a police raid, when all exits were barred and anyone caught drinking under the age of eighteen hauled home to face furious parents, as well as an appointment at the town's juvenile court a few weeks later.

Grace actually laughed out loud at that, Pietronella turning to join in with the unknown joke. These days, with half the pubs in the town closed down, the kids all gathered openly outside the village co-op with their bottles of cider and spliffs. And probably knives. And no one, particularly the police who were too busy either doing admin or asking for warrants to bash down the door of suspected drug dealers, seemed to give a damn.

So it had been a bit of a shock to see an actual, realio trulio, blue-uniformed copper on Harriet and Nick's doorstep asking for Kit.

Kit had always, she admitted now to Pietronella who nodded sagely at her words, been her favourite though she knew she shouldn't have favourites among Harriet's kids, especially when Libby was her own goddaughter. Kit, even when he was a little boy, had the ability to make her roar with laughter. He was the one, at five years old, who'd bought a monster gobstopper for fifty pence, sucked it to half its size and resold it for a pound. He was the one constantly hauled up in front of the head for misdemeanours; the one who, when he was on a high protein, body-building diet had sat at the kitchen table eating nothing but a whole roast chicken, napkin round his neck, tucking in like a modern-day Desperate Dan; the one at whose feet girls – and aunts – fell in a heap of adoration. And, latterly, the one who had the kids' teacher at home in his bed and didn't even realise she was such. And now, it appeared, he was being questioned by the police, while Harriet, almost in tears, was convinced it was something to do with drug-dealing. Grace had left them all to it and driven home with Pietronella. She must keep her phone on if she went out, in case Harriet needed to talk to her about what was happening with Kit.

Grace hadn't anticipated going out at all the rest of this Saturday. Jonty was with his father until the following day and knowing Ross always spent the whole of Saturday with Noah, it was just her and Pietronella. She'd catch up with all the mountain of schoolwork, make popcorn with Pietronella and do some baking. She'd quite got into baking recently, although ended up giving most of it away as she didn't feel too much of it was good for the kids – especially for Pietronella who would try every which way to find the cake tin. And to be fair, she knew herself she'd been eating too many brownies and cherry flapjacks, probably as a substitute for a lack of sex.

But all that was changing. She bent down to give Pietronella a big sloppy kiss, remembering her evening in town with Ross the previous week and smiled to herself, realising she'd not hunted out a single piece of Millionaire's Shortbread since.

She didn't miss Dan one bit. Was that awful of her? Maybe it was, but there was no point in pretending she did. He was up from Exeter the next weekend and she would hand the kids over to him and, she supposed, they'd become like so many other families, living with one parent and seeing the other for pizza and visits to the zoo.

The zoo? Grace actually laughed out loud, reaching for the new loaf of bread and pate she'd just unpacked. What bloody zoo?

'Grace? Noah's just been invited to go to Blackpool for the evening to see the lights.'

'Oh, lucky Noah.' Grace had always wanted to see the garish flashing lights that were Blackpool illuminations, but her mother had point blank refused to be drawn on the matter when Grace had begged to be taken as a little girl. And then, somehow, even though she'd often said, at this time of year, they really *must* go to see the lights, she and Dan had never got around to it.

'Sarcasm doesn't suit you,' Ross tutted down the phone.

'No, no, honestly, Ross, I'm not being sarcastic,' Grace protested. 'I'd actually have loved a trip to Blackpool at Noah's age. And a chance to go in the pleasure beach too; I've always fancied going on The Mouse. My parents never took us: Mum thought it totally non-U to traipse along the Golden Mile with a stick of candy floss in our hands. I really *should* go and take the kids.'

'Please don't invite me – I hold exactly the same sentiments as your mother,' Ross said. 'I can't think of anything worse. So, anyway, Noah is being taken by… Oscar Drake, is it?'

'Oscar? Oh, he's a great kid. I should foster *that* friendship if I were you.'

'It's Oscar's grandparents who're taking them, and then bringing Noah back to Oscar's parents for the night.'

'The night?' Grace felt her toes begin to twitch in excitement at the thought of a whole night with Ross.

'Hmm. So, I er, wondered if you might be er, free? You know, if you've nothing else on?'

'What do you suggest?' Grace did hope he was going to suggest sex.

'Well, I really fancy going over to Leeds…'

For sex and a harvest moon in a beer garden?

'…there's a man behind the curtain…'

'Sorry?' Grace automatically glanced at the sitting room curtains as she stood chatting, one eye on Pietronella's effort with paper and wax crayon, one ear to her phone.

'Sorry, The Man Behind the Curtain. It's a restaurant on Vicar Lane and, apparently, it's got a Michelin star. You have to have booked *years ahead* but one of my mates from uni who still lives in Leeds has had to cancel the table he booked six months ago for his wife's birthday; apparently she went into labour three weeks early this morning, and he's just rung me all excited from the hospital and asked if I want to take it. It's a very early table, so I'd have to pick you up around five.'

'Oh, gosh, Ross, give me ten minutes…' Grace frowned, wondering if her mother was free. 'I'll have to see if I can get a babysitter.'

\*

'Sorry, darling, you know Daddy and I would be up like a shot to babysit if we were free.' (Grace didn't know.) 'So, who are you going out with? Anyone I know. Not David, is it? I know he enjoys lovely restaurants.'

'No, Mum, it's *not* David.' She really was going to have to prick a hole in *that* little balloon her mother was intent on inflating. She tried Lilian.

'Lilian, any chance you can babysit this evening? It's just Pietronella?'

'I'm so sorry, Grace, darlin'. Sure, and you know I'd have been over like a shot (Grace did know) if I hadn't been going out. It's my annual wine-tasting club dinner. I'd hate to miss it.'

'Of course, you mustn't miss it. Don't worry.'

Bugger. Who else could she ask? While Pietronella didn't appear to mind being left with a babysitter, Grace really couldn't think of anyone apart from her mother, Lilian or David. What about Seb and Libby? No, they already had their hands full with the new house and Lysander and Jonty. Harriet? No, not fair when she had all her own kids and this new worry about Kit. She hadn't heard from her, and didn't want to bother her with this. David? Grace hesitated, but couldn't think why she was reluctant. He adored Pietronella and the feeling was mutual, she knew. She just didn't, she finally admitted to herself, want him to know about Ross. For the same reason she'd kept from Cassie and Deimante the fact that she was friends with – OK, having sex with – a child in her class's dad, she certainly didn't think David, as Chair of Governors at Little Acorns would totally approve.

'Grace, darlin'?' Lilian was back on the phone. 'I've just had a word with Niamh. She'll be happy to come over and babysit.'

'Really? Isn't she going out? Saturday night and no hot date?'

'Sure, and I think the poor girl is still waiting for a call from Kit. She's not really going out much at all.'

Well, she'd be waiting for a hell of a long time to come if Kit was now clapped in irons and sewing mailbags. Grace would have to have a word with her and explain, best as she could, that Kit Westmoreland was probably not a good bet as a steady boyfriend, whether this drugs thing was true or not. 'Oh, that would be wonderful if she's happy to do that. Ask her to come over for about four-thirty would you and we'll take it from there?'

Sod the schoolwork, Grace thought. Tomorrow's another day. Instead of analysing the English assessment tests she'd set during the week, as planned, she spent the next two hours shampooing, moisturising, defuzzing and everything else necessary for a night out in a posh restaurant with a new man.

Pietronella saw it as a great opportunity to raid Grace's wardrobe, tripping round the bedroom in every one of her mother's shoes in turn so that, by the time Grace was back at her dressing table to dry her hair, the surrounding area was beginning to look like the House of Fraser shoe department in the January sales.

'Wear the dress, Mumma. The dress for Gwanpa David.'

'I'm not going out with Grandpa. I'm going out with a friend of Mummy's, and Miss O'Connor from school is coming to look after you.' Grace watched carefully through the mirror to see Pietronella's reaction to the news that, instead of Lilian, who usually babysat, Miss O'Connor was going to be in charge, but Pietronella didn't appear to think it at all strange that Jonty's teacher was coming to look after her. She'd seen her having lunch at the twins' house several weeks earlier, so presumably assumed it was the norm for teachers to be part of her life outside school.

Pietronella handed Grace the beautiful long red dress David had helped zip her into a couple of weeks previously and Grace frowned a little at the memory, recalling the frisson of something she'd felt at David's hand on her arm and his dark eyes meeting her own in the mirror. What *had* that been all about? 'Not tonight, darling. This is a *special* dress for going to a ball.'

'Like Cindyella?'

'Yes, just like Cinderella. Clever girl.' Grace smiled down at Pietronella who, with her tongue stuck out in concentration, was now intent on fastening the buckle on the high-heeled gold sandal she'd fitted onto Grace's bare foot. She was doing so well, Grace thought with a surge of pride. Adopting Pietronella was one of the best things she and Dan had ever done, and she was making such good progress, hitting some of the milestones her mother and others had warned her would be only be reached years behind her contemporaries, much sooner than envisaged.

Grace frowned at her reflection as she pulled the hot brush through her hair. She really should ring David, she knew, and offer a shoulder to cry on now that he'd found out it was Dr Scott Butler who'd been with Mandy just before she died, but she didn't want to appear to be a gossip. Did Seb know? Had David admitted to him that his adored mother had been with another man before she died? Best leave things unsaid, she reckoned. If David wanted her to know more it was up to him to bring the subject up.

'Pietronella, let Miss O'Connor into the house before you hug her to death.'

'Aw, sure an' she's grand.' Niamh smiled down at Pietronella who had wrapped her arms round the top of the teacher's long, jeaned legs and was now gazing up at her through her little blue spectacles. Niamh looked round the sitting room, eventually falling with a giggle onto the sofa as Pietronella continued to restrict her movement. 'I don't suppose Kit's here?' she eventually managed to get out.

'Kit?' Grace frowned.

Niamh flushed. 'I did ring him last night to, you know, ask him if he fancied going out for a drink this evening, you know it being a Saturday night.'

'And he said he was *babysitting*?'

Niamh nodded and then shook her head. 'Yes. Well, no not exactly. He said he was busy; said he was probably going to be doing family things. You know, with Jonty being your son but also *his* nephew, I just thought…' She trailed off, embarrassed.

'Family things?' Grace snorted in disbelief. 'Kit Westmoreland? I don't think he's done any *family things* since he was a kid himself.' And even then, she conceded, remembering, he was forever going off by himself, getting stuck up trees so the fire brigade had to be called out or lost on the beach and being hauled back to a worried Harriet and Nick by strangers. Kit – she smiled to herself

– was rarely found in the bosom of his family unless food and drink, money or watching a game of rugby were involved.

Grace looked across at the sofa where Pietronella was now intent on climbing onto Niamh's lap. 'Look, Niamh, my advice to you is play it cool with Kit. Much as I adore Kit as his aunt, I'm not sure he's a good bet when it comes to affairs of the heart.'

'What do you mean, Natasha was with you in Sainsbury's?' Ross put down his glass and stared.

'Well, not exactly *with* us, as such. I didn't *take* her shopping with us.'

'What then?'

'So, she just appeared with chocolate.'

'Chocolate? I've never known Tasha eat chocolate.' Ross frowned in obvious disbelief. 'When she was gearing up to a new modelling assignment, she existed on a diet of champagne, cigarettes and grapes.'

'Blimey, no wonder she's so slim.' Grace frowned. 'Well, she was certainly eating a bar of chocolate this morning. Anyway, *I* adore food.' She helped herself to the tiny spiced prawns in their edible cellophane wrapper that had begun the restaurant's noteworthy flamboyant dining experience and gazed around at the stark white walls and exposed beams that gave one the impression of being in an art gallery rather than a restaurant in the centre of Leeds.

'It's something to do with *The Wizard of Oz*,' Grace said conversationally as Ross, a deep frown between his eyes, appeared to be in a world of his own – certainly not in this world of palate-tickling, epicurean theatre that was being performed in front of them.

'Sorry?'

'*The Wizard of Oz*. I Googled this place and the name comes from a line quoted by the wizard.'

'The wizard?' Ross stared. 'What wizard?'

'The Wizard. Of Oz. Wherever Oz was.' Grace laughed at the rhyming of her words.

Ross didn't.

'The wizard said, "*Pay no attention to that man behind the curtain…*" Ross, are you OK?'

'Why was Natasha in Sainsbury's?'

'Doing the weekly shop, I expect. Like every other poor sod on a Saturday morning.'

'Why was she eating chocolate?'

'Erm, she was hungry? I've been known myself to get through a whole bar of Cadbury's Fruit and Nut while waiting my turn at the till.'

'As far as I knew,' Ross frowned, 'she had a modelling assignment in London for the next week. I didn't realise she was back home.'

'Whatever. Come on, Ross,' Grace stroked his hand. 'You do know no one can *ever* get a table at this place? Now we're here, just relax and enjoy the ambiance.'

'I'm sorry, Grace. I'm being a pain.' He smiled and took up her own hand. 'You're looking gorgeous this evening. I've been thinking about you all week.'

'And what exactly were you thinking?' What was it about this man that had her squirming in her seat at the mere touch of his fingers, cool on the inside of her wrist?

'If I told you that, we'd be thrown out of this place.'

Grace laughed. 'I doubt it. It would just add to the drama, the whole theatre of the restaurant… Making love on this table among the… gosh, what's this…?' She stopped speaking as the third *sequence* (apparently it was de rigueur to name it such, rather than *course*) of the promised ten was placed in front of them.

'Ox cheek with salt and vinegar wild rice,' the young waiter said, before pouring wine from an exaggerated height into their two glasses and gliding off, as though on casters, to the next table.

'So, you were saying?' Grace asked, once they'd marvelled at, and consumed, this particular work of art.

'I was *saying*, Grace, I was so looking forward to spending time with you.'

Grace laughed. 'Thank goodness for Oscar Drake's granny and grandpa then.' Their eyes constantly met and slid away in a heady combination of anticipation and provocation and, as Grace sipped the wine, felt and savoured its mellow tones slipping down her throat, felt also that wonderful crackle of sexual tension build, knowing they had the whole evening and night ahead of them.

Although Ross had allowed himself only one small glass of wine, he eventually began to relax as they journeyed through the sequence of immaculate, incredible, totally bonkers tasting plates: Char Siu Octopus followed Ajo Blanco with frozen tomato and then onto Squab Pigeon with Rhubarb Hoi Sin and Enoki Noodles.

Grace wanted to know everything about his work at RTS Pharmaceuticals and, as he explained, she began to realise what an amazingly intelligent and knowledgeable man Ross Haddon actually was.

'My big worry, with the ease in which street drugs are obtained,' Ross suddenly said, over a Raspberry Macaroon with Fizzy Tarragon, 'is Noah.'

'Noah's ten,' Grace said gently. 'And living in a lovely village, where knocking on doors and running away on Mischief Night is probably the most he'll get to being involved in any criminal activity.'

'I think you're being very naïve, Grace.' Ross frowned.

'I know, I *do* know,' Grace protested waving her spoon in Ross's direction. 'I know Westenbury, and any other village today, isn't the picture-box village with the duck pond and the village bobby it used to be...'

Ross smiled at that. 'Oh, I don't know. Our postman bears a striking resemblance to Postman Pat.'

'And that if I wanted any sort of drugs, I wouldn't have to step too far from my front door.'

Ross nodded. 'I'm sure you wouldn't. I worry that Noah, with the behavioural issues he seems to have, will be particularly vulnerable in a few years' time. I can see him starting off with a spliff on a Friday night down at the youth club and then soon being persuaded onto the harder stuff. There are already a couple of older boys he's met just hanging around down at the rec who seem a bit dubious.' For a moment, he looked terribly sad. 'How do we keep our kids safe, Grace?'

'Well for a start, don't let him hang around down at the rec.' Grace frowned. 'I'm not surprised you're worried if he's mixing with older kids.'

'But I don't want to mollycoddle him. I *want* him playing out until it's dark like I used to. My brothers and I used to be out playing football with the other kids until we couldn't see the ball anymore. The most daring thing we got up to at the age of ten was lighting up the occasional tab we found on the rec and reading the rude bits from the problem page in my mate's sister's nicked magazines. I put more brainpower into understanding the vagaries of the female orgasm as portrayed in *Cosmo* than I ever did into long division.'

'I know.' Grace smiled as she put down her spoon for the last time and leaned forward to kiss Ross's mouth. 'I noticed.'

# 28

Ross was driving slowly through the village taking in, almost for the first time it seemed, the church, the Jolly Sailor pub and Little Acorns school before leaving the centre of Westenbury and turning onto the country lane that led out to Grace's house on its outskirts.

'You don't seem to really know the village you live in?' Grace smiled as he continued to take in the different landmarks she took for granted.

'You have to remember we've only lived here since the end of the summer and, I know it's pretty lax of me but, you're right, I don't really know my way around all of it. I'm usually racing off to the motorway or Manchester airport. Do you know, I've not even been into the Jolly Sailor yet?'

'It's become a bit trendy actually. I preferred it when it was lots of different rooms and you came home full of cheap lager and pork scratchings and smelling of booze and fags.'

'We only moved into the rented cottage because it's next to my mother-in-law,' Ross went on. 'I suppose part of me imagines we won't be here for long. Once Noah is that bit older and we've decided where Noah will go to high school, it may be that we settle back near Manchester.'

Grace didn't like to ask who might be meant by 'we'

but her train of thought in that direction was interrupted by Ross slowing down and pulling up outside the gates of what had to be the most beautiful house in Westenbury.

'Goodness, look at that. What an incredible place.' Ross had hit the button of the car window and the cold autumn air drifting in made Grace shiver. 'Some lucky sod's got it made, haven't they? I suppose it was once the old manor house of the village. Who lives there? Any idea?'

'David Henderson,' Grace said shortly.

'*The* David Henderson?' Ross turned to stare.

'The very one.'

'Actually Jill, my mother-in-law, did mention she thought he might live somewhere round here, but I didn't take much notice at the time.' Ross turned to Grace. 'Do you know him?'

'He's Jonty's grandfather.'

'Sorry?'

'My son, Jonty's grandfather.'

Ross stared. 'I didn't know David Henderson was such an old man?'

'He isn't. He's only in his late forties and, to be honest, doesn't look anywhere near that.'

'Right.' Ross turned back to the house, obviously trying to work it all out. 'So, his son must be *very* young then?' He stared at Grace's face as if seeing it for the first time. 'A bit of a toy boy, was he? You know, when you did it with him?'

'Did it with him? What a revolting expression, Ross, and, I can assure you, the relationship lasted eighteen months, resulted in my son, Jonty, and included a lot more than just *doing it with him*.' Grace felt irritation, anger even at the coarse remark. When Ross didn't say anything, but continued to stare at the long, low, ivy-covered old house, Grace sighed and went on to explain. 'Long story, Ross. Seb's twenty-eight or so now. David and Mandy got together when Mandy was in her first year at Oxford. She was pregnant, they married and had Seb and, with the help of both his and Mandy's father, set up his business empire – it's just grown and grown.'

'The Richard Branson of the North?'

'So they say… Look, can we get back…?' Grace was beginning to feel terribly uneasy parked at David's gate, and actually jumped as a tentative knocking suddenly came on the window at her side. She turned and pressed the button and the glass slid down to reveal a figure wrapped up against the cold night air.

'Can I help you? Oh… Grace?'

'Yes, it's me.'

'What *are* you doing?' And then, obviously realising she wasn't alone, the figure bent to peer in through the window, pulling back in some confusion when he didn't recognise Ross.

'Oh, you know, just driving home.'

'Driving? You're parked. Have you broken down?'

'We've been to Leeds to The Man Behind the Curtain. Have you been? It's well worth a visit… Great food, amazing ambiance…' Grace trailed off, knew she was twittering nervously when it was obvious, she needed to introduce the two men to each other. 'David, this is my friend, Ross Haddon.'

'Mr Haddon?' David paused. 'I believe we have your son in school?'

'In school?' Ross frowned, glancing at Grace for confirmation. 'You're a teacher in the village?'

'David's Chair of Governors at Little Acorns,' Grace said hastily. 'We were just admiring the house, David.'

'Nothing sinister, Dave. We weren't casing the joint.' Ross held out his hand and Grace couldn't quite work out if it was his defensive tone or his calling David by his derivative first name that was causing her that slight frisson of irritation once more at Ross's words.

'You must be cold sitting out here in my drive,' David said politely, but his accompanying smile didn't quite reach his eyes. 'Would you like to come in?' he went on. 'I've just been walking the dog.'

'No, no, really. Thanks, David, but no. We… I need to get back. Miss O'Connor's babysitting Pietronella.'

David whistled for his black Labrador and without another word raised a backward hand in farewell, heading for the wooden side gate that led into the lower half of the huge garden. It suddenly occurred to Grace that, without Mandy, who had spent much of her time – when she wasn't conducting extra-marital affairs – in the garden, David must now be having to employ extra gardening help.

'Miss O'Connor?' Ross turned to Grace.

'Sorry?'

'You said something about Miss O'Connor.'

'Niamh? She's a teacher at Little Acorns.'

'And *she* knows all my business too, I suppose?'

'Your business?' Grace stared. 'What is it with you and your *business*?'

'Well, David Henderson appeared to know who I was. That I was Noah's father.'

Grace shrugged. 'Maybe as Chair of Governors he's got to be in the know re Noah's safeguarding issues? I really don't know, Ross. Does it matter?'

'Well, yes… no… I suppose not.' Ross tightened his grip on the steering wheel and, crunching the gravel at David's gate, reversed at speed before shooting off in the direction of Grace's part of the village on Westenbury's outskirts. 'I just hate the fact that we seem to be the object of conversation. Yet again.'

'Yet again?'

'Everywhere we move, we seem to end up being discussed by different bodies and authorities.' A slight tick in the muscle of his left cheek gave away the tension Ross was obviously feeling.

'I'm sorry you've been going through all this, Ross. It should get better now, surely?' Grace smiled, gently stroking the inside of his thigh in an effort to restore not only his former good humour but the almost palpable anticipation of good things to come that had been generated over the fabulous food and wine in the restaurant. 'Come on, you can have that drink now we're home and you don't have to drive again tonight.' She leaned over to kiss his cheek, her meaning obvious.

'Has she been good, Niamh?' Grace led Ross through the kitchen and into the sitting room, taking his jacket as she did so. 'Niamh, this is Ross.'

'Niamh.' Ross nodded his head in her direction and Niamh looked up in surprise at his curt response before standing and reaching for her own jacket.

'I'm going out now,' Niamh said in some excitement and, as she stood, Grace could see the girl had obviously spent a lot of time doing her face and hair. 'Sure, and it's a good job I had my makeup with me, Grace.' She almost giggled. 'Just need to get back to Lilian's to change into a dress. Or do you think I should stay in my jeans?'

'Kit?' Grace raised an eyebrow.

'Yes. He rang me an hour ago. I'm going to pick him up.'

'You're picking *him* up?' Grace tutted. 'Get him to pick you up, you daft thing.'

'He's no car, Grace. I don't know what's happened to it, but he said he could only go out if I picked him up.'

'You should have told him you'd think about it.'

'Sure, and I didn't need to think about it. I don't mind driving. No, no,' she protested as Grace opened her purse. 'You really don't need to pay me. She's such a sweetie and she was so excited playing with her new doll.'

'Oh, Niamh, you mustn't spend your hard-earned teaching wage on dolls for Pietronella.'

'No, no, it wasn't me. It was her godmother brought it round.'

'Harriet? Harriet's been round? With a new doll for her?' Grace frowned. 'She didn't say anything about...'

'Oh no, it wasn't Harriet. If it was Harriet, I'd have said, "it was Harriet brought it round", wouldn't I? Sure, now that I've had lunch at Harriet's and know her as Harriet rather than Mrs Westmoreland.' Niamh beamed at Grace.

'I don't know who you mean, then. Pietronella's only got one godmother: Harriet.' Grace stared.

'Her Aunty Tasha? Lovely tall lady with the beautiful

hair?' Niamh paused. 'Very much like yours, Grace. I thought she must be your sister. You look quite a bit alike?'

Grace sat down suddenly, glancing back towards the door where Ross was still standing, taking it all in, his white face set in a grim mask.

'Just tell me what time she arrived, Niamh and what she actually said.' Grace tried to speak patiently at the girl who'd picked up her car keys and was obviously desperate to be off to see Kit.

'Well, we were watching *Toy Story 2* together – Pietronella and me, not Aunty Tasha and me – and then there was a knock on the door.'

'What time was this?' Ross demanded, his tone brusque.

'Oh, not too long after you'd both gone off. Probably only about ten minutes or so. She said she was sorry to miss you, Grace, but she had a present for Pietronella. Pietronella seemed absolutely delighted to see her and went to give her a hug, and then Aunty Tasha brought out the doll for her. She said she was Pietronella's godmother. She didn't stay long as she said her husband was waiting for her and hated it if she was away too long. I have to say, Grace, I thought that was a bit of a strange thing to say. I mean, it was only five o'clock and, I know it's getting dark early now that the clocks have gone back—'

'Where is this doll?' Ross interrupted.

'Where is it?' Niamh shot Ross a strange look. 'You want to *see* the doll?'

'So, was that it?' Grace asked. 'She gave Pietronella the doll and left?'

'Well, she stayed about fifteen minutes, obviously wanted to know where you and Ross were and what time you'd be back. I said you'd gone to some fabulous restaurant in Leeds… but I couldn't for the life of me remember the name.' Niamh started to giggle. 'I'm such an eejit: I think I said you'd gone to somewhere called The Man Behind the Curtain but that can't possibly be right, can it? I mean, there can't be a restaurant—'

'Thanks so much, Niamh.' Grace, her pulse racing, cut Niamh off mid-flow. 'You get off and enjoy yourself with Kit. And just be careful. Play hard to get.'

Grace let Niamh out into the garden, watching her carefully until she climbed into her car before closing the kitchen door and checking twice that it was not only locked but firmly bolted. She then ran up the stairs to Pietronella's bedroom where her daughter was fast asleep, her arms wrapped tenaciously around a large, chestnut-haired doll.

Grace managed to ease the doll from Pietronella's arms and, when she was sure the little girl was once more sleeping soundly, her heavy breathing indicative of such, she walked slowly back downstairs.

If she'd been expecting some sort of apology from Ross, or at least some sort of explanation, Grace was soon put right on that score. He'd found and opened the first of the bottles of white wine she'd earlier put into the fridge in anticipation of their enjoying together once back from Leeds, and was already, by the look of it, several full glasses ahead of her.

'Do you think I could have some of that?' she asked pointedly, handing him the doll at the same time. It wasn't a pretty doll, Grace could now ascertain in the harsher light of the kitchen, its chestnut hair perhaps its only redeeming feature.

Ross threw the doll towards the kitchen sink but it missed the mark and fell, landing awkwardly on the tiled floor, its dress raised, displaying legs rudely splayed at an awkward angle.

Grace picked up the doll, straightened its dress and placed it carefully behind her on the kitchen island. Ross poured a small glass of wine for her and handed it over, still not saying a word.

'So, what do you make of all this?' Grace asked, folding her arms and looking directly at him.

'I think the last thing you should have done was to get friendly with Natasha in Sainsbury's this morning.'

'Friendly with her?' Grace stared. 'Why would I get *friendly* with your ex-wife? It was her that came over with the chocolate and got friendly with us. Well, with Pietronella, anyway.'

'She's not my ex-wife,' Ross snapped. 'She's my *wife*.'

'Oh, so what the hell are you doing here with me then? I appreciate you might not technically be divorced, but I was led to believe you were separated as well as there being a restraining order in place? That she's been physically violent towards you?'

'And what would *you* know about it all?' Ross poured more wine for himself, emptying the bottle before crashing it onto the stainless-steel sink. He downed it in one, glaring at her furiously and Grace began to feel the first stirrings of real fear.

'Of course I know about it, Ross.' Grace spoke calmly. 'I know what you've told me and I was there in Mrs Beresford's office when you had that to-do with Natasha and she thumped you one.'

'You know absolutely *nothing*.' Ross turned back to the fridge, retrieved a second bottle of wine and quickly released its metal top. Grace saw his hand was shaking with anger.

'Look, Ross, you're angry and upset. I think it best if you leave now, don't you?'

'Leave?' Ross held up the second bottle of wine in her direction before filling his glass. 'Why should I leave? I think I deserve more than to be thrown out like a dog into the street when my wife has put herself out to bring your daughter a present, don't you?'

'What?' Oh, Jesus, she'd ended up with a complete pair of nutters. His wife was a bunny boiler (ridiculous thought; an absolute cliché used far too often these days both in novels and common parlance) and the man himself, standing in front of her having downed the best part of a bottle and a half of wine in ten minutes flat, had now turned, like the worm. *Oh Rose, thou art sick, The invisible worm...* Why the hell was she quoting William Blake to herself? *Get a grip, Grace.* 'I'm tired, Ross,' she said. 'I've a headache.'

'Tired? You've not done anything yet except eat your way through all twelve courses at that ridiculous restaurant. Bit of a tease, aren't you?'

Grace felt the shock of real fear now and tried desperately to recall all the psychological thrillers she'd ever read and the best way to deal with psychopaths who'd cornered their victims in their own kitchens. But her mind was a blank, refusing to allow her any access to what was the next logical step in dealing with this irrationally angry man standing in front of her. How could there be a logical next step when Ross Haddon was behaving so illogically? So insanely?

'Ross,' Grace soothed, 'you're being illogical. Irrational...'

'Don't *ever* call me irrational, you stupid bitch.'

Grace felt the blood drain from her face and recognised the rusty iron taste of blood as she bit the inside of her cheek in an effort to remain calm.

'No of course, that wasn't fair of me. Listen, Ross, you've been through a lot lately, haven't you? No wonder you're feeling upset...'

'Upset? Of course I'm upset. You bitches are all the same, especially you chestnut-haired ones. You lead men on, always wanting sex, kinky sex in strange places and then crying rape when it gets out of control and it's not going your way.'

Oh, please, please, please don't say she was dealing with a rapist. 'You're right, Ross. We've got a lot to learn, we women.' Jesus, was she on the right track? *Just don't inflame the situation, Grace. Make him think he's right.*

Ross suddenly lurched in her direction and Grace automatically took several steps backwards. He grabbed at her wrist, twisting it painfully, and then his hand shot out towards her hair and she dodged to one side, causing him to fall against the sink and slump to the floor as his legs appeared to give way from under him. He put his head into his hands. 'I'm sorry, Grace,' he said, his voice muffled as he spoke through his fingers. 'I'm so sorry. I don't know... it's losing Natasha... I love my wife... I love my son... I love Noah... I just want us to be all together as a family again... it's alcohol and the anti-depressants... I shouldn't drink when I'm on them...'

'It's OK, it's OK...' Grace soothed. 'I think I need to get you home, back to Noah as quickly as I can.'

'I never intended staying the night, Grace; wouldn't be

fair on… Natasha… no, not Natasha, I mean Noah, I mean Noah, don't I? It wouldn't, would it?' Ross was beginning to slur his words. He raised his head slightly, squinting through bloodshot eyes at Grace, and then his head slumped forward once more, his empty glass fell from his hand and slow little snores began to escape from his open mouth.

What the fuck did she do now? He was a large man at the best of times, and now rendered almost impossible to move by his unconscious state on her kitchen floor. Even if she were able to get him out of the door and into her car a) she'd had enough drink in the restaurant to put her over the limit and unable to drive and b) Pietronella was upstairs, and there was absolutely no way she was leaving her child alone even for the half an hour or so it would take to drive and deposit Ross Haddon back where he belonged.

The alternative was to leave him where he was, throw a blanket over him and let him sleep off the cocktail of alcohol and drugs that had worked together to bring his real personality to the fore.

But she was frightened of him now. Even if he came around and was all solicitous and apologetic – Grace shuddered at the very thought – she still couldn't bear the thought of him in her house. Couldn't bear the thought of him having either another angry outburst with her as its target, potentially witnessed by Petronella, or him creeping upstairs and sliding into bed beside her. No, she wanted him out of the kitchen, out of her house and out of her life for good.

She'd ring Harriet. Grace looked at the kitchen clock; it was only just past nine-thirty. She'd ring Harriet and borrow Nick. He'd come over and help her. Grace moved to find her phone and then stopped and closed her eyes as she remembered Harriet saying she and Nick were over at Izzy and Declan's for supper. Now what?

There was only one alternative. With one eye on the comatose man on the kitchen floor, Grace scrabbled in her shoulder bag for her phone, took a deep breath and found the contact.

## 29

'Oh, my God, Grace. There was a mad woman with a horrible doll in your house? Do you not think you should tell the police?'

Grace nodded. 'I did consider it. But,' she sighed, 'at the end of the day I don't suppose she was breaking any law. She knocked at the door, was let in and she brought a present for a little girl she'd met earlier that day.'

'So, for heaven's sake, what did you do?' Harriet slipped her arm through Grace's own as they headed for the gate which would take them through into Norman's Meadow, the local beauty spot on the outskirts of the village. 'Hang on, just let me put Sam on the lead or he'll end up chasing the sheep and getting shot. I thought we could start here,' Harriet added, 'and just walk through the fields and woods until we've had enough.'

'Well, until the kids have had enough.' Grace smiled down at Pietronella who was clinging onto her free hand, with no desire to run and chase the devil-eyed sheep as Thea was intent on encouraging Fin to do. While Harriet was solicitous about keeping Sam on a lead, she didn't, Grace noted, appear to have any qualms about the twins facing the guns of any angry farmer. 'I'm not sure how far

Pietronella can walk and she's far too heavy to carry these days.'

'So, go on then, what did you do next? I bet you were terrified he was going to wake up and have another go at you.'

'To be honest, I think having him weeping all over me was even worse.'

'What, he began to cry?'

Grace nodded. 'Once David arrived, he suggested I make some strong coffee and then he bent down at Ross's side and managed to wake him up and get him into a chair. Then we poured coffee down him and, when Ross realised what was happening, he just seemed to shrivel into himself and broke down again.'

'Oh, the poor man.' Harriet frowned.

'Poor man? You're joking? You weren't at the receiving end of his vitriolic diatribe against me, his wife and women in general. I don't want *anything* more to do with him, Harriet.'

'No, I can understand that...'

'I don't think you can, Hat. You didn't see the anger and the hatred on his face.'

Harriet patted Grace's arm. 'You don't half pick 'em, Grace.'

'Well, that's it now,' Grace sniffed, wiping her nose with her sleeve. 'Look, more important than me, what the hell is happening with Kit?'

'Kit? What about Kit? Oh, the police coming round yesterday? Sorry, I should have rung you. It wasn't anything. Well, not in the general scheme of things. You know, compared to what you went through yesterday. They wanted to speak to Kit because it was just something about his car. It had been stolen.'

'Oh, his car was stolen? Is that all? That's why he got Niamh to pick him up, was it?'

'No, no, it wasn't stolen *from* Kit. When Kit bought the Audi a couple of months ago, it was apparently a stolen car.'

'Where did he buy it from? Surely the garage where he bought it are to blame?'

Harriet tutted. 'Oh, come on, Grace, you know what Kit's like: daft as a brush. He met some bloke in a pub in town and the next minute, he's the owner of an upmarket Audi. He should have known it was dodgy when he saw the spare tyre was for an old Escort.'

'Do Audis even carry spare tyres these days?' Grace laughed at the thought of Kit opening the boot of his new car to find a useless spare tyre.

'It's not funny, Grace. Not funny at all. Nick is furious with him. He could be up for receiving stolen goods.'

'But when he brought it home, didn't the pair of you say something? You know, like, "how the hell can a twenty-year-old like you buy a posh car like that?"'

'He did have quite a bit of money and now the stupid boy has lost the lot; the police sent round a pick-up and towed it away. The thing is, Grace, apparently my son is a brilliant salesman. He might not be overly academic, didn't go off to university and obviously can't tell a dodgy car when it jumps up and bites him in the bum but, according to David and Nick, he can flog ice to the Inuits. He pulled off such a good deal for Luomo during the summer, I mean a *really* amazing deal according to Nick, that David gave him a ridiculously huge bonus. Told him to bank it for when he's ready to buy himself a house. Nick knew this and didn't want to worry me that Kit had blown the money on a fast car. God, he's just like my brother John was at his age.'

Grace dithered: should she tell Harriet about seeing Kit in the pub in the town centre on Friday night? Maybe she'd got it all wrong and Kit had just been having an innocent chat about his car with those hoody types. Listen to herself – hoody types, for heaven's sake. God, she was getting old. What kids got up to in pubs these days was totally different from the *half a lager and a packet of smoky bacon crisps* scenario when she and Harriet were Kit's age.

'So, you're not worried about Kit then?' Grace ventured.

'I'm always worried about the little blighter,' Harriet said. 'That's kids for you. Wait until Jonty is twenty and into fast cars...'

'...and fast women?'

Harriet laughed. 'But if Kit wasn't still living at home, if he'd gone off to university, he'd have been getting up to all sorts, you know he would, and it would have been a case of out of sight, out of mind and I wouldn't have his little transgressions staring me in the face every day. Look, Grace, I'm far more worried about you at the moment than my daft son. How do you feel about it all now?'

'Shaky,' Grace said. 'Ashamed, embarrassed, frightened. Fed up. I just don't know why I end up choosing the wrong men. Look at you: same man and still in love with Nick twenty- odd years later. What have I got to show for the same period of time? Two attempts at a marriage to a man with a roving eye – wouldn't be at all surprised if Dan's not already shacked up with someone down in Exeter. And then I fall for Seb, a man – no, let's face it, Hat, a *boy* – almost fifteen years younger than me for heaven's sake. And he and I *know* it's not right and then he falls in love with Libby.'

'You mustn't regret that relationship, Grace,' Harriet soothed. 'Without Seb, you wouldn't have Jonty.'

'I know, I know. Jonty and Pietronella are my constant. You should never regret anything you do in life. All part of life's great tapestry as someone, I believe, once said.'

'The women who sewed the Bayeux one, do you reckon?'

'Sorry?' Grace frowned at Harriet, not really listening. 'Anyway,' she sighed, 'and so then I meet Ross Haddon and it all seems exciting and a bit daring and I'm beginning to feel alive once more after years of relationships that weren't right.'

'And that turned out to be totally not right too?'

'The man is a psychopath with a psychopathic wife. They're in a toxic relationship, constantly trying to get the upper hand with each other, playing games with their lives and that poor kid's in the middle of it all. I wouldn't be surprised if Ross Haddon isn't just as guilty as Natasha of physical violence. They probably get their kicks from beating ten bells out of each other and then get more kicks from having sex to make up.' Grace paused and added, without looking at Harriet. 'And probably somewhere almost in view of the general public. You know, to heighten the kicks; the actual danger of it all.'

'Oh?' Harriet glanced across at Grace whose face was inscrutable. When she saw Grace wasn't about to expand further, she asked, 'So, David drove him home?'

'Hmm.' Grace nodded, before turning to look down at Pietronella. 'Try not to drag your feet, sweetheart. Come on, best foot forwards.'

'Which my best foot?' Pietronella gazed down at her red wellingtons.

'You choose, darling. Your choice.' Grace turned back to Harriet who was searching for biscuits in her rucksack. 'Hat, he was furious.'

'Yes, you said. Oy, you two, stop chasing that poor sheep and come and have a biscuit.'

'No, not Ross. David.'

'David? I thought you said it was Ross who was totally angry?' Harriet turned to look at Grace who seemed suddenly overwhelmed, trying not to cry in front of the children.

'Ross *was* angry, horribly so and I was really, really frightened. I *never* want to go through anything like that ever again. But David was just as angry.'

'What did *he* have to be angry about? Ross didn't turn on him as well, did he?'

'Oh no, not at all. David just saw the snivelling remnants of a drunken, pathetic man. I helped him get Ross into the back seat of the car and, luckily, I remembered Noah's address from the register at school. Once we'd belted him in, I was saying thank you again to David and he turned on me. Said I wasn't fit to be a mother, having strange men in the house and leaving my daughter with a daft babysitter who opened the door to mad women with horrible dolls. He shouted at me, Harriet, said I was an absolute disgrace. Said I should have let him babysit and none of this would have happened.'

'And why didn't you? Ask David, I mean? He is Pietronella's adopted grandpa, after all.'

'I know,' Grace said miserably, tears now running

unhindered down her cheeks as she walked. 'I didn't want David to know about Ross.'

'But why ever not?' Harriet passed Grace a tissue and Grace trumpeted loudly making Pietronella giggle.

'Ephalant, Mumma,' she chortled.

'I don't know. Harriet, I really don't know. I'm more upset at David being so angry with me than that pillock Ross Haddon.'

'Grace, you have to remember David's not in a good place at the moment. He's grieving for Mandy, has just found out that she was having a fling with Scott Butler and, also, I think he's had enough of his mother living up here with him. She doesn't half fuss over him.'

'Have you spoken to him?'

'Not really. But Nick has. They go for long sessions down at the Jolly Sailor, ostensibly to talk about work but really so David can offload, man to man over a pint, and then Nick reports back to me.'

'OK.' They walked on in silence, enjoying the sensation of the pluvious terrain beneath their boots and the incredible stillness of the damp November day. There wasn't a breath of wind, just that late autumn feel of a tenacious grasping on to any last vestige of the previous season before winter, with its snow and icy winds, would begin to take hold.

'So,' Grace finally broke the silence, 'you're OK with Kit then? Not worried about him?'

'What?' Harriet stopped.

'Nothing.'

'Come on, Grace, there's something you're not telling me. Is it about Kit? Oh God, he hasn't got the teacher pregnant, has he? Please don't say there's going to be *another* baby to add to the Westmoreland tribe? We're already top of the class in adding to the world population explosion. And if she's Irish Catholic, her mammy won't let her back home in case the priest finds out. *I'm* not looking after it, Grace, I'm *not.*'

'Oh, for heaven's sake, Hat, as far as I know Niamh O'Connor *isn't* pregnant.' Grace glanced at Harriet's set face as she set off at speed up the hill in front of them. 'Hang on, Harriet, we can't keep up...' Grace puffed along after her. 'Anyway,' she stopped to catch her breath, 'far more likely to be Maya Burkinshaw up the duff than Niamh.'

'That's fine,' Harriet snapped. 'Esme's responsibility, not mine.'

'I don't know why you think Kit is daft enough to not be practising safe sex.'

'Probably for the same reason he doesn't practise buying safe cars.'

Grace started laughing at that, the tension of the last twenty-four hours momentarily beginning to seep away as she and Harriet linked arms and started giggling, unable to stop.

'We're nearly back at the car, Thea. Stop whining.'

An hour later they'd completed the circuit around the fields and through the beautiful woods on the outskirts of Westenbury and were dropping back down through Norman's Meadow to their parked cars.

'Horsey, Mumma, horsey.' Pietronella pulled away from Grace's gloved hand and set off towards the horse that was grazing languidly on the long, wet grass ahead of them.

'Hang on, Nella. Come back. You can't just go talking to strange horses.' Grace shielded her eyes against the low, very weak, midday sunshine that had managed to break through the murk of the November day and ran after her daughter, who obviously thought she could.

'Harry! Bloody, sodding horse. Come here, you damned thing.' A woman, blonde corkscrew curls bouncing as she ran from the direction of the nearby terrace of large Victorian houses that bordered the edge of Norman's Meadow, stopped dead when she saw the others.

'Oh, hello, you lot. Are you out for a walk?'

'Juno? I always forget your house backs onto this beautiful place. I wouldn't have thought horses were your thing?' Grace grabbed hold of Pietronella who was getting dangerously near the animal's back legs.

'They're not. Harry's Tilda's pony and he's found a way of opening the gate and getting out. He thinks he's on his holidays now and there's no way he's packing his bags and coming home without some bribery and corruption. You couldn't help me, could you?'

'Hat?' Grace called over her shoulder. 'You any good at catching horses?'

'Me? I'm terrified of the great beasts. He lives with you, Juno. Have you no control over him?'

'As much as you have over your kids,' Juno called back, laughing as she saw Thea push Fin headfirst into a large area of black mud where rainwater had drained down from the meadow and collected against a drystone wall.

'Horsey.' Pietronella, one hand firmly grasped in her mother's, had taken hold of Harry's bridle with the other as the pony grazed, and the others had turned to watch the twins. 'Nice horsey.'

'Hell.' Grace whirled round. 'Put the horse down, Nella. Now.'

'Actually, do you mind if she hangs on to him?' Juno whispered, inching her way towards girl and grazing pony. 'If I can just grab the rope… got him.' Juno breathed a sigh of relief as she fed bits of Eccles Cake to the animal. 'He's addicted to this stuff. It's the one thing that'll get him back. You can't put Fin in the car covered in mud. Come on, I'll make coffee and you can clean him up a bit.'

Once a wailing Fin had been cleaned up, a pouting and unrepentant Thea well and truly told off and Pietronella praised to high heaven for her catching Harry Trotter, the three children were put in front of a cartoon with a plate of ham sandwiches while the others took off coats and sat at the kitchen table.

'God, I needed that.' Grace sipped the mug of hot tea and closed her eyes. 'Where's Tilda? How come she left you to chase after Dumbledore?'

'Harry Trotter,' Juno corrected, laughing. 'She's down at my dad's. He's teaching her Latin.'

'Right.' Grace pulled a face. 'Blimey, all I was interested in at the age of eleven was adding to my collection of Care Bears.'

'And Amanda Goodners at school,' Harriet put in. 'Don't forget Mandy.'

'Yes, yes,' Grace tutted. 'And Mandy. Can't forget Mandy.'

'You OK, Juno?' Harriet put down her mug and looked

directly at Juno as Juno passed a tin of biscuits and finally sat down herself.

'OK?'

'David told us about Scott.'

'Yes, I suppose he would.'

'Did you have no idea? You know, that he'd been seeing Mandy?' Grace patted Juno's hand as she saw tears well in the other's eyes.

'Nope. Not a clue.'

'So, how are you dealing with it? I mean, is it all off now? Between you and Scott, I mean?'

'Yep. All off.'

'But were you and Scott together at the time? I mean, were you actually an item?'

'Yes, absolutely. We really got it together just as the last rehearsals for *Jesus Christ Superstar* were going on. That was back at Easter, Grace. I'd like to think that by August which was when Mandy had the accident, Scott and I had made some sort of commitment to each other. As far as I knew we were together. We were an item.'

'So, you can't forgive him then? Allow him one mistake?' Harriet frowned. 'You know, sometimes—'

'No.' Juno left the other two in no doubt as to her feelings as she pushed a couple of unruly blonde curls from her face and smiled. 'No,' she repeated.

'So, have you and David, you know, discussed all this?' Harriet asked.

Juno nodded. 'He's such a lovely man, isn't he? He actually called in to the surgery yesterday morning to see how I was. You know, it's him that should be absolutely devastated at finding out his wife was messing around with

Scott, and yet he's been more concerned about *my* reaction, about how *I'm* feeling. Which is a bit daft really seeing Scott and I had only been seeing each other six months or so and he'd been married for over twenty-five years to Mandy.'

'That's David for you. He's one truly nice human being…' Harriet stopped suddenly and smiled in Juno's direction, 'Hey… so… David… you know?'

'I know *what*, Harriet?' There was a ghost of a smile on Juno's face but she raised a questioning eyebrow at Harriet.

'Well, there's David, single. And you now single, Juno. You obviously like him. You're very gorgeous and, being a doctor, obviously an intelligent woman…'

'Cut it out, Harriet.' Juno smiled. 'I'm not interested in starting again.'

'No, no, obviously not,' Harriet protested. 'Far too soon for either of you. You know, when you're both nursing your broken hearts. No that would be *ridiculous*. But, when you *are* interested in getting back out there, in the saddle as it were…?'

'God, is she always this persistent?' Juno smiled across at Grace and then frowned. 'You alright, Grace? You're very quiet?'

Why was her pulse racing at any thought of David and Juno together? Grace hid her face in her mug of tea, trying to work out why the idea of David with another woman was making her feel as though yet another body-blow was hitting her, head-on. David was her friend, her mate, and she, Grace, didn't have any first dibs claim whatsoever over that friendship. Of course he was going to end up with someone else at some point. But so soon? And with Juno, her other mate…?

'Oh, Grace has been having men trouble too.'

Grace shot Harriet a warning look and Harriet shut up. She'd known Grace far too long to not know when to put a sock in it with regards her best mate's private life.

'Actually, Juno,' Harriet hastily changed the subject as Grace continued to glare at her, 'how's the King of the Jungle?'

'The King of the Jungle?'

'I can't remember his name – you know, the stripper Izzy took us to see?'

'Leo? Leo Hutchinson? Back on the drugs, big time, unfortunately. It's a real shame as he was totally clean as far as we knew. We hold dependency clinics down at the surgery now – Izzy's idea, and I have to say, one of her better ones – but we can't get Leo to sign up for help. Why do you ask?'

'I saw him the other day.'

'You recognised him with his clothes on?' Grace started to laugh. 'Seriously?'

'Well, yes.'

'In the town centre, was he?' Juno asked. 'It's his usual hangout.'

'Well no, that's the strange thing. If he'd been in the town centre, I probably wouldn't have looked at him twice.' Harriet frowned. 'He was walking up the lane from Libby and Seb's place when I was driving down to look after Lysander. He actually stopped me and asked if I knew where the bus stop was, back into town.'

'Down at Holly Close Farm? Where Dad and Arius are renting their cottage?' Juno frowned. 'It wouldn't have been him, Harriet. There's no reason for him to be down there.'

'No really, it was him. I knew I recognised him from somewhere – as he was talking, he was a bit wheezy from the walk up that country lane and he got out his asthma inhaler.'

'Oh heavens.' Juno suddenly put down her mug.

'What?'

'Oh, it's nothing.'

'Go on. What?' Grace and Harriet both leaned forwards.

Juno sighed. 'It's just that Ariadne is convinced that Arius – you know, my half-brother who's moved into one of the Holly Close Farm cottages with my dad? – is part of all this county lines stuff Clem is always banging on about. He and Pandora's son, Hugo – my nephew – are constantly going over to Manchester on the train and then, according to Pandora, are always holed up together either at Pandora's place or down at Dad's cottage. Pandora thought it was great to begin with. You know, Hugo, who's been away at boarding school, has suddenly got a readymade mate here in Midhope, but she's getting a bit worried now. I saw her a couple of days ago. Hugo has become really secretive. He's always on the phone, and strange kids keep turning up at the house. She found a mobile phone in his bedroom she didn't recognise.'

'Hat?' Grace suddenly turned as Juno stopped talking. 'Is Kit down at Holly Close Farm much?'

'Kit?' Harriet stared. 'Yes.' She didn't say anything for a while, and then blurted out, 'He's *always* down there.'

'Well, he would be,' Juno interrupted. 'He's seeing Maya – Scott and Esme's daughter – isn't he?'

Harriet didn't say anything for a while but sat, biting her lip. 'I knew it. I *knew* he was involved with drugs somewhere along the line—'

'The *county* line?' Grace murmured.

'—and you're not telling me the bonus David gave him would have paid for that Audi, stolen or otherwise.'

'The thing is, Hat, it's just that, well, I think you should know.' Grace hesitated. 'Look, Kit was doing some sort of deal outside the Black Bull pub the other night. He didn't know I'd seen him and I wasn't going to say anything. But if Kit, Arius and Hugo are involved in something, and Holly Close Farm appears to be their safe house, you need to put a stop to it. Right now.'

## 30

It seemed to Grace as she lay wide awake in bed the following morning, watching the luminous red digits tick away the minutes and then the hours from 3 a.m., there was only one way forward in all this mess. She'd tell Cassie she couldn't continue with the class. She didn't *want* to continue, couldn't *bear* the thought of having Noah Haddon in front of her every day reminding her of his dad. She turned over, pulling the duvet across her body while desperately trying to rid herself of Ross Haddon's face, distorted with fury, as he'd stood in her kitchen knocking back the whole bottle of wine in what must have only been five minutes, moving towards her and grabbing at her wrist as though he wanted to really hurt her.

That was the beauty of supply teaching: she could quit, just like that. Cassie would want to know why, of course, but she could say it was all too much for her, that she shouldn't have taken on full-time work when she was suddenly a single mum. She could say her dad was ill, frail, and her mum needed help with him. What rubbish, Grace. Anyone who knew Katherine and Robert Greenwood striding out on the golf course, at bridge or setting out on yet another cruise, would know she was lying. And it was tempting fate. What if she said that and her dad dropped down dead the next day?

Grace turned over once more, closing her eyes against the regular march of time insistently portrayed by the damned digital clock, but the alternative was Ross's face and his hate-filled words, and her eyes snapped open once more. She was so tired. But she was giving in her notice: she could come home and sleep through the whole day tomorrow once she'd taken the kids themselves to school. Cassie would just have to get onto the supply agency. Not her problem, Grace told herself, thumping the pillow and wondering if it were possible to fall asleep with her eyes open.

She woke with a start, her pulse racing. How in God's name was it now 8 a.m.? Hell. For a brief second she considered ringing in and saying she couldn't move, she'd been struck down by some dreaded lurgy, but her professional head got the better of her. But only just.

Both kids were still fast asleep and Grace knew there was no way she was going to be in for the bell at 8.50. She might as well be upfront and ring Cassie; tell her she'd slept in and she'd be there when she could.

She found her mobile in the veritable turmoil of duvet and pillows in which she'd spent the last few hours. Honesty was the best policy.

'Cassie? Grace.'

'You OK?'

'Really sorry, Cassie. Going to be late. Was just setting off and found the car had a puncture.'

'Right, OK. Do you want me to come out and fetch the three of you?'

Heaven forfend. 'No, no it's fine,' Grace twittered. 'All

under control. Next-door neighbour helping. Just wanted you to know I'll be a bit late.'

'Don't worry. I'll send Deimante in to hold the fort once she's done her lollipop stint. Get in as soon as you can.'

'Which tyre was it?' Cassie was in the hall talking to Stan, the caretaker as Grace hurried through, ushering Jonty and Pietronella to their respective classes.

'Sorry?'

'The tyre? You had a puncture?'

'Which tyre?' Grace felt herself redden. 'Oh, it was a tyre… you know… on my *car*…'

'Mummy was still in bed at breakfast time, Mrs Beresford,' Jonty piped up. 'And I think I've got the wrong shoes and socks on.' He looked down almost in some surprise at his battered old trainers with the accompanying pair of *Toy Story*-emblazoned socks belonging to Pietronella that had somehow replaced the usual polished black school shoes and grey socks. 'This isn't like Mummy at all,' he added sagely for the headteacher's benefit.

'OK, Cassie.' Grace felt all the fight go out of her. 'I need to speak to you.'

'Lunchtime? My office?' Cassie patted Grace's arm. 'Don't worry, Atilla the Hun is with your class.'

Five minutes later she was in her classroom, the kids sitting at their tables, mesmerised as Deimante came to the end of a Lithuanian folk tale with its accompanying actions:

'… so, se horrid monster wis se great big ears, wis se big black beard and se great big green staring eyes who had frightened her so badly go away and se loffley fairies who live by se lake hear her and run up to her. "Why you cry, young lady? Why you sigh so much?" Se girl tell sem what is wrong and se loffley fairies begins to comfort her. "Here is soft pillow for you, and quilt and loffley pair of... of pjs. Here is loffley big... gins and tonic and a... a giant Toblerones. You not be unhappy. You go to sleep." Se fairies make bed for her, another sing her loffley song and so se sad lady go to sleep. She sleep very sweetly, and in morning when she open her eyes all is better. Se end.'

If only, Grace thought, as she thanked Deimante and ordered the kids to get changed for their Games lesson, that were really the case.

Jesus, it was cold out here on the playing field. It seemed forever since the worm-divining caper out here back in September, when the weather was still warm and she hadn't yet even heard of Ross Haddon. Grace shivered, pulling her thin coat around her shoulders, cross with herself for forgetting her games kit and trainers. Normally, she'd be fully kitted out and joining in with the skipping and ball skills. She'd not felt it fair to berate a couple of the kids who'd also forgotten their kit – Noah Haddon, as usual one of them – and who, like her were dressed in outdoor shoes and coats rather than the regulation tracksuit and trainers.

The class was split up into six groups working on a circus of activities with Deimante, dressed in a rather strange dayglow orange tracksuit, in charge of football, her tiny five-foot frame darting here and there as she endeavoured to teach goal-keeping skills. Noah, even though not in his football boots, was way ahead of the others in the group and for a split-second Grace felt resentment that Deimante was so easily able to control and empathise with Ross's son through their shared skills in, and love of, football.

Grace herself felt so tired, so fed up at yet another relationship coming to nothing and ending so horribly, that she took the easy way out and, hands in pockets, walked around the other groups, supervising where necessary and advising on a teaching point when and if it arose. It was a copout, she knew, the worst possible way to teach Games, but she'd had enough, she just wasn't a good teacher at the moment. It was time to tell Cassie so.

Grace blew her whistle to move each group on to its next activity.

'I'm staying here, Miss,' Noah called from the football area.

'That's not fair, Miss. Why should *he* play football all lesson?' Edward Granger was most put out.

'*No one* is staying on in any one particular group,' Grace raised her voice. 'All of you, you included, Noah, move yourselves to the next group please.'

'I'm not playing with those silly rubber rings!' Noah shouted. 'They're for babies.'

'Well, you're acting like one. Move it, please, Noah. Now.'

Noah was just about to retort, when Deimante, instead of her usual riposte at any recalcitrant behaviour, whispered something in Noah's ear and he put down the football – but not without kicking it crossly into the bushes first – and moved on with his group who were already making up a team game, as instructed, with the different-coloured rubber quoits.

'I can't be arsed with these bloody things,' Grace heard Noah mutter to anyone listening. Normally she'd have hauled him right out but a) sometimes confrontation just wasn't the answer and b) she couldn't, she realised, be arsed herself. She stuck her hands in her pockets once again and set off to see what the skipping rope group were up to. Skipping, she supposed.

Grace turned around five minutes later to find Noah wandering off and called, 'Noah, where's your quoit?'

'Hanging up in t'cloakroom, Miss.' He grinned at his own witty repartee and carried on walking off.

'Get back over here!' she shouted, but he was intent on the field boundary wall separating the school area from the main road running through the village, and ignored her. She saw there were a couple of other kids sitting on the wall and was just about to shout at them for being there when she realised they were much older than Little Acorns' pupils, probably in their mid-teens.

'Come on, Noah, back to the class,' Grace said calmly as she caught up with him. 'You're out of bounds here.'

'You don't have to do what she says, Noah lad,' one of them, a cliché in a dark hoody and back-to-front baseball hat, jeered.

'He most certainly does,' Grace smiled. 'OK, lads, off you go. You shouldn't be here, you know that.'

'But Noah's our mate. We've come to talk to him.'

'That's as may be but, at the moment, he also happens to be my pupil.'

'Fuck off, you old bat.' The taller of the two spoke for the first time, but jumped down off the wall and back onto the road as he did so. 'See you tonight, Noah, down at t'rec. Don't be late.'

For once, Noah did as Grace requested, shocked, she realised, at her being addressed with such foul language by these mates of his. 'Sorry, Miss,' he said as he walked back with her. 'That were rude. You know, what Liam just said.'

'Yes, it was, but I'm not blaming *you*.' Grace stopped. 'How come you know these big lads, Noah? Does your granny or your dad know you hang out with them?'

'I play football on the rec with them. Spider, that's the other one, wants to play for Man U.'

'Well, his not going to school won't get him there,' Grace said.

'He's left school. He says he can't get a job. But soon, he's going to be earning *millions* when he plays for Man U. He goes over to Manchester all the time and they give him a bit of money. You know, to keep him hanging on so he doesn't sign for Man City or Everton.'

'Right. Has he told you that?'

'Yes, he's my mate. But to be honest, Miss, I don't think he'll make it professionally. He can't play as good as me. In fact, I bet he's making it all up.'

'I think you might be right, Noah.'

Noah looked up at her with his father's green eyes, shrugged and walked off to join the others.

'Grace, come in.' Cassie pulled out a chair and indicated she should sit.

'I can say what I'm going to say, standing, Cassie.'

'Unfortunately, I can't say what *I* have to say with you standing. Come on, sit down.'

Grace sat down gratefully. Why was she so tired? Why did she feel if someone said something nice to her, she'd burst into tears?

'Grace, I've had Noah Haddon's mother in this morning.' Cassie stopped to gauge Grace's reaction.

'Oh?' Grace felt her pulse race.

'She says you're having an affair with her husband.'

'Yes, I am,' Grace said as calmly as she could. 'Well, I was.'

'Oh, bloody hell, Grace. I wasn't expecting that! So, you *were*? As in, you're not anymore?'

'Nope. Look, Cassie, to save you and the school any further embarrassment, I'm handing in my notice.'

'You're on supply. You don't have to give notice. You can just leave…'

'Right then, I'm leaving.' Grace began to get up.

'But there's no way I'm letting you. You know how much I rate you as a teacher, Grace. You're one of the best here – but don't tell Josh I said that.'

'Look, Cassie, I'm a crap teacher at the moment; if you'd seen me teaching Games this morning, you'd have fired me.'

'Oh, don't be so daft. It's Monday morning; we all have our off days. I assume there was no flat tyre this morning?'

Grace shook her head. 'Sorry about that. Wrong of me to lie. I'd been awake most of the night worrying about Ross Haddon.'

'Why? Had he hurt you?'

Grace stared. 'What makes you think he might have hurt me?'

'David and I had a meeting with social services re the Haddons after school on Friday. We wanted to know more about what is going on in that little boy's life.'

'And?'

'Well, it seems – and Mrs Haddon confirmed it this morning – Ross Haddon isn't quite as squeaky clean as he'd have us believe when he first sat here a couple of months ago. Though there was no implication from social services that either Ross or Natasha Haddon have physically abused *Noah*.'

'No, I really didn't think for one moment they had.'

'But the pair of them are embroiled in a very toxic relationship, and unfortunately poor old Noah sees things and hears things he shouldn't. We knew there was a restraining order against Mrs Haddon...'

'Was?' Grace raised an eyebrow.

'Apparently restraining orders can be indefinite or for a set term. This one included an occupation order, which states who can live in the family home or enter the immediate surrounding area, and was granted at the magistrates' court after Mrs Haddon was up for assault. But it was just for six months, presumably to give the pair of them time to cool off.' Cassie frowned. 'When she turned up here at school, you know, when we had that first meeting with Mr Haddon a couple of months ago, she wasn't actually breaking the order as far as I can see. What I mean is, she was allowed to come into school if Ross himself wasn't here. But the actual contact with Ross Haddon, as well as thumping him while she was on the order, could most certainly have had her back in court on a new charge of DV.'

'DV?'

'Domestic violence. As well as, of course, her breaking the order which she blatantly had. Mr Haddon obviously made the decision not to report her to the police after that.'

'Well, he wouldn't, would he?' Grace sighed. 'It would have meant the restraining order carrying on. And as far as I can see, Ross didn't want that.'

'The six months is just about up, according to Mrs Haddon,' Cassie said, 'and I suppose there's nothing to stop the pair of them being together again in the next few weeks.'

'I think they deserve each other,' Grace said tiredly. 'Ross Haddon certainly wasn't who I thought he was, you know, who he led us to believe was the bad guy in all this mess.'

'I can see why you fell for him, Grace. He's a very charming, intelligent and good-looking man.'

'Until he turns.'

'Did he turn on you?'

'Hmm.' Grace couldn't stop the tears as she remembered how frightened she'd felt, violated even, at his behaviour in her kitchen. 'Sorry, Cassie.' She reached for one of the tissues on the desk, embarrassed. 'Not physically as such, although he did grab and twist my wrist and his furious face was right up against mine. I keep seeing it, you know, sort of distorted, twisted with rage. But it was more that Natasha Haddon had been round with a horrible doll for Pietronella while Ross and I were in Leeds.'

'A doll? She knew where you lived?' Cassie stared. 'Oh my God, Grace. Did she hurt Pietronella?'

'No, no, Pietronella loves her. Keeps asking when she can see the lovely lady again. And wants to know where her dolly is. I buried it deep in the dustbin.'

'I'm a bit lost with all this, Grace.' Cassie looked at the

clock above her door. 'Hell, it's nearly time for class. Is she stalking you? Do you need to report this to the police? No wonder you can't sleep.'

'Daren't sleep, I think,' Grace sniffed trying to smile. 'The thing is, when I'm in school and see Noah, I just see Ross Haddon now and feel really anxious. I need to leave, Cassie. I...'

'Go home, Cassie. You look wiped out. I'll take your class this afternoon – I'm getting a big backside sitting here at my desk all day, sorting all this bloody admin; it'll do me good to go a few rounds with Noah Haddon – and then see how you feel?'

'I'll have to be back in a few hours to pick up the kids.'

'Can't you ask David to pick them up? He and Ben Carey are coming in this afternoon to see Josh about something. Something to do with the Christmas concert Josh is organising. Hell, silly season here again already.'

'David's not happy with me.'

'Over Ross Haddon?'

'Hmm. I had to ring him the other night to get Ross physically out of my house.'

Cassie stared. 'Oh blimey. But you're such good mates normally. Why wasn't he happy?'

'He said I wasn't fit to be a mother. That I'd put Pietronella in danger.'

'Oh, that's ridiculous.'

'Look, Cassie, I will go home if that's OK with you; my head is absolutely banging now. I'll ask Harriet to pick the kids up for me.'

Grace gathered her bags and coat and headed for the main door.

'Grace.' David Henderson, ever the gentleman, held the door open for her as she walked through.

'David... I...'

And without another look or word in her direction, he set off through reception.

## 31

'A re we ever going to get round to discussing this book, or what?' Ariadne demanded. 'I mean, that's what we're here for isn't it?'

Juno glanced across at the others, deep in conversation over their respective plans for Christmas. It wasn't even December yet and the last thing she wanted in her present state of mind was to be reminded of the whole commercial overindulgence when there were still several weeks to go. And she'd been so excited, so looking forward to having the Full Monty of Christmas dinner at her place with Scott. She'd even worked out a little plan of the table seating with the kids, with her dad and Arius – with Maya and Esme even. With Scott...

'You're absolutely right, Ariadne, let's get on with it,' Harriet was saying placatingly. She was always a bit in awe of Ariadne, she'd recently confided to Juno, particularly as Juno's sister's choice of book, last month, had been way above the comprehension of mere mortals such as herself.

It had been Izzy who, feeling somewhat bereft after the final performance of *Jesus Christ Superstar* back in the summer, suggested they carry on the camaraderie they'd enjoyed at rehearsals in a monthly book club. 'We were just talking about what we're doing for Christmas,' Harriet went on, obviously for Ariadne's benefit, 'but come on, books out, what did we think?'

'I want to be as far away as possible.' Ariadne sighed, reaching for the paperback in question on the sideboard behind her, but nevertheless drawn into the Christmas chat. 'I'd really like to go to Italy.'

'Ooh, Grace and I spent a week in Cortina d'Ampezzo one Christmas,' Harriet enthused, and then laughed. 'Actually, I hated every minute.'

'Well, that's not really Italy, is it? You know, the *real* Italy. Just a load of posh people with more money than sense flinging themselves down mountains and then drinking themselves senseless at the bottom. I really want to visit Locorotondo in the Puglia region or Trento in Trentino. I've been reading up about the area, with its Buonconsiglio Castle, galleries and outdoor frescoes.'

'Stop it, Ari, you're becoming a patronising, grumpy old woman,' Juno tutted. 'Ignore her, Harriet, she's been in a foul mood all week.'

'What's up, Ari?' Izzy asked. 'Didn't the book I chose do anything for you?'

'Not really, Izzy. I guessed who did it from the get-go.' Ariadne was still unsmiling.

'Oh, I didn't,' Izzy said cheerfully. 'I didn't have a clue.'

'I'm sorry, Izzy,' Ariadne finally relaxed and smiled. 'It wasn't a bad read. Quite good actually, for getting me off to sleep at night.'

'I think that's called damning with faint praise.' Izzy sniffed, helping herself to a handful of the nibbles Ariadne had put out on a low table in front of the sitting room open fire. 'So, what's up then?'

'Oh, I just want to be off somewhere. I've had enough of living in a small parochial town and teaching kids who're not really interested in what I'm saying.'

'Why *don't* you get off then?' Grace had just arrived, joining the others by the fire and immediately joining in with the conversation while taking off her coat. 'Sorry, I'm late. Lilian got the time wrong for babysitting. I mean, Ariadne, there's nothing to keep you here, is there?'

Ariadne glanced across at Juno. 'I worry about my sisters.'

'Hey, don't make me the excuse for your not packing up and setting off,' Juno protested. 'I'm fine.'

'Not fine actually, Juno,' Izzy interrupted. 'You know, the little crying session you had at the surgery this week?'

'Do you mind, Izzy?' Juno snapped crossly, embarrassed. 'Not telling everyone my business?'

'We're your mates, Juno,' Harriet soothed. 'We need to be kept in the loop on how you're coping. We can listen, and feed you wine and crisps. Stop eating them all, Izzy and pass them to Juno.'

'See what I mean?' Ariadne raised an eyebrow in Juno's direction. 'Juno's staggering around under a broken heart, Tilda still hates school and Pandora's worried stiff about Hugo and whatever it is he's getting himself involved in. I'm not convinced Lexia, going through the breakup of her marriage and still living with Mum, is totally happy either.'

Grace glanced across at Harriet who gave a barely perceptible nod of the head. 'Listen, Ariadne, Juno's told us how you're both worried that Hugo and your brother—'

'Half-brother,' Ariadne snapped. 'Arius.' Ariadne frowned across at Juno who put up her hands in acquiescence.

'—that it looks like Hugo and Arius might be involved in this drug problem in the village. Harriet won't mind you knowing that she's worried Kit may have something to do with it too. He's had enough money to buy himself a racy Audi which turned out to be dodgy; he's obviously mixing with some shady characters.' Grace paused. 'And I saw him down in town, in the Black Bull being handed some money by a couple of men.'

'So why haven't you asked him outright, Harriet?' Ariadne asked crossly. 'Why are you pussyfooting around him?'

'I'm *not* pussyfooting around him,' Harriet said, stung. 'I did manage to catch him and sit him down and tell him I was worried, as well as ask him exactly where he was getting all his money from after Grace finally told me what she'd seen. He just thought it really funny that I should think he was a drug dealer. He's been away all week in Holland.'

'Holland?' Izzy exclaimed. 'Well, that's it then. He's *obviously* bringing in drugs if he's working in Holland.' She frowned. 'Or *diamonds*. He's a diamond smuggler, Hat.'

'For heaven's sake, Izzy,' Grace snapped, glancing across at Harriet's stricken face. 'Harriet and I have spent the last couple of evenings, incognito as it were, down at Holly Close Farm where Juno said she saw Leo Hutchinson.'

'Who's Leo Hutchinson?' demanded Ariadne.

'Oh, of course, you weren't with us, Ari, when we went to see the stripper.'

'I most certainly wasn't.' Ariadne frowned. 'I wouldn't choose to go and see a stripper.'

'We weren't actually there by *choice*,' Grace retorted, raising her eyebrows in Izzy's direction. 'Leo Hutchinson is a known drug addict.'

'*Who* knows him?'

'*We* do, Ari. He's on our books at the surgery. Will you stop damned well interrupting?' Juno was getting cross.

'Juno saw him down at Holly Close Farm,' Grace continued.

'Where Dad and Arius are living? I knew it,' Ariadne said crossly. 'Why didn't you tell me this, Juno? Arius and Hugo are obviously dealing down there.'

'Ari, will you shut up and just listen?' Juno glared at her sister.

'So,' Grace went on, 'Harriet's asked Libby and Seb to keep an eye out, but they've seen absolutely *nothing* untoward.'

'Well, they won't have if Kit's been in Holland all week,' Izzy said, matter-of-factly.

'Thanks for that, Izzy.' Harriet glared at her in turn.

'Lilian has come over to look after the kids the last couple of evenings while Hat and I have kept watch down the lane at the farm,' Grace explained. 'And we saw absolutely nothing at all either.' Grace smiled. 'Except a couple of foxes and a rather amazing badger. They're big bloody things, aren't they, up close? I think we've got things totally out of proportion, you know. I listened to Clementine who, because of Lucy, is constantly on the lookout for any problems with drugs, and got caught up in the drama of it all.'

'The young kid who served us at Clementine's was very obviously on *something*,' Juno interrupted. 'David

Henderson had to actually send him away and take over himself.'

'The knight in shining armour to the rescue, yet again,' Grace sniffed pointedly while the others look at her in surprise. 'So, as I was saying,' Grace continued, refusing to be drawn on her curt response, 'there were no strange cars down there, no comings and goings. We quite enjoyed ourselves actually,' Grace laughed. 'We took a flask and some flapjacks and spent the time catching up—' Grace broke off as Harriet's phone rang.

'... You think it's Kit's hire car?' Harriet was asking. 'You can see him? OK, don't let him know you've seen him. Grace and I are going to come down; I want to catch him red-handed before he gets into any real trouble.'

'He's probably just there to see Maya, Hat,' Grace protested. 'Especially if he's been away all week.'

'Maybe,' Harriet replied, throwing her phone into her bag. 'Probably. But I want to see for myself. Sorry to break up the party before we've even got the book out,' Harriet said, almost running to put on her coat. 'Kit's just arrived down at the farm. I want to watch and see what he's up to.'

'Well, if there's something going on down there, I want to come too.' Ariadne snatched up the jacket she'd thrown onto the sofa on her return from school. 'I need to see if Hugo is there.'

'He's *my* nephew as well,' Juno said crossly. 'I should be there as well.'

'Well, don't go without me,' Izzy said. 'I'm coming too.'

'The five of us?' Ariadne shot the others a look. 'We're not the effing Famous Five, you know, off on some adventure.'

'Of course we're not,' Izzy retorted. 'We haven't got a

dog between us. You should have brought Sam, Harriet. You know, made it a bit more authentic.'

'Just bark a bit and sniff at your bottom, Izzy,' Juno snapped, the good-humoured demeanour she'd desperately attempted to assume in the wake of Scott's outing at Clementine's finally deserting her. 'I'll drive, Harriet,' she ordered. 'Kit won't recognise my car and your two will be full of child seats.'

'You never said you were in your Mini,' Izzy complained, squashed between Grace and Harriet on the back seat. 'I assumed you were in Fraser's Volvo.'

'Never assume anything,' Juno said impatiently, driving off at such speed Ariadne's head shot back onto the head rest of the passenger seat. 'The Volvo went shortly after Fraser himself; I never liked either of them very much.'

'Do you not think we're all being overly dramatic here?' Izzy retorted. 'Grace, could you possibly get off my foot and move that way a bit.'

'No, I couldn't. My ear is already squashed against the window. Are you insured for five of us, Juno?' Grace attempted a new position but her arm was firmly wedged under Izzy's large backside.

'No idea,' Juno replied. 'Just let me concentrate on driving and we won't need it.'

'Is that Kit's car?' Ariadne asked, once Harriet had instructed Juno to drive the Mini through a farm gate into a field, pulling up where her car couldn't be seen from the farm cottages but where they themselves were able to view what was going on.

'I think so.' Harriet nodded. 'It's a hire car so I can't be certain…' She broke off as a much smaller car came slowly down the lane, appeared to hesitate and then shot through the gate, bouncing haphazardly through the ruts in the field and coming to a standstill at the far end of the field.

'Get down,' Izzy ordered.

'I can't with you in the middle,' Grace hissed.

'What if it's a dealer?' Harriet whispered. 'If he finds out I'm Kit's mother he might take it out on him. Or me. He might have a gun.'

'Probably a machete,' Izzy said sagely. 'Leo once said his dealers carry them for protection.'

'Thanks for that, Izzy,' Harriet replied, suddenly feeling very frightened.

'Car door's opening,' Grace whispered.

'Get down,' Izzy ordered once more.

'I can't, I told you.' Grace was getting cross as she attempted to peer out of the now steamed-up rear window. 'It's a girl,' she said in some surprise.

'Presumably drug-dealing isn't solely the domain of men,' Ariadne turned to the others in the back. 'You know, women—'

'Oh, don't start a bloody lecture on gender now, Ari,' Juno hissed.

'It's Miss O'Connor.' Grace and Harriet spoke as one. 'What's she *doing*?'

The girl moved stealthily towards the field's dry-stone wall, her white coat stark against the blackness of the Yorkshire-stone.

'Do you think she's not who she says she is?' Harriet whispered. 'Oh, hell, I bet she's an undercover cop and has gone after Kit, you know pretended she's a bit of a dope—'

'Because she is, you know, pretty dizzy,' Grace confirmed, nodding.

'—in order to lull him into a false sense of security to find out what he's really up to? Mind you, she's had sex with him. Is that allowed? Wasn't there some case in the news about an undercover cop being sued for having an actual relationship with some woman he was surveying?'

'Perk of the job, I'd have said,' Izzy said, nodding. 'You know, who *wouldn't* want sex with your exceptionally gorgeous son, Hat? She's not very good at subterfuge though, is she?' Izzy went on, craning her neck and breathing heavily the remains of the cheese and onion crisps into Grace's ear. 'She needs to get a balaclava and a black coat.'

'I'm going to have a word with her,' Grace said, suddenly. 'Find out what's going on.'

'No, no, don't do that. She might turn nasty.'

'Miss O'Connor?' Grace frowned, suddenly remembering how Niamh had accidentally spilled red wine in the lecherous Judge Fitzgerald's lap that Sunday lunch when she'd first appeared at Harriet's house. Was it no accident and she was really executing her revenge at Harriet's father-in-law's sweaty palm on her knee? 'Oh Jesus, look.'

They all sat totally still, staring as four cars sped down the lane, past Holly Close Farm itself, three of them pulling up directly outside the two farm cottages while the fourth slewed across the drive, blocking any potential exit.

'Oh my God, look at this lot,' Juno cried, terrified. 'Arius is in there and possibly Hugo. Ring 999, Ariadne. Do something. Get the police.'

'They *are* the police,' Ari said grimly, as uniformed, plain-clothed and body-armoured men ran towards the cottages. 'They've come for them. Miss O'Connor must have tipped them off.'

'Mum, what's going on?' Libby's frightened voice could be heard in the dark, silent car as Harriet answered her phone on its first ring. 'Is it Kit? Are they after Kit?'

'Stay where you are, Libby. Is Seb with you?'

'No, he's still at work.'

'Just stay where you are, Libby,' Harriet hissed, ending the call abruptly.

Niamh O'Connor didn't appear to be striding forth from her hiding place behind the wall, job completed, to meet the other police. Instead, she sort of crumpled, her back towards the wall, her face, the others could now see, frightened.

'I'm going in,' Ariadne said, opening the passenger car door before the others could stop her.

'Don't be so bloody stupid,' Juno hissed, grabbing onto Ariadne's jacket.

Ariadne shook her off and set off in the direction of the gate. She stopped, said something to Miss O'Connor who then, throwing a look of utter surprise in the direction of what she must have previously assumed to be an empty car, scuttled back in the direction of her own.

'Come on. We might as well all try and get as far as we can,' Juno said, jumping out and leaving the doors open for the others to follow her. 'My dad's presumably in there with the boys. It's not going to do his blood pressure any good that lot knocking the door down. Hell, they are as well, listen to that.'

'Police, police, we're coming in...' rent the cold night air, followed by loud bangs and crashes as the door of the first cottage was bashed in with a small metal battering ram.

'Oh God, they've bashed down the wrong door,' Juno shouted as she cautiously led the others towards the cottages. That's not Dad's cottage, it's Esme's. She'll have an absolute fit.'

'Harriet, they must be after *Kit* then,' Grace said, holding Harriet's arm to stop her rushing in after the police.

Within a few minutes two lads, handcuffed, were brought out and led to one of the waiting cars.

'I know them,' Grace said, staring. 'They're Noah's mates. You know, Harriet, the ones I was telling you about who told me to eff off the other day on the playing field?' She paused, hand to her mouth. 'I bet anything Noah's in there with them. Oh God, he's only ten, for heaven's sake.'

'Kit,' Harriet shouted as her son was next to be brought out, handcuffed. She made a dash towards him, but was held back by a police officer in uniform as one of the plain clothes officers yelled furiously in their direction. 'Get the fucking rubberneckers out of here. It's not a fucking show, you lot.'

'Mum? Mum, I haven't got a clue what's going on.' A white-faced Kit turned back towards Harriet as his head was pushed through another of the car doors. 'I've only just got back from Amsterdam, Mum,' he continued to shout from the depths of the open car, 'and came down to see if Maya wanted to go out for a drink, and I was just waiting for her because she's not back yet...'

'Is there a little kid in there, Kit?' Grace shouted, braving the wrath of the police officer walking towards her. She might find Noah Haddon bloody hard work but any ten-year-old would be terrified with what was happening in there. As his teacher, didn't she have some sort of responsibility for his welfare? How long after school hours did *loco parentis* continue, because his granny, and bloody Ross and Natasha Haddon – only interested in their own toxic relationship – were effing useless. Did they not wonder where Noah was at eight-thirty in the evening?

'Yes, there is,' Kit shouted back. 'I've no idea who he is. I assumed he was some relative of Esme's.'

'Shut it,' one of the armed officers snarled in his face before slamming the door and, ignoring Harriet and the others, hurried back inside Esme's cottage once more.

'What the hell is going on?' Patrick Sutherland, dressed only in a bath towel and jaunty pink shower cap, suddenly appeared at the newly built garden wall separating the pair of semi-detached cottages, Arius at his side.

'Go back in, Sir. Close your door. Someone will come round later and explain.'

'Ariadne?' Patrick, without his spectacles, peered into the darkness. 'Is that you? And Juno as well? What, in God's name, are you doing?'

'Sir, I won't tell you again, go inside.' The police officer turned on the women, clutching each other as they stood watching. 'And you lot,' he snarled, 'unless you get back where you came from, I'm arresting you all on suspicion of aiding and abetting as well as interfering with the police in the execution of their duty.'

'I'm a teacher at the local primary school.' Although she

was trembling with the aftershock of it all, Grace spoke authoritatively. 'I think there's a young child in there. And, isn't there some law about search warrants? I'm sure the bashing down of doors shouldn't be carried out if there is a minor on the premises...'

She broke off as Esme was led out, handcuffed, between two armed officers. Esme stopped as she saw Juno. 'I never understand what Scott saw in *you*, anyway.' She gave a sardonic little laugh and walked towards a waiting car.

'Right.' There didn't seem to be any answer to that, Juno thought, although, in the days to come, she would come up with plenty: pithy and full of expletives.

'Look, can I just go in and get Noah?' Grace asked in some exasperation.

'No need, love, we're bringing him out now.'

Grace hurried forwards as Ariadne, Izzy, Juno and Harriet continued to stand and stare. One of the uniformed officers led the way as the boy followed in his wake.

'Gabe? Gabriel?' Juno ran towards her son. 'What are you doing? What are *you* doing here?'

## 32

The custody sergeant on duty down at the main Midhope Police Station on Princess Street looked up in surprise. 'Dr Armstrong? What you doing down here, love? Been pushing your prescription drugs to the town's addicts?' He grinned widely and then, almost immediately, frowned as he saw Juno was in no mood for being teased.

'Hello, Mick.' Juno had seen Mick Staveley only the previous day when he'd been at the surgery complaining that his psoriasis was getting out of hand. 'I need your help here. I'm not quite sure what's going on but, as I'm sure you know, there's been a drugs bust over at Holly Close Farm. My son was there.'

'Your son?' Sergeant Staveley frowned again. 'He a dealer? Or a punter?'

'Mick, he's a thirteen-year-old boy. He's shy and gauche and has somehow got caught up in this mess.'

'Not unusual, love. We've had kids as young as ten...' he turned to the uniformed woman police officer for confirmation. 'Nine? Nine, Dr Armstrong. Nine-year-old kids involved. So, thirteen isn't unusual. I know, I know—' he put up a hand as Ariadne who up until then had said nothing, attempted to speak '—it's *always* a mistake and it's *never* your kids that could ever be involved, but—'

'Right, I think we need our solicitor here,' Ariadne snapped.

'Well, have you got one?' Juno snapped back. 'Because *I* haven't.'

'You're in the middle of a divorce, Ju,' Ariadne tried to speak calmly. 'Ring *him*.'

'He's a *divorce* lawyer. What would he know about drugs and kids?' Juno turned back to the desk. 'Look, Mick, Gabriel is thirteen. Surely he's too young to be arrested?'

Mick Staveley laughed. 'Hey, love, you should see *some* of the little toe-rags we get in here. I tell you, what goes on over in the Youth Court would make your hair curl.'

'Not *born* toe-rags, surely?' Ariadne was cross. 'Kids are not *born* bad; they do what they do because of how they've been brought up. Lack of parental guidance, lack of education, the physical violence they have to live with, lack of family.'

'If you say so, love.' Sergeant Staveley raised an eyebrow followed by a short guffaw of cynicism, that would, Juno knew, only inflame Ariadne's argument.

'Pandora,' Juno suddenly said, before Ariadne's could respond. 'She's a criminal lawyer.'

'Not practised for nearly twenty years though,' Ariadne said doubtfully.

'She'll know somebody though, won't she? Pandora will know what to do.'


'Have you seen him yet?' Pandora was at the police station

within the next hour, a smart, booted and suited, young Asian man at her side.

'Yes, of course,' Juno said. 'A parent or appropriate adult has to be with a child before they can question him. You should know that, Pan.'

'Of course. Absolutely. Just making sure they're following procedure,' Pandora replied importantly. 'Now, this is Rizwan Mahmud. I made a couple of phone calls, called in a couple of favours, and was told he'd know what's the best way forward.' Pandora lowered her voice. 'He's young, but very good. Knows his stuff.'

Juno got the impression Pandora was enjoying the drama of it all now, as far as she was aware, Hugo wasn't involved in the evening's raid.

'Just because Hugo wasn't actually round at Esme's place tonight, doesn't mean he and Arius are not part of all this, you know, Pan,' Ariadne hissed as Pandora made to sit down.

'He's not. Neither is Arius,' Pandora was at her most condescending. 'Richard, Dad and I had it out with both boys last night. Found out why they keep going over to Manchester and why different phones are ringing day and night.'

'And?' Ariadne and Juno spoke at once.

'We're very proud of Hugo. And Arius. He's been *such* a good influence on Hugo. That's all I'm going to say...' Pandora put up both hands in a dramatic little protestation that her sisters should not question her any further.

'Oh, come on, Pandora, you know you're dying to tell us,' Juno said tiredly, rubbing at her eyes.

'I promised.'

'Yes, well secrets between sisters don't count,' Ariadne snapped. 'Come on, Pan.'

Pandora moved away from the custody sergeant's desk and, leaning forwards and making sure only Ariadne and Juno could hear, whispered proudly, 'Extinction Rebellion. The pair of them are *very* high up in the organisation in Manchester and are *determined* to save the planet from the mess *we've* left it in.'

'Speak for yourself,' Ariadne said irritably.

'Oh no, we're speaking for others,' Pandora smiled. 'From now on, Richard and I will be joining the boys in their protest marches and sit-ins and... and, you know, whatever else it is they do, and we shall be speaking, not for *ourselves*, but for the whole planet.'

'Fine, fine, all very admirable, Pan, but can I just remind you why we're here this evening?' Juno snapped. 'At this moment in time I'm far more interested in helping my son than Mother Earth.'

'Shouldn't we have someone from the Youth Offending Team?' demanded Ariadne. 'You know, Gabe is thirteen.'

'You're running away with yourself, Ms Sutherland,' Rizwan said. 'If he admits to some involvement, if he's actually guilty of an offence – and he's *not* actually been charged yet, you know – then what we'll be hoping for is a Youth Caution issued by the police. *Then* YOT will have some involvement. Better still, if it's not in the public interest to prosecute, then let's hope for no case to answer and he'll be allowed to leave. We'll go back in with you and let him tell us what's been going on.

*

'Gabriel, just tell us everything, darling. Tell us why you were down at Esme's house this evening. Were you at Grandpa Patrick's to begin with after football practice and then, you know, you just went next door to call in and see Esme? Is that what it was?' Juno asked hopefully. 'And suddenly the police were there? Were you as shocked as we were to see them there?'

'Dr Armstrong,' Rizwan said, a hand on her arm, 'you've asked over five questions there. Just let Gabriel speak.' The lawyer turned to Gabriel. 'Do you want to tell us, right from the beginning, Gabe? You know, what's been going on?'

For a good minute Gabriel sat in silence, his reddish fair hair standing out starkly against his pale freckled skin (he was so his father's son, Juno thought with a pang) unable or unwilling it seemed to speak and then, once he started, it all came out in a rush.

'Dad had left us—'

'But, Gabe, I thought you were OK about that. I asked you if you wanted to visit him in the summer and you said no—'

'Let him speak, Juno,' Pandora said.

'Dad had left us and I missed him. *You* were so happy with Scott. Every time I wanted to speak to you, you didn't seem to want to listen.'

'Oh, Gabe, that's not fair.'

'Juno…' Pandora frowned at her.

'You were so happy. Because, you know, you *hadn't* been happy for a long while. I knew that. And then you were off singing all the time or with Scott or tired out after working extra at the surgery. It was OK when I was playing cricket during the summer. And then when I went back to school, when I went into Y9 I *hated* it. Everyone started calling Tilda *the Weirdo* and I was really embarrassed about what she was like at school and on the bus. And then they started calling me *the Weirdo's Wee Brother*. And I couldn't do the maths. And then I couldn't understand the English stuff or the Science...' Gabe gave a short bark of laughter which turned into a sob. 'And me with a research scientist for a dad and a doctor for a mother. And some of the lads in one of the other classes kept laughing at me and mimicking me because of my Scottish accent. I've tried hard to speak Yorkshire like the rest of them but it doesn't work. And then I started crying...' Gabriel broke off, unable to carry on as huge fat tears rolled unhindered down his white face. Eventually he said, 'And they took a video on their phone of me crying. Mum, I'm thirteen and I was crying like a wee baby... and then they said they'd leave me alone if I gave them some money. And so I did.'

'But, Gabriel, why on earth didn't you tell me?' Juno brushed away her own tears as Gabriel put his head down on the table in order to hide his face in his arms. 'I'd have been up to school like a shot. You know I would.'

'No, I *didn't* know,' Gabriel, his spectacles askew on his tear-stained face, almost shouted from the depths of the table. 'Tilda was really miserable too because she hated school and had lost all her junior school friends, and was being laughed at by the other kids, even those she'd been really friendly with at Little Acorns. She kept crying and all *you* said was, "It'll get better, darling, you'll see. Come on, man up."' Gabriel affected a high-pitched voice and Juno immediately recognised herself. What had she done? She'd been so in love – in lust – with Scott, she'd not taken her kids' unhappiness seriously enough. Shame shot through her like molten liquid.

When Gabe didn't seem able to carry on, Rizwan said, gently, 'Tell us how you got involved with Esme Burkinshaw, Gabriel.'

'It was just a week after we'd gone back to school and school was *unbearable*.' Gabe almost spat the words as he lifted his face from the table and glared at Juno. She felt as if her heart was being pierced, such was Gabe's look of anger. 'I knew I had to get money for Monday or the video of me crying like a wee baby would go v... v... I can't think of the word ... *everywhere*. Esme had called round at the house for the first time, but you were out. I think you were over at Aunt Lexia's or something. I was at home and Scott was there and Esme arrived and they were sitting in the garden, drinking wine. Scott had left his jacket in the kitchen.'

'And? What happened, Gabe?' Juno took Gabriel's hand but he shrugged it off.

'I took his wallet out and pinched forty pounds.'

'Oh, Gabriel.' Juno closed her eyes momentarily.

'Esme came in and saw what I was doing. She was really nice, asked why I needed the money and so I told her. She said we mustn't tell Scott because he'd be so angry, he might not want anything to do with you again, Mum. And you were so happy with him. I didn't want to be the reason he left you.'

'Gabe, you were thirteen, for heaven's sake. Come on, why would Scott leave me because you'd taken some money of his?' Juno couldn't quite take it in.

'Esme said he could report me for theft and I'd end up at

the police station. And then you'd find out and Scott would go. And you'd be all unhappy again.'

'*Surely* you didn't believe all that?'

'Juno,' Pandora interrupted. 'He's telling you he *did* believe that.'

Gabe gave Pandora a brief, grateful glance and carried on. 'Esme told me to put the money back and then she gave me fifty pounds out of her own purse. She said I could pay her back by doing a couple of errands for her and, if I needed more money, she could give me a little job. She had a village vacancy.'

'I *bet* she did,' Juno fumed.

'She had a new beauty business in the village, she said, and the parcel post was so bad these days it would be quicker if I got on my bike and delivered packages for her. She said she had other places in Manchester and Sheffield and someone who worked for her would bring over the vitamins she was selling in the salon, on the train, and I was to bike down to her cottage or to Blush and Blow in the village and help deliver it.'

'But you didn't find it all a bit odd?' Ariadne was staring at this nephew of hers.

'I'm not *stupid*.' Gabriel glared at Ariadne. 'I soon realised what it was in the packages. I opened one and had a look.'

'And you carried on?' Rizwan gave Pandora and Juno a worried look, part of his defence, that Gabe had no idea what was in the packages, starting to crumble.

'I suppose I began to enjoy it. I liked being out on my bike in the dark when you thought I was at football or at one of my friends. But I haven't actually *got* any friends at school – no one wants to be mates with the Weirdo's Wee Brother who's thick and speaks with a Scottish accent, who has ginger hair and freckles and glasses and cries if you look at him... and... you know... hasn't... you know...'

'Hasn't what?' Juno and Ariadne leaned forward to hear.

'I think he means, hasn't hit puberty like most of the other boys,' Pandora said calmly. 'Is that what you're trying to say, Gabriel?'

Gabe flushed scarlet and nodded. 'There was a joke going round at school: *What's the difference between the Weirdo's Wee Brother and a brick...?*'

'Oh Gabe.' Juno went to hold his hand but, again, Gabe threw it off.

'Do you know the answer?' Gabriel glared at his mother. 'Do you? *Bricks get laid...*'

Juno reached for Gabriel's hand once again and this time Gabriel allowed it to stay there.

'*You* were always so busy at work, Mum, or out with Scott and I began to really like going down to Esme's. It was a bit like having a new granny. She made me omelettes: lovely cheesy ones and *really* lovely ones with salami and red pepper.'

Juno closed her eyes once more knowing if that fucking woman walked in here, this minute, she'd go for her: she, Juno, was always the one who made Gabe his omelettes.

'And Liam and Spider really liked me too. They were always down there, or on the train to and from Manchester.' Gabriel shot a look of defiance at Juno. 'I went with them once.'

'OK, let's just stop there, shall we?' Rizwan smiled faintly and glanced over at Pandora once more. 'I think, when you're questioned and making a statement, I shall be advising you, Gabriel, to answer "No comment"…'

# 33

'They let him come home,' Nick Westmoreland said tiredly as he walked into the kitchen, Kit following behind. 'Accepted, for the moment at any rate, that he'd been down at the cottages because he was going out with Esme Burkinshaw's daughter and had no idea what was going on. Regular little Fagin's den down there by all accounts.'

'Oh Kit, darling...'

'For heaven's sake, don't *Kit darling* him, Harriet,' Nick snapped crossly. 'It's after midnight and I've a plane to Brazil to catch in the morning. I know exactly what he's been up to now,' he added, heading for the stairs. 'I suggest you enlighten your mother where all this money you've got has been coming from, Christopher.'

Hell, Nick was obviously fuming to be calling Kit by his full handle.

'You go to bed, Nick. I've packed your case while you were down at the station and ironed a couple of shirts. Do you want anything to eat?'

'No, I just need sleep.' Nick turned back and, picking up his briefcase, set off once more.

'I wouldn't mind something,' Kit started, but seeing Harriet's face went, instead, and sat at the kitchen table.

'So, promise me, Kit, you've had nothing to do with Esme Burkinshaw's little set up?'

''Course not,' Kit pulled a face of irritation. 'For heaven's sake, it was only a matter of time before they were on to her. It all seems a bit amateurish, and she can't be overly bright if she didn't think one of those kids would eventually let on what they'd been up to.'

'So, where have you got all this money of yours from then? Who were the men giving you money down at the pub when Aunty Grace saw you?'

'Poker.'

'Sorry?'

'You heard, Mum.'

'Well I might have heard but that doesn't mean I understand. Poker as in card game poker?'

'Yep. I just happen to be a bloody good poker player.'

'Well, I don't know how,' Harriet sniffed in disbelief. 'I've always been able to tell from your face when you've been up to something.'

'Obviously not. Look, I *am* pretty hungry. I've not had anything except a miserable sandwich at lunchtime on the flight back from Amsterdam. I *was* planning to take Maya out for a meal.' When Harriet didn't appear to be making any inroads into resolving his hunger issue, Kit wandered over to the fridge and stuck his nose into its chilly depths as he'd done on so many other occasions. He brought out a triple pack of the twins' *Frozen*-emblazoned strawberry yoghurt and proceeded to make his way methodically through all three.

'So how long have you been playing poker?' Harriet demanded. 'I don't ever remember you being interested in, or being any good at, card games when we tried to get you to play with us? You wouldn't even play Monopoly. In fact, you've always hated any kind of games.'

'I love rugby.'

'You know what I mean.'

'It's depressing and a bit lonely being in foreign hotel rooms when I'm away working for Dad and David. What does someone my age do? Go down to the hotel restaurant and sit there by myself looking like a right loser with a starched napkin on my knee?'

'*I've* always taken my Kindle if I've been somewhere where I've had to sit and eat by myself,' Harriet shrugged. 'I actually rather enjoy it. You know, the peace and quiet of it.'

'Mum, I don't *have* a Kindle. I don't damned well read. You know that.'

'OK,' Harriet conceded the point. 'So instead you took up poker? What, in foreign cities? In Italy? Bloody hell, Kit, you could have been mobbed and murdered by the Mafia.'

'No,' Kit tutted irritably. 'I played Poker online. You know, in the hotel rooms. It's absolutely fascinating once you get into it.'

'But at the end of the day, you're gambling.' Harriet shook her head. 'And we all know where gamblers end up, don't we? Same place as drug addicts and alcoholics,' she went on, answering her own question when Kit didn't appear to know, or couldn't be bothered to come up with, the correct answer.

'Mum, I might not have been overly academic at school. Couldn't be doing with it all, you know that. But there are three things I *am* jolly good at: I can sell – Dad and David both know that – and now, it appears, I'm bloody good at poker too. I don't take risks; in the same way I don't take risks when I'm selling. You have to sit for literally hours when you're playing online. It can take all night.'

'You're playing poker all night when Dad's paying for a bed in a nice hotel for you? Well, tell him not to bother next time. Just sit in your car in the carpark and play poker.'

'It takes ages to build up a reputation when you're playing online. You have to be patient and really, really concentrate. You can end up sitting in front of the computer all day and sometimes all night. So, yes, I made a lot of money playing online poker. Together with that brilliant commission David gave me in the summer, I was able to buy the Audi. It was a bargain.'

'It was dodgy.'

'*I* didn't know that,' Kit said mulishly, starting on the block of cheese Harriet had intended for the following day's mac'n'cheese. Obviously, mac'n'fresh air now.

'So, what about these young kids down in the pub? The ones giving you money in the Black Bull?'

'So, I was having a drink at the Jolly Sailor down in Westenbury during the summer and got chatting to some blokes about online poker and was introduced to a poker-playing consortium held at different blokes' houses…'

'Well, surely that can't be legal?' Harriet interrupted. 'Don't you have to have a licence to gamble?'

'Bit of a grey area really,' Kit said. 'You can play games of poker, in your own home and between friends.'

'But these *weren't* your friends, Kit,' Harriet broke in. 'They were blokes you met in the pub.'

'I'm very friendly.' Kit grinned. 'They *wanted* me as their friend. To be fair, you can't just invite members of the public to join in. There was a village vacancy – you know in the consortium – one of the blokes had just died, heart attack apparently.'

'Are you sure he didn't have his boots filled with concrete and is now at the bottom of the cut?'

'Will you let me finish?' Kit said irritably. 'So, they bought me a few drinks, I became their *friend* and they invited me round for a game to see if I'd be any good. See if I could fit into the other bloke's shoes.'

'Concrete boots,' Harriet repeated.

'There's absolutely no limit on the stakes and prizes when you're playing at home,' Kit went on. 'Honestly, Google it if you don't believe me. I did.'

'Well, I can't see you're going to remain their friend if you're constantly winning,' Harriet said. 'And why did shifty-looking kids in hoodies have to meet you outside the pub in town to pay you?'

'They weren't shifty-looking,' Kit protested. 'Look, the people I've been playing with include a financier, a surgeon and a lawyer. They were very impressed when I told them I worked for David Henderson. *With* David Henderson. They're in their fifties and started playing at university years ago. One's a woman.'

'You can get dodgy women, you know,' Harriet snapped. 'Look at Esme Burkinshaw.'

'The group I've been playing with are totally above board. Honestly, Mum. Laurence Gardener's a divorce lawyer in Leeds, but didn't have the money on him when I had a big win last week. Didn't think I was going to take so much off him.' Kit laughed at his own obvious good fortune. 'He was going on some cruise the following day and asked if it was OK if his son met me in the pub down in town that he's always in, to give it to me.'

'Why not pay it directly into your bank account?'

Kit looked shifty. 'You know, tax and all that. Not sure if you're liable but, anyway, I wanted it cash in hand. Wanted to have cash to buy another pair of wheels. You can get good deals for cash.'

'More dodgy cars? I suggest, Kit, you go down to the dealerships this time. Go with your father. Driving to see Luomo customers in dodgy cars, no matter how good a salesman you think you are, isn't on, as I know Dad's already warned you.' Harriet paused. 'So, you said there are three things?'

'Three things?'

'Three things you are good at? *Jolly* good at?'

Kit grinned, reaching for the biscuit tin that was on a high shelf out of reach of the twins. 'Just ask Niamh O'Connor,' Kit laughed. 'Or Maya Burkinshaw.'

'Oh, for heaven's sake. Can your head *get* any bigger?' Harriet shot him a look as he sucked chocolate somewhat suggestively from a Twix finger. 'So, what *about* Miss O'Connor? And Maya? You do know Miss O'Connor was down at the farm tonight? Hiding behind the wall?'

'Oh God, again?'

'I assume she's stalking you?'

'Stalking's probably a bit strong; she does keep following me. I'm totally honest with them both, Mum. I'm not exclusive to either of them. Unfortunately, Niamh does keep popping up wherever I seem to be. Going to have to knock that relationship on the head I reckon.'

'I would think the ending of the relationship with Maya

Burkinshaw is *far* more imperative, Kit,' Harriet said crossly. 'You're not telling me she didn't know what was going on with her mother? She's a very bright girl by all accounts – you do know she's my friend, Juno Armstrong's ex's daughter? And it was Gabriel, Juno's thirteen-year-old, who was the kid in there this evening?'

Kit stared. 'No, no, I really didn't know that.'

'Grace was convinced it was one of the children in her class. Poor old Juno,' Harriet went on, almost to herself as Kit rummaged once more in the biscuit tin. 'So, do you think Maya was in on it all?'

'Dunno. Possibly. Probably. She always had pretty decent gear – you know the clothes and the bags – to say she's still a student.'

'Well, I should keep well away if I were you. In fact, I'm ordering you to. Keep right out of it, Kit.'

'Yes, I know, you're absolutely right.' Kit paused as he crunched a ginger biscuit and swallowed. 'Do you know, Mum, I ended up sitting next to this really gorgeous girl on the plane back from Holland. Got her phone number and have arranged to meet her in Manchester at the weekend. Right, one more biscuit and then I'm off to bed. Been rather a stressful day.'

# 34

'Ah, Grace, just the person.' Cassie Beresford popped her head round the office door and beckoned as Grace walked quickly down towards her classroom. December had suddenly arrived with Grace hardly realising it, and its accompanying dark days of cold sleety weather had left the kids cooped up in the classroom, frustrated at its restraint. Hell, she hadn't done a single thing about Christmas yet. Not thought about a turkey. She didn't even know what Dan was doing. Would he be spending the day with herself and the kids at her parents? What about Jonty? She didn't want his Christmas day split between her and Seb.

'What have I done now?' Grace frowned, impatiently looking at her watch but nevertheless changing direction and heading back to where Cassie held open the office door for her.

'Why do you always think you've done something wrong?' Cassie laughed. 'Sounds like a guilty conscience to me.'

'You won't persuade me to stay,' Grace said, smiling. 'As soon as you find someone suitable from the agency, I'm off.'

'Even if I tell you Noah Haddon's gone?'

'Gone? Where's he gone?'

'And that April Harrison has just rung me and assures me she'll be back after Christmas to teach your class?'

'Oh. Right.' It was alright, Grace thought, herself deciding she was leaving, but she felt (illogically) miffed that she was being shoved out in order to give her class back to its rightful owner. 'So, what do you mean, Noah's gone?'

'Well, as you know, he wasn't in yesterday and I've just had an email from Ross Haddon. He and Natasha…' Cassie paused to gauge Grace's reaction. '… Are moving over to Manchester. The pair of them have spent the last few days looking at rented properties near where he works apparently, and then yesterday let Noah sit the entrance exam to one of the independent schools in the area. Although Noah'd have us believe otherwise, he's a bright boy as you well know. Ross Haddon says they've chosen a school which is big into Games so he'll be playing either rugby or football on a daily basis.'

'Goodness.' Grace felt slightly depressed and couldn't for a moment quite articulate what she was feeling.

'You OK, Grace?' Cassie asked, concerned. 'Are you upset that the Haddons are back together? Have you still got a bit of a thing for Ross?'

'Oh, God, no, no, absolutely not.' Grace felt an actual shudder go through her as she recalled, yet again, that look of fury on his face as Ross Haddon cornered her in her own kitchen. 'You couldn't be further from the truth.'

'What then? I thought you'd be really pleased Noah was out of your hair. Although, you know, I'm not convinced a rough tough boys-only school is the right place for him.'

'No, I'm not sure either. I suppose I hate feeling that I

was unable to get through to Noah. Professional pride, you could call it.'

'Hang on, back up, Grace. Between you and Deimante – especially Deimante, who really worked wonders with him – you certainly got through to him. He's a quite different boy from when we inherited him over three months ago, and his latest assessment scores, particularly in literacy, have improved dramatically. All down to you, Grace.'

'I'm just concerned for him. Poor kid facing yet another school. And you know how he'll react to another new situation, Cassie: by being badly behaved. He'll be euphoric that Ross and Natasha are back together again, but constantly anxious that they'll be at each other's throats and that social services or the courts will be involved once more. And he won't have his granny for backup this time.' Grace paused and then gave a little laugh. 'I actually think I'll miss him.'

'Oh, you want me to email Ross Haddon back and say, don't go, let him stay?' Cassie raised an amused eyebrow.

'Er, no thank you very much. I won't miss him that much.'

'No, I didn't think you would. Although, you know, the other afternoon, when you went home and I took your class, he was the one who wanted to know where you were. Kept asking when you'd be back.'

'Really?' Grace was pleased. 'Kids like Noah need stability – they don't react well to change, however slight that might be.' Grace laughed once more. 'And I think I probably impressed him by not batting an eyelid when his mates told me to eff off. He was actually embarrassed.'

'You could have *really* impressed him by telling his mates to eff off back.' Cassie held up a hand. 'Only joking... So, you'll be pleased at my not having to beg you to carry on then? You know, with April Harrison coming back?'

'I feel a bit put out, if I'm honest.'

Cassie laughed. 'I knew you would. I know you, through and through Grace Stevens. You're a born teacher and think your class belongs to you. I bet the hardest day of the year is you seeing your beloved old class with someone new at the start of every new school year?'

'Might be.' Grace found herself laughing back. 'Right, need to get on. So, I'll work the couple of weeks left of term and then hand them back to Miss Harrison?'

'Thank you.'

Grace turned and made to leave.

'Grace?'

'Hmm?'

'How do you fancy two days a week?'

Hope flared in Grace's heart. 'What do you mean?'

'Kath Beaumont's just been in for a chat. You know both her parents have dementia? She's determined to carry on working but wants to cut down to three days after Christmas. We can only let her do that if I know we can get someone who'd work really well with her the other two. Job-shares, as you know, can be tricky.'

'Two days a week with the heavenly Y4 class? Oh gosh, yes please, yes please. That would be wonderful.' Grace, who'd not admitted, even to herself, how drained, no, actually *down*, she was feeling re the events of the last couple of weeks, felt something akin to enthusiasm, to pleasure – to hope even – when there'd been only the fear of a creeping despair which she'd tried desperately to keep at bay.

'Hang on, hang on. Don't say anything yet, I'm only just

thinking aloud here. It will have to go to the governors. I can't make any decisions without David and the others, you know that.'

'OK, OK, I'll leave it with you. But you know I'm interested. *More* than interested.' Grace smiled in delight.

'It's just getting *hold* of David,' Cassie said, almost to herself. 'He's so busy organising this sale of his.'

'Sale? What sale?'

'Bell's gone, Grace.' Cassie looked pointedly at the door and then back at Grace. 'You know, this big sale he's having. I assumed you'd be in there helping to organise it?'

'I don't know anything about any sale. What's he selling? Not the house? He's not moving back down South with his mother, is he?' For some reason, the slight sense of despair Grace had felt start to evaporate at Cassie's news about a possible part-time job began to nibble away at her toes once more. History told her she needed to keep it at a distance, like a threatening, circling dog, before it pounced and sunk its teeth into her.

'Not as far as I know. Although that house of his is absolutely huge. Far too big for one man on his own, don't you think? No, you know, the sale of all Mandy's clothes and bags? All going to a charity to get drug addicts off the streets. The sale of one of her Hermes bags alone would be enough to get a rough-sleeping kid off the street for a month or two. I've got my eye on a Mulberry.' She laughed excitedly. 'I keep dropping hints to Xav I'd like him to bid on one for Christmas for me. Bell's gone, Grace. Come *on*...'

Grace opened the office door and then, even though a stream of children was already making its way down the corridor, turned back. 'When is it?'

'When's what?' Cassie was already engrossed in something on her computer and didn't look up.

'This sale?'

'Of David's? It's actually at his house, I think. The week before Christmas. Ask Juno Armstrong.'

'Juno?'

'Grace, kids are *in*.'

'Juno? Why Juno?' Grace felt her pulse race as it always seemed to now whenever Juno's name was mentioned in the same breath as David's.

Cassie peered over her reading glasses and frowned. 'Well, David's having a bit of a thing with her, isn't he? That's what *I* heard. Not very up on the latest gossip; if they *are* getting together, I think it's great. They really suit one another. Ask Harriet, she'll know.'

Grace threw the last of the marked Y5 Science books onto the teetering pile of blue, sat back at her desk and glanced up at the classroom clock. Five minutes before the kids were due back in after the lunch break and the tables were already covered with their red oilcloths and allotted glitter, glue, dowelling, tinfoil and fabrics, and whatever else the children fancied, to create the 3D snowflakes that would – once they were completed – festoon the hall in readiness for the Christmas concert in just over a week's time. Art and craft stuff, like this, was right up her street; it was one area of the curriculum she wouldn't mind teaching every single day. Forget Maths, Science and English – she was more than happy to be permanently up to her eyeballs in glue and glitter. That's why the job-share she'd done with

Harriet, when Cassie had first taken over as head, had been so successful. Harriet hated anything arty – constantly reiterated she didn't have an artistic bone in her body – and had left it all to Grace who was more than happy to take it all on. Noah Haddon had been a brilliant artist, Grace mused, recalling the concentrated effort on his face whenever he was engrossed in a particular piece of artwork. Mind you, she also recalled, that hadn't stopped him turning over the whole table of powder paint and water jars when he'd totally lost it after poor Alexandra Sandon had accidentally knocked her own water jar over his almost finished painting of Westenbury church.

Would she miss Noah? She certainly wouldn't miss his need to disrupt the class when things weren't going his way. And she certainly wouldn't miss those incredible green eyes of his, narrowing in preparation for yet another outburst of bad behaviour. They were his father's eyes, and just the memory of Ross Haddon's eyes turning furiously upon her in her own kitchen was enough to make her feel anxious.

It was good, yes very good, that both Noah and Ross had moved on, but that didn't stop her feeling a certain sense of failure that she hadn't been able to totally win Noah over.

As well as yet another bloody relationship gone to dust.

What was the matter with her that she obviously picked the wrong men? Did she intentionally pick the ones who weren't right because she didn't want the responsibility of total commitment or, deep down, did she feel she wasn't worth a really good man's love? Maybe she should ask Santa for a few sessions with some psychoanalyst this Christmas? Mind you, she wasn't alone. Look at poor Niamh O'Connor lusting after the irascible Kit. Or Juno being totally let down by the gorgeous but two-timing Dr Scott Butler. At the thought of Juno – *come off it, Grace*, she censored herself, reaching for her mobile, *you've done nothing* but *think of Juno ever since Cassie told you the news about Juno and David getting together* – she decided to bite the bullet.

'Do you fancy a night out, Harriet?' Grace asked as Harriet answered on the final ring.

'A night out?' Harriet asked suspiciously. 'I know your nights out, Grace. What is it this time? More dressing up as nuns and German officers? Another session with Leo, King of the Jungle?' Harriet was laughing now. 'More drug-busting…? Hmm…? Grace…? You OK…?'

'I just wanted to be with someone who loves me…' Grace broke off, dashing away an angry tear.

'Aw, Grace, sweetie pie, we *all* love you.'

'Just feeling a bit sorry for myself. I'm fine, I'm fine. Forget it, I need to go; the kids are coming back in after lunch.'

'No, no, don't go. Nick and Kit are both away at the moment so I've no babysitter. Bring your two round after school for tea. Go on, do that. I've just made an *enormous* lasagne. We can stuff the kids with carbs and *Frozen 2*.'

'*Frozen 2?* Is it out yet?'

'It is at our house, courtesy of Kit.' Grace could feel Harriet's raised eyebrow, if she couldn't actually see it.

'He'll be arrested again, Hat.'

'Tell me about it. Anyway, come for tea and I can tell you *all* the gossip about David and Juno.'

# 35

Grace pulled up in Harriet's drive alongside a car she didn't recognise: a low, sleek little number in racing green that she immediately thought must be yet another of Kit's new acquisitions. That boy must have been out playing poker until the cows came home, she thought, as she pulled Jonty away from trailing admiring fingers along its shiny wing.

'Granny C,' Jonty shouted as he ran into the kitchen followed by Pietronella.

'Gwanny C,' Pietronella immediately followed suit, butting her dark head into Caroline Henderson's stomach as she sat at Harriet's kitchen table, a prettily painted china cup of tea held aloft in mid-air.

'Hello, my darlings, how are you?' David's mother gave each of the children a warm hug before turning to Grace. 'Hello, Grace.' Was Caroline Henderson's vibrant welcome for the children somewhat tempered by the time she was able to release herself from their embrace and address Grace herself? Grace smiled warmly at David's mother and bent to kiss the older woman's cheek but there didn't appear to be much of a reciprocal welcome on Caroline's part.

Grace had only met Caroline Henderson on a couple

of occasions since she'd moved up to be with David on Mandy's death four months earlier and, to her shame, she did keep forgetting that this handsome, dark-eyed woman, sitting and watching speculatively, was Jonty's great-grandmother and, as such, her son's blood relative. In the same way that David had wholeheartedly adopted Pietronella as his granddaughter, Caroline too had obviously had no qualms about also doing the same with Pietronella who had now climbed onto Caroline's lap and was sharing the lemon drizzle cake on the plate in front of them.

'Oh Grace, you're here. I was going to ask you to bring my two back with you as well but then remembered Caroline was popping over so I picked them up at the usual time.' Harriet lowered her voice. 'I have to constantly try to avoid Miss O'Connor these days,' she went on. 'She always wants to know where Kit is and what he's up to. I just grab the twins, twitter on about having to rush, and get out of the playground before she can corner me. Poor girl, she's so pretty.'

Grace could feel Caroline Henderson's cool gaze still upon her and smiled in what she hoped was a friendly manner. 'How much longer are you staying, Caroline?' she asked pleasantly and then, seeing Caroline's raised eyebrow, realised it was something of an ambiguous question. 'Up here in the North, I mean? You know, with David? I don't mean here in the, you know, here in Harriet's kitchen...' Grace trailed off, embarrassed.

'I think I shall be here with David until after Christmas,' replied Caroline. 'This sale of Mandy's things is taking up a lot of our time, and then of course it's Christmas itself. I do hope you're going to allow Jonty and Pietronella to join us at some stage?'

No invite for herself then. Grace felt that creeping feeling of being left out, of being surplus to requirements and had to force herself to smile. 'Of course, Caroline. Whenever you and David would like them.'

'The thing is, David is *so* much better than he was when I first came up to be with him. I know it's only been four months or so, but I'm sure I'm not speaking out of school when I say David had not been happy for *years*. Much as I loved Mandy as my own daughter – and who couldn't help but adore Mandy? – I do feel it would have been better all-round if they'd perhaps gone their separate ways and moved on from each other.'

'Oh?' Harriet, to Grace's relief, had returned after settling the children in front of the dodgy recording of *Frozen 2* and a pile of breadsticks and had now joined the other two at the kitchen table. 'Is there any tea left in that pot, Caroline? So, you think Mandy and David had sort of outgrown each other then?' Harriet sat down, relishing the idea of a few minutes' gossip, straight from the horse's mouth as it were.

'Hmm, but don't ever let on *I've* said that. I've had long, long talks into the night with David and I've been most upset to hear what Mandy has been up to over the years. I don't understand it, one little bit. When *I* married, it was to forsake all others, not to have little liaisons whenever the fancy took me.' Caroline sighed. 'They married far too young, of course. Although, I myself was only nineteen when I married David's father. It was ridiculous David not finishing Oxford in order to follow Mandy back up here.'

'Well, I don't think David's done too badly without a

degree from Oxford, do you?' Grace smiled. 'You must be very proud of all he's achieved?'

'Naturally.' Caroline nodded dismissively in Grace's direction, appearing totally uninterested in any opinion she might hold with regards her son.

Something wasn't right, Grace thought, shooting a quick glance at Harriet who was listening attentively to Caroline and wasn't giving any indication she'd noticed the *froideur* coming off Caroline in waves, hitting Grace head on.

*She doesn't like me*, Grace thought.

Caroline Henderson suddenly turned in Grace's direction, her dark, shrewd eyes holding Grace's own in a long drawn out stare. 'So, Grace,' she finally said, a chilly smile playing on her handsome face, 'how are you coping now that you've split up from your husband *once more*? You've not had an easy time, I understand, over the past few years?'

'An easy time? I'm sorry, I don't...'

'Well, your husband left you I hear, and you went after my grandson, Sebastian?'

'*Went after...*?' Grace couldn't believe what the woman was saying.

'And *that* relationship finished because of your postnatal depression? And you were reunited with your husband – Daniel? – but now he's gone to live in Exeter?'

'Well, yes, but we'd not been getting on...'

'I believe you *know* my friend Natasha Haddon's husband...?' The emphasis on the word *know* left Grace in no doubt as to Caroline Henderson's implication that there was knowing and there was *knowing* and Harriet, now realising something was going on between Caroline and Grace, glanced at Grace and frowned.

'Oh, *dreadful* woman from all accounts,' Harriet trilled as Grace, obviously deeply embarrassed, seemed unable to speak. 'How do *you* know her, Caroline?'

'Natasha? Dreadful?' Caroline's eyes narrowed. 'Not at all, dear; she's a charming girl. We met at that new Turkish Hamman in the village and were sat together over tea once we'd been scrubbed and were waiting for the massage. We got talking and the poor girl obviously needed to unload. She was terribly upset that her husband was having an affair with her son's teacher...' Caroline looked pointedly at Grace.

'It wasn't like that,' Grace protested, her face scarlet. 'I'm sorry, Caroline, you're making it out to be quite sordid; as if I *pinched* her husband.'

'I'm only going by what she told me, dear. Terribly upset, she was. Anyway, really none of my business. Now, Harriet—' Caroline deliberately turned her back on Grace '—shall we get down to business? The sale is only just over two weeks away and Juno and I could do with a bit of help. What an absolute *treasure* that girl is.' Caroline lowered her voice in Harriet's direction, but it was obvious her intention was for Grace to hear. 'I have high hopes that that little friendship of David's might develop into something, shall we say, more serious?'

'What the hell was all that about?' Harriet asked half an hour later once she'd seen Caroline to the door with the promise of spending the following afternoon helping to price up Mandy Henderson's clothes, bags and shoes. 'What have you done to upset her?'

'Honestly, Harriet, I really don't know. I've only met the woman two or three times before. I wonder if she thinks I'm in the habit of dumping my kids on David. You know, taking advantage of his good nature so that I can go out and shag every available man – married, toy-boy or otherwise – while he looks after them?'

'I did get that impression, Grace. Not helped by Natasha Haddon sticking in the knife. Honestly that woman.'

'Who? Natasha or Caroline?'

'I meant Natasha. I've always really liked *Caroline*; found her just as kind and pleasant as David. I just think maybe she was being very protective of her son. You know, after finding out more about Mandy's little predilections for flirting and liaisons with other men?'

'Well,' Grace retorted, still feeling a bit trembly after the onslaught from Caroline Henderson, 'we don't need to worry about Natasha anymore. *She's* gone.'

'Oh?'

'Hmm. The restraining order is up and she and Ross and Noah have legged it back over to Manchester.'

'Best place for them.'

'So, what do you think about David and Juno then? Great, isn't it?' Harriet intent on lifting the lasagne she'd made earlier from the depths of the huge American fridge, wasn't able to see Grace's reaction to her question. 'Nick said they were together in the Jolly Sailor the other evening and she was round at the house at the weekend... Look at this bad boy for a lasagne... Grace? What is it? What's the matter? Has David's mother got to you? Or is it Ross getting back with his wife?'

Grace could only shake her head as she put up a hand to

wipe away the tears. 'No, no… I'd be happy for the toxic Haddons to be in Timbuctoo.'

'What then? Caroline?'

Grace could only shake her head. 'It's David.'

'David's been unpleasant to you? That's not like David. You're his mate, his friend.'

'Harriet, David falling out with me is as bad as you falling out with me. But… but…'

'But what?'

'Harriet, I can't bear the thought of David and Juno together.'

'Can't you? Why not? I thought you liked Juno?' Harriet, still holding the giant lasagne, frowned.

'Because I think I love him.'

'Well, yes, we all love David. *Everyone* loves David.'

'No, really love him. As in, *in love* with him.'

Harriet sat down still holding the dish.

'Hat, will you put that effing lasagne down. Look,' Grace went on, wiping her eyes, 'I know this sounds stupid, but I've only just realised myself, the last few weeks or so, that's how I feel about him.'

'Are you sure this isn't just because he's seeing Juno? You know, suddenly wanting something you can't have?'

'Harriet, I'd no idea he was having a thing with Juno until Cassie told me this morning.'

'So, what then? How's this all suddenly come about?'

'It was the night I first went out to meet Ross over at Upper Clawson. Pietronella and I were dressing up and she brought David upstairs to zip me up. It was his hand on my bare back, on my arm, and those lovely brown eyes of his meeting mine in the mirror… I didn't even acknowledge to myself what I was feeling. I mean, this was David, for heaven's sake…'

'Hang on, just let me put this food in the oven or we'll never get to eat…' Harriet reached for her lasagne once more. 'Well, you've picked a fine time to realise this. Couldn't you have laid claim to him as soon as Mandy died? You know, before Juno did?'

'For heaven's sake, Harriet, he's not a box of chocolates to be picked up at will when the last owner's had enough. Now, you promise you don't repeat any of this to *anyone*?'

'Not even Nick?'

'Especially not Nick. And please, please, not Libby. Can you just imagine her trolling off back down to Holly Close Farm and telling Seb that I've fallen in love with his dad? No, this is totally between you and me, Harriet. And if I thought, for just one minute, you'd breathe a word of this to *anyone*, I'd have to kill you.'

'OK, dib dib dob, scout's honour.' Harriet poured two glasses of wine. 'Have a drink and tell me more.'

'When I look back, Harriet,' Grace said thoughtfully, ignoring her glass of wine, 'I think I loved him from the moment I met him.'

'When you were dressed as that Nazi German officer?'

'Hmm. I'd always loved Mandy from school days. I suppose it was obvious I'd end up loving her husband too.'

'You don't think that's why you ended up with Seb? You know, because he was David's son?'

Grace shrugged. 'Dunno. If you psychoanalysed me then there's a good chance that's in there somewhere. Anyway,' she sighed, wiping her eyes determinedly and taking a deep breath, 'I'm going to put a stop to all this nonsense right now: a) David is seeing Juno, b) he's totally fallen out with me thinking I'm a bad mother and have awful taste in men and c) any relationship I have appears doomed to failure.'

'You've forgotten d)...'

'D)?'

'And d),' Harriet added sagely, 'you'd never get past his mother!'

# 36

'How long are you going to keep this up, Juno?'

'Keep this up? Keep *what* up?' Juno, intent on scanning the results just through on her computer from old Mr Lloyd's bowel referral to Midhope General, didn't look up as Scott leaned against her desk, arms folded, awaiting her attention.

Juno glanced first at the practice room clock above the sink, and then briefly up at Scott. He'd made an effort; she'd give him that. But then, she supposed, he always did. His navy linen shirt, immaculately ironed as ever, was her favourite and a perfect foil for both his short, thick dark hair and those amazing eyes she'd so fallen in love with almost a year previously. A year of believing in herself, believing that yes, despite both her husband and now Scott cheating on her, she was a strong, intelligent woman with the ability to make the right decisions for herself and for Gabriel and Matilda.

'I'm sorry, Scott.' Juno offered up a wintry smile in his direction. 'I really need to sort this lot out before letting in the hordes.'

'I miss you, Juno.' Encouraged by the fact that Juno hadn't told him to eff off as had been her usual mode of greeting whenever he tried to mollify her – to let him explain – Scott moved a warm hand to Juno's hair, gently caressing the nape of her neck.

Juno didn't move, didn't react, except to say. 'I miss you too, miss you an awful lot...' She eventually stood and walked over to the sink, washing her hands before pressing the button to alert Marian in reception that she was ready for her first patient of the day. 'But, unfortunately, Scott, I miss my children more.'

'Miss them?' For a second, Scott looked startled. 'Why, where are they? Where have they gone?'

'I was so wrapped up in *you*, Scott, so intent on acting out my happy ever fantasy with the dishy New Zealand doctor – you know, like something out of a Mills and Boon novel – I didn't realise both my kids were desperately unhappy and in a place I didn't appear to be able to, or want to, reach out to them to help them.'

'You don't think you're being a bit over the top here, Ju?' Scott smiled somewhat condescendingly. 'Come on, stop beating yourself up; lots of kids go through bouts of unhappiness when they're forced into the challenges and new situations life throws at them.'

'And *you'd* know all this would you? You know, with your – how long is it now...?' Juno held up her fingers and counted off in some exaggeration. 'Six months of being a father?'

'Gabe just got caught up in something he didn't understand. And Tilda will be fine,' Scott said almost heartily. 'She's a tough little cookie. Just like her Aunt Ariadne. She'll eventually settle at the comp or, why don't you do as Ariadne suggests and move her over to the grammar school. Or fee-paying, even?'

Despite having wrangled with both those options during the sleepless nights that had ensued after Gabe's arrest, Juno shook her head slightly, giving Scott such a look of disdain he visibly flinched. 'Both Ariadne and Tilda might both appear to be tough, to be able to cope with whatever life throws at them, but they're very similar: deep inside they're both hurting. I never realised just how badly affected Ariadne was at losing the love of her life in California.'

'But that was fifteen years ago, for heaven's sake. Surely she's been able to get over it all by now?' Scott smiled winningly at Juno, trying to take her hand as she sat back down once more.

Juno shook it off crossly saying, 'Just go, Scott, would you? There are patients waiting.'

Instead, Scott folded his arms once more and settled himself seemingly for the duration. 'Come on, Juno, don't be like this. You know I'm in love with you.' He moved a hand once more towards her, massaging her shoulder gently.

Every fibre of Juno's being wanted to lean into Scott's embrace, to write off the fact that he'd had a fling with Mandy Henderson, to start again with a clean slate. How tempting it all was. Instead, she hissed, 'Get off me or I'll have you up for harassment in the workplace.'

'Ah.' Scott's smile slipped slightly. 'So, it's true then?'

'What is?' Juno asked irritably as a timid knock sounded on her door.

'You and David Henderson.'

That was when, in exasperation, Juno reverted to the same retort she'd been flinging at Dr Scott Butler ever since she'd learned of his dalliance with Mandy Henderson. 'Just fuck off, will you, I'm busy…'

'Oh, sorry…' Eighty-year-old Mrs Rogers, in search of relief for her chronically painful hip, spoke apologetically through the half-open door, 'I'm *so* sorry, Dr, I didn't realise you were busy. I thought it was my turn.'

'You're *what*?' Both Izzy and Declan stared at Juno as she stood, back towards the closed door in the tiny room that served as kitchen and rest room in the surgery. Not that there was ever, it seemed, time to rest.

'You heard me. I'm giving in my notice.'

'Juno, no, don't be silly. Just because you and lover boy have had a tiff doesn't mean you have to be the one to leave.' Izzy frowned before turning to her husband. 'I knew he'd be trouble,' she snapped crossly. 'I knew I shouldn't have listened when you insisted on taking him on as locum.'

'It's got nothing to do with Scott,' Juno said determinedly.

'Oh, of course it has,' Izzy snorted disparagingly. 'You were perfectly happy here until *he* turned up.'

'Is it Gabriel?' Declan asked, frowning across at Izzy in an attempt to shut her up. 'Do you need some time off from work to sort things out for him, Juno?'

'Yes, do that,' Izzy interrupted Declan. 'Take the week off and give yourself time to sort things out. Take sick leave until after Christmas.'

'That's really not necessary although, to be honest, I do have more appointments with Gabe's school, with his solicitor and with the youth offending team and so there are a couple of mornings or afternoons that'll need covering.'

'Any news on what's going to happen with Gabe? You know, with the police?'

'He's been charged.' Juno closed her eyes briefly. 'Possession with intent to supply.'

'That's *ridiculous*.' Declan stared, wide-eyed. 'Surely he was coerced? Groomed even?'

'He knew what he was doing, Declan. Admitted even going over to Manchester with those kids a couple of times. It's all my fault. I wasn't there for him.'

'So, what happens now?'

'Rizwan has advised Gabe to plead guilty. He's from a good family, never been in trouble before, and was, as you say, coerced into it. Rizwan will put up a really good defence for him when he appears in the youth court after Christmas.'

Izzy put out a hand to Juno. 'He's not going to be sent down, Juno. He's thirteen, for heaven's sake.'

Juno sighed. 'According to Rizwan, when a child is in the Youth Court for the first time, he's usually already had several police cautions before he gets there. Gabriel obviously hasn't, which is all in his favour. Anyway, apparently there's only one of two things that can be handed out to a child for a first offence under the age of eighteen.'

'Oh?'

'He'll either be given a DTO...'

'Detention and Training Order?' Declan raised an eyebrow.

Juno nodded. 'The nick, basically. Or he'll be given what's called a Referral Order. Rizwan is totally convinced that's what he'll get. The Youth Offending team will write a report on him and, Rizwan says, try to convince the Youth Magistrates that's the best way forwards. Bit like being on probation really. And, Gabe won't end up with a record that he'll have to admit to when he eventually starts writing his CV and personal statement.'

'There you go then,' Declan said, putting an arm round Juno and giving her a hug. 'Izzy and I – and Scott – will cover for you when necessary.' Declan paused. 'Just don't give in your notice, Juno. The patients love you.'

'No, they don't,' Juno almost laughed. 'And don't try to make me stay by massaging my ego. I actually told Mrs Rogers to eff off this morning.'

'Did you?' Izzy was momentarily silenced. 'Blimey. She's a nice old dear as well. Why take it out on her? Oh well, she's as deaf as a post,' Izzy went on comfortably. 'She won't have heard you. So, have you been head-hunted elsewhere? Because that's not on, you know, Juno. I know we banished you to the stockroom so Scott could have your practice room, but...'

'I'm going away,' interrupted Juno, feeling her pulse rate quicken now that her plan was actually out in the open.

'A holiday? Yes, that's what you need, Juno,' Declan said kindly. 'A week in Tenerife or somewhere. Get some winter sunshine. You'll feel a whole load better after that.'

'No, I'm going away for a long time.'

'Now you're being bloody dramatic.' Izzy stared at Juno. 'In fact, you sound like *you're* going to prison. You're not, are you? I mean you weren't actually involved with Esme's little business, were you?'

'Oh, for heaven's sake, Izzy.' Declan and Juno spoke as one.

'OK, OK.' Izzy held up her hands. 'So where *are* you thinking of going?'

'Ariadne and I are going to buy a great big Winnebago and travel Europe.'

'A Winnebago? Oh, don't be so soft,' Izzy scowled. 'Who's going to look after Gabriel and Matilda?'

'I'm not going *without* them,' Juno tutted. 'They're coming with us. Once Gabe's done his Referral Order – Rizwan says probably six months which, if he does well on it, can be revoked to three – the four of us are going travelling.'

'But what about school?' Even Declan was beginning to look concerned. 'You're fined these days if you take your kids out of school even for a week. How long are you thinking of going for?'

'Six months? A year? Who knows?' Juno was warming to her theme. 'And I don't think missing two terms from Westenbury Comp is going to make a huge difference to Tilda's intellectual output, do you?'

'But Gabriel?'

'Gabriel needs to be away from school. My dad and I will home tutor him until we're able to leave. And then, Ariadne will take over once we set off. Don't forget, she's a teacher. We've thought it all out: we'll visit the coliseum in Rome and look at the history and geography of Spain; we'll visit art galleries and museums; we'll walk and climb mountains. we'll swim in the sea…'

'Well, I can just see a thirteen-year-old wanting to visit dusty old museums with his mother and his maiden aunt. You're just asking for trouble, Juno. Don't go,' Izzy wheedled. 'We need you here.'

'No, you don't.'

'What about your house? What about the mortgage?'

'I'll rent it out. My dad already knows someone at the university who might be interested. And, if not, well, I'll just extend the mortgage time and Fraser will have to pay a bit more. He's got off fairly lightly so far. It's just for a year at the most.'

'OK.' Izzy narrowed her eyes. 'What about David?'

'David who?'

'David You-know-perfectly-well-who,' Izzy retorted with a slight smirk.

'Oh, for heaven's sake,' Juno said once more raising her eyes to the ceiling and noticing a silvery cobweb in the corner of the architrave. 'Can we knock that little rumour on its head? David Henderson and I have become friends that's all.'

'Ha, that's what they all say.'

'He called round not long after we both found out about Mandy and Scott. He just needed to talk about what had happened, to find out if I'd actually been aware of what was going on between the pair of them. We discussed it over an early supper at Clementine's, and then I volunteered to help him, his mother and Harriet with the sale of Mandy's clothes and bags he's having next week. So, I've been over at his house sorting through things and pricing them up ready for the auction. Anything to get me out of the house and give Gabe – who thinks I'm constantly watching him – some space...'

'And, of course you are? Constantly watching him?'

'Of course. Gabe's spending a bit of time down at my dad's place with Dad and Arius and Hugo. It's not the best *place* to be, given the circumstances, but I think he's with the best *people*. Dad's already helping him with his schoolwork and, knowing he doesn't have to go back to the comp – at the moment anyway – he seems much happier.

I think he might spend some time with Fraser in Boston at some point...' Juno sighed. 'If the Americans let him in, of course, with a record for drugs.'

'So, let's just get back to David,' Izzy demanded, folding her arms.

'Why?'

'Well, you mustn't miss this great opportunity for your having a bite of ...'

'Opportunity?' Declan rolled his eyes. 'A bite? You're making David sound like a piece of cheesecake.'

'Much more delicious,' Izzy sniffed.

'I'm simply helping him with Mandy's *things*,' Juno said in some exasperation. 'I can't tell you how much stuff there is. And when we've had a session—'

'A session?' Izzy's eyes gleamed.

'A session sorting and deciding what can go to the hospice shop and what will go into the sale, then we've ended up in the Jolly Sailor, talking about Gabe mainly...'

'Ah, you see, it's all coming out now. A drink in a pub is always how it starts.' Izzy appeared almost triumphant. 'And that's it?'

'What else do you want?'

'Well, you know, has he flirted with you? Has he made a move on you? I suppose if he did that would fit nicely with Scott having a thing with Mandy Henderson. You know, just desserts and all that? Give him chance, work on him and then he'll fall in love with you and you won't have to think about swanning off on this ridiculous trip of yours. And *we* won't be one man down and having to find another doctor.'

'But I *want* to go,' Juno said quietly. 'I want to get the

kids away from here for a while and there's no reason *not* to have a bit of an adventure. So, we'll be off, if all goes to plan, after Easter. You know, just as spring is arriving and, hopefully, once all this ghastly mess is sorted with Gabriel.'

'But what about David Henderson?'

'Sorry to disappoint you, Izzy,' Juno shot an eyebrow in her friend's direction. 'There's only room for one woman in David Henderson's heart and it certainly isn't me.' Juno smiled at the two of them and headed for the door.

'One woman? Does she mean Mandy? Yes, I suppose she means Mandy. Anyway, Declan, *I* want to have an adventure too.' Juno heard Izzy's plaintive tone as she pulled the kitchen door behind her. 'And I tell you now, Declan, RandyPants Scott bloody Butler can jolly well be demoted down into Juno's dungeon of a practice room. There's no way on this planet we'll ever recruit anyone half-decent if they know they have to work in that hellhole. So, shall *we* go somewhere, then, Declan? Shall we have an adventure before we're too old and decrepit to get out of this surgery? Shall we…?'

Juno smiled once more, to herself this time, before descending the stairs to her practice room.

## 37

'Snowing, Mumma.' Pietronella gazed in wonder at the huge gobstoppers of snowflakes descending from a mustard-yellow sky, before slipping precariously down the garden path and landing unceremoniously on her backside.

'Santa'll be able to come on his sleigh.' Jonty, still in his *Superman* pyjamas, a pair of hastily donned wellingtons his only concession to the weather, followed his sister into the garden and, head thrown back, endeavoured to catch the flakes in his open mouth, giggling as the soft coldness met his teeth and lips.

'Inside, the pair of you,' Grace shouted down the long, increasingly white stretch of garden from the warmth of the house. 'Santa's got a whole week to get here yet, Jonty and your Daddy will be over to pick you up in an hour.'

'Santa here *now*.' In her excitement at seeing a red coated, Santa-hatted figure making its way through the mesmerizingly-dancing snowflakes, Pietronella found herself horizontal once more.

Even Grace began to wonder if she was a week out as Santa, laughing, picked Pietronella up and carried her up the path towards the house.

David.

Wrapped up in a huge red ski jacket and red scarf against the cold, his dark eyes peering out from lashes fringed in white, David Henderson trod slowly and carefully towards her as Pietronella batted playfully at the white bobble on his red hat.

Grace's pulse raced. She'd not seen him for weeks; he'd not been to pick up the kids as usual and, when she'd finally acknowledged to herself, after the awful put down from his mother at Harriet's the other day, that she was going to have to be the one to break the ice, she'd texted him. It was a friendly little text, saying she'd be more than happy to come and help with both the sorting of, and actual sale of, Mandy's things.

He'd not replied.

Grace knew, in his capacity as Chair of Governors at Little Acorns, David would be attending both the infant and junior Christmas performances in the coming final week of term, and she'd comforted herself with the knowledge that she'd at least be able to speak to him then. He wouldn't really, in all politeness, be able to ignore her at school.

But he was here now. Grace automatically ran a hand through her unbrushed hair and wished she'd had least put on a slick of lipstick.

Except David *wasn't* here. It *wasn't* David.

'Daddy's here,' Jonty shouted excitedly, hanging on to his father's red ski jacket.

'Seb? I thought it was your father.' Grace pasted a smile on her face in order to mask the disappointment surging through her as she did so. 'You're early.'

'It started snowing as soon as we got up. I knew I'd never get the car up the farm lane if I left it any longer so decided to set off straight away.' Seb lowered his voice and mouthed the next bit: 'I didn't want Jonty to miss out on being taken to see his first football match. I'm not convinced it won't be cancelled, but I thought I'd get here early just in case. I'm sorry, Grace, I ought to be taking Pietronella off your hands as well…'

'No, you shouldn't,' Grace said, shaking her head. 'You're always including her. You and Libby are not responsible for Pietronella. Anyway, I would have thought watching twenty-two men racing after a ball in the freezing cold would be the last thing she wanted.'

Seb placed Pietronella down on the doorstep and smiled. 'The forecast says this little lot will be gone by tomorrow – just a freak storm, they reckon. You still OK with Jonty staying over with Libby and me on Christmas Eve, Grace?'

Grace turned back into the kitchen and Seb followed her in as she sent Jonty upstairs to get out of his pyjamas and ready himself for the weekend with his father, Libby and Lysander. No matter how often she shared him with Seb, it never really got any easier. Happening everywhere, she supposed, children being shared out between their estranged parents like a bag of sweets… *One for you, one for me*. Grace went to the coffee machine and held up a mug in Seb's direction.

'Please,' he said, as Pietronella clambered onto his knee. 'So, Christmas, Grace? Is Dan back up for Christmas?'

Grace nodded but then shook her head. 'He is, but he isn't.'

'Oh?'

'He's back up from Exeter, and at his mother's place the few days before Christmas, and he'll see the kids then.

He's been invited to my parents' on Christmas Day but he's ducking out of it. I don't blame him really: he'll have my mother glaring at him over the bread sauce, asking when he's coming back to the wife and children he's abandoned yet again.' Grace gave a rueful smile.

'Do you *want* him back, Grace?' Seb frowned, accepting the coffee and patting her arm as he did so.

'No.'

'Right, that's alright then.' Seb smiled, but when Grace didn't expand added, 'Isn't it?'

'Hmm, it is. We should never have got back together again once you and I split up.'

'Grace, you and *I* should never have really got together in the first place. You know that.'

'Of course I do.' Grace laughed brightly, but felt a sharp stab of hurt. Seb had never before actually said, in so many words, that their relationship had been a mistake and, while she herself conceded that they'd really had nothing in common, as well as their thirteen or so years' age difference, one never wants to be told, blatantly, that it should never have happened. That it was one big mistake.

'Mind you,' Seb laughed, tickling Pietronella until she chortled, 'your mummy, Pietronella, was very hard to resist.' Seb glanced up at Grace. 'Grace, you are one of the most attractive women I've ever met. You're kind, you're funny, you're pretty gorgeous and, of course, you're Jonty's mum. Quite a heady combination really.' He stood and put both his still full mug and Pietronella down before reaching for Grace, enveloping her in a bearhug. 'You are very special, Grace Stevens. I just wish...'

'What?'

'I wish... I just wish...'

'What?' Oh please, Grace thought, please, please don't say Seb was coming on to her.

'I just wish you could fancy my dad.'

'Your *dad*?' Grace pulled herself from Seb's embrace and stared.

'I know, I know, I'm sorry. I should never have said that.' Seb was totally embarrassed and, unable to meet Grace's eyes, reached for his Santa hat before putting it down once again in exactly the same place. 'Right, where's that son of mine? Shall I go upstairs and chivvy him along?'

'Your dad?' Grace repeated.

'Forget it, forget it.' Seb's face was flushed almost as red as his jacket and hat. 'It's just that the two of you have always been such good mates.'

'Sebastian, your mother only died five months ago.'

'Yes, Grace, I'm well aware of that and I can't tell you how much I miss her. How much I wish she was still here, but you must know that Mum and Dad's marriage died long before Mum did? It's very difficult for me, as their only son, to acknowledge openly that, to all intents and purposes, they had the perfect marriage when really, you know, it had been crumbling, being eaten away, bit by bit, for many years.'

'I miss her too, you know. Your mother and I might have always seemed to be at odds with each other—'

'I think you both really enjoyed winding each other up.'

'—but really she was a bit like the big sister I never had. I loved Mandy, Seb.'

'I know you did. Not once, never once, would you ever admit it though.' Seb actually laughed aloud at this. 'And she may have been my mum, but she led my dad a right dance. I mean, I know she loved him, but there was always *something* – or somebody – going on with her.'

'You knew?'

'Come on, Grace, all that stuff with Harriet's brother, John? Don't forget John's Libby's uncle. Do you not remember that awful Christmas day at Harriet's? When Uncle John's wife, Christine, threw her wine over Mum? Of course, I knew all about it. Just as Dad did.'

'You never really said, Seb. You know, when we were together, you never actually discussed it with me?'

'I was being loyal to Dad. And Mum. I never told you about how I bunked off school with a couple of mates when I was sixteen and we went into Leeds. I saw Mum going into a wine bar with some man then.'

'John?'

Seb shook his head. 'Possibly, but I don't think so. This guy was blond whereas John, now I know him, is obviously very dark. So, no, I'd say she was with someone else. To be honest, Grace, I think Mum had calmed down a bit in the past couple of years or so and she and Dad were making a go of it again. Until...'

'Until?'

'Dr Armstrong's your friend, isn't she? You must know Mum was with Dr Butler before she died on the M1.' Seb raised an eyebrow before lifting his coffee cup and draining its contents.

'I only just recently found out.' Grace shook her head. 'Juno is absolutely devastated as you can imagine. And your dad must be too.' Grace gave a surreptitious glance at Seb's face in the hope of ascertaining whether he knew about his father and Juno. She wanted to be pleased for the pair of them – that they were finding new happiness with each after being dealt such a god-awful hand with regards Scott Butler and Mandy. But she couldn't. She wasn't big-hearted enough. In fact, let's face it, she was downright jealous. Not a nice trait she knew, but there it was. If she could only get rid of the images of Juno and David that kept crowding, unbidden and uninvited, into her mind: David running his fingers through Juno's blonde curls; Juno pulling David's lovely navy sweater over his dark hair in order to get to his shirt buttons. Grace shook her head slightly and wrapped her arms protectively around herself to dispel the pictures.

'You OK?' Seb was staring at her.

'Hmm? Oh, just a bit chilly.'

'Really?' Seb frowned doubtfully. 'Mind you, I'm dressed for Siberia,' he laughed. 'Anyway,' he went on. 'Dad? Upset, yes. But as much for Dr Armstrong as himself: I actually don't think anything – or anybody – Mum ended up getting involved with, surprised him much towards the end. So, devastated? No, I don't think so… Look, Grace, have you and Dad had a bit of a fallout?'

'What makes you say that? Has he said something to you?' Grace felt her pulse quicken.

'You and the kids don't seem to be a huge part of his life at the moment? I've not seen you over there for ages. I know he's missing having the children to stay; he really dotes on them.' Seb paused. 'And you as well, you know.'

'Me?'

Seb smiled and Grace knew he was wondering whether he was saying too much. 'He always has. I think Mum knew that too.'

'I'm sorry if you think—'

'What I think, Grace… what I *know*… is that Dad loves you. He's always loved you. There, I've said it. He and I went on a long walk several weeks ago and he never stopped talking about you. I soon realised he'd got me out on a walk, without the kids – just him, me and the dog – and was trying to tell me how he felt; how he'd always felt about you. Very, very difficult for him when you and me used to be together and Mum only just passed away, but I know he really wanted to open up to me. Test the waters as it were…'

'Right.' Grace felt a huge heavy load beginning to lift from somewhere near her heart. Maybe it actually *was* her heart?

'Grace? Oh hell, I hope I haven't said something I shouldn't.'

'No, no, really—'

'Dad kept going on about a dress,' Seb frowned. 'Something about a dress? A red dress? That he only admitted, even to himself, how he really felt about you when he helped you with some zip on a dress?'

'Right.' Grace's heart was singing, soaring somewhere up above her where she couldn't reach it. But she knew she had to; she had to pull it back. There was a reason. Grace took a deep breath. 'So, this er, this walk of yours, Seb. With your dad? When was it?' She exhaled slightly as she and her heart waited for his answer, unable, it seemed to take another breath.

'The walk?' Seb frowned. 'Several weeks ago? Why? Libby and I have discussed you both. You know, should I drop a hint to you if Dad hadn't plucked up the courage to tell you how he felt…'

So, Grace thought. David had said these things to Seb before he knew she'd been seeing Ross. Before he'd been forced to help her to clear up the fall-out in her kitchen. Before he'd found out about Scott Butler. Before he'd got to know Juno… Grace felt her heart descend with a thump back into its rightful place.

Seb was saying, 'If you and Dad have had some disagreement, Grace, some falling out, the pair of you need to sort it. He's like a bear with a sore head at the moment. All, I'm saying is, don't lose each other…'

Sebastian trailed off, reaching for his Santa hat and scarf once again as Jonty bounded into the kitchen ready for the off. 'Changing the subject, I think sorting Mum's things ready for this sale will have been terribly hard for him, but I know it's what he wants to do, a sort of catharsis. Have to say, *I* don't want to be there.' Seb gave a rueful smile. 'You know, seeing my mum sold off as it were.' For a couple of seconds, Seb looked distraught and then he smiled. 'I'm going to look after the boys before I take Jonty to the match this afternoon while Libby goes over to Dad's place to help. Are you alright taking Pietronella over when you go over there yourself? Hopefully the roads will have cleared by this afternoon.' Seb paused. 'Look, Grace, all I'm saying is, take a chance. Don't let that red-dress-feeling, whatever it was, go.' Seb laughed and then bent to kiss Grace's cheek before taking Jonty's hand in his own and waving a farewell with the other. 'You and Dad are both very, very special to me…'

*And David is so very, very special to me*, Grace thought as she and Pietronella spent most of the morning building the snowwoman now standing in the garden. Resplendent in the blue plunging lacy Lepel bra Grace had bought in anticipation of a night of passion with Ross, the cross-eyed, almost lascivious look on Sandra Snowwoman's carrot and tangerine features must surely be a come-on to any snowman being created in their neighbours' adjoining gardens.

Ross Haddon. How could she have been taken in by Ross? Thank goodness he was out of her life. If she was such a bad judge of character when it came to choosing men, she'd be better off spending the rest of her days with just Pietronella for company. And she *was* good company, Grace realised, laughing as her daughter attempted to fill the bra with handfuls of snow. 'For bosoms, Mumma,' she said sagely, her tongue held out in concentration as Sandra's accentuated bust began to resemble something more usually displayed in a porn mag.

'More is less, I think, darling,' shouted Grace, once Pietronella had kitted Sandra out in Katherine Greenwood's best Hermes headscarf she'd left behind the previous week, tying it around the snowwoman's white head so that she looked uncannily like the Queen. 'A rampantly busty Queen,' Grace laughed out loud, 'but the Queen nevertheless.'

By early afternoon the accumulated snow was starting to melt and, despite constantly checking her phone to see if there was a message from David – or even Harriet – accepting her invitation to help out at the sale, none was forthcoming. Grace looked out of the sitting room window where she was helping Pietronella with a jigsaw, and seeing a weak sunshine already making inroads into taking Sandra from a 38 GGG down to a more becoming 32B, shouted,

'Come on, let's go sledging, Nella, before all this snow disappears.'

She managed to ferret out the two large red plastic sledges that the previous year's mild winter had rendered redundant, Dan obviously tidying them away behind the plethora of gardening implements in the shed at the bottom of the garden. She and Pietronella spent the next hour on the long sloping meadow behind the house after joining a small group of others who'd made their way up from the village, and who'd had the same idea about sledging.

One of the dads, obviously with the romantic – if somewhat daft – intention of recreating former good times skiing in Val d'Isere, produced a hip flask of something alcoholic from the pocket of his trendy ski-jacket and, after wiping the top of the flask, offered it across to Grace together with a smile and what she recognised as a bit of a come-on. Declining both the flask and any potential flirtation, Grace pulled Pietronella onto her knee and together they set off on the first of the descents that kept them outside until the rapidly melting snow was just very wet slush and the green of the meadow was winning its battle against the white.

They were both soaked to the skin, Grace realised, as the endorphin rush, created by an hour attempting to sledge in slush, was evaporating as surely as Sandra's bra size.

''S'cold Mumma,' Pietronella wailed as they squelched their way back through the slush and mud at the bottom of the field towards home. 'Wet botty and wet feets and hands hurts.' She held up mottled, frozen hands and began to cry.

'Where are your gloves?' Grace asked. Oh, sod it, she wasn't going back up that muddy slippery hill to find them. 'Come on,' she encouraged, 'we're nearly home.'

'Want Jonty,' Pietronella now wailed. 'Want to see Jonty's daddy. Want Gwanpa. Want Gwanpa David. Feets cold. Hands cold. Want to go to see Gwanpa... Want Gwanpa David...'

*Oh, so do I. So do I,* Grace thought as she made encouraging noises in Pietronella's general direction and hoisted the two unwieldy red sledges out of the mud and slush where they were fast becoming immobile, wedging one under each armpit before reaching for Pietronella's hand. 'Nearly home.'

For some reason the house was no longer warm. In fact, there was a distinct chill in the air. Grace felt at the radiators. Stone cold. While Pietronella stood, dripping in the kitchen like a badly defrosting fridge, continuing to wail about how cold she was but seemingly unable or unwilling to divest herself of wellingtons and wet clothes, Grace headed for the boiler in the utility room. Stone cold as well and, although all the dials and switches were giving every indication that heat was pumping throughout the house, it wasn't.

'Bugger, buggering bugger,' Grace swore under her breath. 'The boiler's buggered.'

'Bugger,' Pietronella sobbed as she finally attempted, but failed to remove her wellingtons. 'Bugger, Mumma. Hands cold. Buggery feets cold.'

'Shhh, sweetie. OK, let's get your wet stuff off and you into a nice hot bath and your lovely *Toy Story* onesie on.' Grace left the recalcitrant boiler still sulking and ran upstairs to fetch a towel before starting to peel off Pietronella's clothes. She was wet right down to her vest and pants, her pale skin mottled blue with cold once she stood, naked, except for her bobble hat and glasses, sobbing and shivering in the middle of the kitchen floor.

Grace thought of Juno, at this moment very probably cosily ensconced in David's beautiful warm kitchen after the sale, sipping mulled wine while David stirred something tantalisingly tasty on his dark blue Aga, and found that she too was crying, great fat tears that joined with Pietronella's until they were both sobbing in sympathy with each other.

'Grace? What is it? What on earth's the matter?' David Henderson was standing in front of her, looking on in bewilderment while a still-naked Pietronella patted Grace's back and sobbed, 'Gwanpa David, the buggering boiler's buggered.'

# 38

'*I thought* it was cold in here.' David shivered slightly and, not quite meeting Grace's eyes, patted Pietronella on her cheek before heading off in the direction of the utility. 'Boiler in here, Grace?'

While David fiddled around, attempting, presumably, to resurrect the dead boiler, Grace reached for the pile of clothes she'd finally got round to ironing the previous evening. Accompanied by a rerun of *Dad's Army*, as well as a reward of one Malteser for each completed article, she'd managed to put aside all thoughts of David and Juno together, concentrating on artistically ironing every last piece in the basket, as well as on Captain Mainwaring and his men. She now found pants, vest and socks as well as Pietronella's jeans and hoody and coaxed her still shivering daughter into them before she impatiently tottered off to help David.

God, she must look a mess. Grace hastily pulled a brush through her hair and rubbed at the mascara underneath her eyes before divesting herself of her own extremely wet outer clothing and searching in the pile of ironing for her favourite warm fleece. Her fingers were so cold she could barely lift the kettle and she shivered as she held it to the tap, but whether from the cold or having David suddenly appear, she wasn't quite certain.

'You won't get any heat out of that today, Grace, I'm afraid. It's had it.'

'Right, OK, well thank you for trying anyway.' Grace didn't quite know what else to say. 'I'll ring for a plumber.'

'Do you know one?'

'No, but I'm sure there's one in the *Yellow Pages*.'

David laughed at that. '*Yellow Pages*? Does anyone have *Yellow Pages* anymore?'

'Online then. I'll find one online.'

'Well, for a start, I doubt that you'll get one out over the weekend. And, to be honest, Grace, I think it's beyond redemption.'

*As am I?* Grace wanted to ask, uncomfortably recalling Ross Haddon, slumped drunkenly against the dishwasher and David's angry words towards her as he'd moved the offending article from her kitchen and driven it away. 'Well, we can always snuggle down in our ski gear and sleeping bags in front of the fire,' she attempted cheerfully.

'You won't have any hot water.' David raised an eyebrow.

'Immersion heater? Kettle?' Grace smiled and turned to switch off the now boiling article. 'Tea? Coffee?'

'Look Grace, I'm sorry.' David folded his arms, obviously embarrassed.

'For what? Not being able to mend my boiler?'

'Don't be facetious, Grace. You know damned well what I mean. I was out of order, yelling at you like I did the other week.'

'I think you probably had every right to yell at me,' Grace sighed. 'It was all very nasty and could have been

a lot nastier. I'm obviously a terrible judge of character…'
She trailed off and, when David didn't reply, smiled. 'So,
changing the subject, how did the sale go?' she asked
brightly. 'Did it all go well?'

'Kit was brilliant as auctioneer.' David smiled. 'He has a
real gift for selling, does that kid; he'll go far. And, with Ben
Carey as his assistant, they made a real pair. I tell you, once
he gets to heaven, Ben will be selling off the Pearly Gates to
the angels… Look Grace, I'm sorry, I should have replied
to your text.'

'You were angry with me. I can understand you thinking
I'd put Pietronella in danger, with that crazy woman
coming round while I was out. And, knowing what you
did about Ross Haddon…'

'Gwanpa, can I come to your house for tea? S'cold here.'

'Pietronella.' Grace frowned at her daughter.

'You'll have to ask Mummy.'

'Mumma? Gwanpa's for tea?'

'I'm sure Gwanpa – Grandpa – is busy. It's Saturday
evening and I'm sure he'll have plans.' Grace bent down
to Pietronella, unwilling to see the confirmation on David's
face when she continued, 'Perhaps Doctor Juno is there for
tea.'

'Like Doctor Juno,' Pietronella said excitedly. 'Want to
see Hawwy Twotter again, Mumma.'

'Hawwy Twotter?' David looked bewildered.

'Harry Trotter, Juno's daughter's pony.' Grace raised her
eyes to David's.

'Ah, right. Well, Pietronella, as far as I know, neither
Doctor Juno nor Hawwy Twotter is at my house for tea, so
I would very much like you to come over.'

'To sleep?' Pietronella was ecstatic. 'In my bed at Gwanpa's, Mumma?'

'I very much want your company, Pietronella,' David said gravely.

'Mumma, Gwanpa David want my company,' Pietronella said importantly, her brown eyes behind the spectacles feverishly scanning the kitchen. 'Where my company?'

'That's really kind, David. At least she'll be warm with you. And Juno?'

'Juno?' David frowned. 'As far as I know, she's now at home with her children, planning their big trip overseas in the new year. Why do you keep asking about Juno?'

Grace stared. 'Juno's leaving?'

'Not for a while. Not until all this business with her son and that dreadful Esme woman is sorted. Didn't you know?'

'No, I had no idea.' Hope flared briefly in the general direction of Grace's heart, but began to fizzle out at the thought of her mate, Juno, actually leaving Westenbury, and completely went out when David said, 'OK, Pietronella? Just you and me for tea then, is it? What do you fancy?'

'Pizza.'

'Well, there's a surprise.' David smiled down at her. 'Come on then, grab your PJs and whatever else you want to bring with you.'

'I'll go and get them, for her.' Grace headed for the door and upstairs, when David put a hand on her arm.

'Grace?'

'Hmm?'

'You'll be cold here by yourself.'

'It's fine. Really.'

'There's a rather lovely casserole bubbling away in the

Aga as well as a Brie which, if it doesn't get eaten, is in danger of walking off by itself.'

'Your mum's casserole?'

'My mother's? No, not at all. I've been having lessons with Clementine, Betty and Sarah in the kitchen over at the restaurant. I can now do a pretty mean casserole as well as a nifty tarte tatin.'

'Blimey, I've never mastered those.' Grace was momentarily impressed but then said, 'David, you don't have to feel sorry for me. You don't have to *always* be on hand to rescue me.'

'You're my mate, Grace. That's what friends do.'

'Will your mother be there? She doesn't like me, you know.'

'Doesn't she? Why not?' David began to laugh. 'Have you been mean to her?'

'Mean to her? No, no *of course* not. It's because she… I mean…' Grace trailed off. How could she say Caroline Henderson didn't like her because she thought Grace was after her son? 'I think it better if I stay here.'

'Oh?' David folded his arms. 'Why?'

'Come on, Mumma, let's go. S'cold here. Want pizza.'

'My mother has gone off to the ballet in Sheffield with Sarah Carey, Ben's wife.' David's eyes were full of humour. 'The coast will be clear.'

Grace raised her eyes to his and found she couldn't look away. She'd loved this man for so long, never admitting even to herself the strength of her feelings for him.

'Grace, I miss you so much when you're not there. It's, it's… it's ridiculous how often I come into school when I don't really need to, just on the off-chance of seeing you.

And how let down I feel when I don't see you, when I don't bump into you down the corridor.' David continued to stare down at her with an intensity that she knew must only mirror her own. He took a tentative step towards her before moving a warm hand to her face, stroking it gently while she closed her eyes allowing herself to relax into the gesture.

The first kiss when it came was hesitant, gentle, finding its way and then, as they moved apart slightly, both seemingly transfixed, despite its subtlety, by the intensity of feeling it had ignited, David smiled down at her once again.

'All will be well, Grace, darling,' he whispered. 'I promise you; all will be well.'

# Acknowledgements

A huge thank you to DCI Andy Farrell who sat with me and advised on the many aspects of County Lines, as well as the way in which children are used in the carrying and distribution of drugs both throughout the county, and the country as a whole. His explanation for the whole concept of County Lines was invaluable when researching and writing this book.

I need to mention a reader from Ireland who asked whether Grace would ever be making a reappearance in a book and, if she were about to, could she perhaps be accompanied by a young Southern Irish teacher? This request set me thinking and was the basis for *A Village Vacancy*.

I hope the book says a lot about female friendship and, as such, I'd very much like to acknowledge my own lovely female friends who've supported me in my writing by offering their time, a listening ear, advice – and wine. You know who you are.

Thanks, as always, to my lovely agent, Anne Williams at KHLA Literary Agency, and to the ever-fabulous Hannah Smith, my editor at Aria, Head of Zeus who, together with

Vicky, Rhea and the rest of the team continue to make my books the best they can possibly be.

And finally, to all you wonderful readers who read my books and write such lovely things about them, a massive, heartfelt, thank you.

# About the Author

JULIE lives in Huddersfield, West Yorkshire where her novels are set, and her only claims to fame are that she teaches part-time at 'Bridget Jones' author Helen Fielding's old junior school and her neighbour is *Chocolat* author, Joanne Harris.

After University, where she studied Education and English Literature, she taught for many years as a junior school teacher. As a newly qualified teacher, broke and paying off her first mortgage, she would spend every long summer holiday working on different Kibbutzim in Israel. After teaching for a few years she decided to go to New Zealand to work and taught in Auckland for a year before coming back to this country.

She now only teaches when the phone rings asking her to cover an absent colleague, but still loves the buzz of teaching junior-aged children. She has been a magistrate for the past twenty years, and, when not distracted by Ebay, Twitter and Ancestry, spends much of her time writing.

Julie is married, has a twenty-six-year-old son and twenty-three-year-old daughter and a ridiculous Cockerpoo called Lincoln. She runs and swims because she's been told it's good for her, but would really prefer a glass of wine, a sun lounger and a jolly good book.

# Hello from Aria

We hope you enjoyed this book! If you did, let us know, we'd love to hear from you.

We are Aria, a dynamic fiction imprint from award-winning publishers Head of Zeus. At heart, we're committed to publishing fantastic commercial fiction – from romance to sagas to historical fiction. Visit us online and discover a community of like minded fiction fans

You can find us at:
www.ariafiction.com
- 🐦 @ariafiction
- 📘 @Aria_Fiction
- 📷 @ariafiction